GREENIES

Book One

Alan Steiner

To all the people in my life who have put up with my crazy writing hobby all these years. Thank you for reading my earlier stuff even though much it wasn't that good, for putting up with me tuning out while I was writing, and for all the encouragement.

Book Title Copyright © 2006 by Alan Steiner. All Rights Reserved.

All rights reserved. No part of this book may be reproduced in any form or by any electronic or mechanical means including information storage and retrieval systems, without permission in writing from the author. The only exception is by a reviewer, who may quote short excerpts in a review.

Cover designed by Alan Steiner

This book is a work of fiction. Names, characters, places, and incidents either are products of the author's imagination or are used fictitiously. Any resemblance to actual persons, living or dead, events, or locales is entirely coincidental.

Alan Steiner
Email me at alsteiner237@gmail.com

Printed in the United States of America

First Printing: October 2018
Amazon self-publishing

ISBN- 9781729007785

PROLOGUE

June 30, 2171
Eden, Mars

Laura Whiting was a politician, and she was doing what politicians were expected to do at times such as these. She was "touring" the area of devastation. Whenever something was devastated—be it by war, by industrial accident, or by acts of divinity—an elected official was expected to tour it, to see the damage firsthand. As to *why* they needed to perform this tour, as to what possible good was being accomplished with their presence, the answer to that depended upon who one talked to. Most politicians would answer that they needed an "eyes-on" assessment of the damage in order to help calculate the cost of replacing it. That sounded good on the surface, the sort of thing that played good on Internet, but, of course, it was not really the reason. There were engineers, insurance claims settlement specialists, and hundreds of other people who were much more qualified than a politician to assess damage and calculate cost. Laura, who had the unusual political trait of brutal self-honesty, knew that the real reason was so the politician in question could give the impression that he or she cared about their constituents and their neighborhoods. Such affairs were always rife with Internet cameras. The politician was expected to look properly solemn while viewing the destruction and then give an appropriately moving speech promising aid or an end to the cause or some other such thing.

Laura, though she was only a city council member, was expert in the art and science of politics. She should be. Her father, now retired and living the life of luxury on Earth, had had a long and distinguished elected career that had climaxed with two terms as the Governor of Mars. She had begun to learn politics about the time she had begun to learn to walk. Conventional wisdom among the Martian movers and shakers was that Laura herself would follow in his footsteps by the time she was fifty. Laura was a little more optimistic than that. She hoped to take the oath of high Martian office in ten years—by the time she was forty. She did not, however, wish this for exactly the same reason everyone thought.

"As you can see," intoned Assistant Chief Henderson of the Eden Department of Public Health and Safety, "the blast doors that were designed into the basic structure of the city did their job very well. They activated within two seconds of the laser strike and sealed off the damaged section, preventing further loss of life and property. Without those blast doors, we would not be able to stand right here at this moment. This entire building would have been reduced to the outside atmospheric pressure."

Laura and the other two city council members who had gone on the tour with her were standing on the sixty-eighth floor of the MarsTrans building looking downward through the thick plexiglass windows. Around them rose countless other high-rise buildings, stretching upward into the red Martian sky. The high-rise was the staple of life on Mars. People lived in them, worked in them, did business in them. A Martian city was nothing more than a compact collection of tall buildings that were located in a grid pattern of streets. The street level was where people moved from one building to another. All streets were enclosed by a steel and plexiglass roof thirty meters above the ground, and by plexiglass walls on the sides. This kept the air pressure inside, where it belonged, and the thin Martian atmosphere outside, where it belonged. The buildings did not actually touch each other, but they were all connected to the street level complex making Eden, in effect, one giant, interconnected, airtight structure that was home to more than twelve million people. Then entire city was kept at standard Earth sea-level air pressure by means of a system of huge fusion powered machines that extracted the traces of oxygen and nitrogen from the thin Martian atmosphere and pumped it inside. This system of pressurization and air supply was what made human life on Mars possible, but it was a system that depended upon the airtight integrity of the city remaining intact.

The MarsTrans building stood across the street from the Red Towers housing complex—an upper end luxury apartment building. From their vantage point, they could clearly see the large hole that had been burned through the steel of the building from the fortieth floor all the way to street level and below. Several floors of the building had collapsed from the force of the blast, burying the victims beneath tons of rubble. Many other sections had remained intact but had decompressed, smothering those inside of them. The street outside the building had also lost pressure, killing all who happened to have been walking about at that moment. The death toll from this one blast had been confirmed at more than nine hundred so far and was expected to rise even higher as more rubble was cleared away. Eden Department of Public Health and Safety workers, commonly known as dip-hoes because of the acronym of their department, could be seen patiently digging through the debris or moving about within the building. All of them were outfitted in protective biosuits that covered the body from head to toe. The biosuits were the only way people could exist outside of the pressurization.

"Those blast doors and the other safety features were indeed a godsend," proclaimed Councilman Dan Steeling, a senior member and, according to the movers and shakers, the man slated to be the next mayor of Eden. He was pretending to address Assistant Chief Henderson but was in actuality talking to the group of Internet reporters who were standing clustered behind them, just in front of the group of uniformed Eden police officers providing security. The reporters all had digital image recorders with microphones attached to them and they were all pointing them at Dan. "It is fortunate indeed that, even in the midst of this horrible tragedy we are viewing, we are able to at least receive reassured proof that the safety systems in place in this great city work as they were designed. While it is true that the loss of life and property from this strike, and from the others that took place on other parts of Mars, was horrific, it could have been much, much worse."

Laura, who knew she was partially in the frame of some of the cameras, kept the proper expression of saddened, though elated agreement on her face. She nodded a few times during his statement, just slightly, just enough to relate to anyone taking notice of her on the Internet screens that she was just as torn up about all of this as everyone else. In truth, had her natural expression been allowed to come through, it would have been one of horror. As she looked at the twisted steel and exposed apartments of the Red Towers, she had to clench her fists in anger at what had happened. Eden, her city, the city she had been born and raised in, had been attacked by EastHem atmospheric craft. Attacked! They had blown holes in it, decompressing entire sections like a child popping a balloon, killing thousands so far. And it was not just Eden either. Though Eden was the largest city on the Western Hemispheric Alliance's federal colony of Mars, it was just one of twelve large cities on the surface. So far, with the war only one week old, six of them had been hit, two quite badly. Triad, the orbiting space-platform that was home to more than six hundred thousand, had been attacked particularly fiercely, with more than six thousand citizens dead up there. And what was it for? Why were all of these Martians dying?

Because of greed. Simple greed.

They were calling it the Jupiter War, although the point in dispute was actually one of Jupiter's moons: Callisto. The atmospheric gas of Jupiter, which was composed primarily of hydrogen, was used as propellant for fusion-powered spacecraft and as conventional fuel for tanks, aircraft, and surface to orbit craft. It was a substance that was vital for continuation of the space-faring society and particularly for military operations. WestHem, of which Mars was a part, currently held the monopoly on the supply of this gas. Nearly one hundred years before, WestHem corporations, most notably Standard Fuel Supply and Jovian Gases Inc. constructed a large space station in orbit around Ganymede, Jupiter's largest moon. From the space station, which was actually an orbiting city, collection ships made the short trip to the gas giant and dove into the atmosphere, collecting a hold full of the hydrogen concoction before clawing their way back out and returning. The raw gas would then be refined into liquid hydrogen and stored in huge orbiting pressure tanks. Tanker ships, the largest moving objects ever constructed, would then fill up and transport the gas across the solar system either to Mars or Earth.

Nearly half of this gas was sold to EastHem who, although they were bitter enemies of WestHem and had been since the end of World War III, needed a fuel supply as well. Since EastHem did not have a secure supply of its own, it was forced to buy it from the two WestHem corporations at top dollar. Not only was this expensive, and not only did it take EastHem currency out of the hemisphere, it also meant that their fuel supply was subject to being cut off during times of crisis, which was usually when they needed it most from a military standpoint. It also meant that WestHem held an advantage in the complex relationship between the two halves of the Earth.

Three years before, tensions between the two powers began to grow as it became apparent that EastHem was constructing the components of an orbiting fuel refining and shipment platform in lunar orbit using mined steel from beneath the surface of the moon. These components, which were loaded into cargo ships nearly as large as a fuel tanker, could only be destined for one of the moons of Jupiter. Though Saturn was gas giant planets with an atmosphere very similar to Jupiter's, colonizing it was clearly impractical due to the distance involved and because such a supply line would be impossible to defend during a conflict. WestHem, realizing this, insisted in the sternest manner that the *entire* Jupiter system belonged to them, not just the single moon of Ganymede. EastHem, not bothering to deny its intentions, countered with the argument that WestHem had no right to claim an entire planetary system when they had no settlements on the planet in question.

This war of words went on and on as the construction process neared conclusion and the cargo ships, with an escort of heavy battle cruisers and stealth attack ships, began to prepare for departure. As the armada left lunar orbit heading for Jupiter, WestHem issued an ultimatum. It warned EastHem that if any of its ships entered the Jovian system, they would be attacked. EastHem ignored this threat and continued, probably figuring that WestHem would back down. WestHem didn't. When the first of the ships crossed the invisible line that had been drawn, the WestHem Navy attacked with short-range space fighters based at Standard City. The cold war that had been the status quo for the past one hundred and twenty years suddenly became very hot.

Mars, as a strategically placed point located between the orbits of Jupiter and Earth, was immediately bombed once hostilities commenced. The WestHem navy had a large base in orbit around the red planet with many of their ships stationed there. Aside from that, Triad, the orbiting space station in geosynchronous orbit, was home to the three major shipbuilding companies that supplied warships for the navy and for cargo transportation. EastHem forces, as they passed, had dropped off three battle cruiser groups complete with attack craft, assault landing ships, and support vessels. They were on station just outside of laser range of the WestHem battle groups, which had been forced to stay in position to counter them. It was ironic indeed that the Martian cities, which were hundreds of millions of kilometers from both the moon in dispute and from the planet that had spawned the combatants, were the most heavily damaged during the fighting. Even on Earth itself, where the two powers were separated by a mere twenty kilometers at the Bering Strait, not so much as an artillery shell or a bomb was detonated.

Laura Whiting, as she looked at the devastation that a single laser blast from a single EastHem attack craft had caused, felt an angry hatred she had never experienced before. It was not EastHem she directed this anger towards, however. It was directed towards WestHem, towards the so-called government that supposedly represented and protected the interests of the Martian people, and towards the powerful untenable corporations that controlled that government.

The official WestHem reason for attacking EastHem and trying to prevent their colonization of Callisto was that they, WestHem, needed to protect their deep space defensive positions and not allow those godless fascists of EastHem a toehold in the same planetary system. They told their citizens and their soldiers that to allow EastHem to establish themselves on one of the moons of Jupiter would be as good as signing the death warrant for the glorious WestHem way of life. Within a decade, it was suggested, EastHem would have enough forces and enough equipment on Callisto to evict *us* from Jupiter and to strangle *our* fuel supply. A few years after that, EastHem tanks would come rolling into the western hemisphere itself, bent on the final takeover. The rhetoric was unwavering from its course. No EastHem ships will enter the Jovian system. No EastHem installations will be established on Callisto or any other moon. Jupiter and all that orbited it were WestHem property.

Of course, it was apparent to any thinking person—and Laura White, like most Martians, certainly fit that category—what the *real* reason for the war was. If EastHem began gathering and refining their own fuel from Jupiter's atmosphere, Standard Fuel and Jovian Gasses and the other industries that relied upon gas refining and shipping for their profits would lose more than half of their business. The WestHem government, which imposed export taxes upon those sales, would lose all of that income from its yearly budget. In addition to the loss of revenue, WestHem would lose one of its trump cards in any future conflict. It would never again be able to threaten EastHem with a fuel embargo. That could simply not be allowed. And so, even though there was enough hydrogen in the atmosphere of Jupiter to supply both halves of the Earth and all of their colonies for thousands of generations, a vicious war erupted over the issue.

But Laura, above all, was a politician. She could not show, could not say how she really felt about the subject. She could not even say what the people she served wanted her to say or feel. She said and felt, in public anyway, what her sponsors—those who had contributed to her campaigns, who had bankrolled her election—wanted her to say and feel. That was how you stayed in the game. There had been a time when she had not wanted to stay in the game anymore, when she had not wanted to be a part of the perverse and sickening process that was modern government. That time had not been so long before. But now that Martian cities were having holes blasted in them, that Martian citizens were being killed because those corporate sponsors didn't want to lose their profit margins, she had decided it was her duty to stay in the game. She did not like the game, but she would play it and she would play it well. She would kiss every ass, would spout every company line, would do whatever she needed to do to advance her political career. And hopefully one day, years from now, when she was in a position much higher than a mere Eden city council member, she would *change* the game.

She turned her face from the window before her, putting the view of the destroyed housing building out of her sight. The reporters approached her, fishing for a statement. Laura had a gift for public speaking, an ability to turn even the most benign utterance into a passionate narrative. She cleared her throat and began to spout about devastation and the evils of fascist EastHem and how the great people of WestHem were going to defeat the tyranny that was trying to destroy all they held dear and sacred. The reporters loved it, as they always did statements from her. All except for one.

"Ms. Whiting," said a short, Asian descended reporter from MarsGroup Information Services. "There has been much worry about the landing ships EastHem has stationed near our planet just outside of orbital range. In the event of an EastHem invasion of Mars, I was curious how you would rate our city's defenses?"

That was a loaded question and it was not surprising that Mindy Ming, the MarsGroup reporter, was the only one to ask it. All of the other reporters represented either InfoServe Internet Communications stations or SpacialNet Communications stations. Those were the two major providers of Internet media and literature in WestHem and, though they pretended to be antagonistic to government and corporate motivations and elected officials, they were actually little more than the propaganda arm. Again, anyone with any thinking capacity knew this. But MarsGroup was a Mars based, independent Internet media corporation. It's owners and investors were all Martian-born who had no financial ties to any Earth-based corporations. They were often derided in the popular press and had been sued for libel so many times it would be years before all of the cases came to court. They were a constant thorn in the side of many a politician or corporation. Laura, though publicly she denounced MarsGroup like everyone else, secretly admired them greatly. MarsGroup news services, in her mind, was what news reporting *should* be like. They strove to find the truth instead of simply repeating what their masters told them to repeat.

"Well," Laura said lightly, as if the question were a ridiculous annoyance, "I don't think we really have much to worry about in terms of an EastHem invasion. My understanding is that our space forces in orbit and at Triad are more than sufficient to keep them from attempting such a feat."

"Really?" Mindy said, raising her eyebrows in disbelief. "Is it not true that a good portion of our space-based attack craft were destroyed attempting to repel this battle group?"

Laura feigned a sigh, as if she were dealing with a complete paranoid. Again, this was just for appearances. Mindy's military source, whomever he or she was, was obviously very highly placed. Though the general public did not know it yet, both sides in the conflict had recently discovered the fallacy of trying to attack heavily defended space cruisers or stations with small attack craft. The anti-spacecraft lasers could pick them off like ducks in a skeet range. Well over three quarters of the front-line defense craft based at Triad had been blown to pieces in three separate attacks without putting a single EastHem ship out of commission. Well over half of the crews of those ships had been killed or captured.

"I am not the one to ask about military matters," Laura said shortly. "I'm just a councilwoman. I have every confidence however, that our armed forces have the situation above our planet well in hand. And as for city defenses, as you are aware by the itinerary we supplied you with, we will be visiting the staging area for the WestHem marine forces that have been assigned to Eden next."

The two strong-willed women locked eyes for a moment. Laura could see the contempt Mindy held for her reflected in those brown orbs. *Sell-out*, those eyes said to her. *You're nothing but a corporate, WestHem sell-out*. She ignored the look. She had seen it many times before and would see it many times again. Though it still hurt a little, though it still bothered her to be seen as a traitor to her people, to their ideals, to be considered a tool of oppression, she was getting used to it.

*****

The staging area for the 103rd WestHem Marine Battalion, the battalion responsible for defending the city of Eden in the event of an EastHem invasion, was a city park located just on the edge of the city perimeter. The park was the showpiece of the business district and was nearly five square kilometers in size. It was surrounded on all four sides by towering high rises, the biggest on the planet. The AgriCorp building itself—the tallest building in the solar system at 325 stories—stood across the street from the eastern entrance to the park grounds. The park was mostly grassy fields, groves of trees, and winding walkways that snaked in all directions. There was a zoo and a golf course as well as football and baseball fields and a large duck pond. The roof of the city, which was usually ten meters above the ground over the streets, rose to more than a hundred meters above the park grounds. In addition, the roof here was mostly plexiglass instead of a mixture of glass windows and steel support beams. This allowed the pale Martian sun to shine brightly in the park during the daylight hours instead of being broken up into shadow.

Usually, the park was filled with a mixture of business types taking lunch hour walks through the nature areas, daycare providers walking groups of children to the play equipment, and unemployed lower-class thugs and gang-members. But that had been during peacetime. Now, the marines had occupied the sports fields, the golf course, and every other piece of open land in the park. They had set up inflatable tents in geometric clusters near the west side. Near the south side was a collection of mobile command posts and latrines. In between, a calisthenics and jogging area had been fashioned. Near the north side entrance, the closest entrance to the actual edge of the city, was a storage depot for weapons and biosuits. Off duty marines could be seen walking everywhere through the park, most dressed in the blue shorts and white T-shirts they wore inside of a protected area. Most were between the ages of twenty and thirty years old and, since they were combat troops, all were men. They gathered in clusters of two, four, six, sometimes more. They walked to and from the mess hall. They exercised in the calisthenics area. To the uneducated eye, their numbers appeared generous indeed, more than a match for any EastHem invasion force, particularly when you considered that nearly a third of them were on-duty outside of the safety of the city, out in the Martian wastelands.

Their commanding officer, Lieutenant Colonel Ron Herald, greeted the tour of Eden city council members personally. He was dressed the same as his men, in a pair of blue shorts with the marine emblem upon the leg and a white T-shirt with his name and rank on the breast. His hair was short, as were all marines' hair, and his body was trim and fit. He looked like that kind of man that you would like to have in charge of your city's defenses. He practically oozed confidence.

He greeted each council member personally, addressing him or her by name and offering whispered reassurances that their city was perfectly safe in the hands of his men. "Landing here and attacking this city," he told Laura, "would be the worst mistake those EastHem fascists ever made. My battalion would eat them for breakfast."

"That's good to know, Colonel," Laura beamed right back, putting the reassured expression upon her face.

Herald gave them a tour of the staging area, leading them around from place to place and pointing out every cluster of tents. The entourage of reporters followed along behind, Mindy Ming included. They saw the inside of a typical tent, in which squads of marines were housed on small inflatable mattresses. They were shown the primitive latrine facilities where the marines took care of their bodily functions. They walked through the mess hall, which was full of empty tables and filled with the smell of dinner being constructed. Finally, they were led to the staging area itself.

A large guarded reinforced tent housed the marine equipment. Herald led them past two armed guards out front and into the interior, which was mostly a huge locker room. Rows of gray plastic storage cabinets sat before rows of plastic benches. The smell was that of locker rooms solar system wide; of stale sweat and dirty clothing.

"It is in here," Herald explained, "where the marines under my command change into the biosuits which allow them to operate outside of the pressurization of the city. The biosuits are completely self-contained and supply oxygen, food paste, water, and even excretory containers for the soldiers wearing them. With the supply carried within the suit, the soldier can stay outside the safety of this artificial environment for up to twelve hours at a time. The suits are somewhat bulky, of course, but modern WestHem engineering and manufacturing have managed to keep the fully loaded weight down to less than forty kilograms. That is five kilograms less, I might add, than the standard EastHem biosuit. This weight advantage, which translates into increased mobility in the field and the ability to carry more equipment, is but one advantage that my soldiers have over their EastHem counterparts."

He then led them to the other side of the room, towards another guarded opening to the tent. This one led to the park's exit and the wide, heavily traveled 3rd Street, a major downtown movement corridor.

"From here," the Colonel continued, "each company of soldiers, after donning their suits and gathering their personal weapons, will march down 3rd Street to the airlock complex in the city corporation yard. Just outside of those airlocks is the staging area for our tanks, armored personnel carriers, and hovers. Upon deployment, most of the soldiers will enter the armored vehicles and proceed to their defensive positions near the approaches to the city. Others will climb into the hovers and be transported to the artillery emplacements or antiaircraft bunkers. Of course, I cannot give you the exact locations of these defensive positions for security reasons, but rest assured, they are formidable."

The tour wrapped up a few minutes later with Laura and Dan Steeling both giving inspirational speeches to the Internet cameras about how safe they felt in the presence of Colonel Herald and his marines. Steeling even managed to throw in a pitch about buying war bonds. There were only two pointed questions from Mindy Ming and Herald, though new to such blatant inquiries, handled them very well. Everybody thanked the Colonel for his time and for the steadfast watch he was providing. The Internet reporters, with nothing left to report on, quickly left the scene.

Herald, his work done, excused himself and asked his aide, a young lieutenant, to lead his "honored guests" back to the entrance of the park and their police department security detail. Halfway there, as they were passing a group of marines doing push-ups on the trampled grass, a voice hailed Laura.

"Ms. Whiting?" it called, its owner trotting over from his position near the physical training leader. He was an African-American descended man of about thirty, and Laura had already placed him as a Martian born person based on his accent. A better look revealed his identity. Though she had not seen him in well over ten years, she had once known this man very well.

"Kevin Jackson," she said, putting her politician's smile upon her face. She stepped towards him, holding out her hand for a shake. "Or should I say, Captain Jackson," she corrected, reading the insignia upon his shirt.

Jackson had been a college classmate of hers at the University of Mars at Eden. She had been going for the required degree in political theory prior to law school and he had been working on his military science degree. The very fact that he had been admitted to an institute of higher learning had spoken volumes about his family connections and intelligence. In modern WestHem society, less than two percent of those who graduated high school were admitted to college. Most young men and women of the working class were doomed to self-funded technical schools that taught them the specific job skills they were striving for. She had shared several general education and history classes with Jackson over the years and they had developed a very close friendship that eventually led to a brief love affair. They had parted amicably enough after both had been advised by betters of the potential career damage their relationship might cause. Though interracial love affairs carried no stigma in Martian culture, they were still considered an anomaly in WestHem culture and those who participated in them were deemed to be somewhat less than normal. Though the physical aspects of their affair ended, their friendship had continued until graduation. From there they had parted. Jackson had gone on with his career in the corps. Whiting had gone on to law school and her political career.

"Captain as of five days ago," he told her, grasping her small hand in his large one and shaking vigorously. "Easy promotions are the one fortunate aspect of wartime."

Laura, ever the lady, made the required introductions to her colleagues. Hands were shaken and kind comments were passed between Jackson and Steeling and the others. Laura saw that, despite their jovial expressions, her fellow councilmen were impatiently awaiting the end of her conversation. She put an accommodating look upon her face and told them to go on without her, that she would find her own way back to city hall.

"But, Laura," Dan Steeling said worriedly. "What about security? Surely, you're not thinking about walking back to city hall alone, through downtown?"

This was a legitimate concern, and not just because she was an easily recognized person. With Martian unemployment at approximately twenty-two percent, the crime rate was frighteningly high. Large, well-organized street gangs roamed about with near impunity in certain parts of the downtown Eden area. "Have one of the police wait for me," she told him. "Tell him I won't be long. Captain Jackson is an old friend from school and I'd like to talk to him for a few minutes."

Steeling reluctantly agreed to this plan and took his leave, heading across the park towards the entrance.

"So," Jackson said, his smile warmer once he had gone, "you're making quite a name for yourself in the political arena, aren't you? I've heard stories even down in Argentina about the charismatic Eden city council member."

Laura smiled. "I have a gift for making myself known to the right people," she told him.

"You always did, Laura, you always did."

"And yourself?" she asked. "You say you were in Argentina. I hear it's pretty nasty over there."

He shrugged a little. "Poorly armed fanatical nationalists who have never accepted WestHem rule. They love to hide in the mountains and shoot at us with old World War III era weapons. It's not that dangerous as long as you have a little common sense and don't venture far from the base. The worst part is being in that hellish environment. For someone who grew up on Mars where the temperature is always the same and it never rains, it takes a little getting used to, I'll tell you."

"I'll bet," said Laura, who had never been to Earth before and had therefore never experienced anything but the constant 22 degrees Celsius of the artificial environment.

"Do you have a few minutes?" Jackson asked her. "Maybe we can go over to the mess hall and scrounge up a cup of coffee or something."

Laura sensed that his offer entailed a little bit more than simply catching up on old times. However, it did not seem that renewing their romance seemed to be his goal. That could only mean that he had news for her; news that she might not otherwise hear. Never one to shun a potential source of information, she agreed to join him.

They talked of inconsequential things as they wandered through the calisthenics area and to the large mess tent Herald had shown her earlier. It was still empty of soldiers and still filled with the aroma of cooking meat spiced with onions. Jackson led her to a mess table in the center of the room, within easy sight of the entrances, and bade her to sit. She did so and he disappeared behind the serving counter, reemerging a few minutes later with two steaming metal cups. He rejoined her and they sipped the strong brew as they appraised each other.

"How do you find the political life, Laura?" Jackson asked her, seemingly lightly, but obviously very interested in her answer.

Laura hesitated before answering him. During their past friendship they had been as close as two people could be. They had spent many a night sharing their views of the solar system over coffee or beer or marijuana. Jackson was one of the few people in existence she had discussed her peculiar ideas about an ideal government with. Was that what he was thinking about now? Was he trying to equate Laura Whiting, the idealistic realist, with Laura Whiting the politician? "I find it," she told him carefully, "pretty much as I always expected it would be back in college."

He gave her a pointed look. "You used to say that politics was the most corrupt, soulless profession in existence; that it was worse than working for a law company or a corporate management team."

She returned his look. "Yes," she said. "I did say that."

"So, that's how you've found the life to be?"

She took a deep breath. This could be a set-up of course. In the world of politics, you could never discount that possibility. But her instincts, which had always served her well, told her it wasn't. Jackson was just trying to see if his old friend and lover was still the same person she had once been before he talked about whatever was on his mind. Finally, she nodded. "That's how it is," she told him. "And I hate every minute of it. I've almost quit in disgust a few times."

"Why do you stay if you hate it so much?"

"I believe you remember our past conversations," she replied slyly. "The ones about why I needed to go into politics." She smiled a little in fondness, remembering the closeness that accompanied those talks. "You used to think I was crazy, remember?"

"I remember," he said warmly, remembering the same thing. Yes, this woman before him was the same person he had once loved. "But I also remember being impressed by the complexity of your ambitions. I wish you the best of luck in them."

"I appreciate that, Kevin," she told him.

"But, in the meantime," he said, turning to business, "there's this war going on."

"I've noticed," she answered. "I toured the blast site in the Calvetta district today. It's rather frightening to see what one blast of an EastHem laser can do. One tenth of a second of energy release from eighty kilometers away and more than nine hundred people are dead. And that wasn't even one of the bad ones. Those are up on Triad."

"Triad is getting the shit beat out of it, that's for sure," he agreed. "But the laser blasts are not the concern here."

"The invasion fleet?" she asked softly.

"Yes," he answered. "I saw the briefing by Admiral Graves of the navy on an Internet terminal earlier. He did a good job of blowing smoke up the asses of all the citizens here."

"And the citizens believe him about as much as they do anyone else in such a position," Laura put in. "That's the biggest failing of Earth natives when they deal with Martians. They assume we're just as easily cowed by reassurances as people in Denver or Buenos Aires."

"Underestimation," Jackson said with a nod. "You always said that that was the key to your plans."

"And it still is," she assured him. "If we can survive this war, that will still be the key. So, tell me. How much at risk are we? I know we're in danger of invasion from that fleet up there, but I don't know how bad it is. You do, don't you?"

He leaned back a little bit, taking a quick glance around the room, searching for eavesdroppers. Seeing none, he leaned forward a bit and lowered his voice. "They have three divisions of combat troops up there," he said. "Those landing ships are loaded with heavy equipment and troop-carrying landers that can be down on the surface in less than an hour with every last one of those men, as well as their tanks, their APCs, their artillery, and enough hovers to guarantee air superiority over an advance. If they left the landing ships right now, they could be in occupation of all the Martian cities except Triad in three days."

"Three days?" she asked, feeling fear coursing through her body. She had known it was bad, but *that* bad? "What about your marines? You won't be able to hold them off at all?"

"Our presence here is nothing more than a public relations tour," he scoffed bitterly. "We make the public feel better and we look good parading around the park in our shorts. See, Mr. and Mrs. Greenie? You're nice and safe on your planet. The marines are here to protect you from those evil EastHem fascists."

"But surely you can hold them back for a little bit?" Laura asked nervously.

"We're a goddamned battalion, Laura," he said, letting a little of his own fear show now. "A battalion! That's four companies of soldiers. Twenty platoons! We have thirty tanks, forty APCs and a few artillery guns we managed to scrounge up. We have six anti-tank platoons and one anti-air squad. If the EastHems land here, they're going to throw at least a division at Eden, complete with hover support. The battalion we have as a defense here would be nothing more than a warm-up exercise for them. It's even worse in New Pittsburgh and Proctor. We weren't even able to spare complete battalions to defend those cities. They have no artillery at all and only a few tanks. This planet is virtually defenseless."

"Christ," she said, shaking her head in disbelief. "It's much worse than I thought. And I'm a realist. How did this happen, Kevin? How is it that the most valuable planet in the solar system, the planet that grows more than half of the food for WestHem, that supplies ninety percent of the steel, that generates trillions in profits for all of those corporations, was left wide-open to capture? How?"

"I think you know the answer to that," Jackson replied.

"Money," she spat.

"You got it," he said, nodding. "The WestHem government did not want to spend the money to station a defense force here. Why should they? It's never been invaded before, has it? The only soldiers that are ever on the planet are the ones who occasionally come to train at the extraterrestrial proving grounds. And even then, there are usually only a few battalions and they only have outdated equipment because the armed forces do not want to spend the money to transport front-line tanks and APCs here. They always figured they could transport troops here from Earth if EastHem ever made a move. After all, the EastHem troops have to come from Earth as well, don't they? But they never figured on a two-front war. The possibility that those troops might be needed on one of the Jupiter moons apparently never occurred to them. And now that EastHem has made landings on Callisto, the forces that were slated to prevent an invasion of Mars have been sent there and they only left a token holding force here."

"That doesn't make any sense," Laura said. "Callisto is of no real strategic value to them. It's only worth is as a staging body for a fuel refining operation."

"That's true," he agreed. "But that's what you get when you have politicians on Earth, acting on behalf of Standard Fuel and Jovian Gasses, making the military decisions. The executive council ordered all available troops to the Jupiter system to eject the EastHem marines from Callisto. General Kensington, who's in command of this particular clusterfuck, practically begged them to reconsider and allow him to reinforce Mars first and foremost. But they wouldn't listen to reason. Standard Fuel and Jovian Gas want that EastHem refining operation destroyed and those EastHem marines off of Callisto. They don't give a damn about Mars. All they're concerned with is preventing EastHem from becoming self-sufficient in fuel."

"But if EastHem invades Mars," Laura said, unable to keep the exasperation out of her voice, "WestHem loses their food supply, their steel supply, and most of their shipbuilding and armament industries. The entire economy of WestHem could very well collapse if those things are lost. At the very least, EastHem would be the one with the power. They would be able to strangle us."

"And do you want to know the real irony of all this?" Jackson asked, sipping from his coffee.

"What's that?"

"That battle group that has been sent to Callisto, the one that was supposed to defend Mars, it's going to be slaughtered when it tries to eject that landing force. There's no way in hell it's going to be able to retake that moon if the commander of the EastHem forces is even halfway competent at his job."

"What do you mean?" she asked him. "You said that they would have been able to keep EastHem from invading Mars. Why won't they be able to take back a moon? What's the difference?"

"The difference," he explained, "is that here on Mars that battle group would have been the defenders. They would have dug in and set up their forces and just waited for the EastHems to try and make a move against them. But on Callisto, the situation is reversed. The EastHem forces were able to make the landings. It is now they who will be dug in, their tanks and artillery all set and pre-positioned in the optimum places. In any battle, the advantage goes to the defender. A military rule of thumb is that it takes three times as many troops and equipment to dislodge a position than it does to hold it. The EastHem forces on Callisto are roughly equal to the forces that will be trying to retake it. They're going to be massacred."

"Christ, Kevin," Laura said. "Do you have a lot of friends among that group?"

He nodded. "Hundreds of men I've trained with and served with everywhere from Ganymede to Cuba. Most will probably be killed during the assault phase. Others will be captured and sent to an EastHem POW camp. The lucky ones will be those who are just wounded and pulled from the battle area. They might just live through the war. Not that we have it much easier here. If EastHem makes landings here, we'll fight them as hard as we can but we'll all be killed or captured within a day." He snorted a little. "They'll probably write songs about us and make Internet shows and erect monuments to us, just like the Snoqualmie defenders back in World War III. That'll make my mother real proud, won't it?"

"Is there a solution?" Laura asked, knowing that Kevin had to have a reason for telling her all of this.

"Not for the current crisis," he said. "Like I told you, if EastHem wants to take this planet, then it's theirs. But there is a chance they won't do that."

"Why wouldn't they?" she asked eagerly.

"EastHem doesn't really want this war," he explained. "At least that is my impression as a military historian. I know that all the Internet channels and the news services are telling us that EastHem is the aggressor and that they are bent upon ruling the entire solar system, but I don't really think that's the case. They just want Callisto and they felt they had a right to colonize it. Whether they are right or wrong is not the issue here. The fact is, that they just want to become self-sufficient in fuel so they don't have to pay WestHem corporations for it. All they were trying to do was set up a fueling operation on Callisto and we attacked them for it."

"But why wouldn't they invade Mars though?" she asked. "I'm not a military expert or anything, but I know that in an all-out war like this, doctrine is to press any advantage you have. Invading Mars and cutting WestHem off from their food and their steel, as well as denying them a strategic staging area between Earth and the Jupiter system, would certainly seem advantageous to me."

"It is," he agreed. "And I'm not sure they will be able to resist the temptation now that those idiots have left us wide open, but I'm quite sure that occupying Mars was not one of their original goals. They positioned that invasion force here only as a diversionary tactic, figuring, as any sane commander would, that WestHem would then have to reinforce Mars, which would draw troops away from Callisto and therefore give them more time to dig in there. To tell you the truth, I'm pretty impressed by the way EastHem has fought this war so far."

"We should have such leadership," Laura observed sourly.

Jackson dismissed this thought. The situation was what the situation was. "In any case," he went on, "EastHem has Callisto now and we're not going to be able to take it back from them any time soon. With any luck, they will be satisfied that their war goals are met and try to push for an armistice instead of drawing out the fighting by landing troops here. If that is the case, then that invasion force will stay where it is for now."

"Will WestHem consider an armistice with them though?" she asked him. "This is edging into my area of expertise now. If politicians are controlling this war on behalf of their corporate sponsors, then they won't give a damn how many marines die trying to take Callisto back. They'll keep sending wave after wave of troops there to try again."

"I have no doubt about that," he told her. "And that's exactly what I wanted to talk to you about."

"Oh?"

"If WestHem does not sign an armistice soon, if they keep trying to retake that moon from EastHem, then EastHem is eventually going to *have* to invade this planet in response. Whether they want to or not, they will have no choice. I think you can help prevent that from happening though."

"Me?" she asked. "What can I do? I'm just a city council member."

"You're a politician, Laura," he reminded her. "And as a prominent, upward moving lawmaker, I'm sure you have established certain connections with certain powerful people in the Martian corporate world."

"Sponsors," she said. "Of course. You can't get elected to the PTA board in this life without a corporate sponsor to donate money and tell you how to vote. But I don't have any sponsors from Jovian Gas or Standard Fuel. I only have connections with corporations that operate on Mars."

"That's my point," he said. "Would AgriCorp be one of those sponsors?" AgriCorp was the owner of the majority of the Martian agricultural industry, which was considerable. Martian crops, which grew in huge greenhouse complexes that surrounded the equatorial cities like Eden, made up the bulk of the exports from the planet. It was an industry worth trillions and AgriCorp was easily the most powerful of all of the WestHem corporations.

"Yes, they would," she said. "One would not get very far in one's political life, either here or on Earth, without AgriCorp's consent." She started to gleam a little of what he was getting at. "So, you think that they'll be able to... influence things?"

"If they understand the seriousness of the situation," he replied. "AgriCorp wields a whole lot of political clout, as I'm sure you're aware. Especially with the executive council. If someone could impress upon them just how serious this threat of EastHem invasion is, how easily their entire industry and holdings could suddenly be in EastHem hands without any sort of compensation, then I'm sure they'll see to it that defensive troops are sent here to prevent that invasion. AgriCorp has more pull with the council then the gas refining industry, don't they?"

"Yes," she said. "Nobody has more pull with the council than AgriCorp. They have their fingers in everyone's pocket. The question is whether or not they will listen to me. Remember, I'm just a city council member right now. I have a reputation as a future force to be reckoned with, that's true, but right now the lobbyists I deal with are pretty low level."

"I think you need to try, Laura," he said. "If they don't listen to you, then they don't listen to you. But you have to try. Be persuasive."

She smiled a little. "Now that," she said, "I know how to do. I'll get online with my contact as soon as I get back to my office. Can I mention your name?"

"You can," he said, "but I don't know how much good it will do. I'm just a greenie like you, remember? Corporate haunchos probably won't have a lot of respect for what a greenie has to say. Remember, we're all the descendants of welfare sucking losers who were chased off of Earth. I think you'll do better mentioning the name of Colonel Herald."

"Colonel Herald?" she asked. "Does he know you're talking to me?"

"He gave me his permission to have this talk with you," Jackson confirmed. "Herald is a halfway decent guy for an Earthling and he's just as worried about the strategic situation here as a non-Martian can be. He'll tell your people what I've told you as long as he's assured that it remains in confidence."

She nodded slowly. "Then he'll face to face with them?"

"He will," he confirmed. "If they are brought here and if they are of high enough level to make a difference. Don't bring your low-level lobbyist down here, bring the guy who can whisper in the ears back on Earth. Herald will be taking a pretty significant risk by talking. It doesn't take much in the armed forces to completely derail a career, believe me. Make sure the risk is worthwhile for him."

"Right," she agreed. "I'll get right to work on it."

They sat in silence for a moment, each contemplating the conversation that had just taken place. Finally, Laura said: "It's kind of ironic in a way, isn't it, Kevin?"

"What's that?" he asked.

"That I have to enlist the aid of the most powerful corporation in existence, that I have to utilize the very power of corruption I hate so much in order to save the planet they are desecrating."

He gave her a meaningful look. "The solar system is full of ironies," he told her. "The best you can do is use them to your advantage. Look at me. I'm utilizing the same process of manipulation of the military that has left us in this mess in the first place. Does that make it wrong?"

"No," she said. "Sometimes the ends really do justify the means."

"Sometimes they do."

*****

April 2, 2172
Eden, Mars

The view from Riggington's Restaurant was impressive. The four-star facility sat atop the 230 story Emmington Group building in the heart of downtown Eden, right at the very edge of the city. From the picture windows near their table, Kevin Jackson and Laura Whiting could see the rolling red plains of equatorial Mars stretching off into the setting sun. The landscape was framed by the towering Sierra Madres foothills to the south and by the geometric squares of the greenhouse complexes stretching to the north. On the other side of the room, out the far windows, the other high-rises of Eden, including the AgriCorp building, crowded the sky around them, their lights just beginning to shine. It was truly a commanding view and one that Jackson was sure to enjoy, Laura figured. That was why she had chosen this particular location for their discussion.

Martians, as a culture, did not stand too much on glittery displays of status. For that reason, the dress code in Riggington's, as in most Martian facilities, was quite casual. The majority of the diners were dressed only in shorts and light cotton short-sleeve shirts of varying colors. This was the favored casual wear in a world where the temperature never changed and where weather conditions were never a concern. This was how Laura was dressed, though as a politician she usually pained herself to wear Earth-style business attire when out in public. It was expected of such a station in life. But today she did not wish to call much attention to herself; an endeavor she seemed to have been successful in.

The two friends had just come from the Eden Spaceport where they had been a part of the crowd greeting the returning POW's from the Jupiter War. The armistice had been signed nearly two months before and the first group of those naval and marine personnel who had been taken prisoner during the Callisto battles or the space battles had finally made it back to WestHem soil. They had emerged from the C-10 surface to orbit craft onto the tarmac of the spaceport's airlock where the Martian governor and two members of the executive council had greeted each one with handshakes and warm words of meaningless thanks for their sacrifice. The ceremony itself had actually been quite moving, even for a hardened politician like Laura or a hardened military commander like Jackson. After so much death and destruction during the bloody course of the war, seeing survivors, seeing those that had been thought lost returned, was enough to trigger powerful emotions. There had been hardly a dry eye among the assembled crowds as wives, parents and children greeted their loved ones after all of those long months away. The ceremony was capped with patriotic speeches and flag-waving and horns blowing and a mass singing of the WestHem federal anthem. To see the portrayal, to feel the emotion of it, one could almost forget that the entire war had been for nothing.

More than twenty thousand WestHem marines had been killed in three separate attacks on Callisto. Twice that number had been wounded. More than ten thousand naval personnel had been killed and more than thirty front-line ships had been destroyed by enemy torpedoes. Though Mars itself had escaped invasion, thanks in part to the efforts of Laura and Jackson back at the beginning of the conflict, all of its cities had been bombed without let-up and more than thirty thousand citizens ultimately lost their lives. And despite all of this fighting and bombing and death, the EastHem fuel refining operation on Callisto was still there and was producing at high capacity. EastHem was now self-sufficient in fuel and the two major WestHem gas production corporations were in the midst of laying off tens of thousands of workers and mothballing dozens of their tankers.

Of course, the WestHem government's position was not that it had *lost* the war. WestHem, the greatest democracy in the solar system, was incapable of losing a war. No, what WestHem had done was "negotiate a settlement" to the dispute. They claimed that the settlement reached was consistent with their original war goals. They had been misunderstood back at the beginning of the conflict when they stated those goals as being the unconditional withdrawal of all EastHem forces and civilians from the Jupiter system. All they wanted was to keep EastHem from attempting to expand their holdings in Jupiter and from attempting to impede WestHem fuel production. EastHem had agreed to this in writing, so the war was over. The goals were met. Everyone was happy, right?

Laura had never been to Earth and did not know the extent of the Earthling's stupidity in such manners. Did they really believe all of the bullshit their government was laying upon them? She thought it entirely possible they did. But on Mars, even the most common citizen knew the truth. WestHem had gotten its ass kicked and kicked royally. And Mars had been damn lucky to avoid a brutal enemy occupation.

"What's the occasion, Laura?" Jackson asked her as they sipped from glasses of white wine imported from Earth (Mars had very little wine or alcohol production). "You didn't bring me up here to get me drunk, did you? You seem too serious for that."

"I'm concerned about the pull-back of the marines from Mars," she said, nibbling on a piece of bread. "I understand the withdrawal will start next week."

"That's correct," he said. "The mechanized units will start loading up their equipment onto the landing ships for return to orbit. The troops will all be sent back to their bases on Earth after that."

"And we'll be defenseless once again," she said.

"Not completely," he corrected. "It's been decided by the powers-that-be that a division of marines will be permanently stationed at the training base outside Eden. Their heavy equipment will be stored in a group of heavy landing ships which will be kept at anchor at Triad Naval Base."

"So, they're going to kick loose a little bit of funding for us huh?" she said cynically. "How rankin' of them. Will a division be enough?"

"It could potentially be enough if it was used correctly, but you have to understand that this division, though it will be stationed here, is not specifically intended for the defense of Mars."

She raised her eyebrows a little. "It's not?"

"No," he told her. "It will be a fast reaction force that is capable of being moved away from here in less than twenty-four hours. Its primary function will be to respond if there are any other problems in the Jupiter system. It has been suggested that the reason we were forced to 'negotiate a settlement' in the war was because we were unable to respond quick enough with enough troops and equipment to prevent the occupation of Callisto."

"That's a bunch of bullshit," Laura said. "We had all of the troops that were supposed to protect Mars in orbit around Ganymede when the war started. They were there long before the EastHem marines occupied Callisto."

"Right," Jackson agreed. "That was because WestHem didn't believe that EastHem was really going to try to forcibly install troops on Callisto. They thought it was all a big bluff. Since they thought EastHem was bluffing, it was decided that our marines shouldn't be landed there in advance. Another stupid political decision made against the advice of the commanders. That one was probably the worst one of all. If we had had those troops down there, the entire momentum of the war would have been on our side instead of theirs." He shrugged lightly, as lightly as one could when one was talking about a flawed decision that had cost twenty thousand men their lives. "What can you do?"

"What indeed," Laura agreed sadly.

"In any case," he went on, "that is the excuse our political leaders have settled on for why we could not evict those EastHem forces from Callisto. So, in response to that, they've kicked loose enough funding to form this fast reaction division. It will be stationed here because it's too expensive to station it on Ganymede. They would have to build an entire base on the surface in order to do that. God forbid they spend a couple of billion of the budget for that."

"Will these troops be of any value to Mars whatsoever?" Laura wanted to know.

Jackson offered another shrug. "They could theoretically help defend us in the event of an attempted invasion, but they would only be able to hold for a little while before reinforcement became necessary. Reinforcement from Earth, as I'm sure you're aware, takes anywhere from four to twelve weeks depending on planetary alignment. Worst case scenario is that EastHem hits us with a surprise invasion when Earth and Mars are on opposite sides of the sun."

"A surprise invasion?" she asked. "I thought that was impossible. Wouldn't we see the ships coming from the moment they left Earth?"

"Not anymore. Now that EastHem has a supply line stretching from Earth to the Jupiter system, it would be relatively easy to launch a surprise attack upon us during certain times of the year."

"What do you mean?" she wanted to know.

"Well," he told her, pouring each of them a little more wine, "they could hide their invasion force in specially modified fuel tankers. When Jupiter and Mars are approaching alignment, we would be accustomed to seeing groups of EastHem tankers passing within a few hundred thousand kilometers of us. We wouldn't think anything about it. But suppose a few of those tankers contained not fuel, but a dozen assault landing ships apiece. They're easily big enough for that. The EastHems, if they did it at the right time, could have two or three divisions of troops secure in their beachheads before our marines even had a chance to get their own heavy equipment on the surface."

"Unbelievable," Laura said, shaking her head. "If you want to hear a doomsday scenario, just ask a marine commander."

"And ask you did," he said. "And that's just one surprise attack scheme. I can think of five or six others just off the top of my head."

"Has any of this been brought up to the executive council or congress?" she asked.

"It's been suggested that a permanent force of soldiers dedicated completely to Martian defense would be a good idea," he explained, "but the suggestions have only come from the command level. Once the suggestion moves into the offices of those idiots in Denver, it gets shot right down as being unnecessary and too expensive."

Laura sighed in disgust. "Money," she said sourly. "That's what it always comes down to. We don't want to spend the money right now to prevent a crisis later."

"It's the way of the solar system," Jackson agreed.

Though Laura was morally upset with the situation her planet was being left in, she was also elated. Though Mars would be left nearly defenseless in the short term, it did open up an entire new aspect to her long-range plans. The idea she had been mulling over ever since she heard of the impending pullback of the marines began to click more firmly into place.

"Tell me something, Kevin," she said, lowering her voice just a little. "What if there was a Martian planetary guard? A force made up of volunteers from Mars itself and equipped with modern weapons. Could such a force be trained efficiently enough to repel an invasion?"

He mulled that over for a second. "A planetary guard huh? I suppose such a force could be drilled and trained enough to cause EastHem quite a headache. I would even venture to say that a good number of Martian citizens would participate in such a program if you had one. But where would the funding come from? You have the same basic problem as stationing professional marines here. Nobody wants to pay for it."

"The Martian citizens could pay for it," she suggested.

Jackson blinked. "Come again?"

"A voluntary income and sales tax increase," she explained. "Say an extra two percent on sales and maybe an extra three percent on income. I haven't done the exact math, but that would generate in excess of four billion every year. With four billion a year allocated for equipment and training expenses, you could buy a lot of tanks and artillery and guns, couldn't you?"

"Yes, you could," he said. "But you don't really think the people would volunteer to tax themselves that much, do you? We already have ten percent sales tax and we already pay more than forty-five percent in income taxes to the feds, not to mention an additional six percent to the planetary government."

"On the contrary," Laura retorted. "I believe the citizens would vote overwhelmingly for such a thing as long as it was for planetary defense. Remember, we were hit very hard during the war and most of our citizens know it was because we were largely undefended. Trust me on this. If there's one thing I know how to do, it's read the mindset of our citizens. They would vote this in."

"I'll have to take your word for it," he said doubtfully. "But that's not the only factor involved in such a thing."

"No," she said, "it's not. It would also require the approval of congress and the executive council. But if the funding was available, what possible objection could they have to it? Their prize moneymaker will be protected from invasion at no cost to them. It would also require the approval of the various corporations that control this planet. They would be concerned about an additional income tax affecting their Martian sales. Granted, with only seventy million people on the planet, Martians amount to only one percent of any WestHem corporation's paying customers, but you know corporations. If they think they'll lose ten cents a year, they'll want the measure killed and they'll spend billions killing it."

"Do you think they would approve of such a plan?" Jackson asked.

"If it was presented to them in the right way. That would be my job and I think I can do it. Now that I'm a member of the planetary legislature and not just a council member, my contacts have become more powerful—a little higher up the ladder. You have to remember that the corporations were particularly nervous during the war. After all, we citizens only had our lives to lose. They had their very holdings put in jeopardy."

"You seem to have this all figured out," he observed. "What do you need from me?"

"I need a military expert to draw up plans for such a force," she told him. "I need minimum staffing recommendations, minimum supply recommendations, and minimum deployment recommendations. I need facts, figures, and presentations to show just how such a force would be used and to explain to those complete idiots of the corporate boards and congress just how it would be an effective deterrent."

"I see," he said slowly.

"I would put you in touch with various auditors, accountants, and lawyers from the various corporations that supply the equipment so you could develop estimations for both initial start-up costs and yearly operational costs. Most of the military hardware manufacturers are based here on Mars. That should make things a little easier. We wouldn't have to deal with shipping costs."

"No," he said, his head spinning with the request. "I don't suppose we would."

She took a deep breath. "And most of all," she continued, "if such a project were approved, I would need someone to lead it."

There was silence as he digested her words and tried to grapple with all of the ramifications of it. "You would want *me* to lead it?"

"I cannot think of a better person," she replied. "Of course, unlike the bulk of the members, you would be paid a salary for your position and you would be expected to devote your full-time energies to it. You would be allocated a command staff and a training staff, the composition of which would be your discretion. The governor would have to appoint you to the position and the legislature would have to confirm you, but I'm pretty sure that if I can get things that far it will not be a problem. A few whispered words to the right people would be all that was required. For instance, I could assure Alexander Industries that you would buy your ammunition from them if they pressured the politicians they own to vote for you."

This was all moving too fast for Jackson. "I would have to resign from the marines in order to accept your offer," he said. "I would have to give up my rank, my pension, and everything I've worked for over the years."

"Yes," she said, not pulling her punches, "you would. As I said, you would be paid for your position and given all of the perks you would expect from it. Comparable salary, medical and lawyer insurance, and travel expenses would all be covered. But you would have to leave the marines behind."

He took another sip from his wine, swallowing it slowly. "You're asking a lot of me, Laura."

"I know," she said, wondering if she should tell him the rest of her plans for this force. To do so would be a horrible risk. If her instincts about his planetary loyalty were the least bit wrong... But on the other hand, he would have to be told eventually, would have to agree. And there was no one else that she could even begin to trust with what she had in mind. There were undoubtedly others who would do it, but she had no way of picking them out. Though her political connections were many, her military ones were almost completely limited to this one man.

"Look, Laura," he said, intruding upon her train of thought, "I'll be happy to draw up your plans for you and provide any manner of expertise that I can offer. I'll even take an unpaid leave of absence to help you get it up and running. But as for giving up my commission... well, I'm not sure that I can..."

"Kevin," she said softly, making her decision, "why don't I explain a few other things to you?"

"Other things?"

She nodded, feeling her hands wanting to tremble as she laid her proverbial cards on the table. "I'm going to be governor of this planet someday," she said. "Probably within twelve years."

"I'm sure you're right," he said, "but..."

"Listen to me for a minute," she interrupted. "Listen to me very carefully. I want to be absolutely sure that you do not misunderstand anything I'm about to say."

That got his attention. He snapped his mouth shut.

With that, she began to talk.

Jackson listened to her, his eyes widening as the story developed. When she was done, he only sat there, stunned.

"What do you think?" she said at last. "It's certainly a risk, I'll be the first to agree. But it's a risk worth taking and I think that together, we can pull it off."

"My God, Laura," he finally intoned. "What you're suggesting is... is..."

"I know what it is," she told him. "The question is, will you help me?"

He scratched his head a little and took a few breaths. Would he help her? Would he risk not just his career but his very life? He could easily imagine the consequences of failure. But at the same time, he could imagine the rewards of success. They would be the greatest rewards a people could imagine. "I'll help you," he said at last. "You get me a planetary guard established and I'll lead it."

She smiled, holding her hand across the table. "Welcome aboard," she said as he shook with her. "Someday they're going to name cities after you."

"Yes," he said, feeling both elation and fear at what he had agreed to. "They do that after you're dead, don't they?"

CHAPTER ONE

January 28, 2186
Eden, Mars

Lisa Wong drove the black and white police cart slowly down 5th street, cursing as she had to detour around city hall. Uniformed Martian Planetary Guard squads, part of Governor-elect Laura Whiting's security detail, had closed the streets to all traffic for a block in each direction in anticipation of an inauguration party that would be taking place all day tomorrow, after the new leader of Mars was sworn in tonight in New Pittsburgh. They had erected plastic barricades and were standing by with M-24 assault rifles slung over their shoulders. Combat goggles were settled upon their faces. The soldiers and the police department usually got along well together—after all, a good portion of the police force served on their days off—but not well enough to invite the cart to pass through. They had their orders, direct from General Jackson himself.

"Fuckin' politicians," Lisa groaned to her partner as she turned onto 16th Avenue, winding her way through a group of pedestrians that were watching the soldiers. "There won't be a single fuckin' dignitary down here until tomorrow afternoon, but they're closing everything off tonight. What the hell is up with that? Sometimes I think they have all that security as a goddamn status symbol instead of out of any real need. Who the hell would want to kill a politician anyway? All they'd do is elect another one."

"Yep," Brian Haggerty replied from the passenger seat of the cart. He took a drink from a large bottle of soda and then belched loudly, as if to express his opinion. "If there's one thing there's no shortage of, it's elected officials. They oughtta use all of those troops to come out here and run some of our calls for us. Maybe that could cut us down to eight a shift instead of twelve."

"And maybe let us get a chance to eat lunch once in a while," Lisa agreed, honking impatiently at a group of gang members that were taking too long to clear out of their way. On Martian streets it was generally the pedestrian that ruled since walking and the elevated trains were the principal means of transportation. But what little vehicular traffic did exist—police carts, dip-hoe carts, delivery truck—was legally given the right of way. Apparently, this street gang had not been briefed on that particular provision of the municipal code. Two of the gang members raised their middle fingers to the black and white without even glancing at it. Two others did glance at them, but only long enough to make eye contact while they contemptuously grabbed their crotches.

"Fucking vermin," Brian said sourly, glaring at them through the reinforced mesh wire that covered the windshield. "I'd like to cram my tanner up their back doors and crank it up to full."

"They'd probably like it," Lisa replied, finally achieving enough room to maneuver the four-seat electric cart around them. She picked up a little speed and continued down the avenue, turning at the next block and circling back around to 5th Street once more.

Lisa and Brian were uniformed patrol officers of the Eden Police Department. Both were nine-year veterans of patrol services and both had recently been assigned to the downtown division. Downtown Eden was not exactly the most desirable district to work. Once away from the office buildings and the expensive housing complexes, which were patrolled by high seniority foot patrolmen anyway, the streets were as dangerous as anything in the ghettos. Downtown was rife with armed gangs of welfare class youths that trafficked in *dust*: a cheap, illegal drug that was synthesized from stolen agricultural chemicals. Dust was the intoxicant most favored by the lower classes when they ran out of, or grew bored with, their monthly allotment of marijuana and alcohol. Those who chronically used dust were prone to fits of violent paranoia while on a binge. Between the sellers, the manufacturers, and the users, all of whom were concentrated in high numbers in the welfare housing buildings of downtown, the district was a busy, dangerous place to work. Downtown forced patrol partners into a sometimes fierce protective bonding with each other.

"What's this bullshit for again?" Lisa asked, referring to the latest call that they had been dispatched to. She knew she was heading for the lobby of the Apple Tree public housing complex at 5th Street and 65th Avenue, but aside from that, she had not heard the particulars.

"Assault in progress," Brian told her, reading from the terminal mounted between their seats. "A young man of Asian descent is apparently beating upon someone with a piece of lobby furniture."

"So, what the hell do they want us to do about it?" she asked, shaking her head. "Those fuckin' animals are always beating the hell out of each other. We haul them off to jail and they're out two hours later beating on someone else."

"Maybe he'll kill him," Brian said with a shrug. "At least that way he'll spend a few months in the slam."

"And give us more reports to compose too," she pointed out, slowing up for another group of gang members that were ambling from an intoxicant store across the street to the entrance of their housing complex. They all carried bottles of Fruity—the potent concoction of fermented waste juices from the bottling facilities. It was the favored drink among the welfare class because it was both cheap and powerful. One bottle of Fruity was more than enough to give a person of average weight a therapeutic alcohol level. Though the taste was horrid, it was very economical. This group of gang members seemed to be in a better mood than the last. Only one of them flipped the bird at the patrol car and one of them, an African descendent, actually blew a kiss at Lisa.

"It's good to see public support for the police, isn't it?" Brian asked, grinning at his partner.

"Yes," she said, shaking her head in amusement. "It makes me all warm inside."

As they continued on their path towards the Apple Tree, their talk turned to the upcoming inauguration. Lisa was of the opinion that Laura Whiting, whom she had voted for, was not quite as corrupt as the others of her species. "I mean, I actually voted for her," she said. "Me. I haven't voted for anything since I was twenty years old because it seemed like a complete waste of time and mental effort. But there's something about her that's... well... different. I just can't explain it, you know?"

Brian was a little more cynical. "She just had a better campaign manager," he said. "She's smart enough to realize that we Martians are not as dumb as the Earth politicians and the corporate assholes seem to think we are. She just played to our intelligence a little. You watch. She won't be any different. Remember how she got to where she is."

"I know," Lisa said. "By cramming her nose up every corporate ass that's been stuck in her face since law school. I'm not saying that she's going to make a real difference or anything. I'm just saying that she seems to have a little empathy for us working folks."

"Hmmm. Then you seem to be of the opinion," he paraphrased, "that she won't totally fuck us, that she'll just partially fuck us?"

"Right," Lisa agreed, chuckling. "She'll put on a little bit of lube before she sticks it in."

The two partners were still mulling over that analogy when Lisa pulled to the sidewalk a half a block from the Apple Tree main entrance. They opened their doors and stepped out onto the street, taking a moment to adjust their weapons belts and resettle their Kevlar armor upon their torsos. As part of the standard patrol load-out they had blue and white, bullet resistant helmets upon their heads with combat goggles mounted to the top, where they could be pulled down for easy use. Their belts contained 5mm pistols with thirty round clips in addition to three pairs of handcuffs and a tanner, which was a one-meter metal club capable of delivering an incapacitating electrical charge. They had military style M-24 assault rifles in their possession but these were usually kept under the seats of the cart and rarely taken out. On their lower bodies they wore blue shorts but their knees were protected with Kevlar guards and their feet were encased in steel-toed boots.

"Shall we do it?" Lisa asked, slamming her door shut. She pushed a button on the patrol computer/communicator on her belt and the door locks clanked into the locking position. A chirp indicated the alarm system was active.

"We shall," Brian agreed with a sigh.

Above them, the red Martian sky, which was visible through the dirty plexiglass roof, was darkening with sunset. Soon the stars would be out and shining in all of their brilliance. The ninety-story low rent building, most of its windows darkened, rose above them, somewhat cutting off the view. On the street before them there was not much activity. A drunken group of youths, not quite badass enough to be considered a street gang, were sitting on a planter in the middle of the street passing a marijuana pipe back and forth. The youths watched the two cops impassively, hardly seeming to notice them. Brian and Lisa gave them a once over and then turned their attention forward. They walked carefully to the entrance of the complex, keeping a wary eye on everything within view. The police department was not terribly popular with members of the welfare class and ambushes by gang members or just plain crazy people had been known to occur. Despite the armor they wore and the weapons they carried, an average of thirty patrol officers were killed each and every year in Eden alone. It was a dangerous profession where Darwinism ruled.

The main entrance to the complex consisted of glass panels reinforced with steel bars. Two sets of automatic sliding doors allowed access to the lobby area. An elderly man lay curled up and snoring next to the closest door, an empty bottle of Fruity next to him. He smelled strongly of urine and stale sweat. The two police officers stepped over him and sidled up to the door, peering through into the lobby. It was best to get an idea what you were walking into before you went and walked into it. The lobby of the Apple Tree, like the lobby of any housing building of the welfare or working class, was typically used as a gathering area for the residents. Any Internet packages or grocery shipments were delivered there before being carried up to the rooms. A large crowd of fifty or so people was gathered around the bank of elevators on the far wall. They seemed very upset and excited.

"I hate crowds," Lisa said, trying to see what the focus of the excitement was about. "A group like that could stomp us both to death in about a minute flat."

"I'm sure these fine citizens wouldn't do something like that," Brian joked, a little nervous himself. Having those that a police officer was trying to help suddenly turn on him or her was an all too frequent phenomenon in modern law enforcement. The welfare class hated the cops and the cops hated the welfare class.

"Well," Lisa sighed, stepping forward to activate the door sensor, "let's get it on."

"Right behind you, babe," Brian replied, taking up position.

The glass door was badly in need of a routine maintenance regiment. It rattled and clanked its way open with agonizing slowness, ruining their hopes of a quick, unobtrusive entry. Finally, it provided them with an opening big enough to walk through and they stepped inside. The lobby was covered with various bits of trash that overflowed from the garbage containers and seemed to spread out from there. Everything from empty Fruity bottles to empty marijuana packages to empty food containers lay in piles on the carpet and the lobby furniture. The smell was of poorly ventilated air scented with sweat, urine, vomit, and even a hint of feces. It was a smell that both had long since ceased to notice, they smelled it so often.

"Yo, motherfuckers!" screamed a middle-aged Caucasian man from the rear of the crowd as he saw them enter. "Git yo asses over here! They killin peoples!"

"Yeah!" yelled an elderly Asian woman standing next to him. "Motherfuckers is dusted out!"

Hearing the words: "they" and "dusted out", both officers drew their tanners from their belts and charged them. *Dusted out* was street slang for dust psychosis, the paranoid, violent state of mind that came from a two or three day binge of the powerful amphetamine. One strange effect of such psychosis was that it often encompassed more than one person. If two or three or even five people binged together over a period of days, they would all tend to dust out at the same time and with the same paranoid fantasies.

"How many 'theys' are we talking about here?" Lisa, still in the lead, asked the elderly Asian.

"They's two of 'em!" she yelled. "They fuckin' killin' people! Do somethin' 'bout it, goddammit!"

They could hear cusses and screams coming from within the crowd now, and the occasional thump of an object striking a human body. They began to push their way through. "Police!" they barked. "Move aside, let us in!" Reluctantly the crowd parted, more in deference to the charged tanners the two cops were waving than out of any respect for authority. As the onlookers parted, the scene became visible. Lying on the ground were two elderly men and one middle age female. One of the men was obviously dead, his skull split open and the bloody gray matter of his brain clearly visible. He lay in a twisted heap next to a broken lounge chair. The other man was alive but unresponsive. He was on his back while a young Asian male, shirtless and sporting multiple tattoos, kicked him repeatedly in the body while hitting him in the head with a piece of firm plastic that had once been the lounge chair's armrest. About two meters away the female, who was African descended and in her forties, was being choked by a Caucasian man in his twenties. He too was shirtless and bore an impressive array of both jailhouse and professional tattoos upon his torso. The woman he was choking was still struggling weakly, her arms beating ineffectively at his head and chest.

"I'll get the left, you get the right," said Lisa to Brian as she stepped forward.

"Sounds good," he replied.

They moved in, gripping their tanners in their left hands, keeping their gun hands free in case the tanners proved not to be effective. Sometimes with dusters, the electrical charge didn't work all that well.

"Drop it, asshole," Lisa barked at the man with the armrest.

He didn't even look up, he just continued to kick and hit with a fury, sending little sprays of blood upward with each blow. He was yelling at the man as he went about killing him. "You wanna spy on me, motherfucker? You wanna spy on me?" he demanded, over and over. Yes, this guy was dusted all right. He and his friend had probably gotten it into their heads that these three welfare class public housing residents were members of "them", that shady group those in dust psychosis always convinced themselves were after them.

"Put the club down, asshole," she yelled a little louder. "And I mean *now!*"

Again, the man did not even seem to hear her. Mentally sighing, she stepped forward, cocking the hand with the tanner backward. She had to be careful to not actually shock the assailant while he was touching the victim. If he were, the electricity would course through the victim's body as well. Granted, the electricity would not actually hurt the victim any worse than he was already being hurt by the piece of plastic, but cops were not allowed to inconvenience or cause pain to anyone that was not a suspected criminal. Years of civil law precedence had been established in that manner. A cop that caused pain to someone, even in the act of saving them, could be sued successfully. It was insanity, but it was modern reality.

"I hate this fucking job," Lisa muttered, as she swung the tanner sharply into the man's right knee. It struck right at the junction, hard enough to cause the leg to buckle but not hard enough to cause any physical harm. If she actually broke the man's knee, he could sue her for excessive force, pain and suffering, and a civil rights violation. She did not key the tanner as it struck him, using it as a club only. The man did not fall but he stopped hitting the victim and surged just enough off balance to allow her to step forward and, holding the tanner with one hand at either end, give him a shove. He stumbled backward three steps and then hit the broken lounge chair, falling into it and breaking it even further. Plastic splinters went spraying out across the room.

"You bitch!" the man screamed, a mad glint in his eyes as he tried to scramble back to his feet. "They was followin' us! They was fuckin' followin' us!"

"Lay on the ground!" Lisa barked, backing up a step and holding her tanner out before her once more. "Get down on your stomach or I'm gonna zap your ass!"

"No!" he returned, continuing his efforts to stand up. He was hindered by the fact that he was tangled up in the chair. "Them motherfuckers was followin' us. Gotta kill 'em, gotta fuckin' kill 'em!"

She yelled at him to get down one more time and, when he failed to obey her, she put the end of the tanner against his chest and pushed the discharge button. Thirty thousand volts surged out of the end and into his body, overpowering his nervous system. Whatever damping effects the chronic use of dust had did not seem to be present in this case. He stiffened up as if in seizure and then crashed to the ground, his hands splayed out before him.

"Could use a little help over here, partner," Brian grunted from her right side.

She turned and saw him struggling to pull the other duster off of the woman. He had his tanner wrapped around the man's neck and was trying to yank him backwards, but the duster would not release his grip on her. Again, the easiest, sanest course of action would have simply been to zap the man right there where he stood, but the contact would have resulted in a liability incurring shock to the victim.

She gave a nervous glance towards the man she had just dropped—there was no telling how long he would remain unconscious—before hurrying over to assist her partner. If was for damn sure that none of the concerned bystanders were going to help him. They would stand and watch impassively as the two dusters tortured and killed him, drinking Fruity as they did so.

"Get his arms, Lisa!" Brian barked. "Get his arms and I'll be able to pull him free!"

She bent down next to the victim and put her hands on the duster's forearm, yanking at it with all her strength. Like most cops that worked the dangerous areas, Lisa was a physical fitness fanatic. Her work-out regiment was augmented by her own volunteer work with the MPG, who's physical agility requirements, even for non-combatant positions like Lisa's, were stringent. The duster, though quite a bit larger and in the midst of psychosis, was no match for her. His arm popped free into hers, releasing its grip upon the woman's throat. She twisted it upward, putting it into a lock with her right hand so she could make a grab at his other hand. Before she could do this however, the duster released that grip on his own and swung his fist upward, striking her sharply in the face.

Pain exploded in her head, centered on her nose, and she staggered a little, seeing stars. She felt wet blood running down her face.

"Motherfucker!" she yelled, jamming the elbow of her free arm into the duster's stomach hard enough to cause tingling in her funny bone. The duster coughed and gasped as the air was expelled from his lungs and fell backwards, pulled that direction by Brian. Lisa kept her grip on his arm as Brian spun him around and slammed him to his stomach onto the filthy carpet of the lobby. She twisted the arm up further on his back while kneeling down and placing her knee on the back of his neck to keep him from rising up. Brian, releasing his grip on his tanner and allowing it to roll to the side, kneeled on the man's back. He grabbed the free right arm, which had been flailing around trying to strike something and twisted it up to join the left one.

"I got the cuffs," Brian told her, reaching to the rear of his belt and pulling out a set. In the last hundred and fifty years of law enforcement technological advances, the basic set of wrist restraints had changed little. Though they were now unlocked not with a key but with a command from the arresting officer's belt computer, the mechanism was the same as cops in the early twentieth century had utilized. He snapped the bracelet first on the wrist that he was holding and then the one that Lisa was holding.

They stood up, each breathing a little harder than normal with the effort. Brian picked up his tanner and holstered it. The duster, dismayed to have his arms immobilized and still trying to refill his lungs with air, began to kick his feet up and down, desperately trying to make contact with one of them.

"Chill out with that shit," Brian told him, "or I'll hobble your ass too."

The duster, though not exactly in his right mind, whatever that might be, was coherent enough to know that he did not want to have his feet tied together and attached to the handcuffs. More than likely he had experienced that particular form of restraint before. He let his feet lie still.

Lisa looked over at the first duster, the one she had zapped. He was moaning now and beginning to stir. Picking up her own tanner and holstering it she hurried over to him and kneeled down on his back.

"You got him okay?" Brian asked, taking a few steps in that direction.

"Yeah, he's still pretty much out of it," she replied, quickly grabbing his twitching left arm and applying a cuff to it. She twisted it up behind his back and then grabbed the right arm, bringing it into position and joining it to its companion. He offered no resistance.

Done, she stood back up. Her face was throbbing rhythmically, with the beat of her heart, from the blow she had received. She brought her fingers up to her face and touched the nose. Her fingertips came away bloody. "Asshole," she spat, wanting to go over and deliver a kick to the restrained duster, knowing she would do no such thing. A cop could end up bankrupt and in prison for doing something like that.

"You okay, Lisa?" Brian asked her as he ran a scanner over the prone body of the first duster. The scanner was low-yield ultrasound device that identified and inventoried everything in the possession of a suspect.

"Yeah," she said, reaching down for the transmit button on her belt computer. "It's just a bloody nose. I'll make it." She keyed her radio. "Four delta five-nine," she said into it, speaking to the dispatch computer back in the communications center, "we have two in custody, three victims down. Send us two dip-hoe carts for medical treatment of victims and a full homicide assignment."

"Copy that, four delta five-nine," said the cheery female voice of the computer. "Two suspects in custody. I'm responding two health and safety carts and a homicide assignment right now."

"And," she added, "inform the watch commander that physical force was required for the arrest. One subject immobilized with a tanner and one struck with an elbow."

"Notification will be made," the computer assured her.

Lisa shook her head in disgust, hating herself for feeling worried about the blow she had given to the scumbag duster and hating the department for making her feel worried about it. Any use of physical force at all required a report and notification of the watch commander. That was routine. But any use of force that was not outlined in the field training manual—and blows to the stomach were most assuredly not outlined—were subject to intense scrutiny by the department brass and the internal affairs division. Cops had been suspended, fined, fired, and even criminally prosecuted for such things.

"Good thing it's Lieutenant Duran tonight," Brian, who had overheard the transmission, told her. "You know how that prick Wilson rants about excessive force."

Lieutenant Wilson was one of two watch commanders that they dealt with on a weekly basis. He, unlike his counterpart Lieutenant Duran, was firmly in the loop for a rapid climb up the administrative ladder. As such, his every action was designed to show that he was in *control* of the cops he commanded. Duran, on the other hand, was an older cop rapidly approaching retirement age. She had capped out her climb up the ladder long ago and all she asked of her subordinates was that they not screw up enough to get her fired before her pension was secure. She had also spent many more years working the streets as a grunt before achieving her promotions. This tended to make her much more sympathetic in use of force cases.

"I don't know," Lisa said worriedly. "Duran or not, you know how they feel about hitting people. Those fuckin' personal injury lawyers have a field day with that shit."

"I wouldn't sweat it," Brian said soothingly. "He hit you in the face. That was the only way you could react to the situation."

"If they'd just let us tan those assholes instead of making us wrestle with them," she said, taking out her scanner.

"I know," he told her. "And if ten percent of the working population weren't lawyers, we wouldn't have to worry about any of this shit."

"But the solar system is what the solar system is," Lisa said fatalistically, repeating an often-heard motto in those times.

"Goddamn right," Brian agreed.

Once their suspects were searched for weapons and dragged off to the side, the two cops took a look at the victims of the attack. The man with the brains leaking out of his skull was, of course, beyond salvation and the man next to him, the one that Lisa had rescued with her tanner, was not looking terribly well either. Though there was no actual brain matter visible, his entire face was a bloody pulp. One eye was fixated off to the right while the other stared unblinkingly forward. His breathing was ragged and irregular, sometimes racing along frantically, sometimes slowing to almost a halt. The woman who had been choked was in a little better shape. Though she was gasping for air and having a little trouble getting her throat and lungs to work properly, her eyes were open and she was at least able to nod or shake her head to questions.

Now that the excitement of the fight was over, the crowd of onlookers began to react in a predictable manner. "Y'all took your fuckin' sweet time gettin' here, didn't ya?" a middle-aged man asked angrily. He was a Caucasian descendant and looked like he had put away more than his fair share of Fruity over the years. His bare, hairy stomach bulged alarmingly over the waistband of his shorts and his jowls jiggled with each word he spoke. "If you'd a been here when we called, them fuckin' dusters wouldn't a killed Jeff!"

"Yeah," added an Asian descendant woman next to him. She was smoking a cigarette and dipping the ashes on the floor. "I bet if it'd been someone that had a fuckin' job that'd called, your asses woulda been over here for we got off'n the terminal!"

The other members of the crowd quickly picked up the thread of this argument—a common one in such places. Within a minute, the angry shouts and accusations intensified to the point that Lisa and Brian began anxiously looking for the arrival of the two additional patrol carts that were being sent to assist with the homicide investigation. Crowds like this, in which many of the participants were either drunk on Fruity or a little dusted themselves, had a way of getting out of hand very quickly.

"They got fuckin' cops on every goddamn corner down in the Garden," a drunken African descendant shouted. She was referring to the Garden Grove area of Eden, just outside of downtown, where most of the wealthy and elite resided. "A duster wouldn't a been able to even get within a klick of one of them buildings, let alone go an' kill someone in one!"

"Yeah," added a companion, a Hispanic descendant this time. "But with us it just: 'be there when we get 'round to it!' Shit, we lucky you showed up at all!"

Lisa, working hard to maintain her composure, faced the crowd with a blank expression on her face. "I hate this fucking job," she mumbled to herself for perhaps that tenth time that shift, the hundredth time that week. While it was true that response times to the ghetto addresses and public housing buildings were considerably longer than they were in the areas where employed people lived, this was not due to any apathy on the part of the cops. When a call appeared on their screen, they went to it. It was the same with the other patrol units. The simple fact was that the ghettos were just not staffed adequately enough even though they were the busiest districts in the city by far. Eight out of every ten calls to the police department originated in one of the ghettos. But did the ghettos contain eighty percent more cops? Not even close. The ghetto was staffed with no more units than any other section of the city, except of course for Garden Grove and other areas like it. By contrast, the areas where the elite lived enjoyed the highest per capita ratio of cops to citizens. As the drunken African descendant had so delicately pointed out, there were foot patrol teams on damn near every corner. It was, without question, a serious misallocation of resources that was based upon money and social inequality. But was any of this Lisa's fault? Was it Brian's, or any of the other rank and file cops'? Was it the fault of those high seniority cops that worked in Garden Grove? No. But the inhabitants of the ghetto, who were perpetually plagued by violent street gangs, drug dealers, and poor response times when they needed help, perceived that this problem was because of the line cops. After all, the line cops were the only cops they ever saw. They could not take their complaints or frustrations to the city council or the department brass. So they blamed the most visible members of the organization and in the most angry and sometimes physical ways.

Lisa and Brian were both experienced enough in the realities of their job to know that trying to explain any of this to the crowd pushing in at them would be useless. They did not want to hear explanations or excuses. They wanted to vent. The best the two partners could hope for was that the crowd would stick to verbalizations to achieve their venting and not resort to physical stress relief. Things would get real ugly in a real hurry if that happened.

"'Get yourself assigned to downtown', the lieutenant told me," Brian was muttering to himself, although his words were easily picked up and transmitted to Lisa through the tactical radio link they shared. "'It's a lot mellower than Covington Heights,' he says. 'The AgriCorp building is downtown. Nothing bad could happen near the AgriCorp Building, could it?'"

"And why the fuck ain't you helpin' those people now?" a Caucasian near the front of the crowd demanded of them. "First you wait a fuckin' hour to show up and then, after you beat up on the people doin' it, you just fuckin' stand there! Them people's hurt!"

"We have the dip-hoes on the way," Lisa intoned mechanically, thinking to herself that the Caucasian, who was about her age, though looked ten years older, was going to be the first one she zapped if push came to shove. He had the biggest mouth. "They'll take care of them and get them to the hospital."

"Yeah right," the man said in disgust, taking another step forward. "And they'll sit there in the fuckin' hall whilst the doctors treats people that have jobs first! They'll let 'em die out there in the hall whilst they take care of people with stubbed toes that have insurance!"

"Yeah," agreed several members of the crowd. "You tell 'em, man!"

Neither of the cops bothered to dispute this point. Both knew it was true, had seen it happen just that way more than once. "That's not my department," Lisa told him, putting her hand on her holstered tanner. "But I do need you to step back out of the crime scene!"

"Or what?" he demanded. "You gonna zap me too? You gonna send me to jail? Fuckin' do it why don't you? I'll eat better and live better if'n I's in jail!"

"Goddamn right!" added the Hispanic who had spoken earlier. "Them motherfuckers in the jail get private rooms, room service, and better pot. They even get them premium Internet channels! They live like them pricks in the Garden. What kinda fuckin' punishment be that?"

"Step back, *now*!" Lisa said, raising her voice and locking eyes with the Caucasian. She gripped the handle of her tanner and pulled it upward a little.

The man spat on the ground at her feet, barely missing her boot with a yellow wad of phlegm, but that remained the extent of his defiance of her authority. At last, he stepped backwards. The crowd took a step back with him. Lisa and Brian both let a small sigh of nervous relief escape their lips. Though the crowd continued to shout insults and accusations, they kept their distance. In the world of modern law enforcement, that was perhaps the best that could be hoped for.

The first of the two-person emergency medical teams from the Department of Public Health and Safety arrived a moment later. They were dressed almost identically to the two police, lacking only the combat goggles and the weapons belts. The design on their blue helmets and on their bulletproof armor was a little different—it featured a star of life instead of a police oval—but except for that, they were virtually indistinguishable from their law enforcement counterparts. Lisa and Brian watched as they wheeled in a stretcher upon which blue bags of equipment were resting. As soon as the medics came through the rickety front door they paused, eyeing the obviously hostile crowd nervously. The ghetto class often verbally and physically abused the dip-hoes as well, and for much the same reasons; misallocation of scarce resources and widespread abuse by other aspects of the medical system.

"It's okay, guys," Lisa called to them before they could slink away. "It's safe. C'mon over."

Plainly trepidatious, they nevertheless approached and went to work. They pronounced the first of the victims, the one with the exposed brain matter, officially dead. The second victim, the one that had been beaten with the arm of the chair, they paralyzed with a stasis drug and then installed an artificial breathing mechanism. By the time they were done doing that, the second team had entered the building and gone to work on the woman that had been choked. As they performed their duties, the crowd stayed at a reasonably safe distance, only shouting the occasional accusation about how if they'd been employed people they'd be getting better treatment.

"Fuckin vermin," Brian said softly into his throat microphone as he kept a wary eye on the crowd.

Lisa, who was watching the two suspects on the ground (they were stirring around and shouting insults of their own now) heard him but did not respond. Though most cops, like most employed people in general, disliked the welfare class immensely, Brian's hatred of them was unique in its fury. Six years before, his pregnant wife had been raped and killed by a group of welfare class thugs as she got off of the public transit train in the notoriously dangerous Helvetia Lowlands section of the city. Mandy Haggerty had been twenty-eight years old at the time and working as a fifth-grade teacher in one of the public schools of the Helvetia district. She had dedicated her life to teaching the welfare class children and had been quite good at it. But some of the welfare class youths in the neighborhood, emboldened by a combination of Fruity and dust, had spotted her one morning on her way to work and that had been the death of her. Brian had long since gotten over the grief of her loss but his flaming hatred of the vermin, as the derogatory term for those of the welfare class went, had never so much as flickered in its intensity. Lisa, who had yet to marry and produce her one legally allowed offspring, knew that she could not fathom the depth of his feelings. But at the same time, she knew that working among the very people he hated so much ten hours a day, four days a week, was poisoning his mind.

By the time the DPHS teams carted away the two surviving victims of the attack the homicide investigation, such as it was, was in full swing. Two additional patrol units had arrived and were questioning members of the crowd (and taking a lot of verbal abuse) about what had transpired. They were just going through the motions. The answers were all the same, no matter who was talked to. "I didn't see nothin," was recorded for the reports more than twenty times. Though everybody present had seen what had happened, nobody would admit it. They all knew that the accused murderers had a right to face their accusers in court. Bearing witness against dusters or street gang members was not a healthy thing to do in the ghetto. It went without saying that no matter how ironclad the case against them was, the two dusters would not spend more than a year in prison. There simply was not room to lock up every duster that killed a piece of vermin in Eden, not for very long anyway. Those rooms in the prison had to be kept free for more serious criminals, like those who pirated software that was produced by the media corporations or those who illegally distributed commercial music or video files.

Sergeant Franklin, their immediate supervisor, arrived a few minutes later. He brought in a digital camera, which he used to photograph the crime scene just in case the two dusters did not cop a plea or were not set free due to lack of evidence. Lieutenant Duran, the watch commander, showed up right behind him. She was not part of the standard homicide investigation assignment but her presence was required to take the use of force report. She was a tough, battle-hardened cop in her mid-fifties that had seen a little bit of everything during her twenty-five years on the job. She pulled her two subordinates aside, out of earshot of the suspects and the crowd, and offered each of them a bottle of flavored water.

"Thanks, Lieutenant," Lisa said, opening the plastic bottle. The label identified it as "Raspberry Surprise", produced and bottled by JuiceCo, a subsidiary of AgriCorp. She took a large drink, soothing her parched throat.

"Yeah," Brian agreed, opening his bottle of Apple Delight. "This'll help wash the taste of these vermin out of my mouth."

"Watch your language," Duran intoned gently. "You wouldn't want to get caught using a forbidden term now, would you?"

Brian snorted in disgust. The use of the word *vermin*, as well as many other derogatory slang terms, was deemed a firing offense by the public relations oriented department. General terms such as "asshole" or "dirtbag" were considered distasteful though acceptable, but specific slurs having to do with social status were not. The distinction dated back to a civil court case more than fifty years before in which a third-generation unemployed man had successfully sued the New Pittsburgh Police Department for referring to him as vermin during a physical altercation. "You know something, Lieutenant," he told her, taking a drink of his juice. "Every time I come into a place and run a call like this and deal with a bunch of... people like that, the idea of losing this shitty job seems like less and less of a threat."

"I know what you mean," she soothed, patting him on the shoulder. "But remember, if you get fired from here, you'll be unemployed too. You'll have to move to public housing and live off welfare donations. You'll be considered vermin along with everyone else that's unemployed."

"And you'll have to quit the MPG," Lisa added, a little worried about her partner's mental health. "You won't get to fly your Mosquito anymore." It was this argument that would carry more weight with him than anything else. Unlike Lisa, whose MPG assignment was administrative, Brian, as a male, was a member of the elite air guard portion of the service. He flew the winged attack craft that had been developed by New Pittsburgh Enterprises and were specifically designed for operation in the thin Martian atmosphere. Though the WestHem armed forces considered them to be quaint, useless wastes of money, the pilots who drove them and the ground forces they protected considered them to be the finest piece of military engineering since the stealth attack ship. Brian was no exception to this. His one great thrill in life was climbing into the cockpit of his Mosquito and rocketing down the runway.

"I know, I know," he said, frowning a little. "Sometimes that's all that keeps me here. I don't know why the hell I didn't listen to my old man and spend my career training money on engineering school instead of the fuckin police training school. I could be workin at the damn water plant or the fusion plant or the air production plant instead of dealing with these animals every goddamn day."

"Well, you're stuck with us now," Duran told him, "so you're just gonna have to hang in there. Keep your sanity intact another four years or so and you'll be able to transfer to a working-class neighborhood."

"I keep that vision before me like it was expensive pornography," he told her, seeming to lighten up a little. "Imagine, dealing with people who have jobs every day, who don't suck the money right out of my pay before I ever see it. It would be like paradise."

"It will be paradise," Lisa, who kept the same image at the forefront of her brain, assured him. "Four or five more years of hell, and you're in."

Now that Brian seemed to have calmed himself a little, Duran proceeded with her investigation. She questioned each of them regarding the events that led up to the use of force and as to why they thought the use of force was needed in the situation. Their answers were recorded and instantly transcribed by her investigation computer program. Both were veterans of such investigations and kept their voices neutral and professional, not allowing any sort of emotion to leak through.

"Can you think of any other option to the situation," Duran asked Lisa near the end, "other than striking the homicide suspect with your elbow?"

"No ma'am," she replied. "As I stated earlier, the suspect was quite agitated and was refusing to release his grip upon the victim's throat. Furthermore, he had struck me in the face with his free hand at that point. Due to his contact with the victim and with my partner I was unable to apply electricity to him with my tanning device. It is regretful that such violence needed to be employed to diffuse the situation, but I saw no other option."

Duran smiled and clicked off the recorder. "Very good, Lisa," she told her. "I particularly liked that last bit about it being regretful. If your asshole ever sues for excessive force, that'll play well in court."

"Shit," she said, "he'll have to get in line." Lisa, like most cops, had more than thirty abuse of force suits pending against her in various stages of negotiation. Thank god there was a such thing as lawyer insurance and lawsuit insurance. True, the premiums for such coverage for law enforcement officers were almost as high as they were for doctors and lawyers themselves, but without those policies Lisa would have been bankrupt ten times over.

"What do you think, lieutenant?" asked Brian. "Is Lisa gonna get banged for hitting that piece of shit, or what?"

"It'll go to internal affairs of course," Duran told them, informing them of nothing they did not already know. "But I wouldn't worry too much. They tend to go with the investigating command officer's preliminary report and my report will be favorable to you. I honestly don't see anything inappropriate about elbowing that shitheap in order to get him to let go of the victim. In fact, I'm going to put a note on the end of my report stating that I thought the both of you exhibited admirable restraint for not kicking the crap out of both of them."

"Thanks, lieutenant," Lisa said gratefully.

"But in the future," she cautioned, "I would watch what I was doing if I were you. If Lieutenant Wilson had been the watch commander today, you probably would've found yourself under suspension by now. Wilson spent about twenty minutes or so working patrol before he got promoted into management, so he doesn't really have much of a shake on how things work out here on the streets. Nor does he care how things work on the street. His interest is in making deputy chief before he's forty. Right or wrong, good or bad, Wilson thinks that collecting two-week suspensions for excessive force is putting him in favor with the brass. You get too many two-weeks under your belt and you'll find yourself on the fast-track to vermin status, if you know what I mean."

"I know what you mean, lieutenant," Lisa said. "I'll try to watch what I'm doing in the future."

Duran sighed a little. "That's just the thing, Lisa," she told her. "You shouldn't have to watch what you're doing. Not like that. Those assholes in city hall charge us with protecting the public and then do everything in their power to see to it that our hands are tied behind us and that our authority is mocked at every turn. Then they wonder why crime is so fucking high." She shook her head. "I don't know sometimes. Laura Whiting says she's going to empower the police when she takes office. Maybe she's our savior." The sarcasm of her last remark was quite evident in her tone.

"Yeah right," Brian said with a cynical laugh. "She'll make it easier for us to go after those farm workers that steal apples and oranges and marijuana buds from the AgriCorp greenhouses. What the hell else did they fund her campaign for?"

"The solar system is what the solar system is," Duran told them with a shrug. "And we're the ones that get paid to shovel the shit."

*****

Lon Fargo brought the electric truck to a halt near the southern end of greenhouse A-594. The truck was ten meters long and featured a thirty-meter extendible hydraulic boom that was currently retracted. At the end of the boom was a portable airlock that allowed a person to pass from inside of the pressurized environment of a greenhouse building onto its roof by utilizing one of the access panels. One such panel was directly above the truck now.

Lon and his fellow agricultural complex maintenance technician, Brent Shimasaki, stepped out of the cab and onto the dusty macadam surface of the narrow access road. This particular greenhouse, one of more than ninety thousand in the Eden area, was two square kilometers in size. The ground inside of it, which had once been gently rolling hills and gullies, part of an ancient wetland water shed, had been bulldozed to a nearly perfect flatness when the complex was built forty-six years before. Golden stalks of wheat, less than a month from harvest, stretched from wall to wall in all directions, broken only by the geometric rows between them and by the access roads that divided the field into grid quadrants. The air was dry and warm, kept at the perfect growing temperature and humidity by the environmental simulation machines on the roof. It was one of these machines, which were powered by a fusion plant just outside the city, that the two men had come to repair.

They stepped lightly and carefully as they walked from the doors of the truck, which were emblazoned with a brand new AgriCorp decal, to the rear where a storage cabinet was mounted. The greenhouses, though pressurized and warmed, did not have artificial gravity fields in place. Inside the city buildings or on the city streets, magnetic simulation fields were sent through steel conductors that were built into the base construction. This field kept gravity at a comfortable and healthy Earth standard 1G. It had long been known that human beings could not live long term in anything less than .8G without losing dangerous amounts of bone density and muscle mass. The development of artificial gravity in the late 21st century had been the key factor in allowing the biggest mass migration of humans in history to take place. It was the artificial gravity that allowed sixty million people to live and work on Mars and above it. But in the agricultural fields, the artificial gravity was not necessary. Not only was it cost prohibitive to maintain and install, it was also somewhat of a hindrance to operations. The crops actually grew better in the considerably weaker Martian gravity. And the harvesting machines and maintenance trucks could carry more and used less electricity since they and their cargoes were lighter. But for human beings used to walking around and functioning in 1G, performing tasks in one third of that was something that had to be done carefully. It was quite easy to push a little hard during a step and suddenly find yourself a meter in the air and tumbling towards the ground.

This greenhouse, and in fact all of the greenhouses in the surrounding eight hundred square kilometers, had once been the property of Interplanetary Food Products, which had been the fourth largest agricultural company on Mars. As of two weeks before, however, IFP had ceased to exist. AgriCorp, thanks to a multi-billion dollar merger of assets, was now the owner of everything that IFP had possessed. It was a merger that had been much lauded in the business sections of the Internet services as being far-reaching and progressive. AgriCorp stock had increased nearly fifteen percent since the merger became official.

"I hope we get this thing done real quick," Brent said as they opened the storage compartments and removed their folded blue biosuits. "It's almost quitting time. The overtime would be nice, but a couple a hits of some good green at the bar would be nicer."

"Shit," Lon said, kicking off the canvas shoes he wore and tossing them up on the truck, "we can't work overtime anymore, remember? We work for AgriCorp now. Overtime has to be approved by management in advance or you work for free."

"What do you mean?" Brent asked, wondering if his coworker was joking or not. "That doesn't apply to overtime we pull trying to finish a job, does it? I thought it was just for shift work."

"Nope," Lon replied. "It applies to all overtime, for anything. I checked with Jack before we came out here. He says if we're not done with this blower by the time 4:30 rolls around, to just pack up and leave it until tomorrow. Nobody is to run past their scheduled shift for anything. No exceptions."

Brent shook his head at the idiocy of that. "They would rather have us leave a blower open to the dust all fuckin' night then pay us time and a half for thirty or forty minutes?"

Lon gave a cynical smile. "Ain't our new bosses smart? You ask me, I'm honored to work for the biggest corporation in the solar system. Their vision and frugality are something to be admired and imitated."

"God almighty," Brent said, kicking off his own shoes. "Now I've heard just about everything."

The biosuits they wore were designed and manufactured by the same company that made suits for the Martian Planetary Guard. They were constructed of form fitting reinforced carbon fiber that provided near-perfect insulation. An inner sleeve that formed to the body when the suit was activated served the dual purpose of maintaining the proper body pressurization—for the atmospheric pressure on Mars was considerably less than the minimum required to sustain human life—and maintaining proper body temperature—for the outside temperature of Mars, even on the equator, rarely climbed above 0 degrees Celsius. Lon stepped into his suit and pulled it tight, making sure it was properly positioned. Having a suit activate while a portion of the inner sleeve was askew could be a painful and even dangerous experience, particularly if the askew portion happened to be near the genitals.

Once things seemed to be aligned properly, he pulled his helmet from the storage compartment and placed it on his head. The helmet was a lightweight, airtight vessel that would pressurize when the suit was turned on. The air supply came from a small, flat tank on the front of the suit. Attached to the tank was an oxygen and nitrogen extractor, a much smaller version of the machines that kept the air flowing in the cities. The extractor would continually draw in those two elements from the thin atmosphere and keep the tank full of breathable air. Lon, as a member of the MPG, was in top physical shape. As such, except during heavy exertion, the extractor on his suit would be able to supply the tank faster than he could breathe it down. This meant he could stay outside all day if necessary, urinating into a sponge device inside his shorts and drinking water from the small storage vessel that fed a straw in his helmet. Only the need for food or defecation would force him inside; two biological functions that were addressed in the military version of the biosuit but not the civilian version.

Lon gave his helmet a final twist, locking it into place. A small green light appeared in the corner of his visor display. This told him that the seal was intact and the suit was ready for activation. He spared a glance over at Brent, seeing that he was still struggling to pull his own suit tight over the bulk of his body. Brent was not a member of the MPG and was not particularly fond of physical exercise. What he was fond of doing was sitting in a bar or at home and smoking bag after bag of cheap marijuana, which in turn led him to eat quite a bit of food. The result of all this was that he was more than twenty kilos overweight and he tended to draw more air from his biosuit than it could replace, even during non-exerting work. This technically placed him in violation of safety standards for an outside worker, but IFP management had always looked the other way about it. As long as the work got done, IFP had not cared how it was accomplished or whether or not it was accomplished safely. But now that IFP management had been replaced by AgriCorp management, who had already proved to be much more stringent and nitpicking about such things, Lon wondered if Brent's next physical exam was going to be his last. But then there was a strong possibility that neither one of them were going to even make it to their next annual exam. The blue collar workers of the former IFP force were still awaiting word on the inevitable merger-related "elimination of positions" that came every time two companies became one. Usually, especially when AgriCorp was involved, it was the smaller of the two merged company's workers who bore the brunt of the cuts.

"Suit computer," Lon said into the throat microphone, addressing the voice-activated circuit that controlled the suit. It was necessary to address the computer by name, such as it was, so that it would not inadvertently mistake some aspect of normal conversation for a command. "User logging on."

"Go ahead," said the artificial, vaguely male voice that the cheap computer had been programmed with.

"User Lon Fargo. 897-78-98-9876-34."

The suit computer quickly accessed the Internet via a cellular antenna in the far corner of the greenhouse. It then accessed the AgriCorp main intranet for Martian operations, searched its employee databanks and found that that name matched that social security number and that that employee was currently authorized to utilize an AgriCorp biosuit. It then compared Lon's voice pattern with the pattern it had stored and concluded that they were both the same. This took a little over two and a half seconds. "Log on accepted," it told him. "Awaiting command."

"Suit computer," Lon said, "testing procedure."

"Stand by." The computer performed a complete safety check of all seals and circuits. This took nearly ten seconds. When it was done and satisfied that Lon would not be decompressed if he stepped outside, it said: "Test complete. Your suit is functioning properly."

"Nice to know," Lon muttered. "Suit computer, activate suit."

"Activation in progress," the computer answered.

Lon took a deep breath and braced himself. The activation sequence was not painful by any means, at least not if the suit was being worn correctly, but it was not exactly one of life's great pleasures either. He felt the entire surface area of his body, from the bottom of his neck downward, being slowly compressed. For a moment it was difficult to breathe at all as the plastic constricted the rise and fall of his chest. But once the proper pressure was reached, the constriction eased up, allowing free movement. No sooner had the body section pressurized than the hissing of air against his face began. That was the pressurization of the helmet portion of the suit. The air had an industrial, almost chemical smell to it that was actually caused by the delivery system, not the air itself.

"Activation complete," the computer told him when it was done. "All systems working properly."

"Suit computer, activate radio link with suit uh..." he paused to look at the number stenciled on the right sleeve of Brent's suit. He had to read it sideways since Brent, having just successfully closed his body inside, was putting on his helmet. "Five seven five nine three two... uh six."

"Link established," the computer said. "Be advised that the specified suit is not currently active."

"No shit, dickwad," he replied. The computer said nothing in return, had in fact not even heard his remark since the proper salutation had not prefaced it.

It took another two minutes for Brent to go through his safety check and activation sequence. Once he was done and had his radio link active, he looked over at Lon. "You ready," he asked.

"I'm ready," Lon said. "Let's do it."

He walked over to a control panel on the truck and opened the access hatch. A small computer screen was beneath it. He activated the screen and instructed it to link up with both his and Brent's suit computers. It asked for authorization in the form of names, social security numbers, and voiceprints. They provided this information. Once that was complete Lon instructed the truck computer to power up the airlock at the end of the boom.

"Airlock active," replied the truck computer over their radio.

The airlock was nothing more than a steel box, two meters square by two meters deep. At the top was a synthetic rubber cushion that would form a seal against the roof of the greenhouse. Lon and Brent stepped onto the back of the truck and picked up their two large tool chests, which had been stored against the hydraulic housing. Lon swung his leg over the side of the airlock first, the thin material of the suit allowing almost normal range of motion. Once he was inside, Brent handed him the tool chests, hoisting them up and over with absurd ease although, had they been in 1G, they would have weighed more than thirty kilograms each. Lon set them on the floor and Brent hefted his own bulk into the box. With the two of them inside, the quarters were a little cramped but they would only have to put up with it for a few minutes.

"You all set?" Lon asked, putting his hands on the boom controls. The glove portions of the biosuits were thin and were designed to allow as much dexterity of the fingers as possible but, even so, any fine movements were awkward. As such, the controls were overly large.

"Take us up," Brent told him, settling in against the wall. "Let's get this shit over with."

Lon pushed upward on the control yoke and the hydraulic boom began to extend, moving the airlock upward and outward. The roof access panel was 1.5 meters square and set into the glass of the ceiling twenty meters above the road. It was marked by an outline of black paint. The idea was to make sure that the entire outline was within the airlock before the panel was opened. If it were not, an explosive decompression would occur when the hatch was opened, causing the blast doors in the 500 meter quadrant around the hatch to come slamming upward from the underground panels in which they were housed. Though the blast doors would protect everyone beyond the immediate quadrant, those unprotected workers inside of it would die a nasty death of decompression and suffocation. Lon's aim with the boom was at its usual level of perfection. The rubber seal pressed firmly against the glass leaving the black outline in almost the exact center. A flip of a switch caused the airlock's hydraulic system to apply constant upward pressure, making the seal airtight.

"Truck computer," he said. "Decompress airlock."

"Decompression sequence in progress," the computer replied.

From below them the powerful exhaust fans began to remove the air from the inside of the lock and expel it out into the greenhouse. The airlock would not be reduced to a complete state of vacuum, as would have been the case had they been in space, but would instead be reduced to the atmospheric pressure outside. The outside air pressure was a greatly variable number on Mars. It changed constantly from day to day as vast portions of the mainly carbon dioxide atmosphere were constantly frozen and thawed and refrozen in the polar regions of the planet. The truck computer automatically established a link with the Martian Weather Bureau, which kept track of current conditions, and downloaded the latest barometric reading. Of course, in addition to the constant shifting of pressure due to polar freezing, the pressure was different from place to place depending upon elevation as well. And, unlike on Earth, there were no oceans in which to base a standard 0 elevation. The MWB, as did the rest of Mars, used the elevation of New Pittsburgh, Mars' first settlement, as its standard. Since the Eden area greenhouse was nearly a thousand meters lower in elevation than New Pittsburgh, which sat atop a huge plateau, the computer had to do some adjustments of the figure it received. This was all a standard part of living and working in an environment where human beings were not meant to live and work. Most Martians hardly gave such things a thought, although they frustrated Earthling to hysterics at times.

"Decompression complete," the computer told them ninety seconds after it had begun. "Airlock seal is intact. It is safe to egress."

"Got it," Lon said, looking up at the number printed on the access hatch. "Suit computer, establish radio link with AgriCorp Eden Operations."

"Establishing link," the computer replied. A moment later: "Link is active."

Lon told the AEO computer that two workers would be atop greenhouse number A-594 near access panel A-594-12 for approximately one hour. He then asked the computer to open that particular panel for him. Once again, he was asked for his name and social security number and once again his voiceprint was compared with that in the files. The computer then took the additional step of comparing Lon's stated mission with the work orders for the day that had been filed in its memory banks. At last, satisfied that Lon and Brent were not terrorists attempting to disrupt AgriCorp operations and cut into profits, it consented to their request.

"Access panel A-594-12 is opening now," they were told.

There was a very slight hiss of mingling air as the square panel above them slid along its track. Red sand and dirt, blown up there by the constant wind that swept the planetary surface, dropped down upon them. Above them, the natural red tint of the Martian sky, which had looked distinctly purple through the tinted glass roof, could be seen in all of its glory. The sky was completely cloudless. Cloud formations, while common in the higher and lower latitudes, were almost unheard of in the equatorial regions.

Lon climbed out first, stepping on the ladder that was a permanent part of the airlock's wall. He pulled himself out onto the glass roof and then kneeled down next to the hatch to pull up the two tool chests that Brent handed up to him. He set them to the side and then stood up, allowing Brent to extricate himself from the lock. This portion of the greenhouse roof was only a few meters from the southwest corner of the large building. Twenty meters below them was a paved access road that ran alongside. The road, which was used to access the roof if major repairs or renovations, those involving heavier pieces of equipment, needed to be done, had not been plowed in a while and had drifts of sand marring its surface. Back at the AgriCorp operations building at the edge of the city (not to be confused with the AgriCorp main building downtown—the Earthlings that ran the company certainly would not wish to work out of the same building as the common field hands) were large hydrogen powered trucks and even tracked vehicles that were used for heavy maintenance and repairs. On the other side of the road there was two hundred meters of open space, just enough to allow heavy equipment through, before the next greenhouse began. A narrow connecting tunnel near the far end joined the greenhouse to its neighbor which was, in turn, joined to its neighbor, and so on and so forth, all the way back to the main tunnel that led from the operations building to the first greenhouse. This allowed workers and heavy harvest machines, as well as container trucks, to get to where they were needed without having to go outside. It was through this system of tunnels and interior roads that Brent and Lon had driven their electric maintenance truck to where it was now parked.

Looking outward from the roof of number A-594, just poking upward from the western horizon, the tops of the Eden high rises could be seen some sixty kilometers distant. Aside from that, the tinted blue of greenhouse after greenhouse, all a uniform twenty meters high and two square kilometers in size, covered the land like a blanket. Lon and Brent were at the near edge of the Eden area's agricultural land. They could only see to the horizon, which was not very far on Mars, so only about a half percent of the total number of greenhouses in the area were visible to them from twenty meters above the ground. And Eden's agricultural holdings, while the largest on the planet, were only twenty-two percent of the total on Mars. Eight other cities, all along the Martian equator, were centered among similar complexes of artificial growing environments. Staring out upon the sea of glass and steel and realizing that you were only looking at a minute fraction of what was actually there, one could begin to fathom why it was that AgriCorp and the other food production companies of Mars were the most powerful entities in the solar system. Within those greenhouses everything from corn to marijuana to soybeans were produced year around, free of the perils of insects or weather. Nearly every type of food that was consumed by human beings or animals, whether they were on Mars or Earth or the Jupiter system, whether it was junk food or vegetables or meat, came from Mars in one way or another. It was hard to believe sometimes that all of this food production, which employed more Martians than anything else on the planet, and all of the wealth that came from it, most of which was sent back to rich stockholders on Earth, had been born as a simple experiment a hundred years before.

The first Martian colonists had come, not to grow food, but to exploit the rich deposits of iron ore that lay beneath the higher and lower latitudes of the planet. The supply of easily mined ore on Earth had been almost completely depleted in the early 21st century by the decade long World War III. The bloodiest conflict in human history had raged on three different continents and had killed more than two hundred million people. During the struggle, the combatants had mined iron ore at a mad pace from every available location on the planet turning it into guns, tanks, aircraft, ships, missiles, and bombs. By the time the last shell was fired and the formal surrender ceremonies were conducted, a large percentage of the reachable iron ore was gone forever, exploded into fragments that littered the battlefields of North America, China, and Eastern Europe.

Aside from wiping out the iron supply, World War III had also spawned the two spheres of influence that were now the constantly bickering entities of EastHem and WestHem. WestHem consisted of the North and South American landmasses and was ruled by Caucasians from the former United States and Canada. EastHem, the larger, though poorer of the two, consisted of Europe, Asia, Africa, and Australia. It was ruled by Caucasians of the former British Isles, Germany, and France. EastHem and WestHem had been the victorious allies of World War III, defeating the Asian Powers alliance of China, Japan, Korea, and India. The Asian Powers launched a surprise attack on January 1, 2029 into Siberia and the Middle East before jumping across the Bering Strait into Alaska, Canada, and, eventually Washington, Oregon, and Idaho. Their goal had been a lightning fast capture of the world's petroleum supplies before the opposition had a chance to gear up to a war footing and stop them. They came very close to achieving this goal in the first months of the fighting. Only a few lucky guesses on the part of the American Army and a few instances of bad luck on the part of the Chinese Army had allowed the Asian Powers to be stopped short of the Texas and California oil fields in North America. Here, the war had stagnated into a bloody stalemate for the next eight years, with millions upon millions dying but with the lines not moving much more than a few kilometers back and forth. Only the development of practical, portable anti-tank and anti-aircraft lasers had broken this stalemate and allowed the WestHem and EastHem alliance to slowly, grudgingly push the Asian Powers back and eventually destroy them with strategic and tactical bombing campaigns against their homelands.

No sooner had the fighting of World War III ended then the long, bitter cold war between EastHem and WestHem began as each vied for superior resource development and strategic positioning. The cold war was marked by an intense space race as each half of the world tried to secure precious resources that were only available in space. It is one of the cruelest ironies in history that World War III, aside from depleting the supply of exploitable iron ore, also depleted the very resource that it had been fought over in the first place. After ten years of all-out mechanized warfare, the world's supply of easily recoverable petroleum had been reduced to almost nothing. Thus, fusion power for electricity and space flight and hydrogen combustion engines for propulsion became the rage of the future. Huge platforms were built in low Earth orbit and large, interplanetary ships—at first only for cargo and personnel, but later, warships—were constructed. An entire new method and theory of warfare developed along with the spacecraft as each side theorized and planned for the best way to fight the other if it came to that.

It was the need for iron ore to convert into steel that led WestHem corporations to Mars in the first place. Though the moon had a significant supply of iron ore beneath its surface, EastHem had had the foresight to claim the lunar surface as its own first by establishing a large mining colony there. With the development of artificial gravity and the second generation of fusion powered spacecraft, the trek across the solar system to Mars became a cost-effective endeavor. Triad Steel Mining and Refining was the lead company that struck out for the red planet. They established the beginnings of the Triad orbiting city in geosynchronous orbit to serve as an interplanetary shipping platform. On the surface of the planet, they founded New Pittsburgh, the first of four mining cities that would eventually develop.

It was only after the New Pittsburgh mines were up and running and the settlement itself was a thriving city of more than a million souls that the great experiment of Martian agriculture was attempted. A water supply was quite easy to secure on Mars since huge underground aquifers existed nearly everywhere on the planet. But food was a different story. Shipping enough food across the expanse of space to feed more than a million people was a very expensive operation. Particularly since most of what had once been prime farmland in WestHem territory had long since been converted to cities and suburban areas, leaving the entire half of the planet perpetually short on food stocks to begin with. The settlement of Eden was begun modestly, with only a few buildings and living areas made out of castaway pre-fabricated construction materials. The first greenhouses were built just to see if there was any possibility of raising Earthly crops on the surface. It was an experiment that was very controversial at first since a lot of money had been spent for it with little hope of success.

To the surprise of everyone involved, it was discovered that crops of all kinds grew extremely well in the iron rich Martian soil when supplemental nutrients were added. The greenhouses made it possible to simulate the perfect conditions for whatever was being grown. Wheat could be given a hot, low humidity environment with just the perfect amount of irrigation. Apples could be given the damp, cool, high humidity environment they favored. No matter what kind of weather, humidity, or temperature was needed, it could be provided for. No matter what the Martian soil was lacking as far as nutritional content, it could be added. Pests, if they managed to infest a particular greenhouse—something that happened from time to time—could easily be eliminated by flooding the greenhouse with carbon dioxide and displacing the oxygen. Gone was the need for fumigation. Gone was the need to worry about an out of season frost or monsoon wiping out entire crops. For the first time in the history of mankind, farmers could be almost completely assured that whatever crops they planted, they were going to harvest.

Naturally, once the profit potential of the Martian agricultural project was realized, investors immediately bought it out. Thus, the great and powerful AgriCorp was born and the Martian Agricultural rush was begun. Greenhouses began to spring up as fast as the materials to construct them could be produced. Immigrants from WestHem, most of them from the ranks of the hopelessly unemployed, climbed aboard cargo ships and made the nine to twenty-seven-week trip across space, lured by the promise of jobs in construction, engineering, or agriculture. Eden, in less than ten years, went from a makeshift settlement with a few thousand botanists and manual laborers to a city of five million. Soon, other cities such as Libby, Proctor, Paradise, and Newhall began to spring up along the equatorial region of the planet;

each one the center of a rapidly growing expanse of greenhouses. All of this construction required extensive supplies of steel, glass, synthetics, and a thousand other resources. New Pittsburgh was simply not large enough to provide it all. And so, the cities of Ironhead, Vector, and Ore City were born, popping up one by one over the next thirty years in the high latitudes to supply the mining and manufacturing demands.

For the longest time, Mars was a complete paradise. It was true that an Earth-based corporation of one kind or another owned everything, but that was no different than life on Earth. On Mars, at that time, there had been no such thing as unemployment. Shipping a person through space was expensive for the corporations involved, so they only did it if a job was available for that person. With no unemployment to worry about, crime was almost non-existent as well. There were the occasional fights in the bars and the occasional domestic problems, but street gangs, robberies, random beatings, drug dealing, and sex crimes were very rare. The Martians, as they began to call themselves, were living in the most modern of surroundings and participating in one of mankind's greatest endeavors. Most importantly, they were employed and making money of their own instead of living off of welfare handouts and public assistance food. To the type of person that took the rather drastic step of leaving their home planet and traveling to another in search of a job, this was a very important distinction.

But gradually, over the space of a few decades, the so-called Agricultural Rush petered out as equilibrium was established. The greenhouse construction slowed and finally came to a virtual halt as the point was reached where there was enough farmland to produce all of the crops that needed to be produced for the maximum amount of profit. To make any more greenhouses, to produce any more crops, would shift the delicate balance of supply and demand upon its axis and drive down the bulk prices. And so, those in the construction and engineering fields were the first to face mass layoffs as construction company after construction company went bankrupt and closed their doors. Their former office buildings, which had once ruled empires of men, materials, and equipment, were converted into the first of the public housing buildings that would soon become the ghettos of Mars. Other industries quickly followed. Though ore mining would always be a very important staple of Martian society, the end of the construction boom caused mass layoff among mine workers and support personnel as the demand for iron ore was slashed to nearly a third of what it had once been.

On the day that Laura Whiting was to be sworn in as Governor, unemployment stood at a firm twenty-eight percent. Each year that number grew a little as corporations merged and created super corporations and laid off personnel as cost-saving measures. It was just this factor that threatened to reduce Brent and Lon from employed status to the welfare class. Those that serviced machinery were particularly vulnerable to post-merger job elimination; almost as vulnerable as middle-management employees. It was only natural that this subject and the impending doom that it implied, would continually dominate their conversation as they went about their scheduled task.

Brent, after considerable grunting and groaning, finally managed to pull himself out of the airlock and onto the roof. Wearily, he stood up, already huffing and puffing and making the discharge warning light appear on his air supply screen.

"You really ought to start getting a little exercise," Lon told him, listening to the ragged breathing in his earpiece. "They have a gym in your housing complex, don't they?"

"Screw that," Brent replied, picking up his tool chest. "If I went up there and ran on a treadmill it would take time away from the finer things in life."

"You mean like smoking green and jerking off to VR porn channels?"

"And eating," he added. "Don't forget eating."

"Of course," Lon said, shaking his head a little.

"Besides," Brent said, "I might as well enjoy my food and good green and premium porn channels now, while I have a chance. As soon as those AgriCorp assholes lay us all off, I'll be stuck with shitty brown grass and welfare channels, just like all the other vermin. And they don't have exercise rooms in the vermin housing complexes, so why should I start an exercise program now?"

"We don't *know* that we're going to get laid off," Lon said with false hopefulness as he picked up his own tools.

"No, we don't know, we just strongly suspect. They won't tell us for sure because that way they wouldn't get the satisfaction of watching us stress about it before they shitcan us."

"That's depressing," Lon said sourly. "Let's talk about something else. I'm sick of talking about AgriCorp all the goddamn time. It's all anyone's ever talked about since they announced the merger plans last year."

"Hey," Brent said, "it's the most progressive merger of the decade, remember? Aren't you thrilled to be a part of it?"

"Oh yes," Lon agreed. "A real boom for the business community. How could I forget?"

The environmental extractor machine they had been sent to repair was one of twelve that kept the greenhouse operating. It was located only ten meters from the hatch they had emerged from. A large steel box, twenty meters square and ten meters in height, it was part of the basic construction of the building. On the side of it that faced the hatch was a hydraulic lift that was big enough to shuttle up to four workers and five hundred kilos of equipment to the top, where the main machinery was located. Lon and Brent climbed aboard the lift and pushed the button. It ground slowly upward in a jerky motion, as if blowing sand had corrupted some of its interior parts. This was a fairly common problem with outside machinery on Mars.

"Shit," Brent whined, feeling the motion, "now we're gonna be out here tomorrow fixing *this* fucking thing."

"Job security," Lon told him, holding securely to the handrail. "You should be grateful that a lot of shit breaks around this place."

"Why should I be grateful?" he countered. "I'm still more than likely gonna be vermin this time next month. All this shit breaking will be fixed by the AgriCorp maintenance guys. They'll get to keep their jobs because they signed on with the biggest, baddest, ass-kickingest corporation to ever rape and fuck Martians instead of the one that only partially raped and fucked us."

"Again with the AgriCorp," Lon said, stepping off the lift as it finally reached the top. They were now on a narrow catwalk that surrounded the perimeter of the machine. "Can't you ever talk about something else? Why don't you give me that lecture on how to get the most for my marijuana dollar again? I liked that one."

"You continue to live in denial," Brent told him, hefting his toolbox over and walking towards the sand filter housing mechanism, "and I'll continue to be a realist. We're future vermin, Lon, have no fucking doubt about it."

Lon didn't answer him. Any reassurances he could offer would have sounded like a lie to his lips. Instead, he opened up his toolbox and removed a rechargeable electric wrench. He kneeled down and began to remove the bolts that held the motor housing in place. Brent, giving a few huffs and puffs, picked up his own wrench and walked around the perimeter of the catwalk to begin work on the other side.

As they went about the task of removing the cover so they could access the main fan bearings, which needed to be replaced, Brent softened his tone a little. "So, what do you think your chances are of scoring full-time with the MPG?" he asked. "You're in the special forces division. That's who they always hire from."

Lon gave a shrug. "The only real full-time positions are in training or VIP security," he said. "I haven't been in special forces long enough to apply for training. Jackson is real stringent about that. A minimum of six years is required before you're eligible for a teaching position."

"That's screwed up," Brent declared righteously.

Lon shook his head. "I don't think so," he told him. "The MPG isn't like other places. You have to know what you're doing before they let you teach. I haven't learned everything there is to learn about all the stuff we do. How am I supposed to teach someone else how to do it?"

"I still think it's screwed up," Brent insisted. "What about VIP security though? Think they'll let you guard Whiting or the Lieutenant Governor or some of those other rich-prick politicians? Maybe they'll let you guard Jackson himself."

"I've applied for it," he answered, his voice far from hopeful. "They're a pretty exclusive clique though. Jackson handpicks them himself you know. Only one out of every two hundred applicants gets picked for testing. And only one out of every ten that pass the test gets picked."

"Well, it's a shot anyway, ain't it?"

"A little shot," Lon replied, dropping the bolt he had just removed into the pocket of his biosuit. "But, truth be known, they tend to take the older guys for the security detail, the ones who have been around. I've only been in the MPG for five years, and in the special forces for two years. I'm only a squad leader for god's sake."

"It's a better chance then I got," Brent told him. "At least you got a hope of something to fall back on. If AgriCorp lays me off, I got nothing. I'll never see a payday again."

"Well," he told her, "if they lay me off, I have to resign from the MPG, remember? You have to have a job in order to serve."

Brent shook his head angrily. "Ain't that just some shit?" he asked. "AgriCorp comes in and buys up our company and boom, our whole fuckin' lives are destroyed. They take away our job, which makes us have to leave our apartments—I been livin' in that apartment since I was eighteen fuckin' years old! We'll have to move into Helvitia Heights or some other vermin shithole where we'll have our food given to us and we'll probably end up getting killed by one of those fuckin' street gangs. And you," he pointed over at Lon, "you'll have to leave the MPG. You worked for years to get into special forces and they'll make you leave just because AgriCorp bought us out. And why does shit like this happen? For money! Because AgriCorp wants to make more profit to send to those fucking rich pricks on Earth!"

"It's the way of the solar system, Brent," Lon told him, trying to maintain his composure. "It's the way of the fucking solar system. Now let's get this bearing fixed before 4:30 so we don't have to come out here again tomorrow."

"Right," Brent said, watching the gauge on his air supply display carefully. Getting excited certainly had not helped it any. "Let's get it done. And then let's get our asses out of here so we can go to the bar."

"Sounds like a plan."

*****

New Pittsburgh, Mars

Laura Whiting was dressed in a smart blue business dress, complete with the obligatory tie and dark nylons. It was a style of dress that was obsolete and shunned in all but political circles on Mars. Not even the most conservative of business people, not even lawyers or insurance agents, wore such things anymore. Laura understood why such clothing had gone out of favor. It was horribly uncomfortable, particularly in the warm environment of a Martian city. The nylons itched her legs and the tie threatened to strangle her. The dress, though not uncomfortable in and of itself, she considered to be demeaning to all of the female gender. Dresses implied servility to men, a concept which still, even after all these years of socialization, pervaded even the highest aspects of WestHem society. Laura was grateful that no matter what else happened tonight, this most important night, this dreadfully nerve-wracking night, she would never have to wear a dress or nylons again. From this night forward, she would be seen in nothing but shorts and a plain blouse.

She was in the so-called green room of the legislative chambers in the planetary capital building. It was a comfortable, friendly room full of plush furniture. Red carpet, the color of the Martian soil, covered the floor. An Internet terminal, which was wired into a service dispenser that could, for a small fee, provide fruit juices, soda, or water, sat upon an imitation wood table. The Internet terminal was blank, having been shut off some time before. The beverage dispenser was unused. She ignored the couches and chairs as well, choosing instead to pace back and forth and round and round. Her nerves were quite on edge. In a few minutes she would leave this room and walk into the chambers where, at long last, she would be sworn in as the governor of Mars.

The election had been three months before, her first attempt at high office, and she had won in a landslide. The race between herself and Governor Jacobs, the incumbent, had generated the highest voter turnout in the history of Mars, with a staggering 84 percent of the eligible populace casting ballots. This number meant that at least ten percent of the votes in this election had been cast by the welfare class, those perpetually unemployed and hopeless Martians that lived in the public housing complexes and made up more than a quarter of the population. These ghetto inhabitants, who typically paid no attention to politics and who were typically very fatalistic, had actually helped elect her. Though voting was not a difficult task to undertake in modern society—all one had to do was access any Internet terminal, and Internet terminals were in every apartment and in every public building—the welfare class rarely bothered voicing their opinions when it came to planetary or federal elections. But this time a significant number of them *had*. They had turned on their terminals, accessed the voting software, identified themselves with a fingerprint and a voice analysis, and cast their vote for governor. That was an encouraging sign for what was to follow. A very encouraging sign.

Now, on the night that this mandate was to take effect, the legislative chambers was packed far beyond its rated capacity. Peering out through a gap in the metal partition, Laura could see her former colleagues in the legislature all in their assigned seats, all dressed in clothing similar to hers. One representative for each district of a million people. Representatives of both sexes, of all racial backgrounds, of varying ages, with only one thing in common: corporate sponsorship. All had allegedly been elected by the people, but only with the say-so of the powers-that-be. The people were just the mechanism that was used to put the corporate favorite in office. All had to vote the way their sponsors wished them to vote if they wanted to continue to be elected and to collect their campaign contributions. Though the people of Mars had elected them, they did not represent them in anything more than symbolic manner. Laura planned to begin the process of changing that tonight. Would she be successful? She did not know, could not predict. But she was going to try.

Behind the suited legislature members were the public seats that were usually, when the body was in session, either completely empty or occupied by nothing more than grade-school children and their teachers. On this night, however, they were filled with a collection of corporate lobbyists and wealthy corporate managers; the people who had propelled her to this place, to this moment, with their support and with their money. Laura had made promises to those people, had helped pass laws for them, laws that took the money out of the hands of the common Martians and gave it over to them. Laura had been so skillful at this that most of the common Martians did not even realize they had been robbed. She was not proud of her association with such people, with such a system, but it had been necessary in order to get her where she was. It was this group that was going to receive the shock of their lives in just a few minutes now. Soon, the Chief Justice of the Martian Supreme Court would swear her in. She would take her oath of office and then she would officially be the governor of the planet. She would then give her inauguration speech. It was a speech she had written long ago, shortly after the Jupiter War when this crazy scheme had evolved from a vague idea into a concrete plan of action. The speech had been modified here and there in a few places, mostly to update historical references or events, but it had survived the years mostly intact. Tonight, it would be heard at last, for better or for worse.

She smiled nervously, going over the words in her mind for perhaps the hundred thousandth time. She did not want so much as a syllable to be mispronounced or stuttered.

"Are you feeling okay, Governor?" asked Lieutenant Warren of the Martian Planetary Guard. Warren was in charge of the security force that protected her. He was in his thirties and had once been a sergeant in the WestHem army. He had seen combat in Cuba and Argentina before being discharged and sent back to Mars where his extensive training had entitled him to a job as a security guard in one of the agricultural fields. His status as an employed person had allowed him to join the MPG (only those with private income were allowed to join the planetary guard—the WestHem congress and executive council had stubbornly insisted upon this as a condition of inception). His previous experience had allowed him to be assigned to the special forces division where he had gradually worked his way up to the security detail and one of the coveted full-time, paid positions in the guard. Like all of the security force that watched over high officials, General Jackson had handpicked him personally for the detail and he had been subjected to intense training. He was a very loyal, very competent leader with a knack for his job. He was also one of the few people besides General Jackson himself and a few close, sympathetic friends that knew what was about to happen.

"I'm fine, Mike," said Laura, who insisted on calling those close to her by their first names. "I'm just fine. Thank you for asking."

Warren nodded, looking a little nervous himself. He was dressed in the standard indoor MPG uniform of red shorts and a white T-shirt with the Martian flag on the breast. Over the T-shirt was a Kevlar armor vest that was capable of stopping handgun fire. He had a 4mm sidearm strapped to his belt and an M-24 assault rifle slung over his shoulder. A helmet with a headset sat atop his head and a pair of combat goggles, which were linked to the combat computer/ tactical radio system, were covering his eyes. In the goggles he would be able to see status reports of his troops, maps of the location they were in, and other pieces of vital information superimposed over the display. The goggles gave him an almost insectile appearance but Laura had long since gotten used to that. "Don't you worry about a thing, Governor," he told her. "I'm not going to let anything happen to you."

She nodded, offering him a smile. "Well," she said, "there are going to be a lot of upset people out there once I give my speech, that's for sure. But let's hope it doesn't come to violence, shall we?"

"It won't," he assured her, adjusting the sway of his weapon a little. "Politicians attack each other in different ways, Governor. But just in case some of those tempers get a little too hot, remember that my platoon and I are watching out for you."

"And I appreciate that, Mike, thank you."

Warren basked in her praise, feeling a wave of protectiveness towards her that was quite similar to what a mother bear feels for her cubs. He checked the time, which was showing in the upper right-hand corner of his vision, seeming to hover in the air before him thanks to the combat goggles. "It's almost time, Governor," he said.

"Almost," Laura agreed. "Almost."

*****

The Helvetia Heights section of Eden was perhaps the worst ghetto on the planet of Mars. Located just five kilometers from downtown, it was a ten square kilometer area that had once been where the financial and business offices of the Eden construction industry had been based. Now, it was nothing but public housing complexes full of third and fourth generation unemployed and their families. The streets of Helvetia Heights were ruled not by the police, who only came in when they were called and only in teams of four or more, but by the street gangs and the dust dealers. One did not leave one's apartment in Helvetia unless one was prepared to shoot it out with a group of hardened teenage criminals. To live in Helvetia Heights was to live in unending despair and hopelessness.

Helvetia Park was almost directly in the center of this most dangerous area. It was a four square block area that had been a quaint showpiece in happier times; a place where smiling parents took their children to play and feed the ducks in the pond. Now, the irrigation system had long since ceased to operate, the trees and shrubs had all been killed and marked with gang graffiti, the grass was an overgrown ugly brown, and the playground equipment was nothing but broken, rusting hulks. Children no longer played in the park. Their parents would have been mad to allow them anywhere near it. These days, the park was the domain and home base of the 51st Street Capitalists, a fiercely possessive and well-organized gang that supplied much of the dust that was distributed in the neighborhood.

Matthew Mendez sat upon one of the scarred plastic picnic tables near the south entrance of the park with his friend, Jeff Creek. They each had a bottle of Fruity that they were sipping out of from time to time and a marijuana pipe that they were smoking out of. The alcohol and the marijuana were part of the monthly allotment that was allowed of them by the Martian welfare system. They both had cheap 3mm pistols holstered to the waistbands of their shorts and concealed with oversized T-shirts. The pistols were mostly worn out of habit at this point in their young lives. The Capitalist members would not harass them in any way. Matthew and Jeff had been respected members of the gang until recently "retiring" as the term went. They had sold dust, had helped produce it, and had fought bitterly with other gangs for territory. Both had drawn the blood of others in the name of dust distribution. As retired veterans, they were entitled to free passage through gang controlled areas and respectful treatment by current members. It was part of the code of conduct that the Capitalists had developed over the years and swore blood oaths to uphold upon initiation. Many other gangs in other parts of the city had similar rules.

Matthew had just turned twenty-two years old a few days before. He was a tall, well-built young man of Hispanic heritage, the descendant of one of the original Martian agricultural workers that fled WestHem at the beginning of the Agricultural Rush. His ancestors had certainly led a more fulfilling life than he was leading so far. Like most Helvetia inhabitants, he had never been out of the city of Eden in his life. He had not, in fact, ever been out of the neighborhood of Helvetia except to make the occasional drug pick up near the agricultural processing plants. He, like his father before him, had been born into unemployment and welfare. His grandfather had been the last of the Mendez clan to earn a paycheck.

"So, you gonna make it official with Sharon, or what?" Jeff asked as he packed a pinch of the brown waste marijuana that was distributed to the ghetto class into his homemade pipe. "You're in your twenties now and you gotta make the big jump sometime. You don't wanna keep livin' with your parents, do you?"

"I don't know, man," Matthew said with a sigh, taking another sip out of his Fruity. This was the same question that Sharon, the lanky, skinny girl he had been seeing for the past six months, continually asked him as well. "Getting married just seems so... I don't know, programmed into us. I mean, I don't love Sharon. We just like to fuck now and then."

Jeff shook his head in amusement. "Love?" he scoffed. "What the hell does that got to do with it? You think I love Belinda? She's a fuckin' bitch and the less I see of her, the better. But she got me my own apartment, didn't she? And pretty soon she'll get me a kid and the extra money and food that goes along with it. If you go waitin' for love, you're gonna be thirty years old and still living at home. There ain't no love in this place."

The Martian Welfare laws stated that only a married couple was entitled to a public housing apartment. For this reason, it was a ritual among the ghetto class to marry young, almost as soon as they were considered adults by the legal system. And, once the couple had the one child they were permitted, they were then entitled to a two-bedroom apartment and an increased food allowance. For this reason, young married couples of the ghetto class tended to pump out their one child before their twenty-first birthdays. But Matthew did not like doing what everyone else was doing. He could not help but suspect that it was all part of some sinister plan formulated by those that kept everyone in hopeless squalor. "I just don't think having your own apartment is any reason to get married," he said, lighting a cigarette. "That wasn't what the institution of marriage was intended for."

"Institution? You belong in a fuckin institution," Jeff accused. "You are sometimes just too goddamn much to take. Like when you insisted on graduating from high school because it might help you get out of here someday. You remember that?"

"Yeah," Matthew agreed. "I remember. I took a lot of shit from the rest of the Capitalists for staying in school."

"Fuckin' A, you did," Jeff said. "Nobody graduates from high school around here. What's the fuckin' point? You think someone's gonna give you a job? You? A third-generation vermin? You just can't accept the fact that you're going to be vermin until you die, can you?"

"I refuse to accept it," Matthew replied, unoffended by the outburst. He knew that he annoyed the hell out of his peers at times. "If there's a way out of this ghetto, I'm going to find it. I don't want my kid to grow up in this shithole, do you understand?"

"This shithole is all we got," Jeff told him. "We're vermin. Our kids will be vermin. Our kids' kids will be vermin. Nothing is going to change that, man. You hop in a time machine and go forward a couple hundred years and you'll see your great, great, great grandkids hanging out in this park and sellin' dust or whatever people use to get high with then."

"That's where you're wrong," he replied firmly, with all the zeal that an early twenties male could muster. "I will not have any kids while I live here, while I don't have a job. I won't bring a kid into this life."

Jeff started laughing, almost spilling his grass out of his pipe. "You kill me sometimes," he said. "Is that why you voted for that stupid bitch Whiting? You think she's gonna get you a job?"

"Probably not," Matthew admitted, "but she seems... oh... different than the rest of them somehow. She caught my attention. She says she'll help the welfare class out."

"Yeah, she's going to take the money away from AgriCorp, who owns her, and give it to us. She's gonna get us jobs picking tomatoes out in the greenhouses. You don't really believe that crap, do you?"

"No," he admitted. "She's probably just smart enough to tell us what we want to hear so she can get votes out of us. After all, no one else has ever tried to tap the ghetto vote. But if she went to all the effort to touch bases with us, the least I can do is take the time to log on and vote for her. Hell, it only took me five minutes and it didn't cost me nothing. Why shouldn't I have done it? And maybe if more of us vermin did that, we'd have a little bit more of a voice."

"A voice?" Jeff chuckled, shaking his head once again. He handed over the pipe that he had just filled. "Here," he said. "Feed this to your voice."

Matthew took the pipe and applied a disposable lighter to it, taking a large hit. The knowledge that the intoxicants were being provided to him by the planetary government as a calming measure did not stop him from imbibing. What the hell else was there to do? As always, the cheap grass, which was mostly stems and seeds, burned his throat and lungs. If you smoked enough of it, however, there was a pleasant buzzing effect, particularly on top of the effects of the Fruity.

Ten minutes later they were pleasantly intoxicated. The pipes and baggies of marijuana had been stowed in their pockets and the bottles of Fruity, now empty, had been tossed aside onto the grass. The two friends leaned back and watched a group of younger Capitalists a few tables over. They were squabbling over whether they should go down to the tram station and try to score some pussy or head down to the border area and try to clash with some members of the rival 63rd Street Thrusters. Matthew was of the opinion that their time would be better spent pursuing the first option—he was a firm believer in the philosophy of sex before violence—but he kept his feelings to himself.

"What you doing?" Jeff asked as he saw his friend remove his personal computer, or PC from his pocket. "Gonna check your stock reports?"

The PC was a small device that everyone over the age of ten or so, ghetto class or not, carried with them at all times. It was a wireless communicator and Internet access machine. It was used for all financial transactions and for identification purposes. Matthew unfolded his and turned it on. The screen lit up with the opening display. "I'm gonna watch the inauguration ceremonies," he answered. "See what kind of bullshit she promises us."

Jeff looked at him in for a moment, convinced he was joking. Finally, reluctantly, he was forced to conclude that his friend was serious. "You're shittin' me," he said. "You're actually going to watch a politician get sworn in? You're going to watch that?"

Matthew shrugged, stubbornly refusing to be embarrassed. "Why not? What the hell else is there to watch? She'll be on every channel." He looked at his screen and spoke to it. "Computer, give me broadcast media mode," he said. "MarsGroup primary."

"Making connection," the pleasant, sexy voice that he had programmed the PC with replied. "Connection active. Enjoy your show."

"Thank you, baby," he told it, peering at the eighty-millimeter screen before him.

Jeff watched all this in wonder. Now he had seen about everything. His friend was truly ready for the nuthouse. He had not only voted for a politician, but now he was watching her on Internet—actually watching a political swearing-in. "Tell me the truth," he said. "You got the hots for this bitch, don't you? You wanna fuck Laura Whiting."

"Oh yeah," he answered sarcastically as the face of a MarsGroup reporter graced the display. In the background could be seen the podium where the ceremony would shortly take place. "I'm really into women that are the same age as my mom. They make me horny as hell."

"Whiting's never been married has she?" he asked next, looking over Matthew's shoulder at the screen in spite of himself. "You think she's a lesbo? I bet she munches the old carpet."

Matthew shrugged again. "So what if she does?" he asked. "The best thing could happen to us is to get some politician up there who hates men. After all, men are the ones who run all the corporations that fuck all of us over. Maybe she'll get rid of them and replace them all with ball-busting women."

"An all lesbo ruling class?" Jeff said, smiling as he imagined the possibilities of that. "Now that's something *I'd* vote for."

*****

The stage was hot beneath the overhead spotlights as she stepped onto it in her high-heeled shoes, a serious expression upon her face. She shook hands with her future Lieutenant Governor, a shallow, career politician like herself who was owned by MarsTrans and Tagert Steel Refining. It was no secret among those on the inside that he and Laura were bitter enemies. Not only were their sponsors competing companies, but they were not even in the same political party. Laura wondered what her second in command was going to think about what she was about to do. Undoubtedly, he would attempt to take political advantage of it and force her from office. Would the drive to remove her gravitate around him? If MarsTrans and Tagert Steel had their way, it would. But what would AgriCorp do? Would they try to form a quick alliance with him? This seemed a likely possibility.

Outgoing Governor Ron Lee, who was enjoying his last five minutes of high office, shook her hand next. He greeted her warmly and introduced her to the audience, smiling graciously and congratulating her just as if he hadn't attacked her viciously on the Internet during his campaign, accusing her of everything from sexual perversion to money laundering for dust dealers. She accepted his congratulations without bitterness. Lee was no worse than anyone else in this business. He had just been doing what everyone else did to win. It was the system that encouraged such things, not Lee himself. What would he think about what was about to transpire? Had it ever occurred to him to use the office for the ends that she was about to, even fleetingly? Probably not.

The Chief Justice of the Martian Supreme Court delivered the oath of office to her. He was a wizened, gnarled old man of ninety-three that had been appointed to the court nearly thirty years before. Once the terror of those who dared challenge the rights and privileges of the agricultural corporations or their subsidiaries, he was now quite senile, his duties having long since been taken over by senior members of his legal staff. His role in the ceremonies was kept as brief as possible to avoid having anyone notice that their lead justice barely had the mental capacity to tie his own shoes. He had been grilled continuously with his lines and shot up with dopasynthamine, a powerful neurological drug that would give him momentary clarity for the broadcast.

"Repeat after me," he told her, his voice barely audible though, of course, it would be magnified by the directional microphones for the broadcast. "I, Laura Whiting..."

"I, Laura Whiting..." she said, holding her left hand up while her right rested upon her heart. She found herself looking a rivulet of drool running from His Honor's mouth and trying not to giggle at the ridiculousness of this production.

"Do solemnly swear..."

"Do solemnly swear..." she intoned.

"To faithfully execute the offices of... uh..." he hesitated for a moment, forgetting what he was supposed to say. Thankfully those in charge of the production had anticipated this. A tiny speaker, mounted in his right ear, provided the missing words for him. He listened to it, took a moment to process the fact that the disembodied voice was helping him with his lines, and then continued. "...uh, Governor of the Planet Mars."

"To faithfully execute the office of Governor of the Planet Mars."

And so on it went. They covered the upholding of the Martian constitution and the laws and challenges of the sacred office, so help her God. The old man before her required only two more prompts to get it right. It was much smoother than the last swearing in, four years before, when he had urinated on himself during the ceremony.

"Congratulations, Governor Whiting," he told her when he finished, holding out his hand to her.

"Thank you, your Honor," she replied, letting a smile cross her face as she shook with him. It was now official. She had been sworn in and, according to the constitution that she had just promised to uphold, she was now the governor. There was no turning back now.

The applause from the crowd went on for better than three minutes. Their enthusiasm was genuine enough. Laura was very popular among her former peers in the legislature, even across party lines. She was regarded as a politician's politician. They knew that if they could enlist her support on one of their bills or amendments, it stood a good chance of being bullied through the system. Laura's way with words and pushiness with opposing views was legendary. While they were clapping, the Chief Justice was whisked quietly away where he would be shoved into a waiting DPHS cart and driven to the nearest private hospital to be treated for the rather nasty side effects of the dopasynthamine.

The applause died down as she mounted the lectern before her. On the front of it was the great seal of Mars, which showed a view of the planet from space, complete with its two tiny moons. A black microphone stuck up from the top of the lectern and a 200mm Internet screen was discretely installed in the top of it. On the screen was the text of the speech she had submitted as her inaugural address; a speech she had no intention of actually giving. Her real speech was in her head.

Now that the time had actually come to show her true colors, she felt the nervousness that had been plaguing her for the past two weeks, whittling nearly five kilograms of her body weight away and destroying her slumber, fade away. A cool calm overtook her as she looked out over the audience, at the sea of political and corporate faces, at the scattering of media members. They were about to receive the shock of their lives. She couldn't wait to see their expressions.

"My fellow Martians," she said into the microphone, her voice not only traveling through the public address system but into the digitizing equipment of more than twenty news services. Her words would be broadcast to everyone on the planet and would even be beamed back to Earth in case anyone cared to watch it there. It would also be instantly transcribed into print and published on news service sites on the Internet. "Let me begin this evening by thanking you for electing me to this most trusted office. Without your support, without your taking the time to cast your ballots for me, I would not be standing here right now, facing you as your newly inaugurated governor. I would particularly like to thank those of you in the welfare class, the residents of those high-rise public assistance complexes in the downtrodden sections of our planet. I have tried to reach you during this campaign, tried to penetrate the wall of cynicism and apathy that has grown up around you through the generations. I am to be *your* governor as well and it has given me hope that a significant number of you listened to my words and took me at least seriously enough to vote for. I assure you, your trust will not be abused."

Confused looks began to pass among the reporters. As was customary, they had all been given advance copies of the speech she was to give and had already read through it. They realized that she was not following the text. She was supposed to have begun by thanking her many corporate and financial supporters and then delivering an endorsement for AgriCorp coffee beans that was thinly disguised as a joke. What was she doing? Thanking the welfare class? The vermin? Was she going as senile as the man that had sworn her in?

"And for you of the working class," she went on, deviating even further now, "I thank you as well. Like the welfare class, you have battled the apathy that our corrupt political system has fostered to cast your votes in record numbers."

There was a gasp from the crowd at her words; a gasp that was echoed by all that were watching the live broadcast. She had called the political system corrupt!

Of course, everyone knew that it *was* corrupt, but politicians were not supposed to *say* that! Was Laura Whiting going crazy?

"You have given me a mandate," Laura went on, hardly able to suppress her glee. Though the true dynamite of her speech was yet to come, she had crossed neatly over the line. There truly was no turning back now. "Working class and welfare class have spoken to me quite clearly and I shall respond to what I believe are your wishes. The intent of our government, of the WestHem constitution, is that laws and legislative functions are to be the wishes of the people. The intent of the Martian constitution is supposed to be the same. Elected representatives are supposed to propose and pass laws that are for the betterment of the people of Mars. The people!" She paused for a second, her eyes tracking over the crowd, seeing just the expressions that she had hoped for: shock and disbelief. "Somewhere along the way, that idea became perverted and twisted. Because of money, because of so-called campaign contributions and lobbyists and corporate sponsorships, the definition of 'the people' has changed to mean corporations. AgriCorp, MarsTrans, InfoGroup, a dozen others just here on this little planet. They bribe us politicians with outrageous amounts of money and call it a contribution. In return, they expect complete loyalty from that politician. They expect that politician to vote for laws and to propose laws that are in *their* best interests. And their best interests are almost always contrary to your best interests; you, the common Martian people; the people who work and live on this planet or who are confined to squalid hopelessness in the ghettos. Who represents *your* interests? Who proposes laws that are for your benefit, for your prosperity? We, the people you have elected to office are *supposed* to do this, but we do not. So, who do you have? Who can you turn to?" She paused again, staring into the collection of cameras. "You have nobody," she said. "Nobody until now.

"This system of government that we have is an atrocity before humankind," she went on. "It operates on the principals of greed and corruption. It has led directly to the horrid crime and unemployment problem that this planet faces. It was responsible for the bloody war with EastHem fifteen years ago in which tens of thousands of innocent Martians were slaughtered to try to protect a WestHem monopoly on hydrogen. Our little planet produces trillions in agricultural products. Our food—food grown, tended, and harvested by Martian workers—feeds the solar system. Our iron ore and other minerals support the space faring society that we live in. Our factories build the ships that travel from planet to planet. Without Mars and the exports we provide, WestHem and even EastHem could not exist as they now do. We are the crown jewel of the solar system. Each year our gross planetary product is a staggering 800 trillion dollars. 800 *trillion*!

"Now think about that for a moment, fellow Martians. 800 trillion dollars worth of products are produced every single year on this planet. That is more money than you or I or any individual person is capable of even comprehending. So, with all of this money being made every year by our hands, or labors, in our agricultural fields and mines and factories, why is it that the vast majority of us are living in abject poverty? Why is it that more than one quarter of us are living in substandard hovels and are unable to escape from them? Why is it that our schools are overcrowded and underfunded, with actual waiting lists for enrollment in some parts of the planet? Why is it that there are only six institutions of higher learning to educate our people; a shortage that is so vast that only the upper crust of the elite is afforded the opportunity for a college education? Why is it that our police departments are dangerously understaffed and that our prison space is so lacking that even those who commit murder cannot be kept locked up? Surely, with 800 trillion a year in gross planetary product, with more than 230 trillion in raw profits, we should be able to fund a few police officers or build a few schools and colleges. Why can't we do this? Where is all of that money going?"

She smiled at the cameras, a conspiratorial smile. "I don't think I really have to tell you all where it goes," she said. "I'm sure you all know just as well as I do. We Martians are, as a culture, blessed with healthy common sense, with keen minds. We are, after all, the descendants of those who left poverty and despair on Earth, who gave up their home planet to come here and forge a new reality. The vast majority of that money, that 230 trillion credits, is sent back to Earth. Some of it is given to the WestHem government as taxes. Some of it goes into the pockets of WestHem executive council members and congressmen as political contributions. But most of it, perhaps sixty percent, goes to rich corporate stockholders; people who have never even been to Mars and consider our planet to be an unsavory though valuable possession. These are the people who are raping our planet, who are keeping us in poverty. These are the people who are the enemy of Mars. And these people are the ones that we need to be free of."

She looked meaningfully into the camera now, a serious, sincere expression upon her face. "You, the people of Mars, have elected me to a four year term as your governor. I have just taken an oath of office that makes that position official under our constitution. Now, as your duly elected and sworn representative, I will share with you what has been my goal the entire time, what has been my dream. It is my desire that, with your consent, we strive to make the Planet of Mars completely independent from the government of WestHem within the year."

*****

The booking area of the downtown police substation was its normal, chaotic self. Located just inside the back door of the facility, near a fenced-in parking area for patrol carts, the intake waiting lounge (as it was called) contained more than two dozen teams of police officers from all over the district, all of whom had at least one and in some cases as many as three, prisoners with them. The prisoners waiting to be processed were sitting on a long plastic bench that ran the length of the far wall, their hands all cuffed to metal rings that were installed every meter. They were a motley collection of criminals, all very dangerous looking, most of them accused of fairly serious crimes since people generally were not arrested and hauled in for mere misdemeanors. The officers with them were gathered in the center of the room on plastic seats that had been put in for this purpose. Every ten minutes or so, a haggard looking booking officer would emerge through the sliding door at the other end of the room and call out a prisoner's name. The officers guarding him would then release him from the bench and accompany him inside where he would begin his latest trip through the Martian criminal justice system, joke that it was.

Usually, the booking area was an extremely loud place to be as the criminals talked and sometimes engaged in verbal fights with each other and as the officers talked among themselves about their jobs and their lives, the latter group's conversation often being considerably more profane than the former's. At this moment however, the room was eerily silent, as quiet as it had ever been, probably since the day before the police station was opened nearly seventy years before. All eyes in the room were riveted to the Internet screens mounted high on two of the walls, all mouths hanging open in sheer surprise as they heard the first two minutes of the new governor's speech. Cops and criminals alike simply could not believe what they were hearing come from the middle-age, though strangely handsome woman's mouth.

Brian Haggerty and Lisa Wong, who were near the center of the room, awaiting their two prisoners' names to be called so they could be booked for second degree murder (which might get them as much as six months in jail if they had priors), were among the cops watching. Both were just as flabbergasted as their colleagues. Had she really just said *independence* from WestHem? Had she really just called the corporations criminal? Granted, Governor Whiting was a favorite among the rank and file of just about every Martian law enforcement agency. Her tough talk on crime and criminals and her cries for increased funding and increased prison sentences almost guaranteed that. She had been the first politician in the history of Mars to actually gain the support of all of the planet's police departments, both at the administrative level and the street level. But what was this madness she was spouting now? Was it a joke?

"Is she out of her damn mind?" Brian whispered to his partner just as she declared her goal for her term. "Independence?"

"This is unbelievable," Lisa said. "She's insane. They'll crucify her for even saying that!"

There were some other murmurs, both from the cops and the criminals that were much to the same effect. Nor were they alone. As Whiting paused in her speech for a moment to let her words sink in, the babble of hundreds of onlookers in the audience chamber could clearly be heard being transmitted live from the capital. The idea of an independent Mars, in which the Martians followed and controlled their own destinies, was certainly not a new one. On the contrary, Martians from all walks of life had expressed that thought many times before. But usually such words were spoken in bars or at parties when alcohol and marijuana was being consumed. Such words were usually the pipe dreams of intoxicated philosophers, striving to save the world with their wisdom but never actually doing anything to forward it or thinking that anyone else ever would. Never had such words been spoken or even hinted at by a politician on live Internet. Never had such a thing even been conceived of before.

But Whiting was not finished with her speech. Not by a long shot. As they watched in growing disbelief, she continued to stare into the camera—the effect being that she was looking directly at each one of them—and she continued.

"Independence," she said, obviously savoring the word. "That is the only way that this planet and the people on it will ever be truly free. And I am not talking about just token independence either, where WestHem declares us free but where we are still their puppet, their plaything, influenced by their monetary system and their corporations. I am talking about complete freedom; *total* freedom from the tyranny of that greedy, corrupt society. That means that all Martian industries, particularly the steel and agricultural industries, will be nationalized and run for the benefit of the Martian people, *not* for the stockholders of AgriCorp and Standard Steel. I am talking about an entirely new constitution and way of life, a government for the people that is run by the people and that benefits the people—*all* people, not just those with money, not just those with jobs. I am talking about removing the corporate mentality and element completely from our society. And the only way to do this is to be free and to completely restructure our society so that it no longer revolves around the acquisition of wealth."

"Holy Jesus," Brian said, hearing this. "She really has gone insane."

"She really has," Lisa agreed, wondering how long it would be before someone actually removed her from the stage.

Whiting, completely ignoring the gasps and shocked words that were rising up from her audience of fellow politicians and corporate lobbyists, simply kept talking as if she were giving a normal speech.

"This may seem a strange concept for me to bring up," she admitted with a slight smile. "A government that does not revolve around wealth? Absurd, you might say. Impossible, you might say. But is such a thing really all that different than what many of you—the Martian people—have talked about over beers or buds among yourselves? Isn't it generally agreed upon at such bullshitting sessions that money and greed are the curse of the solar system, that the way of life we now find ourselves in the midst of is for the benefit of the elite few at the top of the corporate ladder while it is to the detriment of the rest? Isn't it generally noted at such times that Mars does not really *need* WestHem, that the only resource that we are not self-sufficient in is fuel? I have been to the intox clubs, people, I have listened to the conversations of others all of my life. I know that what I am suggesting is not something new. I am just the first politician in a political setting to bring this up in a serious manner. That is why it sounds like such a bizarre concept to you all at them moment."

"That's true," Lisa allowed. She and Brian had discussed that very thing with other cops many times in the past during drunken and stoned after-hours gatherings with other cops. Mars really could produce everything that a society needed to sustain itself without the assistance of WestHem. Food, steel, machinery, clothing, space vehicles, military equipment, electronics and their components, all of that was produced on Mars or in orbit above it on Triad. Hydrogen fuel was the only thing that Mars really needed to import—that and a few luxury items like coffee and alcohol.

"Yes," Brian was forced to agree, "but..."

He was cut short in his argument by the impatient hushes of those around him. They were becoming extremely interested in this speech.

"Now, in order to remove the factor of money from our new government," Whiting continued, "we will have to replace it with something else that we can worship. We will have to base our new constitution and our new society upon another principal. What should that principal be? What should we revere most of all in this life if not money and the acquisition of wealth? This is just my humble opinion, but I'm sure that all of you out there who are not corporate management or rich stockholders would agree, that society should be based upon common sense and fairness for everyone. Common sense and fairness, the two things that our current system of government pays lip service to but that our new government will actually embrace. Common sense in all decisions, in all dealings, in all laws. Fairness towards all people, unemployed and employed alike. I'm talking about a system of government that has enough checks and balances in it to guarantee that the atrocity that we have with us today is not able to repeat itself. I'm talking about a system where the abuses of power that we have now are not allowed to occur. I'm talking about a system in which the people themselves really chose their representatives and those representatives are incapable of being corrupted by the money from huge corporations because there will not be any huge corporations. I'm talking about a system where working is rewarded with the credit to buy nice things but that even those who do not or cannot work are provided with the basic necessities of life. I'm talking about a system where everyone has the right to a superior primary education and the right to a superior college education and that this is provided free of charge. I'm talking about a system where those who commit crimes against us are locked away for an appropriate number of years, where criminals are no longer allowed to walk among us.

"How will we pay for these things? I can hear you asking that right now. You are telling yourself that my talk sounds rather nice, but it sounds like I am describing an ideal world, a utopian society, and things such as this do not and cannot exist. Someone has to pay for all of that great education, for all of those prisons, for all of those police officers. Who will it be?

"The answer is no one and the answer is also everyone. You see, in a system where money and acquisition of wealth is not the primary focus, where betterment of our society and fairness are the goals, there is no reason to pay for any of that. It is just done. We produce food here on Mars and we produce steel and we produce everything else that is needed to run this society. We have skilled workers and the ability to train others in those skills. Once we are off of the WestHem system of government, once we separate ourselves from their economic system, we can do things any way we like. The new Martian government can build a new school or a new college whenever there is a need for such a thing. Since the steel industry is nationalized, we do not have to pay anyone for that steel since we already own it. Since the construction company that builds the school is nationalized, we do not have to hold a bidding process or pay a corporation to build our school. We just build it.

"As for the workers who put on the biosuits and put the steel together to form the building, they are paid in credits at a predetermined rate. These credits are issued by the government and are used to buy food and housing and luxury items from the government. They represent nothing more than credit for a day's work. With these credits, you can buy food supplies that are better than what is issued to those without jobs. You can pay for upgraded housing, vacation trips, luxury items. Everyone who has a job will be paid these credits and, unlike our current system, it will be a constitutional requirement that we, as a society, do everything that we can to make sure that everyone who wishes a job has one. No more layoffs because of mergers, no more elimination of positions just because the profit margin is slipping. We will put an end to profit margins with this system, an end to them for all time."

*****

O'Riley's Intox Club was a moderate sized chain that was owned by DrinkCo Beverages, which was, in turn, owned by AgriCorp. O'Riley's specialized in alcohol and marijuana service and had more than sixty "pubs" as they were known in company documents, throughout the city of Eden. Their target customers were the working class and, in Eden, they estimated that they had more than thirty percent of the "away from home, modestly employed, intoxicant using market". Their pubs all looked the same and all were located in strategically placed locations—generally on the bottom floors of commercial buildings near the industrial tram stations. Brent Shimasaki and Lon Fargo were sitting at the bar in O'Riley's pub number E-24, which was located in the basement of the Westcity shopping complex, a seventy story building six blocks from the AgriCorp maintenance shed. It was a favorite watering and smoking hole for the former IFP employees who were now AgriCorp employees. It was a place they had gathered in with increasing frequency over the last month since word of the impending "reductions in force" had started to circulate.

Two bartenders were currently on duty along with two servers that carried drinks or bongs to the various tables. All of the employees wore the standard green uniform of O'Riley's, a get-up that would be recognized the solar system over; from Sau Paulo to San Francisco, from Eden to Standard City to Triad. The bar itself looked exactly the same as every other. It was a standard twenty-one meters long with barstools placed every meter. Constructed of molded plastic designed to look like oak, it was easily installed and easily cleaned with wet, disinfectant soaked cloths. When it reached the end of its useful service life (approximately six years, according to company statistics) it was easily removed and replaced by another. The carpet on the floor was also standard throughout the chain. It was a dark beige (designed to be pleasing to the eye but to avoid staining and grime, therefore extending its useful service life) patterned with small green four-leaf clovers. Above the bar were two large Internet screens, purchased via corporate contract from Laslow Electronics, an Earth based manufacturer whose large screen Internet receiver factory was located in New Pittsburgh, in the high latitude region of Mars. Laslow small screen multi-purpose terminals, which could be used (for a small fee) by bar patrons for communications, were located at each end of the bar.

This particular O'Riley's, like most of the other 2346 pubs throughout the solar system, was usually a very noisy place in the early evening hours. On this particular evening however, the large crowd was staring raptly at the Internet screens in disbelief as Laura Whiting gave her inaugural address to the planet. The only utterings from the blue-collar workers assembled to watch her were the occasional comments on the more outrageous of her statements.

"Paid in credits?" Brent said in disbelief. "What kind of shit is this bitch spouting? What the hell does that mean?" He was currently on his second rum and coke and had just finished taking his third hit of the potent greenbud that O'Riley's was known for (it was grown in AgriCorp greenhouses). As such, he was flying quite high and complex ideas such as a society not based on greed and money were a little difficult for him to grasp.

"She's talking about pulling us free of the restraints put on the working class by capitalism," said Lon, who had only smoked one hit and was still on his first drink. "It's brilliant, if it can be made to work."

"It's communism," said Tina Yamamoto, an apple juicer repair tech and a former lover of Lon's. "When the state owns everything and pays the workers out of its own coffers, it's called communism. The Russians, the Chinese, and the Cubans all tried it back on earth. It doesn't work. The system leaves too much open for abuse of power."

"Oh? Like we don't have that here?" Lon shot back. "Besides, it's not necessarily communism she's talking about here. It could be just a form of socialism. And that did work in several countries before World War III."

"Yes, but..." Tina started.

"If you two would shut the fuck up," interrupted Stacy Salinas, another juicer tech, "we'd be able to hear just what she *is* talking about."

They shut up and watched, growing more fascinated as Whiting continued.

"The how's and why's of getting this system up and operating," she told her audience, "is really not the important thing right now, however. I have some loose plans drawn up in computer files that I have worked on over the years and I will present some of these ideas to you in the coming weeks during regular addresses to the planet. After independence is achieved, we will appoint scholars and others to form a constitutional committee to pound out the specific details of the plan. What *is* important right now is achieving our independence in the first place. I don't think I have to tell you that WestHem and the corporations that rule it—the corporations that like to think they own this planet—will not be willing to let us go very easily."

"You got that shit right," Brent snorted, signaling the bartender for another bonghit.

"But what those corporations and their puppets in the WestHem government need to understand, is that there is no reason for us Martians not to be independent. No reason except for their wishes and their greed and their profit margin. We are self-sufficient people and we deserve to be independent of their rule. If all Martians stick together and work for this goal together, one way or another, we will be independent within a year. I guarantee it and WestHem is simply going to have to accept it. It is my suggestion and my hope that the WestHem authorities appoint a committee for immediate negotiations on just how our goal can be peacefully brought about. I think that our goals and their sacred profit margins are not mutually exclusive. You see, Mars already produces the majority of the food supply for WestHem and the Jupiter colony. We would be honor bound to continue to produce that amount and ship it to them if they negotiate our independence in good faith. The labor needed to produce this food will be paid to Martian workers in Martian credits by the new Martian government. The food itself will be given to WestHem in straight exchange for the one commodity that we do not produce here: fuel. No money will be exchanged in this deal, making Martian credits useless to WestHem and WestHem dollars useless to Mars. But production will go on as always and AgriCorp and the other corporations that currently own everything on Mars will still be able to sell this food to the WestHem people at normal prices."

*****

"Would that work?" asked Jeff Creek of his friend, Matt Mendez. Both of the former gang members and current members of the hopelessly unemployed, were staring at Matt's PC intently, having gotten much more than they'd bargained for by watching the inaugural address. Despite his former apathy and doomsaying, Jeff found himself intrigued by what this politician was spouting. True, it was probably nothing but a mental breakdown in progress, but it sure sounded good while it was occurring.

"If it's done right," Matt replied, his mind trying to find holes in the theory and failing, "it would work just fine. The Martians buy goods and services from Mars using Martian money, which they are paid by the Martian government for working. Since Mars owns everything and isn't trying to make a profit, prices can be fixed since supply and demand does not depend on outside sources. Even though most of the food production that occurs is to export to Earth or Jupiter, there is no drain on the Martian economy because they are not on the same system of currency as we are. We produce food for them and exchange it for fuel. What they do with the food is their business. What we do with the fuel is our business. As long as we don't depend on them for anything else, it'll work!"

"Static," Jeff said, shaking his head in admiration. He started loading up another load of the garbage grass from his bag. "It's too bad WestHem will never let it happen. They'll send the fuckin marines here before they sign AgriCorp and those other corps over to us."

Matt nodded sadly. "I believe you've got a point there," he said. "But it's a nice concept anyway, ain't it?"

They went back to watching.

*****

William Smith, at the age of fifty-six, was, hands-down, the richest man on the planet Mars. The CEO of AgriCorp's Martian operations, he lived in opulent splendor in a penthouse suite that took up the 217th, 218th, and 219th floors of the most exclusive housing building in the city. He and his wife and three servants were the only people currently living there since their two children (exceptions to the one child per female ratio were available to the wealthy) were back on Earth attending college. Even so, their quarters had more than a eight hundred square meters of living space available to them: an unthinkable amount on a planet where construction costs were five times that on Earth. Their entire bottom floor consisted of nothing but an entertainment room where politicians and lobbyists and other corporate heads could gather for black-tie parties. A state-of-the-art sound and video system, complete with the latest holographic theater set-up, and a full-service wet bar larger than those found at O'Riley's and made of genuine polished oak imported from Earth were the features of this floor. There was also a huge picture window that looked out on the edge of the city, giving an impressive view of the contrast between the barren wastelands of the surface and the modern steel and glass buildings of the inhabited area. On the second floor of the suite, were the servant's quarters, kitchen area and secondary bedrooms, areas where Smith and his family rarely, if ever, ventured. On the top floor, which was also the top floor of the building itself, were two master bedroom suites complete with private baths and sunken Jacuzzi tubs and two complete office suites, one for Smith to work in and one for his wife to organize her charity events and plan her parties in. Smith's office was, naturally, the larger of the two. It featured a picture window that looked out on the financial district of Eden and its many towering high-rises, including the AgriCorp building itself.

Smith and his wife, both of whom were natives of Denver on Earth, hated their quarters. Though they were arguably the largest and nicest on the entire planet, they found them to be cramped and confined, not at all like their monster 2000 square meter mansion in the Aspen section of Denver or their 1200 square meter winter retreat on the island of Maui. It was a constant irritant to the third-generation corporate manager that he was forced to live in a common apartment building while stationed on this dry, boring little planet that just happened to produce most of the products his company sold. He longed for reassignment back to Earth, to corporate headquarters where he could go outside when he wanted to and where he could concentrate his energies on controlling real politicians instead of wasting away playing the game here with ignorant wanna-be greenie politicians.

He was currently sitting in his office suite behind his large, genuine oak desk, sipping out of a martini and smoking an imported cigarette. On the wall above him, a large screen Internet terminal was on and playing the inauguration of Governor Whiting, a politician that had been carefully groomed through the years as she had risen in stature and importance. His cigarette fell unnoticed from his mouth as he stared at the screen and heard the words she was saying. He could not have been more surprised and shocked if Laura Whiting had suddenly spontaneously combusted on the podium. She had called AgriCorp corrupt! She had mentioned them by *name* and called them that! She was up there telling the planet how his corporation and others manipulated the political system with campaign contributions! Worse than that, she was actually telling those ignorant greenies she now governed that she wanted them to be independent! That she wanted to nationalize the agricultural industry! Was she completely insane? What in the hell did she think she was doing? She was their pet politician! She had been *bought*! More than six million dollars in contributions had been transferred to her election account for this run alone. More than two million in unreported bribes had been laundered and sent to her personal account. She had been set up to sign into law more than sixteen bills benefiting AgriCorp that were being passed through the legislature this term. She had been set up to veto more than ten that were considered a detriment. She couldn't do this! It was inconceivable, impossible! It was madness!

Before Whiting was even two minutes into her speech, Smith's Internet terminal on his desk began buzzing, the female voice informing him that multiple vid-links were being requested. Of course, the computer also told him who the callers were and it was no surprise that they were the lobbyists and other upper-management members. He ignored them for the moment, although he knew he would be calling a conference for damage control with them very soon.

"Computer," he said to the desk mounted terminal, "get me Steve Lancaster. Try him at home, he should be there right now."

"Contacting Steve Lancaster at home," the computer obediently replied. The screen, which had been blank, suddenly flared to life showing the interface for the communications software.

"Highest priority," Smith said. "I want him to answer."

"Connecting," the computer told him.

Steve Lancaster was the Martian operations CEO of InfoServe, the Internet and media corporation that controlled approximately forty-five percent of the market share of WestHem and its colonies. AgriCorp and InfoServe had a long-standing advertisement contract and were about as friendly with each other as two unrelated industries could be. Lancaster was not exactly a friend to Smith—people at their height on the ladder did not really have friends, just contacts and associations—but he was about as close to one as possible. They had played golf together many times at the pathetic excuse for country club that Eden boasted and their wives were members of the same charity groups. As Smith had expected he would, Lancaster came online immediately, his handsome face showing shock and alarm.

"It would seem that you're watching the inaugural address," Smith said to the screen, his words and image being transmitted through the Martian Internet to the other side of town.

"I'm watching it," Lancaster confirmed, shaking his head a little. "I'm not sure if I believe what I'm seeing however. She's gone off the deep end. What the hell does she think she's doing up there?"

"I've never seen anyone throw their entire career away in less than a minute before," Smith said. "I don't know what prompted this ranting—whether it's mental illness or low blood sugar or whether, like she said, she's been planning this her entire career—but whatever the reason, we'll deal with her shortly. The important thing is that we cut that broadcast right away before she puts any strange ideas into the heads of these greenies."

"I'm on it," Lancaster said. "I'll call the main broadcast building and have them cut the live feed. We should be able to kill the transmission inside of a minute."

"Do it," Smith said. "And what about ICS and WIV? Do you have contacts with them?" ICS and WIV were the other two major Internet corporations of WestHem. Between the three of them, they owned every major transmission, publishing, communications, and movie-making entity in WestHem. If they all shut down their stations, there would be nothing for the greenies to watch.

"I do," he confirmed. "I'll get them on a conference call as soon as I get us shut down. I can't imagine that they would protest that. That won't completely kill her though."

"MarsGroup," Smith said with a groan as he was reminded of the independent Internet service that was owned by a small collection of Martian investors. Of course, the three big networks had tried to strangle them many times in the past, both by smearing them in their own news programs and publications and by refusing to sell them shows or content. Even so, MarsGroup had managed to survive for more than three decades now. Though they mostly produced low-budget news programs and reports and hokey Internet sit-coms or adventure shows, enough of the greenies tuned in or utilized them to keep them barely in the black each year.

"MarsGroup," Lancaster confirmed. "They have cameras and reporters at the inauguration as well. We couldn't get them excluded. Quite frankly, we didn't really even try since the public relations problems would've outweighed the benefit. I have no say with their CEO. In fact, she is often quite antagonistic to me."

"I'll see what I can do," Smith said. "Perhaps she'll listen to me if I offer her a little advertising business during prime-time. You get the real media shut down and I'll call her up."

"Right," Lancaster said doubtfully. He seemed about to say more but didn't. Instead, he signed off, his image disappearing and being replaced by the communications software screen once again.

"Computer," Smith said, "get me Dianne Nguyen of MarsGroup. Search every database you need to and call any address you have to, but get her. Highest priority."

"Contacting Diane Nguyen," the computer told him and then went to task.

While it was making its attempt, Smith looked back up at the screen on the wall, where Laura Whiting was still ranting about independence and greedy corporations. She was now suggesting that the Martian economy be completely separated from the WestHem economy. Christ, she truly had gone around the bend. As if that would ever be allowed. As if that would work even if it were. She was talking about communism. Nothing more or less than communism. Just as she began to move to the next subject, the screen suddenly went blank as the InfoServe feed was cut. A graphic appeared a moment later pleading "technical difficulties".

"Thank you, Steve," Smith said gratefully. He made a quick check of the other channels, the ones owned by ICS and WIV, and found that they had been cut as well. Even better. "Computer," he told the terminal. "Switch broadcast channel on screen two to MarsGroup primary."

The computer had been programmed not to reply to commands such as that, just to do it. The screen flicked over and he was looking at Laura Whiting once again, still in the process of destroying her career and possibly her life.

"This planet is ours, people," she told her audience. "We, the Martians, are the ones who were born here, who have lived our lives here, who love this planet. We are the ones who plant and harvest the food that AgriCorp and the others sell for profit all over the solar system. We are the ones who built the structures that we live in with our own hands. We are the ones who set off generations ago to colonize this planet and make a new home for ourselves. And we are the ones who are being held down by the people of Earth who claim ownership of everything that we do. Ask yourselves, people, what do the Earthlings do for us? What do they do? They sit in their high-rise offices and count the money that they make from our sweat and toil. They sit up there and make decisions that affect the lives of all of us. A fingerprint on a computer screen and they've just signed an order that puts thousands out of a job. Another print on another screen and they've just bribed a politician who otherwise might have made your lives a little easier. This has got to stop. It has to end and we have to be able to control our own fates."

"Dianne Nguyen coming online," the computer spoke up just as Whiting was gearing up for another rant. The volume was automatically turned down on the broadcast so the communications terminal could be heard.

Nguyen's face appeared a moment later on his screen. It was a pleasantly feminine face of Southeast Asian descent, very youthful, although its owner was actually in her late forties. Nguyen, Smith knew, had once worked for InfoServe as a low-level manager. Her climb up the ladder had been stopped short in her early days because of her Martian birth and education, both of which were considered inferior in Earthling corporate circles. Still, like most Martians, Nguyen was eerily clever at certain things and, after quitting InfoServe, had been one of the prime movers and investors to get the joke that was MarsGroup rolling in the early days. "What can I do for you, Smith?" she asked now as she answered her call. Her expression was serious but it seemed as if she was hiding a smile.

"Dianne," Smith said warmly, as if she were his closest acquaintance, as if he hadn't worked madly over the years to strangle her company and its advertising contracts. "How are you this evening?"

Nguyen wasn't buying it however. "Let's cut the bullshit," she said with typical Martian crudity. "I assume you're calling about the inauguration speech."

He took a second to gather himself. "Why yes, that is why I'm calling," he said at last. "It seems that Ms. Whiting is... well... having a bit of a nervous breakdown up there. She is saying some very embarrassing things. Things that she will likely regret later."

"She sounds pretty much in her right mind to me," Nguyen opined. "I notice that the three bigs have all cut their feed. I presume you're calling to ask me to do the same?"

"In the interests of décor," he said, "yes, I'm asking if you will save this poor woman some later misery. Obviously, the Martian people do not need to hear the kind of drivel she is spouting up there. It would be best for all concerned if their access to the feed were to be cut completely off."

"Forget it," Nguyen told him. "We're sticking live with her. She's beautiful up there. She's saying things that should've been said a long time ago."

"She's committing libel and slander," Smith said, still speaking reasonably, as one colleague did to another. "It would be a breach of ethics to stay online with her as she commits this crime. As a media provider, there is a professional obligation not to broadcast such inflammations to the public. In some cases, I could see how you would even be held accountable for not..."

"Oh please," Nguyen interrupted, rolling her eyes at him. "*You* are preaching to *me* about ethics? About libel and slander? You, who have directed all of your subsidiaries not to advertise with me, who have forbidden your workers to even subscribe to my service? You can just take yourself a nice, high, flying fuck at Phobos, Smith. The feed remains live and any subsequent speeches by Whiting will be carried live as well."

"I'm warning you, Nguyen," Smith said, raising his voice now. "If you don't..."

"Bye now," she said, bringing her hand into the camera's range long enough to offer a small, contemptuous wave. With that, she went offline, her image flickering away.

"Goddamn greenie bitch," Smith said to the communications screen. He tried to several more times to get her back but only received her answering screen, which he left angry messages on.

With nothing else to do at the moment, he turned the volume back up and continued to watch Laura Whiting's speech.

*****

Laura was elated as she spoke into the microphones, as she looked at the sea of shocked faces staring up at her from the audience chambers. No matter what else came of this night, it felt glorious to finally throw aside the mask of proper politician that she had worn for so many years now. She felt as liberated as she hoped to make her planet.

Now that she had everybody's attention, now that she had explained what she hoped to do with her term and why she thought it needed to be done, she moved into the next phase of her speech: the phase in which she tried to prevent her removal before her work was done.

"I have made a lot of new enemies in the last five minutes," she told the planet. "I like to think that I have made some new friends among the Martian people, but you can bet your ass that the wheels of my removal are already starting to turn at this very moment. My guess is that strings have already been pulled by the movers and shakers of this world and this broadcast has been cut off by all of the so called 'big three' Internet providers. If my words were broadcast for more than three minutes, it would surprise me indeed.

"But I would also be surprised if MarsGroup Internet, the only Martian based media, followed suit with the big three. My guess, my hope, is that the one media provider with any sort of integrity is continuing to broadcast my words to you all. That is my hope because you really need to hear what I have to say next. You really need to hear how they are going to try to hamstring my proposals for this planet before they even get started."

She looked at the reserved seating, where the legislature members all sat, her eyes tracking from face to face. Most of them looked away when her gaze fell upon them. "You in the legislature," she said. "You have the power to impeach me from this office. It is written into the planetary constitution and it is your duty to do so if I commit abuses of power or crimes against the people. In this instance however, I have done neither. I have committed no offense against them that you can legally impeach me for. Nevertheless, you will be asked to open an investigation into my actions, probably shortly after you leave the chairs you are sitting in. Representatives of whoever your *sponsors* are will contact you, and they will tell you to begin an investigation and they will tell you to vote to impeach me. And since you are all bought people— bought and paid for in campaign contributions and thinly veiled bribes offered by lobbyists for AgriCorp and MarsTrans and InfoServe and a dozen others—you will be expected to do as you are told and make me go away. That is the way this great political system works, that is the way our planetary government and our federal government works. That is why we vote to tax John Carlton of Eden or Barb Jones of New Pittsburgh, but to cut taxes for AgriCorp or InfoServe. That is the way things are."

She gave them a softer look and lowered her voice a little. "But it doesn't have to be that way. There is nothing in the Martian constitution that mandates you vote or act as those who have given you campaign contributions wish. The reason we all do it anyway is because we wish to be reelected, to pretend that we really have power for another two years or four years or six years. This has been going on so long that most of you have forgotten who you're really supposed to be working for. Well this time, in this instance, I'm going to remind you. You legislature members were elected by the common Martians to serve and to them is who your loyalty and your votes are owed. Every last one of you is of Martian heritage. Every last one of you is the descendent of those who left Earth to seek out employment here, on this new world. You are all Martians and when those Earthling lobbyists start calling you tonight and telling you what you're supposed to do, I want you to remember that you work for Mars and the Martian people, not AgriCorp and InfoServe and the other soulless corporations. If you refuse to impeach me for daring to defy those corporate masters, this planet will be free within a year. If you cave to their pressure and vote me out, we will continue to languish under their rule. Remember who you are and where you came from and do the right thing for once in your careers."

She paused, taking a breath before continuing. "However, since I realize that my words alone may not be enough to convince you, I will take this time to bring up another point. The voters of each of your districts have the right under the constitution to organize and hold a recall vote that is capable of removing you from office. Thanks to media control and various other factors over the years, this is something that has never been done before. The option to do so however, is there and there does not have to be a specific reason for this action. This is something that the people are able to do at any time and there is no appeal process, there is no way that friends in the corporations can reverse such a thing. All it takes to get such a thing started is a little organization on the part of the voters and ten thousand fingerprints on a petition."

She looked from the legislature seats back up into the MarsGroup cameras, the only one that she knew were still live. "This is where the people of Mars come in. This is where those of you that have elected me can help me stay in office so that I can help you be free. An impeachment drive against me is going to begin in earnest tomorrow morning, my first day of full duties in office. If you, the people, do nothing, I will be impeached and drummed out within the week. But if you take the time to email your elected representative, if you tell him or her that you will organize a petition to remove them from office if they vote for an investigation and an impeachment, and then if you follow through with this threat in the event that they do, I guarantee you that they will do what you ask.

"That is my challenge to you, people of Mars. I have taken the first step to get us free of the tyranny we live under. I know that independence is what the vast majority of you wish. Now is the time to act. You can either stand with me and continue to move us towards freedom, or you can do nothing, let me be drummed out, and things will continue here on Mars as they always have. The time is ripe, my friends and it will never get riper. You have a voice in the governor's office for the first time. I implore you, I beg of you, help me follow through with this separation. Let your voices be heard. With your help, all of us will be free.

"That is all I have to say. The rest is in your hands."

With that she gave one last smile and left the podium, leaving the stunned audience and a stunned planet in her wake.

*****

Corban Hayes was the regional chief of operations for the Martian branch of the Federal Law Enforcement Bureau, WestHem's highest law enforcement agency. A native of Los Angeles and a fourth generation FLEB director, Corban hated the planet Mars as much as any Earthling and couldn't wait until his next promotion when he could get out of this dreadful place. Of course, now that Laura Whiting had gone apparently crazy and spouted a bunch of anti-corporation sentiments on live Internet, that promotion just might be swirling down the great toilet of bureaucracy. It had been his office, his investigators—who were supposedly the best in existence—that had done the background check on Whiting back when she had announced her candidacy for high office the previous year. He had put his fingerprint on the documents that had declared her an excellent candidate with no known "conflicting loyalties" or "unsuitable ideals". His agents had poured through her previous life for more than a month, searching for anything that might have hinted at problems for the government and therefore the business interests that controlled it. They had examined every law that she'd authored or voted on, every speech she'd ever given, every financial transaction she had ever made. She had been squeaky clean, which meant of course, that she only took bribes from her sponsors and that she only voted for or authored bills that had been approved by her sponsors. It meant that she had never been heard to utter an unkind word about her sponsors in public. In the world of politics, that was impressive indeed.

What in the hell had happened to her? Where had that communist, radical, independence talk come from? Had she really been hiding that inside of her and putting on an act all of these years? Was that possible?

Hayes tried not to think too hard about the why of the situation. When it came right down to it, it didn't really matter. He was having enough trouble just dealing with the flak that was being thrown at him. His communications terminal had been buzzing madly ever since that miserable greenie had started spouting off. It seemed that every corporate director on the planet was trying to get through, demanding an explanation. And it would only get worse when the replies started to come in from Earth, where the headquarters of all of these corporations were located. Thankfully the planetary alignment was approaching the furthest that Mars and Earth ever got from each other and radio signals currently took more than fifteen minutes to travel from place to the other. That would at least give him a little break between onslaughts.

His office was on the 112th floor of the New Pittsburgh Federal Building downtown, a building located just on the edge of the ghetto. He was looking out his window at the high-rises that surrounded the building, seeing the lights shining brightly in the clear Martian atmosphere. How he longed to be back in Los Angeles with its thirty-six million inhabitants and where the elite could travel by propeller-driven VTOL's that landed right on the roofs of buildings.

"Priority link-up attempt," his computer terminal told him, repeating the same thing it had said more than thirty times so far. "Caller is William Smith, chief executive officer of AgriCorp's Martian operations."

"Christ," Hayes sighed, longing for a nice healthy pipe-hit of some good green. He had some in his desk drawer but somehow, he didn't think this was the proper time for it. "Put him through," he told his computer, knowing that Smith was not someone he could blow off. AgriCorp, after all, damn near ruled the solar system and Smith was the number three man within that particular corporation.

Smith's face came on the screen and, after a brief exchange of the required pleasantries, he began his ass chewing. He ranted for nearly five minutes about botched investigations, incompetent investigators, wasted tax-dollars, and directors that would be sent back to the streets busting software pirates. Hayes took it all like a true professional, nodding in all the right places, agreeing when it was necessary, disagreeing gently when it seemed expected of him. Finally, Smith was able to calm down enough to talk rationally and to actually accomplish what had been the goal of the communication in the first place.

"She needs to be indicted," Smith told him. "Right away. I want her to be in handcuffs in the jail by this time tomorrow."

"Well, sir," Hayes said reasonably, "I'd really love to oblige you of that, but the simple fact is, I don't have anything to indict her with."

"She admitted taking bribes on live Internet," Smith reminded him, as if he were an idiot. "Don't you remember? During her little portion about how our political system works?"

"Well, yes, I remember," he responded. "And while it is true that that is an indictable offense, it might not be such a good idea to pursue that avenue at this time."

"Why not?" Smith demanded.

He gathered his thoughts for a moment, trying to formulate the proper way to say this. "Because," he said, "those... bribes as you call them, were actually campaign contributions put into her political account. The other... uh... offerings, the ones that went into her personal account, while they went unreported and are technically bribery, they all came from your corporation and her other sponsors. If I indict her for receiving them then I will be forced to indict your corporate officers and your lobbyists for giving them. To tell you the truth, that seems rather counter-productive."

Smith paled just the tiniest bit, obviously shaken by what he was being told. It would seem that he hadn't thought of this yet. "But... can't you arrange it so that doesn't have to occur?" he asked.

"Unfortunately, no," he said with just the proper hint of regret in his voice. "While we can bend the law quite broadly in the interests of WestHem security, we cannot bend it quite that much. Especially not in a case such as this, where a popular politician is the target. If we bring up the bribery issue we'll be opening up a huge can of worms."

"I see," Smith said, glaring. "Then what is to be done about this... this... greenie? Surely, she is not going to be allowed to get away with this. What does my company pay you people taxes and contributions for?"

"Well, of course we will launch an *immediate* investigation into the Whiting matter," Hayes assured him. "Believe me, we won't be standing idle on this. I intend to assign no less than fifteen of my best agents to this case and they will go over everything that Whiting has done in the last year. We'll search out any unauthorized Internet calls from government terminals. She was campaigning for governor. Surely, she has done that—they all do. We'll look into her finances again and find out if she's getting wholesale prices because of her position. We'll find *something* on her. And even if we don't, we'll be watching her every move from here on out, waiting for her to do something wrong. She's not a saint, sir, there has to be something and we will find it."

"Good," Smith said, calming a little. "And make it fast. Getting rid of that greenie needs to be your highest priority."

"And it will," he said. "In the meantime, however, might I suggest that you pursue things from the political angle as well. Get your lobbyists together and get the other corporations to do the same. Have them pressure the legislature to do just as Whiting surmised they would do and impeach her. Misrepresentation shouldn't be too hard to prove—after all, she's certainly not what the people elected to office, is she?"

"No," he said, "she's not."

"And you're not really worried about the public pressure on the legislative members that she tried to foment, are you? If you are, maybe…"

Smith scoffed at the very motion. "The ignorant greenies on this planet are completely incapable of doing what she told them to do. That was actually the most amusing part of her little speech. Greenies organizing a recall vote? Ridiculous."

"You see?" Hayes said, smiling a little. "Things are well under control. You attack her from the political level and we'll attack her from the legal angle. She'll be impeached within a week and then we'll indict her and send her to prison for a year or so. That'll serve to get rid of the problem and make any of the other greenie politicians that might consider such a thing in the future think twice."

*****

Perhaps the only politician who was absolutely delighted by what Laura Whiting had done was the one who had the most to gain by it. Scott Benton had been sworn in as Lieutenant Governor of Mars about thirty minutes after Laura Whiting had left the stage. Though he had had a great speech planned—a rambling twelve-page jerk-off about how he was going to work through the differences that he and the Governor had to strive for a better tomorrow—he had been unable to give it due to the unusual circumstances of the Whiting inauguration. After that, the reporters had all left to go compose their stories, taking their cameras with them, and the legislature had voted an early recess to the gathering to give themselves time to return to their offices and think about the spectacle that they had witnessed. Benton's swearing in had been in front of less than twenty witnesses and hundreds of empty chairs, without a doubt the most unceremonious inauguration of a Lieutenant Governor on record.

Benton didn't care and, in fact, had never been happier about anything. He muttered his oath before the associate judge, making himself official, and then he immediately headed upstairs to his new office to begin his work. Whiting had actually thrown the Governor's office away. She had actually insulted and abused her own sponsors on live Internet before millions of people. Amazing, simply amazing. And now that she had done this, he had no doubt that he would be sworn in by the senile old judge as Governor within days. There was no way that that bitch Whiting would be allowed to survive this.

A third generation Martian hailing from New Pittsburgh, Benton had the cleverness of his people but the ambition of the Earthlings. The son of a MarsTrans chief lobbyist, he had chosen politics as his profession while he had still been in the private high school where he received his secondary education. He had always had a keen ear and a warm way with people and he had developed the instincts that went with the job well before graduating from the University of Mars at NP with his degree in political theory. By the end of law school, he had already been marked by the powers-that-be (namely MarsTrans and Tagert Steel) as an up and coming star to be reckoned with. He had done two terms as an NP city councilman and one as mayor before moving into the legislature—the true springboard to high politics on Mars. He had made many friends among the people who counted as he worked his way through three terms on the legislature, but had been derailed in his path towards the Governor's office by Laura Whiting, whose power and influence had always been just a few steps higher than his own. Whiting had a way of getting things done—she had pushed through the Martian Planetary Guard all of those years ago, had led the fight against the feds to have anti-bombardment emplacements installed in all of the cities, had pushed through a dozen or more anti-crime bills—and she was much loved by the Martian people because of this. He and his sponsors had known that running against such a popular candidate would be an exercise in futility and a huge waste of money, so, instead he had been encouraged to run for the number two spot which, by Martian constitutional rules was completely separate from the Governor's race. That he had won easily enough and he had been prepared to settle in for an unpleasant four to eight years under Whiting's thumb before he had another shot at the big spot. But now, Whiting had just handed him the Governorship after less than one hour in office. Amazing. He would have to remember to thank her as she was led away in handcuffs by the feds.

His staff members had set his office up the day before and he was not in there for more than two minutes before the first of the calls came in. It was from Robert Flanders himself, the CEO of operations for MarsTrans, which owned and operated eighty percent of the rail services, both passenger and freight, on the planet.

"I think you know what to do now, don't you, Scott?" he was asked after the preliminaries were taken care of.

"Yes sir," he said. "Beginning tomorrow I'll address the legislature and urge an investigation into Whiting for misrepresentation. I'll have her impeached in a matter of days."

"Very good," Flanders said, offering a fatherly smile. "I can see we did well to invest in you. It's strange how fate works sometimes, isn't it?"

"Yes sir," he replied truthfully. "Indeed, it is. I'll have my speechwriters and my staffers working all night. You'll have a governor in office in no time."

*****

Laura herself was, understandably under the circumstances, getting her fair share of Internet calls as well. Though she had a secretary to screen most of them, her high-powered former sponsors—and there were a lot of those—all had access to her private Internet address and they damn sure made use of it now. Though her fate had already been discussed and decided while she had still been on the stage saying her words, they all wanted to talk to her, to demand an explanation of her.

"Why, Laura?" Smith of AgriCorp, her biggest sponsor, demanded once he got her online. "What were you thinking? What were you doing? Why did you throw your career away like this?"

"I threw nothing away," Laura told him curtly, her voice even and almost teasing. "As of the moment I said, 'I do' I was governor of this planet. And as for why I did what I did, I believe I explained myself quite well during my speech. Surely you caught the speech, didn't you?"

General Jackson, commander of the MPG, was standing just off to the side, out of camera range. He chuckled a little at her words.

"You betrayed us, Laura," he told her. "After all we've done for you, after all we've spent getting you elected, this is how you repay us?"

"You mean that after all of the bribes you gave me, I am now refusing to do as I'm told like a little VR toy. Sorry if I hurt your feelings, Smith. Do you think they'll fire you for this? I'm sort of anxious to find out how the head office in Denver responds." She looked at her watch. "The transmission should have gotten there about twenty minutes ago now. How long until they send a message back? Do you think it's on its way now? Or do you think they'll need more time to figure out how to shitcan you?"

"The head office is not your concern," he told her angrily. "What you should be worried about is your resignation. If it's in by tomorrow morning we'll call off the FLEB agents that are after you. We'll tell the public that you had a mental breakdown and they'll forget about all of this in a few months. I'm sure you have enough of our money stashed away to live comfortably for a while."

"I have none of your money stashed away," she told him. "Every dollar went into my election account. Most of it is still there. Within a year, your money won't be any good on this planet. And as for my resignation, you can forget it. Do your best. I'm here under the constitution and you have no means to get rid of me. You're not playing with an amateur here."

"You think those ignorant greenies that you're so fond of are going to save you?" he asked her. "Is that what you think? You think they're going to call off our legislature members with the little e-mail campaign you suggested? Tell me that you're not really that naïve, Laura."

"I think you'll be surprised by what us greenies are capable of," she told him. "You've been degrading us and underestimating us for so long now that you have no idea of the resentment that most of us hold for all things corporate and Earthling. They'll compose those emails. Take my word for it. Actually, you don't have to take my word. Why don't you call up some of your pet politicians and ask them how many have come in so far?"

"I have no need to waste my time that way," he said dismissively.

Laura shrugged. "You'll just have to hear it in the morning then, won't you? Our independence is coming, Smith. I think you might want to consider the best way to negotiate it with us so that AgriCorp comes out on top. My offer was sincere. You hand your assets over to us and we'll continue to produce food and give it to you. If you cooperate, we'd be inclined to hand all of the food to *you* instead of simply sharing it with the other agricultural corporations. Think about that."

Smith shook his head a little, the way one does when one is dealing with a lunatic. "I'm going to enjoy seeing you led away," he told her. "This is your last warning. Resign now before it's too late."

"It's already too late," she said. "Goodbye, Smith. Don't send any more of your people here. I won't accept them." With that she signed off, making his face disappear. Before ten seconds had gone by the next call came in and then the next and then the next after that. Most were sponsors but a few were reporters. She denied all calls from the big three reporters but gave a brief statement to the MarsGroup reporter, mostly just assuring her that she had been dead serious up on the stage tonight and that she would grant further interviews once she was settled into office. Finally, they slowed to a trickle and she was able to take a breather for a few minutes.

Jackson, sipping out of a bottle of AgriCorp apple juice, sat down across her desk from her. He was dressed in his uniform, namely the red shorts and white T-shirt that were the standard interior dress of the Martian Planetary Guard troops. His rank insignia—that of commanding general—was stenciled on his left breast, just above the small emblem of the MPG. He carried no weapons belt and wore no body armor, relying on his squad of special forces bodyguards to keep him safe. He looked at his boss pointedly. "It's all come down to this night," he told her. "All of the secret planning, all of the underhanded deals with the arms makers, and now the wheels are in motion."

"Everything according to plan so far," she agreed, opening a bottle of juice of her own and taking a sip.

"You were beautiful up there tonight," he said. "Your speech was very moving. Hopefully it will have the results we need. If you get impeached next week, it's all for nothing."

"The people will do what I ask," she told him assuredly. "I know them well and I know how fed up they are with the system we have. They want change; they've wanted it for generations. All they needed was a leader to cling to, one who had the power to get the job done."

"And now they've got one," he said. "Assuming they're not too cynical to embrace you."

"They voted for me in record numbers, didn't they? They'll embrace me. And once I start giving my weekly speeches on MarsGroup, I'll get them fired up the rest of the way, until they're demanding that we be free, no matter what needs to be done."

"No matter what," Jackson said, knowing what it was eventually going to take. "I know we've been over this before, but do you think that there's any chance at all of WestHem actually negotiating autonomy with us? I mean, after the seriousness of the situation becomes clear to them and they realize what the options are?"

"None whatsoever," she told him. "You know that, Kevin. If we're going to be free, we're going to have to fight for it. There's too much at stake for WestHem to even consider the possibility of letting us go. Not even under the terms that I've offered, which are generous indeed."

He sighed a little. "You're undoubtedly right," he said. "It's a nice dream though."

"But in the meantime," Laura told him, "this planet is rapidly approaching maxima from Earth. In another three months the navy will begin sending the bulk of the fleet here for storage at Triad. Will the MPG be ready by then?"

"In terms of ability, they're ready right now," Jackson reminded her. "Our mission is to prevent invasion of this planet and to be able to fully mobilize to that goal in less than twelve hours. Repelling invaders is all that we train for. And over the last three months we've been training particularly hard. The real question you should be asking is whether or not they will obey your orders and repel an invasion by *WestHem* marines. As of this moment, I don't believe that they would do that. That is where you and your speeches come in."

"They'll be ready," Laura promised. "Over the next few months I believe that WestHem's behavior towards us is going to be particularly reprehensible. It's as predictable as the moons. The WestHem way to deal with opposition is to crack down on it, to smear it. Remember the line theory?"

"Oh yes," he said. "I remember." The line theory, advanced by none other than Laura Whiting herself (always in private discussions of course), stated that the way a government such as WestHem remained in power was to identify *the line*. The line was the boundary between how much abuse and profiteering, how much thinly veiled corruption the citizens would take before they would openly rebel against their leaders. WestHem, EastHem, and other governments throughout world history had been very adept at finding that line and keeping themselves just on the friendly side of it.

"WestHem and the corporations will be forced to step over the line in order to deal with us," Laura said. "I don't like deliberately encouraging suffering among our people, but unfortunately it's the only way. And when the time comes, your people need to be ready to do what needs to be done."

"They'll be ready," he promised. "You do your part and we'll do ours."

CHAPTER TWO

Eden, Mars
January 29, 2186

The morning following the inauguration of the new Martian governor was also a Saturday morning in the western hemisphere of Mars, where all of the terrestrial cities were located. Being a Saturday, it meant that a regular training rotation for the MPG was scheduled at the base on the southern edge of Eden. Of course, all of the Eden area MPG members could not train regularly at one time. There were simply too many of them for that to be feasible on a weekly basis. As such, the MPG volunteers—and they were all volunteers except for a few, select positions—were divided into one of four training rotations. This particular week was B rotation's turn. From all over the city, men and women woke up early on what was traditionally a day of rest, donned their red shorts and white MPG t-shirts, and headed for tram stations near their homes. The paid twenty dollars to board the MarsTrans public transportation trains which carried them through a belt line and a serious of spokes to the base, the entrance to which was located in one of the more dangerous parts of town. Once there, they waited in line for more than thirty minutes to clear the security checkpoints and worked their way to their assigned buildings.

    The base itself consisted of four high-rise buildings, a large hangar complex, an armored vehicle parking area complete with airlock complexes, and more than two square kilometers of enclosed, pressurized and gravitated parkland upon which troops could assemble and exercise. Assembly time was typically 0700, except for a few specialized groups that met earlier. By 0730 the vast majority of the troops were out on the exercise grounds, performing the traditional calisthenics or running on the track that circled the base. As they ran and did their pushups on this morning, the normal loose discipline that the MPG practiced was even looser than normal as everyone talked about the events of the previous evening. For the most part, they cheered Laura Whiting and her idea, telling each other that it was about goddamn time that someone spoke up to the corporations. Many of them talked of the emails that they had composed and sent to their elected representatives. Only a few volunteered that they had not composed such correspondence. Those that did were quickly chided by their peers to do so and quickly, before the legislature opened an investigation.

"You don't think that will really work, do you?" asked corporal Salinas of the special forces division of his squad leader, Sergeant Fargo.

They were well into their fourth kilometer of the warm-up run and starting to breathe a little heavy. "It might not," Lon allowed, wiping sweat from his forehead. "But she'll sure as shit go down within a week if we don't. If those prick politicians get enough mail threatening a recall vote if they try to impeach Whiting, that just might make them think twice. And it doesn't take much to compose one either. No real reason not to do it."

"And it feels damn good to tell off one of them fuckers too," put in Lieutenant Yee, their platoon commander and a twelve year veteran of special forces. "I went to bed happy last night after I sent mine off. Give it a shot, you'll like it."

"I guess I will then," Salinas said thoughtfully. "What's to lose?"

After their morning workout, Lon and his squad went into the base operations building for their briefing. They were to participate in yet another field operations drill today, their third in the last four months. The last year had brought a heavier than normal training schedule, particularly for the tank, special forces, and flight crews. No one at the operational level knew why, although rumors always flew about a possible EastHem invasion in the works. Tensions had been rather high between the two governments lately since EastHem was stationing more warships at their naval base on Callisto, pushing the limits of a treaty signed as part of the Jupiter War armistice. None of Lon's squad minded the increased training in the least. It meant that instead of staying in the classroom all day learning new techniques, or instead of going to the gunnery range to practice old ones, they would don their biosuits and fly out into the wastelands to do what they did best: attack things and blow things up. Today's mission was going to be a fairly realistic anti-tank drill performed with real tanks from the MPG's first battalion.

After each of the four squads under Yee's command was given their operational area, they retreated to the bottom floor of the building where they drew their weapons and their biosuits from the armory.

"Okay, everyone," Lon told his men, "the standard loadout will be the M-24 and six hundred rounds per man. Please be sure that you have training ammo instead of the real thing."

Everyone had a little chuckle over that. The training ammunition was an under-appreciated marvel designed by Martian engineers years before. The training rounds were made out of a thin synthetic material injected with helium. They came in everything from four millimeter all the way up to eighty-millimeter tank shells. They were the same size and would fire at the same suicidal velocity out of the various weapons, but, instead of penetrating through the biosuits and the flesh beneath as a standard armor piercing round would, they would simply vaporize on contact.

"Matza," Lon said to his most junior member, "you're on the SAW today. Draw two thousand rounds for it."

"Right, sarge," Matza told him, excited to be in charge of the squad's machine gun.

"Galvan and Horishito, you two have the AT's," he said next, referring to the AT-50s, which were portable, shoulder fired anti-tank lasers. "Be sure to load up at least ten charges apiece, twelve if you can fit them. And again, make sure you have the training charges. We wouldn't want to blow the hell out of our own tanks."

"Right," Galvan and Horishito both agreed.

"Appleman," he said to the squad's medic. "You got your kit ready to roll?"

"I sleep with it, sarge," he assured him, hefting it up.

"All right then," Lon said with a smile. "Let's get to it. Our ride will be ready in sixty minutes."

The weapons draw went relatively quickly but it took them the bulk of their time to get into their biosuits. They wore standard MPG suits, the same as the ones the grunts and the tank crews wore out in the field. Each suit was custom fitted to its user and colored in the shades of red camouflage scheme that allowed it to blend in remarkably well in the bleak landscape of the wastelands. They were a vast improvement over the biosuits that the regular WestHem soldiers wore because the MPG suits were specifically designed for use on Mars instead of for use in *any* extra-terrestrial environment. A WestHem suit had a finite air supply for its user, usually ten to fifteen hours worth. In order to stay out in the field longer, a WestHem soldier needed to have spare tanks dropped to him. Martian suits, on the other hand, manufactured their own air from the thin Martian atmosphere. This added up to a smaller storage tank and a considerably less bulky suit. WestHem suits also emitted much more heat during operation, which made them much easier to detect by infrared sensors. An MPG biosuit was designed to slowly vent the body heat that its user produced, expelling it through evaporation via a series of pores all over the surface layer. In a way, it shed heat the same way a human body did, by transferring it into a liquid and then letting the liquid rise to the surface and outgas. Again, this was something that was only possible to do on the surface of Mars, which had an atmosphere, thin as it was. A soldier attempting to use an MPG biosuit on the surface of Ganymede or one of the other Jovian moons would die very quickly.

Once the suits were donned and powered up, a few minutes were spent dialing in the operations frequency that was to be used and calibrating the GPS links that helped them navigate on the surface. Each member of the squad had a radio link constantly open with Lon, who, as the squad leader, had a second link open with the platoon commander. After the radio and navigation tasks were taken care of, each man calibrated his weapon with the combat goggles built into the helmet. The computer in the goggles was hooked to sensors on the outside of the helmet that measured temperature, humidity, wind speed, and several other factors on an ongoing basis. When this information was calibrated with the particular weapon and ammunition type and tied into a sensor on the front of the weapon itself, a targeting reticle would appear in the user's field of vision when the weapon was brought up, showing where the rounds would hit if they were fired at that particular moment. The sensor on the weapon was of the binocular type, meaning that it could judge distance with fairly good accuracy, thus allowing for wind drift and gravity drop on targets that were further away. A small readout in the upper right of the goggle display showed the estimated distance to the target.

Lon sighted his M-24 back and forth a few times at various objects, testing the equipment. He aimed at the walls of the weapons room and then at the far door, watching as the small red circle followed his every move. The readouts seemed to work fine so he lowered the weapon once more and snugged it against his right side.

"Is everyone ready?" he asked his men once they had all finished their own sight-ins.

They were.

"Then let's do it. We got a Hummingbird to catch."

Hummingbird was the slang term for the ETH-70 transport craft that the special forces teams traveled in. It was one of two types of aircraft that had been specifically designed by Martian engineers for the Martian Planetary Guard. Like the biosuits, the Martian aircraft were only useful on the surface of Mars and had been designed to take advantage of the meager atmosphere. Hovers, which were the primary means that WestHem and EastHem troops moved about on the surface of extraterrestrial bodies, were bulky machines that kept aloft by means of directional thrusters on the bottom and back. Hovers were fairly slow moving and horrible gulpers of fuel, with a range of less than two hundred kilometers in the Martian gravity. The Hummingbirds, on the other hand, had two sets of large wings, which could be folded up for easy storage and extended to their full length once outside. These wings eliminated the need for vertical thrusters while in flight, increasing speed and fuel economy. A Hummingbird could haul twelve fully armed troops into the air and transport them more than six hundred kilometers out into the wastelands and back with fuel to spare.

When Lon and his squad entered the hangar deck of the base at 0945 that morning, activity was everywhere. The staging areas were filled with both the smaller Mosquito anti-armor planes—which were gearing up for some training of their own—and the larger, bulkier Hummingbirds. The crew chiefs were walking around most of the aircraft, making final checks of components and armament while the pilots and gunners went through preflight checks inside the cockpits. The Hummingbirds all had their back ramps extended into the loading position, awaiting the embarkation of their assigned troops. Their thrusters, which were located under each of the four wing positions, were all in the level flight positioning, facing backward, heat shimmering from their nozzles as they idled. The twenty-millimeter cannons, which were attached to a revolving turret below the nose, were all in the neutral position, facing forward.

"How you doin' today, Lon?" asked Mike Saxton, the crew chief for their assigned Hummingbird as they approached. He was a large man of African descent, dressed in pair of oily red and white coveralls. Since the aircraft hangar was fully pressurized and gravitated, there was no need for him to be dressed in a biosuit.

"Not too bad, Mike," Lon told him after making sure the external speaker for his suit was on. "Is this bucket of bolts airworthy today?"

"Don't be making fun of my hummer," he warned, only half-jokingly. "I'll tell Rick to leave your asses out there in the waste."

"My apologies," Lon said, slapping him on the back. "Is this fine piece of machinery ready to take us to our destination?"

"That's better," Mike grinned. "She's all ready for you. Go ahead and board when you're ready."

They boarded, each walking up the thin alloy ramp and into the cramped interior. Though the Hummingbird could transport twelve loaded troops with ease, comfort was not part of the bargain. They crammed in five to a side and strapped themselves into small seats that folded out from the wall. Their weapons, they kept against their chests, their packs full of extra ammo and food paste pushed into their backs. In the cockpit in front of them, Rick, the pilot, and Dave Yamata, the systems operator, were running through the pre-flight checklist. Since the aircraft would be depressurized once outside of the hangar, both of them were wearing biosuits as well.

"Ready to move out, sarge?" Rick asked as the preflight was completed. "The sooner we blow this scene, the less time we'll have to wait for an airlock."

"We're ready when you are," Lon told him.

"Okay," he said, turning to Dave. "Close us up and run through the final pressure check."

"Closing up," Dave said, pushing a button on the panel. The ramp rose up, pulled by hydraulic arms, and latched into place with a firm clank. "Pressure check in progress... and I got three greens on the panel."

"Copy three greens," Rick said. "Let's get clearance to taxi."

The clearance came a minute later and they began to move as Rick throttled up the hydrogen engine just enough to get them moving. The aircraft turned onto the taxiway and began to make its way towards the airlock complex on the far side of the hanger. Only one Hummingbird sized craft could fit into a single airlock at a time so they had to wait for nearly ten minutes while four Hummingbirds and three Mosquitoes went in front of them. As they waited, talk turned back to Laura Whiting and her now famous speech of the night before.

"I couldn't believe she actually said shit like that on Internet," proclaimed Gavin, who was a high school teacher by trade. "I mean, she told it like it was. She laid out how fucked up our political system is for everyone to hear."

"It was beautiful," agreed Horishito, who was a tram technician for MarsTrans. "I thought she was joking at first. When I realized she was serious, I just about shit my pants."

"I bet those pricks at AgriCorp headquarters were the ones to shit their pants," Lon, who was, of course, an AgriCorp employee as of the merger, said with a grin. "I would've loved to seen their faces when she told everyone how evil they were, or how much money they gave her to get her elected. That must've been priceless. Absolutely goddamn priceless."

"Yeah," said Gavin, shifting his AT-50 from one shoulder to the next, "but what are they gonna do to her now?"

"Nothing they can do if the legislature doesn't impeach her," Lon said. "And if everyone sends those pricks the email like Whiting asked, I don't think they'll have the balls to do it."

"They'll do it anyway," Horishito predicted gloomily.

"If they do, then we need to follow through and vote out our fuckin reps if they voted against her," said Mark Corning, a construction worker. "Hell, we need to do that if they even vote to open an investigation. When I sent my letter that's what I told Hennesy I'd do."

"You don't really think Hennesy is watching all of those emails, do you?" asked Horishito.

"Of course not," Corning said. "I bet the bitch don't look at a single fuckin one of them. But someone on her staff does, and if enough people sent them in, she'll have to think twice about doing what AgriCorp or whatever other fuckin corp that owns her, tells her to do."

Even Horishito had to admit that there was a point there. But he refused to accept that Laura Whiting would simply be allowed to stay in office. "There's no way in hell she'll keep the governor's office after what she said. I respect her for it and all, but you can bet your ass they're gonna find a way to get rid of her as quick as they can by whatever means they can."

"I think if they did that," said Lon, "it would be a very big mistake. Maybe the biggest that anyone has ever made."

With that, the talk turned to other matters deemed more important, namely the marijuana they were going to smoke after training today and the women they were going to try to score with. This was a discussion that was as timeless as it was graphic, as crude as it was a part of the male psyche. Just as they were really getting on a roll however, they were given clearance to enter the airlock, something that none of them particularly looked forward to.

"I hate this part," Horishito said, bracing himself against his seat and closing his eyes. He received no words of disagreement.

Rick brought the Hummingbird forward across the taxiway, using small blasts of the thrusters to propel them. The large steel blast doors were standing open on the base side and the aircraft passed through with less than two meters of clearance on each side. He throttled back down once inside, bringing the engines to idle, and then applied the ground brakes when the nose was near the blast doors on the opposite side. "In position," he reported both to the airlock controller and to the special forces team in the back.

"Airlock closing," the computer generated voice replied over the radio link.

The blast doors behind them slid slowly shut upon their tracks, sealing off the airlock from the interior of the base. The moment they were closed, the fans began to eject the air from the inside, lowering the atmospheric pressure to the level of the outside.

"Prepare for cessation of artificial gravity," the computer generated voice told Rick and Dave.

"Okay, guys," Rick told his cargo. "Get ready for lightening."

There was no gradual way to shut off the artificial gravity field that existed inside the building areas. It was either on or it was off. It could not be gently lowered from 1G to 0.38 Gs, the natural gravitational pull of Mars. A computer circuit cut power to the conductor that gravitated the airlock and just like that, everyone and everything—the plane, the weapons, the suit, the fluids within each person's body—lost nearly two-thirds of its weight. It was not considered to be one of life's great experiences. It gave a terrifying, dizzying sense of falling and spatial disorientation that lasted for almost a minute. Most people who experienced the sensation for the first time became sick to their stomach and vomited. Only the fact that all of Lon's team had been through lightening dozens of times kept them from heaving inside of their helmets.

"Ohhhh," Lon groaned miserably, feeling his stomach turning over. "Sometimes I wonder why I took this fucking job."

Everyone else in the aircraft, pilot and gunner included, matched his sentiments. But, as veterans of the process, all of them recovered by the time the fans finished evacuating the air from the lock.

"Decompression complete," the computer voice told Rick and Dave. "Airlock doors opening."

The blast doors on the exterior side of the lock slid slowly open, revealing a long taxiway that led out to the runways beyond. Red drift sand, a common problem on the Martian surface, marred the paved surface in a few places despite the fact that it had been freshly plowed less than an hour before. Rick throttled up a little and released the brakes, bringing the aircraft out of the lock and onto the staging area just beyond it. Once it was clear, the blast doors immediately began to shut behind them to prepare for another cycle.

"Decompressing the aircraft," Dave said, pushing a pad on his computer screen. It was necessary to bleed the air out of the Hummingbird since the troops would be exiting it when they reached their landing area. If this step were not taken, then they would all be blown out quite violently the moment the door was opened.

"I copy decompressing," Rick said. He pushed a pad on his own screen. "Unfolding wings."

The four large wings began to extend outward in sections, each piece pushed by mini-hydraulics and clanking neatly into place until the full thirty-meter span was out and ready for flight. This took about twenty seconds to accomplish and, once it was done, the aircraft, when viewed from above, resembled a very thin letter H turned on its side.

"Six greens on the gear locks," Rick reported.

"Decompression complete," Dave reported right after. "We're now at anticipated pressure for the LZ."

"Copy," said Rick. "Ready to taxi for take-off."

After gaining clearance, he throttled up once more and began to roll forward, bumping along on the synthetic rubber landing gear until reaching the end of the north-south runway. Once in position, he told the troops to brace for takeoff. Though most air and spacecraft were equipped with artificial gravity and inertial dampers to make the ride as smooth as standing on the surface, combat atmospheric craft did not come with that particular luxury. The heat and electromagnetic radiation that such devices produced made detection of the craft far too easy for an enemy.

"Lifting off," Rick said as he pushed the throttles forward to the maximum.

The roar of the hydrogen burning engines filled the craft with noise and vibration as the sudden acceleration pushed everyone towards the rear. Outside, the landscape began to blur by as they went from zero to more than 400 kilometers per hour in less than ten seconds. Because of the thin atmosphere of Mars, the speed one had to travel in order to obtain lift from the wings was considerable. When they reached 480 KPH of forward speed, considerably faster than the speed of sound in that environment, Dave pulled back on the stick and the Hummingbird's wheels broke contact with the runway. They climbed slowly, wobbling a little in the meager ground effect and then climbing above it. Dave pulled a lever next to his seat and the landing gear retracted into the belly of the craft with a thump. He then banked hard to the right, taking them to the east, out over the seemingly endless expanse of greenhouse complexes.

"ETA to the LZ is fifteen minutes," Dave told the troops over the intercom. "This is a combat insertion, as you know. Get ready for a bouncing ride."

"Just the way we like it," Lon groaned, closing his eyes and waiting for it to be over. The flight in was his least favorite aspect of his job.

Rick kept them at two hundred meters above the greenhouses in order to keep from violating planetary flight regulations. Once they passed over the last group of them however, he dropped down to less than thirty meters above the ground, hugging the hilly terrain to keep from being detected. The Hummingbird was a bulky aircraft and not terribly maneuverable, especially at the speed it was moving, but he expertly kept it within two meters of his target altitude as they moved over and between hills, as they shot through valleys and old watersheds. He stared forward intently as the terrain moved up and down before him, his hands making adjustments to the stick and throttle.

In the back, the ten men of Lon's squad fought down nausea as they pitched up and down, banked back and forth, seemingly randomly and with no forewarning of any kind. This, coupled with the lack of outside visual references and the heavy knowledge that only a slight miscalculation on Rick's part would smash them into a hillside at more than 600 KPH, made for very unstable stomachs. They gripped their weapons tightly and most of them followed Lon's example and kept their eyes tightly shut.

Rick circled in a roundabout path through the Sierra Madres Mountains and down to the foothills that bordered it. On the other side of these rolling hills was a broad expanse of relatively flat terrain some five kilometers wide and more than sixty kilometers in length. Such terrain and other cuts through the surface like it were the most likely avenue of advance for any invasion force attacking the planet since they were flat enough to both support a group of orbit to surface landing craft and to move tanks, artillery, and other armored vehicles through. It was in these valleys that the Eden area MPG troops did most of their training.

"One minute to the LZ," Dave announced as they exited from the mountainous area and began to dive through the smaller foothills. "Going in hot."

"Copy," Lon said, fighting with his gorge. It had been a long time since he'd puked during an insertion but it was always a struggle.

Rick slowed to just above stall speed, easing up on the up and down motion a little bit. He banked sharply around the base of a hill and turned back to the east, towards a small gully that was known only by its map coordinates. "LZ in sight," he announced. "Get ready for insertion."

Dave, as the gunner, examined the ground around the landing zone carefully through his scope. An infrared enhanced camera mounted on the belly panned back and forth under magnification, searching for the telltale signatures of biosuits of "enemy" soldiers. It was possible, though very unlikely, that the MPG armored forces that were acting as the opposing force, or OPFOR, in the drill might have sent out patrols of the area. These training sessions were designed to be executed as realistically as possible. "I'm scanning clear," he announced as he saw nothing but empty ground.

"Copy, scanning clear," Lon echoed. He opened his eyes and looked at his troops. "Lock and load guys. It's time to play."

Everyone jacked rounds into the chambers of their weapons. "Let's get the fuck out of this deathtrap," Horishito said.

"Coming in," Rick said, picking his put down spot. He lowered the landing gear. "Brace for landing."

The transition from straight and level flight to a controlled vertical landing was a rather violent affair. Rick pitched upward and simultaneously changed the angle of the engines, directing the thrust downward. The entire aircraft shuddered as if in seizure as airspeed was bled off in a matter of seconds. The nose rose upward at more than forty-five degrees and the occupants were subjected to a jaw-wrenching 3G of deceleration. Once their forward airspeed fell to less than 30 KPH, Rick nosed down, bringing them back level and reduced thrust, allowing gravity to pull them to the surface. The heavy duty, puncture-proof tires slammed down onto the dusty surface, bounced once, and then settled into a soft roll which was quickly halted with the brakes.

"On the ground," Rick said, keeping the thrusters at just over idle.

Dave pushed the button that opened the loading ramp. As it clanked downward, thumping to the ground, he pushed another button that released the restraint harnesses of the back passengers. "Go," he told them, continuing to peer into his scope for enemy soldiers. Had he seen any he could have engaged them with the twenty-millimeter cannon.

"Let's go," Lon said, getting carefully to his feet. Though the image of special forces troops was that they jumped up and ran everywhere, the fact was, that on the surface of Mars in less than a third of normal gravity, you *had* to move carefully.

In an orderly fashion all ten of them moved down the ramp and out onto the surface of the planet, their suit boots tramping through the powdery, rocky soil. Dust blew up from the landing and the continued thrust of the engines obscured the terrain around them. Once outside the aircraft they spread apart in a well-practiced maneuver and lay down on the ground ten meters from the ramp, forming a loose circle with all of them facing outward, weapons ready to engage any targets that might be encountered.

"We're down," Lon barked into his radio link, letting the pilot know that he could get back into the air. As long as the Hummingbird was on the ground, both it and the troops it had inserted were vulnerable.

"Copy," Rick's voice said into his ear. "Lifting off. Kick some ass out here."

A moment later the blowing dust grew worse as the thrusters fired back up to full throttle, lifting the aircraft back into the air. When it was ten meters above the ground, the thrusters turned slowly back to the rear, restoring forward flight. It moved faster and faster until it was once more capable of sustained flight again. It banked around to the north and moved away, keeping low to the ground. None of the men watched it go.

After a moment, the dust began to settle or drift off in the 40 KPH wind and the men began to bark off that the area in front of them was clear.

"Okay," Lon said, gripping the stock of his M-24. "Jefferson, Horishito, Powell, Yamata, Salinas, move off to that group of boulders at my four o'clock. We'll cover. Matza, keep sharp with that SAW."

One by one the five men that Lon had named got to their feet and trotted across the uneven ground. They formed up in a wedge formation, their weapons ready for action, their equipment clanking on their backs. They stepped gingerly, each footfall a deliberate movement designed to keep them from losing their balance in the reduced gravity. Though their movements looked almost comical, they were able to move surprisingly quickly and within a minute of exiting the ramp they were in position in the boulder field.

"It's clear over here, sarge," Corporal Salinas, his second-in-command, told him on the closed radio link they used. It was an ultra high frequency channel of minute power, incapable of being picked up more than a half-kilometer away unless a power boost was used. And even if it were picked up, the transmissions were encoded.

"Copy," Lon said. "We're coming up." He waved to the men left with him and they all got to their feet. Utilizing the same trot as those before them, they moved across the landscape and joined their companions. Once they were reunited, Lon punched a command into the access panel on the sleeve of his biosuit. A detail map of the area they were in appeared before his eyes. A small red dot in the center of the map, placed there by the suit computer utilizing global positioning satellites in geosynchronous orbit, marked his current location on it. "Right on target," he said, studying the view. He looked to the south, towards a series of small hills. "Right over there," he pointed. "Hill 2718 and Hill 2712. They overlook the AOA of the OPFOR. Salinas, take Gavin and Horishito over to 2718 and hole up with those AT launchers. The rest of us will take 2712 and provide anti-personnel cover. Retreat rally position is going to be that boulder field at grid 7C on your maps."

"Right, sarge," Salinas said, shifting his weapon a little. "Let's go guys," he told Gavin and Horishito. They began to trot across the landscape in that direction.

"Powell," Lon said to one of his more experienced privates, "you take point. Matza, linger back with me with the SAW. Let's move."

They moved, the seven of them assembling into a wedge and moving quickly towards the hill.

*****

The ETT-12 main battle tank was state of the art armor for the WestHem armed forces extra-terrestrial operations. Built in the Alexander Industries armament factory in New Pittsburgh, they weighed in at nearly sixty metric tons (in standard 1G gravity) and could travel at more than one hundred kilometers per hour across nearly any terrain. The engine was a high horsepower hydrogen-burning turbine that required very little maintenance. Crewing three, they sported twin high capacity anti-armor lasers protruding from a housing atop the turret. These lasers were their main guns and could put a hole in just about anything that they hit, no matter how thick or how reinforced. However, as handy a thing as lasers were for anti-vehicle or anti-structure assaults, they did have their limitations. Lasers with a capacity high enough to kill required significant amounts of power and they needed to be charged up before firing, something that took an average of eight to fifteen seconds, depending on the capacity and the power source. This made them virtually useless against personnel or massed light vehicles since rapid fire was impossible. For this reason, the ETT-12 was equipped with an 80mm, high explosive round main gun, a 20 mm, high velocity cannon capable of firing nearly three hundred rounds per minute and a smaller, 4mm high velocity commander's weapon capable of firing nearly six hundred rounds per minute. These weapons were compatible with the firing computers of the crewmembers' biosuits making it quite easy to put bullets on target.

The Martian Planetary guard, which was technically an arm of the WestHem armed forces (though you would never hear an MPG member *or* a WestHem marine say so), used the ETT-12 as their main defensive weapon for city defense, which was basically the only thing worth attacking or defending on Mars. Utilizing the sales and income tax that Laura Whiting had proposed and pushed through the legislature after the Jupiter War, the MPG had bought and modified more than a six hundred of the expensive weapons over the years. The 1st battalion of the 6th Armored infantry regiment of the MPG was the main force responsible for point defense of Eden. They had 36 of these ETT-12s as their main striking power. In addition, they had 54 top of the line Alexander Industries armored personnel carriers, each of which sported a lower yield anti-tank laser and two light machine guns and could carry a complete squad of infantry apiece. Backing up this force were four mobile anti-air laser vehicles that could fire up to six shots per minute and packed enough power to bring down an orbital lifter if such a thing was needed.

Lieutenant Colonel Michael Chin, a twelve-year veteran of the MPG (and a middle management employee of Alexander Industries in his *real* life) was the commander of the 1st of the 6th. Chin and the men under his command had been out in the wastelands since before sunrise that morning, their task to play prey for the special forces and air force. It was a role that they had played many times before in the past, pretending to be an enemy column advancing on Eden.

A tall man of Chinese descent and a fourth generation Martian, Chin was in the turret of one of the tanks in the middle of the column, watching through the view screen that was hooked to an infrared enhanced digital camera on the outside. Taking soft, easy breaths of the canned air from his biosuit, he panned back and forth, searching for any signs of the teams that he knew were out there somewhere. Time and time again those teams had cleaned his battalion's clock and, though he knew such training was invaluable for them, he was tired of being massacred by a bunch of kids with toy lasers. Today, he was going to try a new tactic. After all, his orders were to make things as difficult as possible without actually cheating. "Chin to Air-def," he said on the command channel.

"Air-def here, boss," said Lieutenant Garcia, who was in command of the sixteen men who made up the air defense section of the battalion. "Go ahead."

"Get ready for action," he told them. "I can feel those sneaking fucks looking at us now. This is prime ambush ground and they usually call in the Mosquitoes to hit us first."

"Passive scanners are in acquisition mode," Garcia responded. "The lasers are charged and ready to go. Do you want me to go active on the search?"

"Negative on that," Chin replied. "The radar can't detect them worth a shit. All they do is give them a beacon to home in on. Just keep your eyes out. It's coming soon, I can feel it."

"You got it, boss," Garcia told him. "Staying passive and keeping the eyes open."

"Van Pelt," he said next, calling the captain in charge of the infantry squads.

"Yeah, boss," Van Pelt answered right back.

"Get ready to initiate the new plan," he told him. "The moment those Mosquitoes come into view, get those APCs moving towards the hills. Even split, half to the north and half to the south. We're gonna catch those bastards this time and they're gonna be buying every last one of us bonghits and beers after the exercise."

"You got it, boss," Van Pelt said enthusiastically. He had caught some of his commander's optimism.

The special forces teams, though deadly and stealthy, were somewhat predictable in their operation. They had to be with their limited resources. Usually the teams stayed well hidden in the hills above the advance and called in Mosquitoes to make firing runs on the APCs before they showed themselves. MPG doctrine was not to concentrate on the heavy armor but to instead kill as many of the soldiers as possible as far from the battle area as possible, thereby reducing their numbers to ineffective before they got close to their objective. In a battle where the enemy would have to land their ships outside of artillery range of the city defenses (at least 300 kilometers away) and march inward from there, it made the most tactical sense. The MPG was basically a sniping force that fought using guerrilla tactics. Once the Mosquitoes had made their initial runs, the anti-tank crews of the special forces units would open up with their shoulder fired lasers, taking out more of the APCs and forcing the remaining soldiers out into a fight. Once the soldiers unloaded and tried to assemble, the machine gunners and riflemen would open up, picking off as many as they could as quick as they could. They would then withdraw to safety and be extracted by the Hummingbirds before the infantry troops could close with them. Each individual run would not cause serious attrition, but when they came again and again in succession, the numbers quickly added up.

"Not this time," Chin vowed, continuing to scan back and forth. "We're gonna make those fuckers pay this time."

*****

Fifty kilometers to the north, on the other side of the protective hills, two Mosquitoes circled lazily three hundred meters above the ground. Officially called the AA-55 atmospheric attack craft, they were essentially nothing more than flying wings powered by a single hydrogen/methane semi-rocket engine. Looking like a thirty-meter boomerang of flimsy design, they could travel through the Martian sky at speeds up to 700 KPH and pull turns of up to 3Gs. Like the Hummingbirds and the MPG biosuits, they were functional only on the planet Mars and for this reason the regular WestHem armed forces did not possess them or even acknowledge their possible usefulness.

The name Mosquito came from the derisive comments of a regular WestHem marine general back when the Martian designed and produced aircraft first became a part of the MPG in the early days. This general, who at the time had been the commander of the Marine quick response force stationed on the planetary surface, had been interviewed by one of the Earth based Internet stations for a documentary on the alleged waste of taxpayer money that the MPG represented.

"I don't really see the use for winged aircraft on an extraterrestrial surface," he had opined for everyone to hear. "Sure, they're cute to look at and they can move faster than the traditional hovers that the *real* forces use, and I'll even give credit to the Martian engineers who were able to design and produce such a craft in the first place. But when it comes down to practicality on the battlefield, I'm afraid they're seriously lacking. There is no way that such a flimsy target could stand up to modern air defenses over an advancing column. They would be nothing more than annoying mosquitoes buzzing around an EastHem advance, waiting to get swatted. In my opinion, the so-called General who runs this force would be much wiser to invest the Martian taxpayer dollars in more tanks, which are truly the cornerstone of any defense."

The Martians had made a habit long ago of holding in contempt nearly everything that was reported on WestHem Internet news. As such, the intended effect of the report, which had been sponsored by none other than Alexander Industries and had been designed to force Jackson and the procurement committee to buy more of their armor, had failed. And the derisive term that had been casually coined by the general had actually endeared itself to the Martians who flew the AA-55 and by those who trained with it. By the time a year had gone by *Mosquito* was the official name and the fact that mosquitoes had once been one of the deadliest insects on planet Earth had not gone unremarked upon by the Martian forces.

The Mosquito, for all its gracefulness and flimsy design, was basically an armor buster. Mounted on the belly of the craft, in a retractable turret directly beneath the cockpit, was a twin laser cannon nearly as powerful as those on the ETT-12s. This cannon was under direct control of the gunner, who sat behind the pilot, and could be aimed and fired as fast as the gunner could turn his head and put a targeting reticle on a vehicle. The recharge rate of the lasers was a moderate twelve seconds, which meant that the standard Mosquito tactic was to rush in at low level from behind surrounding hills or mountains, blast two pieces of armor—usually the APCs in keeping with MPG doctrine—and then buzz back under cover again before anti-air forces could even acquire it. It was a remarkably simple aircraft, with no autopilot and very little avionics besides standard navigation equipment. It was truly a pilot's aircraft in an age when almost everything was computer controlled.

Brian Haggerty was the pilot of the lead Mosquito. He held the stick lightly in his right hand and the throttle lightly in his left, keeping the aircraft in a shallow bank over the staging area. He and his gunner, Colton Rendes, were dressed in standard MPG biosuits and strapped into Martian designed ejection seats that could rocket them clear of the craft in an emergency and then set them gently down on the surface below. The cockpit was a bubble canopy that gave commanding views of the jagged hills below them. It was a strangely beautiful landscape that neither ever got tired of looking at.

"I'm telling you, Brian," Colton was saying over their open com link, "you have to follow through with this email. This is not the time to be apathetic about politicians. Apathy is what got the human race into this mess in the first place."

Brian snorted a little, half in disgust, half in exasperation. "You're starting to sound like Lisa, my partner," he said. "A goddamn veteran cop and she's spouting on and on about Laura Whiting. She even voted for her. Voted! She was nagging me at end of watch last night to compose that friggin email to my legislature, just like she asked us to do. Like it's really gonna do any fucking good."

"You heard Whiting last night, didn't you?" asked Colton, who was a flight engineer on a MarsTrans surface to orbit craft. "Did that sound like typical political rhetoric to you?"

"That *was* quite an eye-opening speech," he said. "I'll give you that. And I'll even go so far as to admit that maybe Whiting really is trying to push for independence. But if she really thinks that WestHem is ever going to let us go under any circumstances, she's fucking schizo. Why should I waste my time threatening that dick-wipe politician that fucking AgriCorp has assigned to my district? He doesn't give a shit what I say or what I think. All he gives a shit about is what his sponsors, those rich prick Earthling corporate assholes, want him to do. And what they want him to do is impeach Whiting. I'll be surprised if she makes it through the week."

"I'll be surprised if she makes it through the week too," Colton told him. "Believe me, I have as much common sense as any Martian. I know how the fucking system works. But would you agree that it would be better for us to keep Whiting in office than it would be to get rid of her?"

"Well... sure," he said. "Anything that pisses off those corporate fucks is all right in my book."

"And since it only takes five minutes to tell your legislature member that you'll sign a petition to have him recalled and that you'll then vote to do it, why shouldn't you take the time? It's not like it costs you anything."

"I just don't think it'll do any good," Brian said. "They don't listen to anyone who doesn't command a corporation."

"Who cares whether it does any good or not?" he asked, a little exasperated. "If he *does* vote to impeach Whiting and someone *does* put a petition screen in front of you to recall him, would you put your print on it?"

"Shit, I'd do it now," Brian said.

"And if there were enough signatures to recall the bastard and there was a vote scheduled on that very issue, would you log on and vote to oust him?"

"I suppose I would," he said.

"Then compose an email and *tell* the prick that," Colton said. "Tell him. Whiting got up on that stage last night and she showed some fucking huevos. Can you imagine what it took for her to do that? The least you could do in return is stand in front of your fucking terminal tonight and compose a little email. If enough people do that today maybe, just maybe, those fucks will be forced to make a decision. And just maybe enough of them will make the decision that we need: to keep Whiting in office. What can it hurt?"

Brian had to admit that he had a point. "What the hell?" he said with a shrug. "I guess I could do it to pay her back for the sheer entertainment value of that speech."

"See?" Colton said, reaching forward and patting him on the shoulder of his suit. "You do have some damn common sense in there."

*****

"Here they come," Lon said, looking at the cloud of dust that was approaching from the eastern horizon. A complete armored battalion was impossible to move from one place to another undetected. It was not the sort of thing that just slipped by while you weren't looking.

"Fuckin aye," said Jackson, who was all the way over on the next hill, maybe a half kilometer away, but who was connected via the UHF radio link. "Right down the old poop shoot."

Lon and those with him were sequestered among a group of fairly large boulders near the crest of the hill. The ancient lava rocks were nice and solid and had been in place here for perhaps that last billion earth years or so. They would make good cover for the coming fight, especially since the 20mm cannons on the tanks and APCs would be loaded with water filled training rounds. These rounds would hit hard enough to knock a man clean off his feet if impact occurred, but they would not penetrate or cause damage to the biosuits themselves. The rule was that once a man was hit in a vital area such as the chest or head, he was deemed to be dead. His suit, the computer controlling it having been placed in training mode, would then cut off all communications with the other team members unless an emergency override code was given (the utilization of which would automatically cause a cease-fire to be called in the simulated battle) and would render his weapons unable to be fired. Thus the "killed" team member could no longer be of assistance in the battle but could tag along with them as they moved in order to avoid being left behind. The same principal applied to the OPFOR equipment. If a man was hit, his suit computer would take him out of the action. If a tank were hit with the low yield training laser charges, that tank would be shut down and not allowed to participate further in the battle. If an APC took a lethal hit on the sides or top while troops were on board, all of the troops would have their communications links and weapons shut down. If the anti-air vehicles were hit, they too were rendered incapable of firing any further. All of these computer enhancements, be they to the biosuits, the weapons, or the vehicles themselves, were Martian adaptations available only on MPG equipment and designed specifically to make training missions more realistic. The regular WestHem forces, by contrast, exercised mostly in computer simulations to save money and wear and tear on their equipment.

Lon set his M-24 down for a moment and adjusted the magnification of his combat goggles. Instantly, with the help of infrared enhancement, he was able to pick out the individual tanks of the column even though they were still nearly twenty kilometers distant. "Looks like an armored cavalry column of battalion strength," he reported to his men. They had not been privy to what the strength of the OPFOR was going to be. "They have fifty plus APCs, we're talking five hundred troops if they're fully loaded. I also have three... no four SAL-50 anti-air vehicles in the front, middle, and rear of the column."

"I'm reading the same," said Jefferson from his perch. "Moving at about forty KPH."

"That gives us an estimated time to contact of about thirty minutes," Lon said. "I'm gonna get hold of the Mosquitoes." He flipped another switch on his computer panel and dialed into the encoded laser frequency. "Striker flight one," he said, keying the radio link. "This is Shadow team six. Are you there?" In order to avoid giving themselves away by leaking radio emissions, his words were converted to digital pulses, which were shot upward 18,000 kilometers by a laser beam to a communications satellite in geosynchronous orbit. The suit computer used GPS data to keep a constant fix on the satellite's location in the sky. If Lon had been in a position where the laser was blocked by an obstacle, an indicator in his goggles would have lit up, telling him this.

The delay from talking to reception was about three seconds. "Shadow six, this is striker one," came the voice of Brian Haggerty, one of the many pilots they worked in tandem with on a regular basis. "Go ahead. I'm tracking your current position."

"Copy that you're tracking us," Lon said. In addition to providing secure communications, the laser system also carried placement data, allowing support units to have an accurate fix on friendlies. "We have a visual on an armored column of battalion strength moving eastward through the cut. We count thirty plus ETT-12s, fifty plus APCs, and four SAL-50s. The SAL-50s are at the ends and middle of the column. They're moving west at approximately forty klicks. Estimated time to our position, thirty minutes. I repeat, three zero minutes."

"Copy thirty minutes," Haggerty said. "Get back with us five minutes to strike time with an update and we'll wake them up for you."

"Will do," Lon said. "Shadow six out."

They watched mostly in silence as the column drew closer and closer. The dust cloud that it raised expanded and continued to blow off to the south, carried by the prevailing seasonal winds. Though the sound of the advance did not reach them—sound did not travel very far or very well through the Martian air—the vibration and the rumbling of the ground did. The movement of nearly ninety armored vehicles was enough to shake loose small rocks. It was as they began to come into view without magnification assist that Lon began to notice something different about their formation. It took him a few minutes to pin down exactly what it was. Usually the APCs traveled in a protective ring of tank platoons, all the better to cover the soldiers within. Now the tanks were mostly forward and to the rear, with only a few token pieces covering the flanks.

"Look at how the APCs are formed up," he said when it finally came home to him. "That's not a standard marching formation."

"No," Jefferson said. "It sure ain't. Why do you think they're doing that?"

"That crafty little fuck Chin is up to something," Lon said. "He's trying to screw us out of our beer tonight."

"What's he planning?" asked Gavin. "Why would he leave the APCs bare like that? It doesn't make sense."

"It does if he wants them free for a charge," Jefferson opined. "You think he's trying to spring a little trap on us, sarge?"

"I think that may very well be his intention," Lon said, his eyes tracking over the column. He thought for a few moments as he watched them, his mind whirring in overdrive. His troops respectfully remained silent, allowing him to think. "Maybe," he said at last, "we have become a little too predictable. Maybe we should change things just a bit on this attack."

"Change things?" Jefferson asked. "What are you thinking?"

"I'm thinking that Chin left his APCs unprotected on the flanks and maybe we can take a little advantage of that. Jefferson, get on the secure link to our Hummingbird and tell them to lift off and get ready for extraction."

"Right, sarge," he said.

"Everyone else, listen up. This is the new plan." He began to talk. Everyone liked what he said.

*****

Brian listened to the update from the special forces team observing the column. Fargo, the squad leader, wanted to go with a change in normal operations, something that was not particularly discouraged in the MPG. It sounded like a fairly good plan so he raised no objections to it, something that would have been his right had there been some question of the safety of the aircraft.

"That sounds doable, shadow six," he answered back once the details were heard. "We're on the way now. ETA to strike is five minutes. We'll let you know when we're thirty seconds out."

"We'll be waiting," Lon's voice assured him after the normal delay. "Shadow six standing by."

Brian switched his frequency switch back to the channel that allowed him to communicate with the plane on his wing. "Did you copy all of that, John?" he asked.

"I copied," John Valenzuela, the pilot of the plane, told him. "Sounds like fun, going in without much opposition for once."

"Well, don't get too happy about it," Brian warned. "They still have a shitload of handheld anti-air lasers down there. They're harder to track on but it only takes one."

"Happy?" John asked with a laugh. "Who the hell could be happy around here? Let's do it. I'm right on your ass."

"Where you belong," Brian said, applying throttle and banking sharply to the right.

Moving almost as one object, the two Mosquitoes dove down towards the ground and leveled off at less than twenty meters about it. They accelerated to optimum low-level penetration speed and headed for the hills that guarded the valley. Using a map window on his heads up display to navigate with, Brian shot between hills and dove through gullies, cutting back and forth, up and down, but always moving towards the target area.

"Charge up the laser," Brian told Colton. "Targets will be the APCs, as always."

"Charging," Colton said, looking at his panel. "And I confirm we're in training mode. Low yield shots only."

"Three minutes to target area," Brian said, cutting hard to the right to avoid a particularly large hill. "I'm gonna come up from the west, right over the top of the team on the ground and then head back in over the hills beyond them."

"Sounds like a plan," John answered.

They flew on, heading into the larger hills now, forcing them to maneuver more violently. They bounced about, cut back and forth and the red hills flashed around them on both sides, nothing but blurs. The wings bent and flexed, dipping up and down with the turns. The engine thrummed, gulping fuel and oxygen as it was accelerated and decelerated. Brian kept them in the valleys as much as he could, denying the OPFOR infrared sensors even the barest glimpse of them. It was what Mosquito pilots were best at.

"Thirty seconds," Brian announced over the laser net when they got close. "Do your stuff, shadow six."

*****

"Gavin, Horishito," Lon said when he heard this. "Strike is thirty seconds out. Do it!"

"Copy," both said in unison. From their own perches atop their hill, in the safety of the boulders, they aimed their charged AT-50 tubes down on the column below. Both had already been assigned their targets—two of the anti-air vehicles—and, with the assistance of the magnification setting on their goggles, they sighted in and put their crosshairs directly on the sides, where the engines were.

Less than a second apart, they pushed the discharge buttons sending the laser energy out at the speed of light. They scored two direct hits and just like that the advancing column had lost half of its anti-air capabilities.

*****

"Sir," came the excited voice of sergeant Austin, the second-in-command of the anti-air division. "Two laser flashes from the hills. We've lost two of the SALs! The lieutenant was in one of them."

"What the fuck?" Chin said, panning madly to see what was happening. Other reports began to come in on the frequency now, all of them reporting laser flashes on the hillside. What the hell was this? Had the special forces teams changed the way they operated?

To give him credit, Chin reacted quickly to the situation. "All tank units," he said into the tactical channel. "Open up on the hillside where the flashes came from. Put some fire on those fuckers! Van Pelt!"

"Here, boss," Van Pelt said instantly.

"Move your people in! I want every soldier you have converging on that hill group!"

"Copy," he said.

*****

"Displace," Jefferson yelled the moment the lasers were fired. "Get the fuck out of here before the return fire comes in."

Gavin and Horishito did not have to be told twice. They rolled backwards, down the hill, and then crawled to the right, dragging their laser tubes with them. Jefferson, holding his M-24, brought up the rear. Before they could even get ten feet away, training rounds, both large and small caliber, began slamming into the rocks around them, hitting with thuds loud enough to be heard even through the thin air and the insulating biosuit helmet. Vapor from the rounds began to rise into the air while tiny bits of soft plastic shrapnel sprayed over them. Other rounds whizzed overhead, an experience that was more sensed than felt or seen.

As soon as they reached their new positions, both men ejected the spent charging batteries from their lasers, letting them fall to the ground. The charges were plastic, fifteen centimeters square by four centimeters thick, and colored yellow, indicating they were for training only. They grabbed fresh ones from their packs and slammed them into the slots, pushing the charge button as soon as they were in place.

*****

Fire belched from the main guns of the tanks as well as the smaller, commanders' weapons. Hundreds of rounds per second were launched towards the spot where the two laser flashes had come in the hope that the offenders would be hit by one of them. Meanwhile the APCs, on order from Van Pelt, had all turned and were rushing at top speed at the hills, the soldiers inside of them anxious to get in the fight and put a hurt on the special forces teams that had tormented them for so long. They knew that if they could get to those hills in time they could catch the teams before they retreated to the safety of their Hummingbird.

"Keep up the covering fire on that hill," Chin ordered. "Spread it out a little. Plaster that whole fucking area!"

Before the tanks could begin to spread their volume around a little bit however, the Mosquitoes joined the battle.

*****

"Coming into firing range," Brian announced to both his gunner and his wingman. "Let's pop some APCs!"

He pulled up over the last hill, flying almost directly over the top of Lon and his men. With a quick bank to the right he was now paralleling the valley, streaking along the side of it at more than seven hundred kilometers per hour. In the back seat, Colton was looking out the canopy, his goggles placing an X on wherever the laser cannon would hit if fired at the moment. As he turned his head, so did the X, as he looked up or down, so did it. On the belly of the aircraft, the twin cannon complex moved back and forth with his motions as well, swiveling on its turret. The targets came suddenly into view, an entire line of tiny APCs rolling across the ground below. He moved his head and put the X on one of them, simultaneously pushing the firing button in his hand. The laser flashed and instantly was hitting the target, telling its computer to shut it down and to declare the twelve men inside of it dead. Another turn of the head and the X was on another APC. Another push of the button and another vehicle and everyone in it were out of the battle. Behind them John and his gunner did the same.

And then it was time to get out. Brian cut sharply back to the right while the lasers went into automatic recharge mode for another run. Before the remaining anti-air vehicles of the column even realized that an attack was underway, the Mosquitoes were back in the safety of the hills and out of range. It was a picture-perfect Mosquito run.

*****

"Charged," yelled Horishito from his new firing position. A second later this declaration was echoed by Gavin.

"Good," said Jefferson, who was peering out at the column below from between the rocks. He watched the advancing APCs and the flashing of the tank guns. Rounds were now starting to hit around them as the tanks spread out their fire. "Now take out those other two SALs," he ordered. "Gavin, you get the left one. Horishito, you take the right. Let's clear the air for the Mosquitoes before those bastards overrun us."

Without bothering to acknowledge their orders, they aimed their weapons downward, each of them seeking the distinctive box shape of the surface to air laser vehicles. Horishito found his first. He moved his weapon until the firing reticle rested on its side and then he gently squeezed the trigger. There was no kick from the laser as it discharged, nor was there any sound or any light visible in anything other than the infrared spectrum. But down on the target, there was a bright flash as the laser energy expended itself against the steel side of the vehicle.

"That's a kill," Horishito announced, rolling out of his position and preparing to crawl to the next.

Gavin fired a few seconds later, just as the tanks switched their concentration on the new firing hole. His shot was also a kill, which he gleefully announced.

"Strike one," Lon announced over the secure net. "The SALs are all down. I repeat, the SALs are all down. We have APCs closing our position. We could use a little help over here."

"On the way back," Brian's voice replied. "We're coming in from the north and egressing to the west this time."

*****

Chin watched helplessly as his tactical display showed all four of his anti-air assets a lethal red color. He no longer had the ability to fight off the Mosquitoes without dismounting some of his infantry troops. "Those bastards," he whispered to himself, shaking his head. He could not help however, feeling a sincere measure of respect for them.

He keyed up his radio link. "Van Pelt," he said, shouting over the sound of the guns on his command tank. "They've knocked out our SALs. Get some dismounts out with anti-air lasers as quick as you can. Those Mosquitoes will be coming back! They'll chew us up if we don't have something to swat them away with."

"Copy, boss," Van Pelt answered, his voice resigned. Chin understood. A perfect plan to catch the special forces team with their pants down had just gone to shit. By changing tactics, they had forced him to take his soldiers out of their APCs and put them on the ground where they were most vulnerable.

*****

The Mosquitoes shot back over the battlefield, rising up from behind the hills and making an almost leisurely run. Lon, watching them as they passed, saw their lasers flash in the infrared and, just like that, four more of the APCs were dead. They banked off to the left and disappeared, spinning around to make another run.

"We've got troops dismounting," Jefferson announced from his position with the laser team. "Four o'clock."

Lon looked down and saw that eight of the APCs had stopped. Their guns were now blazing to provide cover for the biosuited infantry troops taking up position behind them. Many of the troops had laser tubes in their hands. They began to pan through the sky, searching for the Mosquitoes. "Horishito, Gavin," he said, "keep blasting those APCs as quick as you can get your weapons charged. Displace between shots. Go for the lead ones first."

"Copy," Horishito and Gavin answered in unison.

"The rest of you," Lon said, "start putting fire on those troops."

Following his own orders, Lon aimed his M-24 through a gap in the rocks and put his reticle on a group covering behind one of the APCs. His weapon was set for three round bursts. He pushed the firing button smoothly and the rifle fired with short, high pitched pops, the casings ejecting to the right and behind him, falling with exaggerated slowness in the weak gravity and clattering on the rocks. Though the bullets were being launched from the weapon at extremely high velocity, the recoil was negligible thanks to the design of the rifle's action. The rounds could be seen in the infrared spectrum as rapid streaks of red moving downrange. He moved the reticle slightly and fired again. Vapor began to rise from the area where the bullets were impacting and several of the troops were hit in the chest and head. From around him came the pops and crackles of other weapons, including the 5mm squad automatic weapon being fired by Matza. Lon was gratified to see that the newest member of his squad was operating the bipod mounted SAW very well. He was using short, controlled bursts and aiming at the greatest concentrations of troops.

"Strike one," Lon said into the laser link as he fired. "This is shadow six. Be advised, dismounts are out with hand held SALs. We're engaging them with small arms fire."

"Copy, shadow six," Haggarty's voice replied. "Keep 'em occupied if you can. We're coming up for another pass in about ten seconds."

*****

"Van Pelt," Chin yelled over the continued thumping of the tank guns, "get some fire on those small arms positions. They're killing the anti-air crews!"

"Just gave the order, boss," Van Pelt replied. "Sections five through eight are shifting fire. I'll have the empty APCs keep plastering the AT-50 positions."

"How long until we can get some dismounts on those hills?"

"Another thirty seconds or so," Van Pelt told him. "The first units are coming into position now."

Even as he said this an infrared flash appeared from the hill and another APC died. Two seconds later, before fire could even be shifted to the new position, another flash took out another one.

"Goddamn, they're good with those things," Chin said with frustrated admiration. He already knew he had lost the battle. The simple ten-man squad of special forces soldiers and their air cover had already "killed" fifteen of his vehicles and more than a hundred men. All he could hope to do now was catch them before they escaped; something that was doubtful at best.

"Mosquitoes! Six o'clock low!" someone screamed over the net.

Chin looked behind him and saw the distinctive thin shapes of the anti-tank craft screaming out of the hills and heading directly for them. He could see the cannon turrets on the bottom spinning back and forth, seeking new targets. The dismounted soldiers, most of whom were cowering behind the meager cover of their APCs, began panning their hand-held lasers back and forth, trying to get a fix on one of the aircraft. One of the men stood to free up his range of motion and was promptly hit in the head by automatic weapons fire, the rounds spraying misty vapor off of his helmet and instantly shutting him down. He kicked the dirt in frustration and then sat down to wait out the battle.

The cannons on the Mosquitoes flashed and four more of the APCs were dead in the dirt. Six of the anti-air crews managed to pull off a shot at them but none hit. They whizzed over the far end of the column and disappeared back into the hills.

*****

Tank and APC rounds were now slamming into their positions with alarming frequency. Rocks, dust, and water vapor were flying through the air in an actual cloud, pelting everyone's helmet with debris. Down in the valley, the APC's were pulling up to the hillside, positioning themselves to dismount their ground troops, who would then start moving in force up the slope to engage them. Though the tactical display showing in his goggles told him that all of his men were still alive, he knew that would change if they stayed much longer. It was time to do what special forces did best.

"Displace and retreat," Lon ordered, firing one more burst down at the soldiers below. "Rally at the LZ. Let's get the fuck out of here."

In an orderly fashion, the men pulled their weapons in and rolled down the back of the hill until they were safe from stray rounds. Matza safed the SAW and slung it over his back. Gavin and Horishito did the same to their AT-50s. Everyone else slung their M-24s on their shoulders and began moving as rapidly as possible down the hill.

"Strike one," Lon said to the Mosquito crews. "We're bugging out. No casualties taken. Thanks for the fun, guys."

"Anytime, Lonnie," Haggarty told him. "We owe you guys a bong hit tonight for slamming those SALs for us. This was the most fun I've had in a year."

"We'll take you up on that, Brian," Lon answered. "See you there."

It took them only a few minutes to reach the bottom of the hills. Once there, they trotted as fast as they could to the north, putting a few more hills between themselves and the battle area. They puffed hard as they went, all of them showing discharge warnings on their air supply screen. This was understandable and expected in post-combat maneuvers. Finally, they rounded the last hill and they were at the landing zone.

"Deploy in defensive positions," Lon told them.

They formed a protective circle in the boulder field, weapons trained outward.

"Jefferson," Lon said. "Are you still in contact with the hummer?"

"They're moving in now, sarge," Jefferson responded. "ETA less than a minute."

The ETA turned out to be accurate. From the north, the bulky flying H that was the Hummingbird came over the hills at stall speed, it's wheels down, and then nosed up, it's thrusters showing an intense red on the infrared displays. It dropped out of the sky and thumped to the ground, raising a large cloud of red dust that obscured it completely.

"Get on board," Lon barked. "Move, move!"

They moved, rushing over the sandy soil and into the dust cloud, their infrared sensors guiding them to the open ramp. One by one they trotted up and took a seat, quickly strapping themselves in and securing their weapons. Each person called out their name and the word secured once they were ready for flight. When the tenth person was safe and accounted for, Dave pushed the ramp button and sealed them up.

"Lifting off," said Rick, applying throttle even as he did so. The aircraft shuddered and pushed into the sky, moving forward as the thrusters were directed towards the rear. Within a minute they were out of the area.

"Digital perfect," Lon said, slumping into his seat as they pitched and dived through the hills. "Good mission, guys. Damn good mission."

*****

"Van Pelt here, boss," came the voice over the radio link ten minutes later.

Chin was watching his tactical display as the small blue dots that represented the dismounted infantry moved over the map. More than a hundred soldiers had advanced without opposition to the top of the hills where the ambush had come from. "Go ahead," he said, already knowing what was going to be said.

"We found their firing positions," he responded. "They've bugged out. No casualties left behind."

"Damn," Chin muttered. He had been hoping for at least one "dead" special forces member. Had any of them been "killed" in the battle, they would have been left behind by their companions and forced to endure a ride back to the base with the OPFOR in one of the "dead" tanks or APCs. It was something that had happened a few times before, but not often. "Copy that," he said into the radio link. "Are you in pursuit of them?"

"We are," he confirmed. "Advance elements are already at the bottom of the hill as you can see on you display. It's not looking real good for catching them though."

"Give it a shot anyway," Chin ordered. "We have to go through the motions, don't we?"

*****

Jeff Creek lived on the 63rd floor of the Bingham Tower Public Housing building in apartment 6312. Prior to his marriage to his longtime girlfriend Belinda six months before, he had lived on the 79th floor of the building with his parents. Now that he was married however, he was entitled under the federal and planetary welfare laws to his own one-bedroom apartment. In addition to this, every two weeks he and his wife were given 835 dollars for food and clothing, sixty dollars worth of alcoholic beverage credits, and eighty dollars worth of marijuana and tobacco credits. Of course, these credits were only redeemable at AgriCorp subsidiary intoxicant stores and could only be used to purchase the lowest grades of product available, but you took what you could get.

Jeff, like most of the welfare class, rose late in the morning as a habit. Why shouldn't he? There was no job for him to get up and go to nor was there any point in going out to look for one. It was 10:58 when he pulled himself from the cheap mattress that was his bed. Wearing only a pair of tattered shorts, Jeff walked to the bathroom of the apartment, which was connected to both the small living room/kitchen portion and the bedroom by connecting doors. He urinated into the rust stained toilet and then told the house computer system to turn on the shower. Recognizing his voice pattern and using his preset temperature preference, it turned on the valves, setting free a feeble spray of warm water that trickled down from the old, leaking pipe. He stripped off his shorts, tossing them into the corner of the room and stepped inside, taking five minutes to scrub himself clean.

"Belinda!" he yelled out into the living room once he was done. "Where's the fuckin clean laundry?"

Belinda was watching a romance drama on the main Internet screen and sipping from her second Fruity of the day. "Ain't no fuckin money to do laundry," she yelled back, not even glancing in his direction. "We spent it all on food."

"What the hell am I supposed to wear?" he demanded, stepping out into the living room naked.

"Ask me if I give a fuck," she said. "Now shut your ass. I'm trying to watch this."

"Bitch," he muttered, trotting back into the bedroom. He dug around in the heaping laundry pile by the door until he found the least offensive shirt and shorts that he could. He pulled them on his body and then donned a pair of leather moccasins, the standard footwear on Mars. He ran a comb through his hair, arranging the strands into something approaching presentable, and then picked up his gun and his PC, stuffing both into the waistband of his shorts. He reached into a drawer on a cheap nightstand and pulled out his bag of marijuana and his pipe.

"Where you going?" Belinda asked as he moved through the living room towards the door.

"Out," he said simply.

"Be sure to be back tonight sometime," she answered listlessly. "You have to fuck me tonight. I'm ovulating."

"Whatever," he said, opening the sliding door and stepping out into the hall.

The hallway of the 63rd floor had once been carpeted in a fecal-brown industrial grade covering. Years of being urinated on, having cigarettes tapped and dumped upon it, and being painted with gang graffiti had resulted in its condemnation by the health department on one of their bi-decade inspections. Since then, it had been removed, leaving only the bare concrete of the floor. Now the concrete itself had gang graffiti and puddles of urine or vomit and thousands of other unidentifiable but equally disgusting markings. The walls were also prime canvas for graffiti and overlapping gang epitaphs from various ages lined it ceiling to floor on both sides in every imaginable color. Doors to other apartments were spaced every five meters on both sides and several cross hallways led off into different parts of the building. A few people were wandering around the halls as he made his way to the elevators, most of them shuffling along and trying to look tough. He passed several current Capitalist members, getting respectful nods from them in deference to his gang tattoo with the large R over the top of it proclaiming his honorably retired status.

He lit a cigarette as he waited for the up elevator to arrive, puffing thoughtfully and wondering if he was even going to be able to produce an erection for that bitch Belinda tonight. It was something that was getting harder and harder to do even though he badly wanted the extra income and bigger apartment that parenthood guaranteed him. He couldn't stand her and he was finding that getting sexually excited for someone that you hated was not as easy as it had once been. He found himself thinking, almost against his will, that maybe his friend Matt was right. Maybe it *was* a mistake to marry the first person to come along just to achieve the status that went with it.

The elevator doors slid open revealing the dank interior. Two women were inside chatting to each other about the Laura Whiting speech the previous night, their tones animated and profane. Both had baskets of fresh laundry from the laundry room in the basement of the building. Neither acknowledged him in any way as he stepped inside.

"Ninety-three," he told the elevator computer and it acknowledged him by lighting up the numeral on its display board. The doors clanked shut and the floor indicator began to blur rapidly upward. No movement of any kind was felt inside the elevator itself. Even though they were shooting upwards at more than five floors per second, the inertial dampening properties of the artificial gravity field kept them from feeling it.

The numbers came to an abrupt halt at 93 and the doors slid open once more. He stepped out into a hallway that was virtually identical to the one he had entered from. He turned left and began walking through the halls, following a course he had walked perhaps ten thousand times in his life. Several twists and turns brought him in front of an apartment door marked 9345. A pinhole camera was set into the door at head level and a small button was set into the wall at chest level. He pushed the button, setting off a buzzer inside.

The door slid open a minute later and Andrew Mendez, Matt's father, was standing there. He was a portly man of forty-one years, his considerable stomach, bare due to his lack of a shirt, hanging over the waistband of his shorts. He sported a full mustache and beard and, on his right arm, was the exact same tattoo that Jeff and Matt sported: that of a retired Capitalist.

"What's up, Jeff?" the elder Mendez greeted with a smile.

"My dick, like always," Jeff replied.

They exchanged the age-old handshake of the Capitalists members: two squeezes, a clasp, and a banging of the fists hard enough to cause momentary pain. Both did it reflexively, without more than a passing thought.

"Is Matt around?" Jeff asked once the preliminaries were taken care of.

Andrew sighed. "He's always around," he said. "Can't get the little bastard to leave this place. Imagine, twenty-two years old and still living at home. When are you gonna talk him into marrying that Sharon bitch so we can have this house to ourselves?"

"I've been trying, Mr. M," Jeff told him. "You know how Matt is though."

"Oh yeah," he said, stepping aside and letting him in. "He brews dust with his own recipe, that's for sure. He's in his bedroom, doing something on the terminal like always."

"Thanks, Mr. M," he said, heading that way.

Carla Mendez was in the kitchen. She was a thin woman with prematurely graying hair. That and the hopeless expression that was always on her face conspired to make her look nearly fifty years old instead of the forty that she was. She was scrubbing dishes with an old washrag and setting them in the rinse tray. Though the apartment possessed an automatic dishwasher, it was more than sixty years old and had not worked in generations. It was now utilized for storage space, which was always short in welfare apartments. "Hi, Jeff," she greeted as he passed. "Is your wife knocked up yet?"

"Not yet," he told her politely. "We have a fuck scheduled for tonight. Maybe I'll be able to plant something."

"Best of luck to you," she said, picking up another dish from the soapy water. "It's so nice to have the bigger apartment."

"I can't wait for it," he said sincerely.

He knocked on the door of Matt's room and a moment later it slid open, allowing him entry. Like all secondary bedrooms in public housing, it was very small, only four meters by three. A simple mattress on the floor was his bed and a simple plastic desk beside it held his main Internet terminal. A few bits of laundry and a few empty Fruity bottles littered the floor. Matt himself was sitting at the desk watching a news program on one of the big three channels.

"What's the word, brother?" Matt greeted, leaning back in his chair and extending his hand.

"Fuckin boredom, that's the word," Jeff said. They exchanged the Capitalist shake. "What the hell you watching now?"

"A smear program on Whiting," he said. "It didn't take them long to get one together. It's pretty damn funny actually. They're saying that she's a secret communist with ties to EastHem fascist groups. They even have people that claim to be acquaintances of hers that go to the meetings with her."

"They do work fast, don't they?" Jeff said, rolling his eyes a little. He grabbed a seat on Matt's mattress. He pulled out his bag of marijuana and his pipe. "Strange how none of this ever came up *before* the speech last night. Want to burn some?"

"Sure, fire up," Matt said. While Jeff started stuffing the pipe, he changed back to the MarsGroup primary channel, which was showing a special feature on the inauguration speech the night before. Mindy Ming, one of the senior anchors, was analyzing it line-by-line, paying particular attention to the economic plans.

"Can't you put some fuckin porn on?" Jeff asked. "I'm sick of hearing about that Whiting bitch."

"This is a historical moment, bro," Matt told him. "Mark my words. You'll be glad I made you watch all this shit later on."

"Let's pretend I'm glad now and put on some porn," he replied, striking a light with his laser igniter. He applied it to the pipe and took a tremendous hit.

"You can get porn anytime," Jeff told him, taking the offered pipe and lighter. "How often do you get to see the corporations smeared on Internet? I'm telling you, bro, it's a beautiful thing that Whiting said last night, fuckin beautiful. That speech is going to immortalized no matter how this shit all turns out, it's going to be right up there with the Gettysburg Address and Martin Luther King's I have a dream spiel."

Jeff blew out his hit, releasing a cloud of acrid smelling smoke into the unventilated room. He shook his head a little. "You are undoubtedly the strangest fucking person I've ever hung out with," he said. "Why do I come over here so much?"

"Because deep down, you know I'm right," Matt told him with a grin. He struck a light and inhaled his first hit of the day. He passed the pipe back over. "So," he squeaked, holding the smoke in his lungs, "did you compose that email to Vic Cargill?"

"No, I didn't compose any goddamn email to Vic Cargill," he said. "I told you I wasn't going to. I don't correspond with fucking politicians. They don't represent me or my family and they don't do shit for me."

"Change ain't gonna happen unless we get involved," Matt said. "The only way the legislature is gonna be stopped from impeaching her is if enough emails roll in to convince those sell-out bastards that we're serious about recalling them if they do. That asshole Cargill represents the Helvetia district..."

"He ain't ever lived in the hood," Jeff said. "Who made him represent us? I didn't vote for him."

"Neither did I," Matt said. "He lives on the edge of downtown, just south of the Garden, in a little sliver of the city that was added to the Helvetia voting district just so someone like him could squeak in instead of a true ghetto dweller. I looked up his record on the Internet last night. Do you know that he was elected by less than a thousand votes? And that's not the margin, that's the total. Only those pricks in the two housing buildings that are part of the Helvetia district were the ones to vote in the election is what I'm thinking. But that don't matter. Vermin or not, we're entitled to organize and sign recall petitions and we're entitled to vote in the recall election whether we voted for him in the first place or not. We need to let him know that we'll hold him accountable for his actions."

"It's a waste of fucking time," Jeff insisted.

"So what? Time is all we got here. What else you gonna do? Go to work? Go fuck your wife? Hell, just do it. You don't have to be polite or nothing. All you have do is tell him that you won't stand for him trying to impeach Whiting. If my parents could do it, than you can do it. And it feels good to tell one of those pricks off. It feels real good."

"Really?" he asked, actually starting to warm to the idea a little. He could see how it would be gratifying to talk to a politician in his own words, even if it was a slim to none chance that the politician would ever watch it.

"Really," Matt assured him. "Just give it a shot. You can use my terminal."

Jeff took another large hit, holding it in while he mulled the suggestion over. Finally, he blew it out. "What the hell?" he said with a shrug. "Set me up and I'll do it."

"That's the way to show some common sense," Mark said with a grin. He turned to the Internet terminal. "Computer, bring up email program and authorize user Jeff Creek to patch in."

The screen cleared from the MarsGroup program and brought up the email program in its place. "User Jeff Creek's voice print is on file. Proceed when ready."

Matt got up from his chair and waved his best friend to it. "It's all you, bro," he said.

Jeff handed the pipe and the lighter over and then took his place in Matt's chair, sitting down before the screen. "What do I say?" he asked.

"Just make it short and sweet," he told him. "Identify yourself to him and then explain that you will sign a petition to recall him and then vote for the same if he votes to open an impeachment investigation into Laura Whiting. Don't threaten him with violence or anything like that though. You'd be breaking the law if you did that."

"I wouldn't want to break the law now, would I?"

"Nope, not here," Matt said. "Just tell him the facts and send it off. His address is already in my database so don't worry about looking it up."

"All right," he said. "But give me the pipe back. It's part of my image."

Matt chuckled and handed it over.

Jeff looked at the screen. "Computer, compose mail from me to Vic Cargill."

"User Jeff Creek confirmed," the computer told him. "The address of Martian Planetary Legislature representative Victor Cargill of the Helvetia Heights district is on file. Record when ready."

Jeff thought for a moment and then said: "Record." The red light on the screen lit up and the small camera on the screen locked onto his face. Jeff smiled and took a large hit of his pipe, blowing the smoke directly onto the camera. "Check it, fuckface," he said, putting a tough expression on his face. "The name's Jeff Creek and I'm one of your constituents here in this shithole known as Helvetia Heights. I ain't never voted for nothing or no one before, but you can bet your ass that if you start fucking around and trying to impeach Laura Whiting, I'll be the first motherfucker to sign a petition to kick your ass out of office. And then, once that petition is all signed and legal and shit and they ask us to vote to get rid of you, I'll be signing on to do that shit too. Don't fuck with Whiting, my man. Don't even think of fucking with her. That's all." He put the pipe to his mouth and took another hit. "End recording," he squeaked. The camera blinked back off. "How was that?" he asked Matt.

"Absolutely fucking beautiful," Matt said. "You got a way with words, you know that?"

"Shit," Jeff said. "I can't believe I just did that."

"Email composed," the computer told him. "Would you like to review it?"

"Naw, baby," he replied. "Just send the shit off before I change my mind."

"Email sent," the computer told him.

"Now, how about we smoke out a little more and then go score some Fruity?" he asked.

"Sounds like a plan," Matt said.

*****

The Troop Club was a chain of taverns that was owned by a subsidiary of Barkling Agricultural Industries, the third largest food producer on Mars now that the AgriCorp-Interplanetary Food merger had been consummated. Only a minute portion of the intoxicant distribution holdings of BAI, Troop Club taverns were nevertheless a lucrative, low overhead venture. Located just outside of military establishments throughout WestHem's territory, they had managed to snare an incredible thirty-eight percent of the "off-duty military personnel market" and their very name had achieved the coveted status of "generic product identification" among their target group. What this meant is that when a soldier, whether stationed in Standard City or on Triad or in Alaska or anywhere else, wanted to go for a drink after duties, the phrase used was inevitably "let's go to the Troop Club" whether or not they were actually going to that particular tavern or whether or not there even *was* an official Troop Club branch operating outside of their base. The Troop Club had achieved the same status with this label as Coke had when carbonated cola was discussed or as Tylenol had when over-the-counter acetaminophen was discussed.

Indeed, in Eden there was an entire three-block section lined with drinking and smoking establishments, all of them corporate owned of course, just outside of the main Martian Planetary Guard base and the main WestHem Marine Barracks. Though on Friday and Saturday nights all of these bars would be filled to capacity with both marines and MPG troops, it was The Troop Club that was the largest, with a capacity of more than six hundred, and the first to fill up. Soldiers only tended to spill over to the other establishments when The Troop Club became too crowded to accommodate any others.

The scene inside of the Eden Troop Club was fairly typical on this particular Saturday afternoon. The majority of the MPG troops had finished their training rotations for the day and many of them had gone over to drink reasonably cheap beers or harder alcohol and to smoke BAI Sensimilian buds. Cocktail waitresses, all of them dressed in tight shorts and chest-hugging tops, all of them physically attractive, circulated between the tables and the gaming areas where darts and billiards were being played. Twelve bartenders were on duty behind the three bar complexes that lined the walls mixing drinks and distributing pipes to the customers. Loud modern music, heavy with synthesized bass and drums, played from the surround sound system at a level that was just below the conversation hampering point. As always in this particular part of the solar system, the MPG troops and the marines segregated themselves from each other with the former occupying the largest main bar and the pool tables while the latter stuck to the dart boards and the smaller secondary bars.

Lon Fargo and Brian Haggarty, the two men primarily responsible for giving Colonel Michael Chin the worst pounding of the day, were sitting at one of the tables near the bar drinking icy cold Martian Storm beers supplied by the very man they had pounded. Chin was sitting with them, drinking a Martian Storm of his own and smoking from a custom-made marijuana pipe that he carried with him in a small felt lined case.

"This shit's not bad," he commented, exhaling a fairly large hit of the house Sensimilian. "It's too bad you can't get that nice green that they serve in O'Riley's here though. In my opinion that's the finest bud in the solar system."

"But it's grown by AgriCorp," Lon said, stuffing a hit into a bar pipe. "I should know. I've serviced enough humidifiers in the greenhouse since the merger. They got plants six meters high and spaced every meter that are just packed with buds. The smell in the place is enough to get you loaded all by itself."

"You ever try to stuff a few in your pocket?" asked Brian who, though he was a sworn police officer, had no moral problem with the idea of stealing something from AgriCorp.

"Are you kidding?" Lon said. "The security in the bud greenhouses is as tight as at the damn fusion plants. Tighter even. They scan you when you go into the place and again when you go out. And one of the fuckin security guards follows you around while you're in there and watches everything you do."

"Wouldn't want any of those buds to slip away without someone paying for them, would we?" asked Chin sarcastically. "That might cut AgriCorp's profits down a couple thousand from the trillions that it is."

"Yes," said Brian, sipping from his bottle. "It's a fine line, isn't it? The whole economy could collapse if you let something like that happen."

"That's what's so funny about the whole thing," Lon told them. "All that security equipment and personnel has to cost more every year than they would lose from theft by not having it. The picking is done automatically by stripping machines. Hell, the only ones allowed in the greenhouses are the horticulture teams and the maintenance guys. And the horticulture guys are smart enough to grow their own if they want some."

"Corporate mentality," Chin said. "Protect profits at all costs. We get it over at Alexander too. Even if it means spending a billion to prevent the potential loss of a million, they'll do it. They just can't stand the idea that someone might be getting high somewhere for free."

"Kind of like we are right now?" Lon said, grinning at the man he had defeated. "Those of us that kicked the shit out of a mechanized battalion today?" This caused a burst of laughter from the special forces troops at all of the surrounding tables.

"Fuck you," Chin said sourly, taking a slug from his beer. "You bastards got lucky. It'll never happen again."

"I read your mind out there, Chin," Lon told him, begging to differ. "When I saw your APCs all lined up nice and neat without tanks covering their flanks I *knew* you were up to something. And it wasn't a bad plan either. You *almost* caught us up there."

"Yeah," Chin said, "and I *almost* didn't lose two hundred of my men to those portable anti-tank lasers you have. You little sneaking fucks are unnatural, you know that?"

"It's what we do best," Lon agreed.

As Chin, Lon, and Brian drank at one table, their men drank with their counterparts at others. Captains and lieutenants of the armored cav shared spaces with the corporals and the privates that had massacred them out in the wastelands that day. There was a mutual respect between them that was independent of their respective ranks within the MPG. Though WestHem troops tended to segregate themselves along clear rank lines in their off hours, there was no such custom among the volunteers of the planetary guard. The officers of the cav did not feel superior to the privates of the special forces. All were merely weekend warriors with other, more menial jobs on the outside.

Naturally, a prevalent topic of conversation among the various groups, other than the exercises that had just taken place, was the Laura Whiting speech and the aftermath of it. At nearly every table, as men and women sipped beers and puffed from pipes, the talk would circle around and always end up again with the discussion of the upcoming legislature assembly on Monday morning. The vast majority of the troops agreed with the principal of what Whiting was doing but felt that she had not the slightest chance of succeeding in her venture. Despite this cynicism however, well over three-quarters of those Martians present admitted to having sent email to their representative threatening a recall vote. Of the quarter that had not, nearly every last one took the stance that it was only because they felt it was a waste of time. It wasn't that they liked their representatives or they thought they were representing them honestly and fairly. No one actually expressed that view. They just couldn't conceive of change happening in their lifetime, or in their children's lifetime. The solar system was what the solar system was.

It was here that a queer form of peer pressure took over. As more alcohol and more THC flowed through more bloodstreams, those that had sent email began to chide those who hadn't. They used the same arguments that were being used planet wide by other such groups, although with perhaps a bit more profanity. And, as it was doing all over the planet, the peer pressure began to have an effect. Personal computers were unclipped from waistbands and communications software was accessed. Drunken MPG member after drunken MPG member gave ranting speeches to their respective representatives in the legislature, most slurring their words quite badly, a few forgetting what they were talking about and having to revise, but everyone gleefully having their say. Colonel Chin himself, who had neglected to send an email of his own because of fears of repercussion from his employer (not an unreasonable fear, he was about as high on the corporate ladder at Alexander Industries as a person of Martian birth could climb), took one last pipe hit and then stood up on the table to compose his message. This started a trend among the other members and soon every table had someone standing on it and reciting a rambling, often obscene message to their local politician.

All of this revelry soon attracted attention from the other side of the establishment, where the WestHem regular marines were drinking and smoking. In WestHem culture, the Marine Corps were considered an elite group of fighting men, the most respected and revered in the armed services profession. In a society with nearly thirty percent unemployment, it was deemed a great honor to be allowed to join the marines and usually such appointments were given to those with family connections or those who scored extremely high on the ASVAB testing and the physical agility exam—a test that was grueling indeed. Though the majority of the marines in the bar were either enlisted rank or NCOs, they were all well-built specimens of masculinity and all had been trained in various techniques of hand-to-hand combat. They also tended to be arrogant, almost bullying types that had little respect or regard for their Martian counterparts.

A particularly large squad sergeant was the first to foment the confrontation between the two groups. He had been stationed on Mars, which he considered a shithole, for nearly two years now and he hated everything and everyone that had been born on the miserable rock that they called a planet. And now, just as the football game piped to the bar's Internet screen was starting to really take shape, the ranting and yells coming from the tables on the other side of the room was drowning out all of the sound. He stood up and said a few words to the group of sergeants and corporals around him. They stood up and walked with him to the nearest table where a young MPG private of the armored cav—a man who had been "killed" early in the day when his APC had been blasted by a Mosquito—was just finishing up his email to his representative. Without saying a word, the marine sergeant walked up to the table and kicked it over, sending the young private crashing to the ground and causing his PC to smash to pieces.

"What the fuck do you think you're doing, asshole?" demanded a drunken MPG lieutenant who had been sitting at the table. He stood and stepped up to the hulking marine where the top of his head came to approximately shoulder level.

"I'm quieting you fucking greenies down," said the sergeant. "You're getting on my goddamn nerves."

"You don't like it?" the MPG lieutenant told him. "Go drink somewhere else then."

The marine sergeant's eyes burned into him. "Why don't *you* and the rest of these little pretend soldiers go somewhere else," he countered. "This is a bar for *real* fighting men, not a bunch of greenie want-to-be boy scouts whose mommies let them out once a week to jerk off on their tanks."

This junior high school level insult had little effect on the Martians in the room. They were used to such comments from the Earthlings that lived on their planet. It did seem to cause quite a bit of hilarity among the marines however. They laughed as if this was the wittiest thing they had ever heard.

"Look," said the MPG lieutenant, "why don't you just stay over on your half of the bar and we'll stay on ours. We don't bitch at you when you start cheering and throwing shit at the terminals because of some sports game, so why should you..."

The marine sergeant put his hand on his chest and pushed him backwards, sending him crashing into the young private who had been picking up the pieces of his shattered computer. The marines behind and around all broke up into another round of derisive laughter at this spectacle. Immediately, the men who served in the insulted lieutenant's platoon jumped to their feet, their hands balled into fists, ready to do battle. They moved in on their targets. The moment the other marines saw this, they began to move in as well. Though the numbers were pretty much even on each side, the marines were much bigger than the MPG members. There was little doubt what the outcome of a battle would be.

"Stand down!" a Martian accented voice shouted from behind the MPG members. It was voice with unmistakable command in it. It belonged to Colonel Chin. The MPG members, hearing it, all stopped in their tracks, whether they were members of Chin's chain of command or not.

"What's a matter with the little pussy greenies?" asked the marine sergeant in a baby voice as he saw them halt. "Don't wanna fight the real men? Afraid you might hurt your little hands?"

"Remember our prime directive, people," Chin said. "It applies here as much as it does on the battlefield."

It was exactly the right thing to say. The prime directive of the MPG, penned by General Jackson himself, was: Pick your fights carefully, try not to get hurt, and *never* fight face to face if you could avoid it. The MPG were sneaking, sniping cowards and proud of it. The MPG members all turned their cheeks and walked back to their seats. The lieutenant and the private picked themselves off the floor and dusted themselves off. They swallowed their pride and began righting their table. Though the marines tried to get another rise out of their quarry, they found themselves ignored. Soon, they went back to the bar and started watching the game again, confident that they had bested their enemy.

*****

Vic Cargill had been elected as the representative of district 38 for the past three terms. Though he was responsible for a district of one million Martian citizens, just like every other representative, he had the dubious honor of having the lowest voter participation on the planet three terms running. This was because the vast majority of his district encompassed the huge Helvetia Heights section of Eden, a horrid, squalid ghetto that he had never actually set foot in. Had his district encompassed *only* Helvetia Heights, it was entirely possible that he, or anyone else for the matter, would not have received even a single vote to put him into office. The ghetto inhabitants simply did not vote. But the people that had drawn the district boundaries had been smart enough to extend district 38 just a little bit into the adjoining downtown neighborhood, allowing it to include several upper-end and lower-upper-end housing complexes. It was in these complexes that Cargill himself lived and it was from these complexes that all of his votes came—less than a thousand of them in the last election.

Cargill was basically a minor league player in the great political game that was Martian politics. He was a second generation Martian and a first generation politician, encouraged to go into the business by his father, who was an upper management partner in a semi-prestigious law firm. Vic's main sponsor in his political career was Equatorial Real Estate Holdings, a multi-billion dollar corporation that had made its fortune by developing, purchasing, and constructing housing units in the Eden and Libby areas. In Eden, ERE boasted a 22 percent share of the upper and middle income housing market and a whopping 45 percent share of the government compensated housing market (in other words: the welfare apartments). Vic's job, as one of their mules, was to push through and vote on laws that helped increase the amount that the Martian government would pay to house "disadvantaged" people in ERE apartments. It was a job that he had done fairly well since his first term. He and the other politicians owned by ERE had already managed to increase government rent responsibilities by two percent in the last session alone. This success had led to increased campaign contributions and increased "gifts" from his grateful sponsor.

Cargill had naturally been as shocked and horrified as any other politician when he heard Laura Whiting's speech the night before. This had not been because he liked or respected Whiting. On the contrary, Whiting was in the opposing political party and she was also sponsored by AgriCorp, a corporation whose interests were in opposition to ERE's. After all, if the government paid more money for welfare housing for the vermin, that meant there was less money available for the vermin to spend on AgriCorp products. Whiting and her other AgriCorp sponsored chums had killed several of his bills in committee in the past, actions that always angered the ERE lobbyists that controlled his life. No, the reason Cargill had been so horrified at the events of the previous night had not been personal, they had been professional. The thought that any politician would get up before a live audience and tell them what the political game was really like, the fact that she would denounce all politicians as corrupt and living only for their sponsors, *that* was what was offensive. The public simply could not be told things like that. True, most Martians knew these things anyway, but she had legitimized these thoughts, had confirmed them. Even if

ERE lobbyists from all levels on the ladder had not been emailing and conferencing him nonstop since the speech had ended, he still would have been a prime mover to get that bitch out of office.

He was in his own office now, a small rented space on the 182nd floor of a low-rent downtown office building. He had a window, something that only about a third of the offices in this building featured, but he may as well not have. All it looked out upon was the office building across the street and the ones on either side. Only by standing directly against the window and looking directly upward could he see the red Martian sky. Only by looking directly down could he see the street level. His office was a place that he had rarely been in on a weekend before but the current crisis had forced him, as well as most of the other representatives, in on their traditional day of rest.

At the moment, he was sitting behind his desk, staring at his Internet terminal, kissing the ass of yet another high-level ERE lobbyist, most of whom had also been called in on days off. "I understand," he was telling the suited image before him. "Believe me, I don't think any of the reps, no matter what party they're in, no matter what corporation funded their campaign, will have any problem voting for an investigation into Whiting. She's crossed way over the line. She's no longer one of us."

"That's what we thought as well," the lobbyist told him testily. "But we've already received some disturbing rebuffs from the other reps we do business with. Two of them are starting to hint that public pressure may force them to reconsider their previous stance."

"Public pressure?" Cargill scoffed, feeling nothing but contempt. "What the hell does that mean? There is no such thing, especially not in *my* district, where nine out of ten of the vermin have never earned an honest dollar in their lives. I'd be surprised if those ignorant animals are smart enough to turn on their Internet terminals, let alone use them to vote with. Hell, I would venture to say that most of them don't even know who Laura Whiting is or what she did last night."

"Those are our feelings as well," the lobbyist said, his Earthling accent thick and crisp. "But we just wanted to make sure that everyone that we've... *helped* over the years does the right thing when the time comes."

"Oh, you can bet your ass that I'll do the right thing," Cargill said. "Whiting is as good as gone."

"We're glad to hear you say that," he said with a smile.

They exchanged a few more pleasantries with each other and then signed off. Once the terminal was blank, Cargill sighed and opened his desk drawer, taking out a bottle of Vodka. He poured himself a healthy shot and put it in his stomach. He then lit up a cigarette and took a long, satisfying puff.

His terminal flared to life again a moment later, his secretary's face staring out if it. "Sir," she said to him, "do you have a minute?"

"Why?" he asked wearily. "Is another one of those damn lobbyists calling? How many more goddamned times do I have to reassure them?"

"It's not a lobbyist," she told him. "It's Linda. She'd like to have a word with you."

Linda Clark was his chief of staff. She was also his mistress of more than six years. "Send her in," he said, smiling at the thought of a little sexual tryst in his office.

But Linda was not interested in sexual activity at the moment. Her young, pretty face was all business as she came in through the sliding door. "Vic," she told him, "we have a problem."

"Who the hell doesn't have a problem today?" he asked rhetorically.

"It's about your constituents," she said, sitting in the chair before the desk without waiting for an invitation.

He rolled his eyes upward. "You mean the vermin? What possible problem could there be with them? As long as their Internet programs run and their intoxicant credits keep rolling, they stay in their little shithole apartments."

"They've been sending emails to you," she told him. "A *lot* of emails. All of them threatening recall proceedings if you vote to open an investigation into Whiting."

He was having trouble believing her. "A lot of emails from the vermin? Impossible. How many are we talking about? A few hundred? That can't possibly..."

"Try two hundred and ninety-six thousand," she interrupted. "And that's as of the last five minutes or so. They're still pouring in at a rate of more than a three hundred per minute."

"Two hundred and ninety six *thousand*?" he asked incredulously, sure that he had heard her wrong.

He hadn't. "That's correct," she assured him. "One hundred and sixty-three thousand came in last night, within the two hour time period following Whiting's speech. Now it seems that a second wave of them is underway. The numbers started to pick up about 10:30 and have been steadily climbing since. Of course, we haven't been able to open them all—there's simply too many for that—but we've had the computer scan them all for basic content and every last one of them is a threat for recall if you vote for Whiting's investigation."

Cargill shook his head a little. "Incredible," he whispered, unable to think of anything else.

"Let me show you a typical one," she said, "just so you know what we're dealing with here." She looked at the ceiling, where the computer voice recognition microphone was installed. "Computer, load and play one of the emails received in the last hour. Select randomly."

"Loading," the computer's voice said.

A moment later the screen cleared and showed a scruffy, thug-like young man in his early twenties. The text on the bottom identified the sender as: Jeffrey Creek, Age 23. Creek was taking a puff on a cheap marijuana pipe that had been fashioned from discarded food containers. He held the smoke for a moment and then blew it directly onto the camera lens, momentarily blurring the image. When it cleared, he began to talk. "Check it, fuckface. The name's Jeff Creek and I'm one of your constituents here in this shithole known as Helvetia Heights. I ain't never voted for nothing or no one before, but you can bet your ass that if you start fucking around and trying to impeach Laura Whiting, I'll be the first motherfucker to sign a petition to kick your ass out of office. And then, once that petition is all signed and legal and shit and they ask us to vote to get rid of you, I'll be signing on to do that shit too. Don't fuck with Whiting, my man. Don't even think of fucking with her. That's all." The image blinked off and the computer informed them that the recording was at an end.

"How uncouth," Vic said, disgusted. "Do they really expect me to take that kind of thing seriously?"

"That's a pretty typical recording," Linda said. "I've looked at several hundred of them myself and his sentiments are basically what they're saying."

"Who really cares what those ignorant vermin are saying?" Vic asked. "So they figured out how to log onto the email program and send mail. What of it? You don't really think they'd actually be able to mount a recall campaign against me, do you?"

"I didn't think so at first," she said. "But now... now that two hundred and ninety-six thousand of them have sent email saying the same thing, I'm not so sure."

"What?"

"More than a quarter of a million and counting," she said. "All of them angry, embittered shouts by the people you represent. Whiting told them that they have a constitutional right to vote you out of office and they've apparently locked onto that thought and embraced it. Surely among quarter of a million there are a *few* with the drive and the intelligence to organize petition drives and to rouse up others to go collect signatures."

"I hardly think so," he said. "That requires work, something that the vermin avoid like the plague."

She shook her head. "Don't underestimate them, Vic," she said. "They may be unemployed but they are not ignorant. They're frustrated with the system and they blame the politicians and the corporations for keeping them where they are."

"That's ridiculous," he said, automatically spouting the company line.

"Ridiculous or not," she said. "It's what they believe. They will be watching the assembly on Monday morning. They'll be watching and when the Lieutenant Governor asks the legislature to open hearings into Laura Whiting, they will take note of how you vote. It is all public record under the constitution. And if you vote to impeach her, I have no doubt that by the time the day is over there will be hundreds if not thousands of vermin out in the Heights getting fingerprints on petition screens. Within a matter of days, your recall will be on the ballet and they will vote you out. They can have you back in the private sector in less than a month."

Vic's mouth was wide as he listened to her. What she was saying was so bizarre, so unheard of. "How can I tell my sponsor that I'm not going to vote the way they want? How can I tell them that? If I don't do what they tell me to, they'll withdraw their funding for my campaigns and they'll find someone else to give it to."

She shrugged. "Which action will kill you first?" she asked. "You can at least rest assured that you're not going through this alone. From what I hear, all of the other reps are getting email in even bigger numbers."

*****

Barbara Garcia was a two term representative from the Shiloh Park section of Eden. Her constituents were a mixture of working class Martians that lived in the northern part of the district and welfare class that lived in the southern. She had grown up the daughter of an agricultural worker and she was—thanks to her intelligence and frightfully high placement scores—the first in eight generations to attend college. With her degree in political theory from the University of Mars at Eden, she had gone on to law school and the Eden city council, the usual stepping-stone for a career in Martian politics. From there, her popularity with her main sponsor—AgriCorp—had made her a shoe-in for the Planetary Legislature.

Barbara had always played the game well during her career, knowing that it was the only game in town and that in order to succeed she would have to follow the established rules. She had taken campaign contributions from AgriCorp and others ever since her first run at the city council. She had gone on the all-expenses paid space cruises to Saturn and Neptune and Mercury, riding in luxury cabins and being pampered to her heart's delight. She had even taken unreported contributions when they were offered, contributions that had swollen her net worth to well over two million dollars. But despite these "perks of the job", as they were called when they were discussed at all, she had always felt more than a little disgusted with herself. She knew that politics was not supposed to be this way, that she was part of a perversion that had gone on for centuries now. There had been a time when she had tried to tell herself that she was only staying in the game for the good of the people she represented, but those naïve thoughts had long since died within her.

Except now Laura Whiting had reawakened them. What Whiting had done the night before had been incredible, outrageous, the most shocking thing imaginable and Barbara could not help but feel a strong surge of respect for the woman. She was trying to change the game! After all of these years, after all of the lies and back dealing and jerking off of the public, someone was actually trying to make a difference! Amazing.

Granted, Barbara had initially had every intention of doing exactly what her sponsors wished of her and voting for an impeachment investigation of the new governor. After all, though she respected Whiting for her stand, political survival was still the most important thing in her life. She was qualified to do nothing else in this life but serve in the legislature. As much as she found herself admiring Whiting and her views, she knew that Whiting was as good as gone and the game would then go on as it always had and as it always would. She had planned to have a drink in Whiting's honor the next time she tipped a glass, but also to vote as was required and to even deride the governor in the media if reporters asked her questions.

And then the emails had started to roll in. An incredible three hundred thousand of them were sent to her staff in the first three hours following Whiting's speech. Another one hundred and eighty thousand had come in since. Nearly half of her constituents, including a good portion of the welfare class, had taken the time to compose messages to her and, according to the computer scans all of the messages, every last one said the same thing: vote to open an investigation into Whiting and you're gone. Had someone told her two days before that something like this would happen, she would have thought them insane. Martians never got involved in politics, especially not the welfare class. They rarely voted, they rarely protested anything in an organized fashion, and they never tried to recall their representatives. But now they were threatening just that, and in no uncertain terms either. Barbara and her chief of staff were both of the opinion that these were not idle threats either. Whiting had really riled the people up.

"What are you going to do?" Steve Ying, the chief of staff in question, asked her now as they sat in her office.

Barbara's office was somewhat nicer than Vic Cargill's, mostly because of the higher campaign contribution rate that she drew. She actually had something of a view from her window. She was at the edge of the developed area and could see the spaceport off to the left about twenty kilometers distant. As she considered her subordinate's question she watched an orbital craft, probably filled with agricultural products, lift into the sky, its hydrogen powered engine spewing white-hot flame as it ascended. "I was just sworn in for my second term yesterday," she said thoughtfully after the craft had disappeared beyond the horizon.

"Yes," Steve said. "That's one possible way to look at it. You have another eighteen months before you have to start worrying about re-election. No matter how much you piss off AgriCorp and your other sponsors, you can't be drummed out until the end of your term, at least not unless they take an active role in getting rid of you."

Barbara knew well what that meant. An active role was a drastic action designed to get rid of a troublesome politician in a hurry. It was in fact what they were trying to do to Whiting. It meant that the corporations pulled out all of the stops and did everything in their power to discredit and smear the person and force public outrage upon them. "I don't think that they would go that far for little old me," she said. "If it was just me and me alone who voted no on the investigation, perhaps they would, but it isn't going to be just me, is it?"

He shook his head. "From what I hear, every representative is getting about the same volume of email from their constituents. Even Vic Cargill is being overwhelmed and you know what his district is like."

"Yes," she said, "Helvetia Heights. A most pleasant area of town. It's remarkable that the people in his district have embraced this cause as well. Truly remarkable."

Steve nodded. "My thoughts exactly," he said. "It goes to show just how deep this thing has become. We're truly in uncharted territory here."

"And the water is infested with sharks," she agreed. "What we do now is going to have some very long lasting implications."

"Does that mean you're going to vote no on the investigation?" he asked her.

"I don't really see another option. I should be safe enough from any drastic repercussions. AgriCorp will be mightily pissed off at me and it's possible they may be forced to withdraw their support for me in the next election, but..."

"But?"

"But if Laura Whiting succeeds in her plan, there will be no next election."

Steve looked at her as if she were mad. "You think there's a chance she'll gain independence for us?" he asked her.

"She has the support of the people," Barbara said. "And she has a gift for riling them up. As long as she is given Internet time to speak her views—and MarsGroup will undoubtedly grant her that—there's virtually no limit to what she can do."

"The corporations and the WestHem government will never allow it," Steve said. "The best that Whiting can hope for is to survive the impeachment attempt. She'll probably be able to do that but she'll still be gone within the month. They'll find some way to get rid of her, legal or not. I wouldn't even put arranging an assassination past them."

"Nor would I," Barbara told him. "But did you ever think for a minute that Whiting is smart enough to have taken that into consideration? She's been playing the political game perfectly for years, all the time planning to do what she did last night. Her goal is to make us independent. She has to know that those in power will do almost anything to get rid of her. And knowing that, she has to have taken precautions against it, just as she took precautions against impeachment. She's not naïve, Steve. I believe that she knows exactly what she is doing and I believe that she may even be ultimately successful."

Steve was having a hard time with this concept, although her arguments did sound logical. "What are you saying, Barb?" he asked.

"I'm saying that I'm going to support her."

"Support her?" he asked, wide-eyed. "Surely you don't mean what I think you mean."

"I do," she confirmed. "Start arranging a press conference for me tonight. I'm going to go live and denounce my sponsorship and announce my support for the new governor and for Martian independence."

Steve was appalled. "Barbara, that's madness," he told her. "Even if you think that Whiting has a small chance of succeeding, you must realize that in all likelihood she will not. If you just vote no on the impeachment because of public pressure, you might be able to survive politically. AgriCorp will probably be able to forgive you for that since everyone else will be forced to do it as well. But if you actually announce that you *support* Whiting, you're dead, maybe even literally!"

Barbara shook her head at him sadly. "You don't understand, do you?" she asked him.

"Understand what?"

"Laura Whiting is right for what she's doing. This has gone beyond a political issue. When you have the vermin contacting politicians and threatening recall of them in the numbers that we've seen, you have an issue that they feel rather strongly about. The people *want* to be free of WestHem and it is our job as their elected representatives to do everything in our power to bring that about. I've done what my sponsors have wanted me to do my entire career, ever since I was voting for beverage contracts on the school board. I've never been able to do what the people who elected me wanted done. My soul aches because of that and it always has. I'm a Martian and it's time to start balancing the scales a little bit. I'll probably go down in flames for this stand, but at least I'll go down a hero to the Martian people and not a corrupt politician."

"My God," Steve said frightfully. "You've gone ideological."

She laughed a little. "That I have. You're a very good chief of staff, Steve, but if you do not wish to be a part of what I'm going to be doing, I'll accept your resignation. You shouldn't have much trouble getting hired with someone else."

He thought about that for the briefest of moments. "I guess I'll stick with you," he told her fatalistically. "What the hell? I'm a Martian too, ain't I?"

"I guess you are," she said happily. "Now how about scheduling that press conference for me."

"I'll get right on it."

"And let my secretary know that I'm no longer taking calls from lobbyists."

"Right."

*****

At 325 stories in height—nearly 1800 meters from base to roof—the AgriCorp building was the tallest in the solar system. It stood sentinel over the downtown Eden area, towering more than 300 meters higher than any of its neighbors. More than three hundred thousand people worked in the building, most of them for the entity that had lent its name to the structure. Lobbyists, accountants, security consultants, management types, auditors, and hundreds of other job classifications all poured into the building each and every day and toiled there for eight to twelve hours or more, all of them working to keep the great empire's Martian operations running and profitable.

William Smith, as the CEO of Martian operations, naturally had his office on the very top of the building. The view was commanding. Looking southward from his huge picture window, he could see the thousands of other high-rises that made up Eden and the stark border on the edge of the city where the wastelands began. The Sierra Madres Mountains could easily be seen as well, the peaks poking up over the horizon. It was a view that other men might have killed for in a city where all that could usually be seen out one's window was the bulk of another building. It was a view that Smith had long since ceased to even notice.

As the sun sank behind the horizon to the west, Smith was sitting at his large desk, his bottom planted in a genuine leather chair that had cost more than beginning apple pickers earned in a month. There were two Internet terminals on the desk before him and he was using one to hold a conference call while the other was tuned to a big three station.

"What in the hell is going on around here?" he demanded of his caller. "Has everyone gone completely insane?"

"Sir," said Corban Hayes, the Martian director of the Federal Law Enforcement Bureau office, "I realize that maybe things are starting to spiral a little out of control here, but..."

"A little out of control?" Smith shouted, leaning closer to the screen. "Correct me if I'm wrong, but did I or did I not just watch *three* of the planetary legislature members—politicians who have been bought and paid for and are supposed to be representing our goddamn interests here—go on live Internet and say that they *support* Laura Whiting? That they *support* independence for Mars? Maybe you saw something different than I did, Hayes, but it sure as hell looked a lot like that to me."

"That is true, sir," Hayes told him complacently. "Three of them did do that. And I will also agree that a good portion of the rest of them will be forced to vote against opening an impeachment investigation into Whiting."

"So that greenie bitch is going to remain in office!" he yelled. "She is going to remain the governor of this planet and she has somehow managed to pervert three of our reps over to her twisted way of thinking. This is not a little out of control, Hayes, this is a goddamn nightmare."

"I'll admit that I was somewhat surprised by the response of the greenies to her speech," he said. "Who would have thought that greenies would respond in the sheer numbers that they did to her call for recall email? It's inconceivable."

"It's inconceivable, but it has happened," Smith said. "That woman has to go and go quickly before she does any more damage here."

"You have the big three working on a discreditation campaign," Hayes reminded. "I saw a few of the programs that they managed to get out today. Very impressive. I particularly liked the one that linked her with EastHem interests."

"Yes," Smith said. "That was very good, very fast work on the part of the big three. The problem is that hardly any Martians watched it. I talked to Lancaster over at InfoServe a few minutes before I called you. He says that according to the media tracking computers, most of the greenies are watching MarsGroup channels. MarsGroup! That sleazy, rabble-rousing excuse for a legitimate corporation. And all MarsGroup has been publishing or airing has been favorable profiles and bios on Whiting. They're canonizing the bitch and those greenies are eating it up!"

Hayes shook his head a little, as if bewildered. "That's a pattern we've noted in the past with the greenies," he said. "They put very little stock in the legitimate news programs for some reason. They prefer the bland, left-wing drivel that they get on MarsGroup, God knows why."

"Is there any way to shut MarsGroup down?" he asked. "Some federal law against inciting riots or something like that?"

"We could probably swing a federal order of some sort on that basis," Hayes told him, "but I'm afraid that that would be a bad idea. We would technically be violating our own constitution by doing that and no matter what reason we offered the greenies for doing it, they would perceive that it was to silence the Whiting viewpoint. I don't even want to imagine what chaos would result from that."

"Those ignorant greenies?" Smith said with contempt. "What trouble could they be? I say go ahead and do it."

"Those ignorant greenies have just sent in more than forty million emails to their elected representatives," Hayes reminded him. "Like it or not, they've achieved organization on this matter and they have very strong feelings about it. I'm sorry, sir, but I don't think that shutting MarsGroup down via federal order will serve WestHem interests very well. I'll run it by my superiors in Denver of course, but I'm going to recommend that it not be done. It's too dangerous."

"Then how are we going to keep them from getting riled up any further?"

"The main goal, the *only* goal remains to get rid of Whiting as quickly as possible. Without her leading them, the greenies will quickly go back to the way they always have been: troublesome, ignorant, but controllable."

"Which brings us back to the question of how we do it," he said. "The discreditation campaign is being ignored and the impeachment is probably going to fail. What does that leave us? Can you arrange an accident for her? Or a lunatic assassin?"

"That's a possibility," he said without hesitation. "And it's one that I'll have my most trusted people look into. A more likely possibility is one that we've already discussed: a corruption indictment. Like you said before, Whiting admitted to taking unreported campaign contributions throughout her career. Granted, all politicians engage in this habit, but that does not present much of a problem. We're only talking about Whiting here. We can leave the other politicians completely out of the argument."

"Didn't you say that you would have to indict the corporate people for offering these contributions? I seem to recall you speaking out against this course of action yesterday."

"I did then," Hayes said, "but I didn't realize that more conventional methods of removal would be neutralized. I'm now starting to think we might have to resort to that."

"And what about the return indictments?" Smith wanted to know. "I can't have you discrediting AgriCorp or one of our sister corporations on charges of bribery. It's bad for public relations. Do you have a way around that?"

"You'll need a scapegoat that you can blame it on," Hayes told him. "Pick some upper-level management type that you can live without and make it look like he and he alone got a little overzealous in trying to recruit Whiting. Rewrite your financial records so it looks like he embezzled the money out of your assets to transfer them to Whiting. His motive could be movement up the corporate ladder. He was after your job, sir, and was willing to go to any lengths, break any rules to get it. After all, your position is worth much more in terms of money and prestige than anything he could have embezzled, right?"

Smith nodded his head thoughtfully. "Not bad," he said. "And I think I have just the person in mind."

"Great," Hayes said. "Of course, you'll also have to burn a lobbyist or two and a few middle management types in order to make this work, but I'm sure you'll have no problem thinning a few out."

"No, no problem at all," he said without hesitation or emotion.

"Okay then," Hayes said with a smile. "Assuming of course that the impeachment attempt flops, I'll get my guys working on the bribery investigation first thing tomorrow. It shouldn't take too much to get a subpoena for Whiting's bank account and financial records issued in light of her admissions during her speech. Once we have your money tracked to her, I'll get back with you and we'll work out a way to weave the trail into the people you pick. If all goes well, we should have enough to indict her in about two weeks."

*****

Sunday was usually a day of rest on Mars, much the same as it always had been on Earth. Office buildings were typically closed and empty of everyone but the security force. The public transportation system ran fewer trains across the tops of the city roofs and those that they did run were usually half-empty at best. Even the crime rate had been noted to take a significant dip on Sundays. Seemingly even the criminals needed a day to kick back and relax as well.

On this particular Sunday on Mars there was not much resting going on however, at least not among the movers and the shakers of the planet. Emails continued to roll in to the legislature representatives, at a slower rate than the day before but still quite rapidly. The representatives that received them all spent the greater part of the day in their respective offices, all of them planning strategy on how to deal with the coming flak of the Whiting impeachment proceedings. During the course of the day, eight more representatives—six women and two men, all Martians of more than three generations—called press conferences to announce their support of Whiting and her goal. All of them banned lobbyists of any kind from their offices and publicly denounced all corporate contacts.

The lobbyists themselves spent their day in front of their Internet terminals trying to cajole the remaining representatives to vote for impeachment proceedings the following day. They begged, pleaded, threatened, offered bribes, and did every other underhanded thing they had learned over the years to try to convince the men and women to act in accordance with the corporate wishes. It was all to no avail. Every last one of them, even the Speaker of the Assembly herself, was forced to tell their sponsor's representatives that they simply could not do it this time, that too much was at stake. Most of them apologized sincerely for not being able to play by the rules but they were firm in their refusals and unwavering in their responses.

The corporate heads of the various Martian operations were also forced to spend most of their day in their offices as well. Their job was to take reports from their lobbyists and then call up the various representatives personally to offer one last round of threats and pleas. Again, despite the warnings of removed support in the next election, the legislature stood firm. As Vic Cargill had been told the previous day, it was a simple matter of what would kill the politicians' career first and most assuredly. In every case they were forced to conclude that they would be out for good in weeks if they voted for impeachment proceedings but that they just might survive if they voted against it. After all, the corporations couldn't withdraw support from *all* of them, could they?

The small red planet turned on its axis and Sunday passed into Monday morning. At precisely 9:00 AM, Eden time, the entire planetary legislature assembled in their chambers in the capital building to be welcomed for their new session. MarsGroup and all of the big three media corporations carried the meeting live on their networks. The ratings computers confirmed that more than forty-five million households, an incredible, unheard of ninety-six percent of all viewers, were watching the meeting, most of them on the MarsGroup stations. The speaker conducted the roll and then turned the floor over to the newly inaugurated Lieutenant Governor at the latter's request.

Scott Benton took the podium and gave a very passionate, very moving ten-minute speech regarding the fallacies of the new governor. He was an exceptional public speaker and he almost managed to sound sincere as he lauded the legislature to open impeachment hearings on the grounds of misrepresentation of office. He asked the speaker to please put the issue on the floor immediately and to follow it up with a vote. The speaker, as she was honor bound to do, did so.

"There is a motion on the floor at the request of Lieutenant Governor Benton," she said tonelessly into her microphone. "The motion is that this assembly of planetary representatives open an impeachment investigation into Governor Laura Whiting. Do I have a second for the motion?"

The assembly chamber remained silent as a mouse. The motion died right there on the floor for lack of a second. In a way, it was almost anticlimactic.

"The motion will be shelved," the speaker said blandly, as if she were dismissing nothing more important than a motion on what to have for lunch that day.

"Wait a minute," Benton said, standing and approaching her. "You can't just..."

"You are out of order, Lieutenant Governor," the speaker said, looking at him. "The motion has died. Resume your seat please."

"You don't understand," he said. "This motion has to be..."

"Take your seat," she repeated. "If you do not do so immediately, I will have security remove you."

He took his seat, fuming as he went.

"And now," the speaker said, "I have another special request. This one is from Governor Whiting. She has asked to say a few words to you before we convene the session and I have granted her request. Governor?"

Laura Whiting came onto the stage, dressed in a simple pair of dress shorts and a cotton blouse. Her long brown hair was down around her shoulders instead of pinned into a bun. She had a smile upon her face as she took the podium and thanked the speaker.

"Members of the Planetary Legislature and people of Mars that are watching this broadcast, I thank both of you for the support you've given me so far. With your help I have passed the first hurdle in my path to securing Martian independence."

CHAPTER THREE

New Pittsburgh, Mars
May 7, 2186

Though there had been many advances in communications technology since the beginning of the space colonization age, there was one constant that never changed and probably never would. No matter what carrier for the signal was used, be it encrypted laser beams or modulating radio waves, they could move no faster than the speed of light. As such, it was impossible for a person on Mars to hold a real-time conversation with a person on Earth. Even at the closest approach of the two planets—a mere fifty-six million kilometers—it took a message more than three minutes to travel from one place to another. Now, three months after the inauguration, with the two planets within ten degrees of being as far apart as they ever got, it took just under twenty minutes. And even that was not the extreme end of the communications lag. Once the sun became positioned between the two planets it would effectively block all radio waves from traveling from one place to the other in a direct line. All correspondence would then have to be routed first to a communications array in orbit around Jupiter, a step that added anywhere from forty minutes to two hours to the trip, depending upon just where Jupiter was located in the great scheme of things at the time. This period of "extended relay lag" as it was known in government documents, came once every twenty-four months and lasted for six weeks at a time. The next such period was calculated to begin in a little over five weeks.

William Smith sincerely wished that it were upon them right now.

He sat in his desk chair behind his desk in his office, a place that he felt he had been spending far too much time in during the last twelve weeks. He had just watched a scathing communiqué from Steve Carlson, CEO and chief stockholder of AgriCorp and arguably the richest man in the solar system, a communiqué that demanded the most immediate response. To say that Carlson was displeased with the recent events on Mars—a planet where seventy-four percent of his company's products were grown or manufactured—was the equivalent of saying that World War III had been a little skirmish. AgriCorp stock, once the staple of the New York Stock Exchange, had fallen by more than a hundred dollars a share thanks to the perceived instabilities caused by the current political crisis. And Carlson, who had calmly expected the troublesome Whiting to be either discredited or dead by her second week in office, was now demanding answers of the man that was supposed to have overseen her removal.

"I thought that you knew how to play the game for keeps," he told Smith in his icy, unforgiving voice. "I thought you knew what measures needed to be utilized to protect corporate interests over on that flying dust ball they call a planet. Maybe entrusting you with the day-to-day operations of our most important holdings was a mistake. Please report back to me *immediately* with an explanation of why this communist greenie bitch is still in office over there and still ranting about independence and nationalization."

In the world of corporate politics, where everything was said in doublespeak and innuendo, those were harsh, scathing words indeed. Smith knew that he was within bare inches of losing everything he had worked for over the years. All of the grappling and struggling and back-stabbing he had done to rise to the position he now held, all of it would be for nothing if the Laura Whiting situation was not brought under control one way or the other. What had started out as an annoyance had quickly become the worst crisis of his entire career.

He sighed and opened up his desk drawer, pulling out a sterling silver box that was about the size of a charging battery for a hand-held laser. Inside, was an airtight compartment stuffed with clipped marijuana buds harvested from the AgriCorp greenhouses. The buds were the very finest available, the kind that were only sold in country club bars and exclusive restaurants for more than eighty dollars per hit. Smith received them for free, of course. It was one of the perks of his job. In a felt compartment next to the buds was a small pipe that had been carved from genuine ivory, one of the most expensive substances in the solar system. He loaded the pipe up with a healthy sized pinch and ignited it, drawing deeply. He had been smoking a lot of marijuana lately, just to take edge off.

After exhaling and letting the THC work its way to his tired brain, he put his paraphernalia away and put the box back in his drawer. He then looked at his Internet terminal, which was in stand-by mode, the AgriCorp logo the only thing showing. "Computer," he said, "communications software."

"Communications software up," the computer answered as the screen changed.

"Addressee is Steve Carlson, CEO." He took another deep breath and consulted some handwritten notes he had composed. "Begin recording."

The camera light on his terminal blinked on and he looked at the screen, his eyes making solid contact with it, his face showing the pleasant, subservient expression he used when talking to those higher on the ladder than himself. He spent a few moments spouting pleasantries, asking about Carlson's wife, children, and mistress just as if this were a normal business communiqué. Once that was accomplished, he turned to the meat of the matter.

"I understand completely your concern that the Laura Whiting matter is still going on despite the passage of twelve weeks since her inauguration," he said. "I also understand the fact that you, as the head of the corporation, would question my abilities as CEO of Martian operations for failing to deal with it. I have no doubt that were our positions reversed, I would be asking the same questions of you and would expect detailed answers. I have always been a loyal manager for this corporation and I must tell you that I have done everything within my power here to dislodge Whiting from high office by one means or another. I have pulled out all of the stops and somehow, she has managed to think ahead of us at every step of the way. Whiting is not a typical greenie, Steve, not in the least. Sometimes I'm forced to wonder if she's really a greenie at all. Allow me to summarize the measures we've attempted so far and how she has managed to counter them.

"The impeachment attempt. This was our first attempt to remove her from office and, though it had never been used before, it was the pre-planned method for dealing with such a gross abuse of trust on the part of a politician. The set-up for it was executed perfectly and without anything in the way of opposition from competing corporations. After all, Whiting was not just spouting damaging statements towards AgriCorp, but towards all corporations and in fact our very way of life. Every Earth-based corporation on this planet rallied their lobbyists within hours of her inauguration speech and began putting pressure on the members of the legislature that they sponsored. Between us, we owned every last one of the sixty-two members of this body and she should have been impeached unanimously within a week of taking her oath.

"Well, you already know how that one worked out. Whiting is a very charismatic speaker and she was somehow able to convince the common greenies to put enough pressure on their elected representatives to derail this process before it was even started. What was worse was the fact that she was able to pervert eleven of the representatives over to her point of view before a vote was even called for.

"And I'm afraid that this perversion of the representatives did not end there. As of this morning here in Eden, a grand total of twenty-nine planetary representatives, twelve of whom had been primarily sponsored by AgriCorp, have renounced their previous affiliations and announced support for Whiting and her goals. These representatives will no longer take calls from lobbyists of any kind and will not respond to requests for communications from corporate heads. The Speaker of the Legislature is thankfully still in support of the corporations and she is still one of our employees, as it were, but even she has been muted to a certain degree by the happenings here on this planet. For all of her power, she is still nothing more than an elected representative that is vulnerable to the recall vote from her constituents. This has forced her to walk a very fine line in regards to which laws she votes upon and what other actions she takes. If she is perceived as being too biased towards us or any other corporation, we may very well lose her to a mass recall vote.

"That brings me to the second way we attempted to remove Whiting from office, namely the media blitz of negative publicity. As you are aware, this is the most common and most effective way that we have of dealing with a rogue politician and it's something that has worked well since long before the colonization of this miserable planet. In this case, I'm afraid it has failed. Again, this is not due to any lack of participation on the part of other corporations. On the contrary, each one of the big three media conglomerates have been outdoing themselves in this effort. You receive the feeds back on Earth so I'm sure you know that you can hardly turn on a terminal to one of the big three channels or read one of their publications without finding something negative about Whiting. They've done stories about her past ties with militia groups, they've done stories about her business dealings and skewed votes as a representative, they've done stories hinting that she is a lesbian and a child molester. I'm sure that the people of Earth, if they've been watching this, are completely appalled by Whiting and are probably demanding her immediate removal. But here on Mars, we're not dealing with rational people. These greenies watch the media shows, but instead of demanding her removal or her indictment, they mock them. They regard them as comedy entertainment. Over the past seven weeks it has developed into something of a ritual that they gather in large groups, smoke marijuana and watch the latest show on Whiting so they can laugh at it. They have discussions in the Internet bulletin boards about how ridiculous the accusations were. The more inflammatory the charges brought are, the more amusing they seem to find it. Even Whiting herself has been poking fun at these shows in those damn bi-weekly addresses that she gives on MarsGroup. I'm afraid that we will not be able to count on the media blitz being any sort of deterrent to her behavior or any sort of vehicle for her removal.

"And then there are some of the other options that we've discussed in the past, namely those involving the Federal Law Enforcement Bureau, which has always been a great friend to all things corporate. I've been in constant contact with Corban Hayes, the director of the Martian FLEB offices here on Mars, ever since this crisis began. My instinct as a manager is to try to blame this fiasco on him and his agents, first for clearing Whiting for high office in the first place and then for failing to get her out once her true colors became known. That is my instinct, but in this case, I simply cannot assign any blame to him. As early as the third day of this crisis, Hayes and his agents began a thorough investigation into Whiting on corruption and bribery charges. After all, she admitted during her inaugural address and in several subsequent speeches that she took unreported money from various corporations including AgriCorp. You'll recall that I explained the plan that the two of us concocted to place blame on Sandy Groover and several of her middle-management team for giving those bribes. While this would have cost us Groover and a few others, and while it would have cast a slight pall upon our public relations, it should have resulted in Whiting's indictment and removal from office. Hayes was able to secure a search warrant for Whiting's financial records and bank accounts and everything seemed to be going well and then we hit the snag that killed the plan. All of that unreported money that we gave her over the years, every last dollar of it from the time she was an Eden city council member to her election to governor, is still sitting in her election account. As incredible as that sounds, all twenty-three million dollars was logged and transferred from her personal account to her campaign account and it is still there, duly documented and technically completely legal from her standpoint. She did not spend so much as a dime of it for her own use. It is doubtful that Hayes would even be able to get an indictment of her on that basis, let alone a conviction. So that is how that plan fell through and it also goes to show just how long Whiting has been planning this little scheme of hers.

"That brought Hayes and myself to the final, most drastic plan for Whiting's removal, that of… well… arranging for an assassin to stalk her and remove her permanently.   By the time we reached this point we were desperate, having exhausted almost all other options. Hayes was certainly agreeable enough to making the arrangements and he even had a plan in his files for how to go about such a thing. The problem with this plan is not in the conception or the assets but in the execution. Whiting has an elite battalion of the Martian Planetary Guard providing around the clock security for her. Now, most of the MPG are bumbling boobs that like to dress up as soldiers on the weekend and play with guns, but the VIP security arm are not cut from this same mold. They are full-time members of the MPG and they train extensively with the latest weapons and techniques. They know their stuff and Hayes is of the opinion that it would be almost as hard to get to Whiting as it would be to get to one of the executive council members. He is, of course, still looking into the possibilities of the assassin plot, but I have been told that it probably will not be feasible unless the MPG drops their guard to some degree."

Smith looked up at the ceiling for a moment, taking a deep breath and allowing the camera to keep rolling. He looked back at the screen. "Steve," he said, "that is my explanation for why Whiting is still in office. I hope you accept it and I hope you will agree that I've done all that I possibly can from my end. I'm dealing with greenies here and sometimes I find it hard to believe that they are actually the same species as we are, their thinking is so different. Now that I've had my say, I hope you'll continue to listen to me long enough to tell you just how bad things really are here on Mars and how critical it is that something is done about her.

"Whiting's speeches on MarsGroup are the biggest threat. Twice a week, on Wednesday and Saturday at 6:00 New Pittsburgh time, she goes live and gives a ten to twenty minute speech. I've sent copies of them to you and I'm sure you'll agree that she sounds like a raving madwoman spouting a bunch of drivel about freedom and independence and government for the people. She's a goddamn communist, no doubt about it. That is how *we* perceive her speeches however. These ignorant greenies adore her and they hang on her every word. Each one of those speeches gets more than a ninety percent market share of the viewers on the planet. Ninety percent! Think about that for a moment. Ninety percent is an unheard-of amount for any one show no matter what it is and this politician is achieving that with her rants. And believe me when I say that the greenies are not watching her for the sheer entertainment value that she represents, they actually buy into what she is saying. These greenies are actually starting to think that they should be free of WestHem. There are increasing reports of pro-separatist graffiti on corporate buildings and property. I'm afraid that if this trend continues we may start to have some sort of work slowdown or other job action in the greenhouses. I don't have to tell you what that might do to profits.

"The most detrimental effect that we're feeling down here though is the loss of control over the legislature, which has always been our most powerful weapon for keeping the greenies of the labor pool under control. Because of the defection of twenty-nine of the representatives in this body and because of the public pressure on the others that Whiting is fomenting, we have been unable to push through a single one of the twelve bills we had planned for this session. Six of these bills were planetary tax breaks towards food production operations and would have saved us nearly a trillion over the course of the year. The other six were easements on health and safety rules that would have saved us another half a trillion. How long will it be before things start working in reverse and this corrupted legislature body starts proposing *increased* taxes or *greater* health and safety requirements? I fear it won't be long at all.

"Steve, I've done everything that I can do from my end. I don't think I've slept a complete night since that bitch was sworn in. I've pulled in every favor and I've threatened almost every person with any sort of power on this shithole planet. None of it has worked. I'm sorry I've failed you and failed the company, but please believe that it was not for lack of trying. You can replace me, of course and I would understand completely if you did, but you have to realize that my replacement would be stuck with the very same problems and he would not have the same connections here on Mars that I have developed.

"The bottom line is that all of the solutions available on *this* planet for dealing with this problem have been exhausted. What we need is bigger pressure on bigger people and that means the executive council members and the federal apparatus on *your* end of the solar system. My suggestion would be that you try to get the FLEB director on Earth to allow Hayes and his people to start cracking down on these greenies as hard as they can. Once you start throwing them in jail and hounding them, they'll think twice about being so vocal in their protestations. And most important of all, we need to find a way to remove Whiting from office. That will be the thing that will most effectively defuse this situation. The longer she remains in office, the worse this thing is going to get.

"Awaiting your reply and your instructions. Signing off. End recording."

The camera light blinked off and he let his subservient face slack.

"Email is ready," the computer told him. "Would you like to review?"

"No," he replied. "Just send it off. Use the highest level of encryption."

"Sending mail with level five encryption sequence," he was told. "Would you like to compose more mail?"

"No," he said testily. "Shut down communications software and give me some music. Something classical."

As the soft sound of synthetic instruments filled his office he reached in his drawer and pulled out his sterling silver case once again. He set up another hit and began to wait for the reply.

*****

Meanwhile, 325 stories below, a black and white police cart came driving slowly down AgriCorp Avenue, in no particular hurry. Brian and Lisa were inside, Brian behind the wheel, Lisa clucking in amusement at the text upon their dispatch screen. They were not often sent into this part of downtown, although it was technically their area of responsibility. Not a lot of crime happened in the business district since most of the office buildings, the monstrous AgriCorp included, had their own private security force.

"That must be our victim," Lisa said, pointing as they approached the solar system's tallest building. Sitting outside one of the side entrances on a planter in the street was a middle-aged man in a business suit. He was holding a towel to his face while two AgriCorp security guards flanked him.

"Must be," Brian said, pulling to the curb next to them. "Looks like an officious Earthling prick to me."

"One of the ones that's been fucking and raping us all these years," she agreed. "I can't imagine why anyone would want to assault him."

"He probably can't either," Brian said.

They stepped out of the cart and shut the doors, both pausing to adjust their weapons belts before walking over to their victim. The security guards, both of whom were undoubtedly Martians, were clearly amused by the predicament of the man they were supposed to be protecting. Dressed in light blue armor that was more decorative than functional, they had barely concealed smiles upon their faces. One of them, the male half of the team, walked over and met them halfway.

"What do we got?" Lisa asked, pulling her patrol computer from her belt and flipping it open. "An upset corporate manager?"

"You know it," the guard said, letting his smile come forth now that he was no longer in view of the victim. "Mr. Ronald Jerome the Third there is one of the bigwigs in the subsidiary accounting division. It seems that as he was leaving the building to go home this afternoon, a group of vermin happened across him and roughed him up a bit."

"I guess the vermin are good for something, aren't they?" Brian said whimsically.

"It's only 1500," Lisa said, checking her watch. "What the hell is he doing leaving work now for?"

"He's one of the upper echelon pricks," the guard replied. "They make the fresh meat work ninety hours a week here but the bosses pretty much come and go whenever the hell they feel like it. They come staggering in here between 1100 and 1300 and then go staggering back out again a few hours later. No one is really sure what it is they even do in there, but it must not be very important."

"Are you kidding?" Brian said. "They're the ones that keep this great planet running. Where would we be without AgriCorp and their bad-ass management team?"

"Free?" Lisa asked.

"You got that shit right," the guard said. "Anyway, he's all livid that he got manhandled by this 'gang of thugs' as he calls them. He's demanding that you go find them and take them to prison."

This cracked both of the cops up. "Prison for simple assault on an Earthling," Lisa said, shaking her head a little. "What fucking planet does he think he lives on? Christ."

"Let's go talk to him," Brian suggested. "This oughtta be fun."

They walked over, both making little effort to put their professional faces back on. There had been a time not too long before when an assault by a welfare class person upon a corporate person would have been a big deal. A full investigation would have been launched and teams of police officers would have been sent out to comb the ghettos until the perpetrator of perpetrators were found. Once arrested, they would have had the proverbial book thrown at them, very likely receiving an extended prison sentence. In WestHem society the question was not *what* the crime was but *who* the victim had been. Crimes against corporations and corporate employees were considered much graver than crimes—up to and including murder—against working or welfare class.

But that had been before the inauguration of Laura Whiting and her bi-weekly speeches on MarsGroup. Her dissertations on the inner workings of the various corporations, of how they achieved the blatant political manipulation that kept them in perpetual power, had had a tremendous effect on the people of Mars, both welfare and working class. True, everyone had always known that the corporations were the real government of the planet and of WestHem itself, but human nature had commanded that they not think about things that they could not change. What Whiting had done was force them to think about the way things were and to think about the fairness of the situation.

"Life is not fair," Whiting had said in one of her speeches shortly after the successful deflection of the impeachment proceedings. "That is one of our most common sayings as a species. Life is not fair and there's nothing you can do about it. We're taught that in school, in our Internet programming, in the movies that we watch and in the literature that we read. Everyone knows—they *know*—that life is just not fair and that is that. We know that because that is what *they* tell us. Isn't that right?

"But has it ever occurred to you, fellow Martians, that they only tell people things like that so that we will accept it, so that we will not try to change the system and come up with something that *is* fair? Because when you think about it, who is life not fair to? Is it not fair to you, the common people of this planet, or is it not fair to the leaders and the corporations that rule us?

"I don't think I have to have an opinion poll put out to hear your answers. You know and I know that life is not fair to *you*. The advantages go to those who have the money and the power. And if you were to try and take some of those advantages, some of that fairness, and shift it over to your side, that would necessarily take some of it away from their side. They don't want that. So they tell you just to accept the fact that life isn't fair. They tell you that in a thousand different ways each and every day from the time you are born throughout your entire life until you and everyone else becomes convinced that this is an indisputable fact of life, an unbreakable natural law. It carries the same weight as a law of physics. Parents teach this concept to their children, they believe in it so much. Teachers teach it to their students. Life is not fair and you'll just have to live with that and do the best that you can with the crumbs that you've been given. Isn't that how it is?

"But did you ever stop to think, even for a moment, even just fleetingly, *why* life has to be unfair? There really are no natural laws that say this has to be so. Fairness and unfairness are a human state of mind and their executions are products of human society. Why shouldn't life be fair? Why couldn't it?"

Of all of the speeches of Laura Whiting, it had been this one that had done the most to open the eyes of the Martian people. The power of her words was not in her presentation but in the blatant simplicity. Why couldn't life be fair? Why couldn't a system that insured life was fair to everyone be developed and put in place? There really was no reason except for the obvious one: the corporations and the government that they controlled did not *want* life to be fair. They did not want fairness and they would fight with everything that they had to keep it away, to banish it from the very thoughts of the people who had been without it for so long.

And after the speech in which the Martians had it explained to them that life did not really have to be unfair, Laura Whiting had then followed this up with other speeches outlining just *how* things were unfair in specific instances and just how this benefited those in power. She laid out the inner workings of the Martian and the WestHem systems in a way that high school civics instructors would never have dreamed of. "Money," she told them. "Everything comes down to the common denominator of money. Those that have the most of it are able to use it to pervert even the most moral of us to do their bidding. And who has the most money on this planet? Who controls the flow of money on this planet? Who runs the industries that make this planet such a valuable commodity to the WestHem system?"

Nobody had to be told that Earthlings was the answer to this question. Earthlings owned more than ninety-six percent of the holdings on Mars yet they made up less than two percent of the population at any given time. They made decisions each and every day from their glittering high-rise buildings, decisions that could take away the livelihood of thousands upon thousands of Martians, yet the Earthlings were never laid off and sentenced to perpetual welfare status. The Earthlings employed Martians in their corporations and had them do all of the manual labor, all of the paperwork, all of the cleaning and guarding, yet the Martians were rarely, if ever, invited into upper management positions within those companies. Martians were rarely, if ever, put in charge of decision making. Martians were allowed into the WestHem armed services where they served with distinction in all branches, but they were rarely promoted to officer rank and they were never promoted to command rank.

Whiting pointed out these fallacies and many others to the Martian people twice a week and she had succeeded in transforming what had been seething resentment towards the Earthlings into white hot hatred of them. As William Smith had noted to his superiors, anti-Earthling graffiti had begun to spring up everywhere, on every building where Earthlings could be found. Leaflets expounding everything from general strikes to actual terrorist violence had begun to appear on apartment doors and bulletin boards in housing buildings. And reports of violence against Earthlings—usually random in nature and usually little more than minor harassment—had begun to crop up everywhere on the planet. Though Laura Whiting did not advocate these violent acts in her speeches—on the contrary, she begged her people to show restraint—years of frustration and apathy were being released and it was inevitable that many of the Martians would chose the most basic of human natures to express their discontent.

What was perhaps the most startling about this wave of anti-Earthling violence and vandalism was not its existence in the first place but the acceptance that the Martian criminal justice system showed towards it. There had never been any official memos on the matter, there had never even been verbal instruction from superiors, but through a strange form of osmosis, the message had been passed up and down the ranks of the system, from the lowliest patrol cops to the judges and lawyers that ran the show: Crimes against corporate Earthlings were no longer the big deal that they had once been. Why should they be? Why should those that exploited and raped the planet receive special treatment? Reports were still taken, of course, but gone were the days that resources were wasted in any way tracking down the perpetrators of acts that were being looked at less and less as crimes with each passing Laura Whiting speech.

"So," Lisa asked their latest victim, "what seems to be the problem here today?"

"What seems to be the problem?" Mr. Ronald Jerome III asked, his cultured Earthling accent sounded decidedly high-pitched and whiny. "Look at my face!" He took the towel away revealing a left eye that was starting to swell. "Look at what those vermin did to me!"

"Somebody popped you in the face, did they?" Lisa said.

"A whole group of them attacked me!" he yelled. "They surrounded me when I came out of the building and they started pushing me from person to person, calling me the most horrible names. They took my PC off of my belt and smashed it on the ground!" He pointed to the remains of his personal computer. It was lying against the base of the planter in a heap of plastic parts and microchips, its screen broken cleanly in half. He seemed particularly outraged about this.

"That's a shame," Brian said without the slightest trace of sincerity. "That looks like it was one of those top of the line models."

"Probably set you back twelve hundred bucks getting a new one," Lisa added, making a few notations on her computer. "You look like you can afford it though, rich corporate Earthling like you. Hell, what do they pay you here?"

"That's none of your business," he said indignantly.

"I guess not," Lisa agreed. "I was just asking. Being a poor Martian and all, I can't really afford stuff like that."

"I'm not here to talk about your problems," Jerome said sternly.

"Of course you aren't," she said complacently. "Please continue with your narrative."

"Right," he said, nodding carefully, unsure whether he was being condescended to or not but strongly suspecting that he was. "Anyway, after they smashed my PC up, they threw me to the ground and one of them kicked me. He kicked me right in the face!"

"With his foot?" Lisa asked blankly.

"Yes, with his foot! What else do people kick with? What's the matter with you people? I've been assaulted by a bunch of vermin! I want you to do something about it!"

"We are doing something about it," Lisa told him. "We're taking a report."

"To hell with your report! I want them caught!" he yelled. "I demand you go out and find them right now!"

"You demand?" Lisa said, letting a little chuckle escape. "Listen to this crap, Bri. He demands."

"He does seem very pushy, doesn't he?" Brian said, picking at a piece of fuzz on his chest armor.

Jerome looked at them in disbelief, clearly unaccustomed to being treated this way by mere civil servants—and greenie civil servants at that. "Are you telling me that you're not going to do anything about this... this crime?"

"I told you," Lisa said, "we're taking a report. We'll log it as a misdemeanor assault and it'll go into the tracking computer as such."

"And that's it?" he asked.

Lisa shrugged. "The detective division will take a look at it when they get around to it," she told him. "That'll be when they work their way through the felony assaults that they have pending first."

"And how long will that take?"

"Actually," Lisa said with a smile, "they'll probably *never* get around to it. You see, there are about five times as many felony assaults that come in as there are detectives to handle them. That's because the politicians that your little corporation and the others bribe to do their bidding won't let us kick loose any money to build jails and prisons. Therefore, there's nowhere to put criminals even if we do catch them and since the criminals all know they won't be punished, there's really no reason for them not to assault someone when the opportunity arises. But you don't want to hear all about our greenie problems, do you? My point is that they have a hard time closing out the felony assault complaints, so the misdemeanor assaults— like what happened to you—just sit there and accumulate month by month. I heard there was more than a hundred thousand of them pending, that sound about right to you, Bri?"

"Yep," Brian agreed. "That sounds pretty much on the mark."

"I am an AgriCorp executive," the man said self-righteously. "I was attacked by vermin! Surely you don't consider that an *ordinary* crime, do you?"

"A crime's a crime," Lisa told him.

"And a report's a report," Brian added. "Welcome to the wonderful world of Martian law enforcement. A world that your corporation helped create."

The man kicked at the pieces of his PC angrily. "You can't treat me like this," he told them. "Your administration will hear about this!"

Lisa and Brian both shrugged disinterestedly, both knowing that the captains and the deputy chiefs, career-oriented pricks that they were, no longer officially gave a shit what corporate executives complained about. "You go ahead and tell them," Lisa said. "But in the meantime, you wanna make the report or what? It doesn't really matter to me."

"You'll be vermin by the end of the week," the man threatened. "I swear to you. I'll have your jobs!" With that he stomped off, taking his towel with him as he headed for the MarsTrans station two blocks over.

"I guess that'll be a no then," Brian said.

"I guess so," Lisa agreed, clearing the screen of her patrol computer and putting it back on her belt.

*****

Six o'clock that evening found Matt and Jeff sitting in the latter's apartment, each with a fresh bottle of Fruity in their hands, watching the large Internet screen in the living room. They sat in scarred and battered plastic chairs that were older than their parents, furniture that had been purchased in a welfare store when Jeff and his new bride had set up housekeeping. In the kitchen, Belinda was mixing up some sort of dish made from the cheap hamburger that was sold in the welfare grocery stores. The smell of cooking meat permeated the small living area.

On the screen, Laura Whiting was just getting into her latest speech. The bi-weekly addresses were something that neither of the former gang members ever missed. There was something hypnotic and irresistible about being told by a politician just how they were all being fucked raw by the powers that be. The subject of today's speech was particularly interesting to them. It had to do with the perpetual class struggle between the Martian welfare class and the working class.

"You have to understand," she told her audience, "that this struggle is deliberate and pre-meditated by the corporations and the government that they've imposed upon us. It serves their interests for there to be strife between these two classes of people. If we are busy fighting each other and concentrating our energies on hating each other and what the other group stands for, we are much too distracted to concentrate any energy on the *real* enemy, the one who has put us in this position in the first place. It is a trick that is as old as repressive governments themselves. The British used it on the Irish Catholics and Protestants. The Americans used it on the poor whites and poor blacks of the nineteenth and twentieth centuries. It's the old conquer by division trick and it has worked well here on Mars ever since the end of the Agricultural Rush.

"Most of those that we flippantly refer to as 'vermin' are not in that position because of their own choice. Most of them would sincerely love to put in an honest day's work and take home money that they've earned instead of having it handed to them by the government. But they cannot. There simply are not enough jobs under this system that we have. And every year, the unemployment rate grows worse and worse as the corporations merge and adjust and adapt cost cutting measures in a quest for more profits. How long will it be before we reach forty percent unemployment? How long until four out of every ten people on this planet are called vermin? Not very long if we go on like this. Not very long at all.

"And how, you may ask me, does WestHem and the corporations perpetuate this class struggle between the welfare and the working? I've told you the why, but what about the how? It's quite simple really. They already have human nature working on their side, human nature that just loves to find a group of people that one's own group can hate. All they really have to do is take something from the more advantageous of the two classes and give it to the lesser. In this case I'm talking about welfare money. Working class tax dollars, already outrageously high in comparison to what upper class and corporations pay, is used to buy food, housing, alcohol and marijuana, health insurance, and lawyer insurance for the welfare recipients. It is used to give them their bimonthly allotments of spending money. Now this act in and of itself is not really a bad thing. We *should* help those that are disadvantaged. But what it does, is cast a stigma on the welfare class and cause resentment among the working class. This resentment is turned to hatred when the prices of food and clothing and housing are raised without a corresponding increase in working class salaries. The working class are forced to struggle to survive, working hard every day just to make enough to keep their children fed and their rent paid and they are given no assistance whatsoever in their endeavor. In a way, they are made to feel punished because they work. At the same time, the welfare class are handed everything they need and are discouraged from even looking for work. They are taken care of as far as basic needs, but they are forced to endure prejudice and mistreatment by police officers, healthcare workers, and others that they deal with in their lives.

"People, this has got to stop! If we're going to be successful in gaining our independence, the welfare and the working classes are going to have to work together. Hospitals, doctors, nurses, you need to stop treating people differently because of their employment status and what kind of health insurance they have. If you participate in this prejudice, you are helping the corporations keep us down. Police officers, teachers, transit workers, you need to stop treating the welfare class differently than you do people with jobs. They are human beings just like yourself and they are *Martians*, the descendants of those who came to this planet to escape from the squalor of Earth. Just because your family has somehow managed to escape from this engineered squalor so far, you do not need to look down upon and mistreat those whose families have not. The welfare class do not choose to be put on welfare, they do not enjoy taking our handouts, but they simply have no other choice in this world that has been created for us."

"Fuckin A!" Jeff cried, sitting up a little straighter. "That bitch really knows how to tell it. And to think, I blew her off a couple months ago as just another scumbag politician."

"I always told you she was different," Matt said, sipping from his bottle. "I'm starting to think that she just might pull this independence bid off. After all, she's beaten the corporations at every turn so far."

"So far," Jeff agreed. "She's got a long haul ahead of her, but maybe she will."

"And what if she does?" Belinda asked sourly, her words thick and slurred from the two bottles of Fruity that she'd swallowed while cooking. "What if this bitch that everyone's talking about actually does manage to get us independent? Do you really think anything is going to change around here? We'll still be unemployed vermin living off of welfare money and drinking this crappy brew that they make out of apple piss."

Jeff usually ignored his wife when she talked. If he was forced to acknowledge her at all, it was usually in an argumentative tone. This time however, he spoke calmly to her. "So, what if nothing does change?" he asked her.

"What?" she asked, not grasping what he was talking about.

"What if Laura Whiting takes over and everyone's worst fear comes true and she turns out to be some Adolph Hitler fascist dictator who only wanted to rule the fuckin world? So, what if that happens? Would we be any worse off than we are right now?"

"That's not the point," Belinda said.

"It *is* the point," he told her. "I personally don't think that anything is going to come of this shit. I think that WestHem is going to find a way to get rid of her pretty soon and everything is going to go back to the way it always has been. But right now, she's tweaking some serious sack among those WestHem fucks and I love every goddamn minute of it. And if there's the slightest chance that we might have our miserable lives improved by what she's doing, shouldn't we support her? Shouldn't we help if we can?"

Belinda shook her head in disgust. "You're getting as bad as your friend there," she told him. "Talking about improvement and independence and shit like that. I guess three generations as vermin hasn't taught you much. Wait 'til you're five generations in like me."

"Fuck off," he told her. "You don't understand shit. Why don't you go finish up that slop you're cooking?"

She did so, after only a minor argument to the contrary. In truth, Jeff thought that even Belinda was feeling some hope despite her cynical blabbering to the contrary. Wasn't she always coming in and out of the room when Whiting was speaking, pretending not to be interested but keeping one ear tuned to the screen? Wasn't she always looking through MarsGroup articles regarding the latest Whiting exploits and then pushing them to the background if he happened to come in the room? Belinda's attitude was typical among many of the welfare class. They pretended to be disinterested because they wanted to be able to say "I told you so" if Whiting ultimately failed.

Matt ate dinner with the Creeks, something he did several nights a week, and then, after fortifying themselves with another bottle of Fruity apiece, the two friends donned their darkest clothing and headed out of the building to perform what had become their favorite activity over the last month. They took with them a can apiece of industrial spray paint that they had shoplifted from the welfare mart and they walked through the darkened streets towards the downtown area. They moved beneath the glass roof, a canopy of billions of brightly burning stars visible in the gaps between high rises. Sticking to the sidewalks and walking as close to the buildings as they could get, it took them twenty minutes to reach their target area: a lower-end commercial district on the border between the Heights and downtown. The streets here were lined with shopping complexes and moderate rent office buildings. Since businesses and office buildings (intoxicant shops excepted) were all closed this time of night, there were very few people out and about.

"How about there?" Jeff asked, pointing at the entrance to the FurnitureCorp building. This was a 114-story tower that housed the administration of much of the planet's rent-to-own furniture industry, an industry that preyed heavily upon the Martian welfare class and working poor. It was, of course, owned and operated by Earthlings.

"Nobody's tagged it yet," Matt said with a smile. "Fuckin amazing. Let's do it."

They walked down the street, moving casually, as if they weren't the least bit interested in their surroundings. In reality they were using their peripheral vision to scan all around them, their street senses searching for cops, witnesses, or anyone else that they didn't want or expect to see. Except for a few bums sleeping in the street planters, there was no one. As they passed the entrance to the building, they saw a guard sitting behind a desk inside but no one else. The guard was a Martian, as were all security guards on the planet, and probably nothing to worry about. Experience had already taught them that security guards—the closest working people to vermin in stature—would happily look the other way on this kind of mission. The security cameras at the front of the building were something else though. Matt got the first one. Though it was four meters up, he was able to hit it with a blast of his spray can by jumping up and twisting around before firing. This was a well-practiced technique, garnered from basketball skills, designed to blind the camera without allowing it to get a digital shot of his face first.

"Good one," Jeff said, impressed. "You're getting better at that." He then proceeded to do the second camera, walking towards it with his head hunched down until the last second. He jumped, twisted in mid-air, and gave a pinpoint blast of red paint right on the lens. A direct shot. Now that both cameras were out of action, it was time to go to work.

On the thick plexiglass of the building front, they each painted their epitaphs. Using broad strokes of the can, Matt wrote FREE MARS in red letters nearly a meter high. He double-underlined it for effect. Jeff's writing was a little more artistic. In calligraphic script he wrote: EARTHLINGS GO HOME. The guard inside of the building clearly saw them doing this but ignored their actions completely except for a slight grin and a quick thumbs up. He would pretend to discover the vandalism later on in his shift.

"Goddamn, this is fun," Jeff said as they headed down the street in search of another target. "It's almost as fun as running dust over from the greenhouse supply yards."

It took them awhile to find another target to hit. It was not that there were no corporate owned buildings to deface, it was that most of them had already been tagged several times. FREE MARS, EARTHLINGS GO HOME, FUCK ALL EARTHLINGS, AUTOMONY NOW, and FUCK THE CORPORATIONS were the dominant mottos seen, painted in varying heights and colors on the fronts of nearly every building. Persistence soon paid off and they found the Caldwell Building, home of the fourth largest lawsuit insurance provider in WestHem. The front windows here were agreeably clean, just begging for a fresh coat of anti-Earthling epitaphs. They provided them and then went out in search of yet another building, a quest they were successful in six blocks over at the Logiburn and Meyers high rise, home to the sixth largest law firm on Mars.

After defacing the law firm's front windows, they moved north along the street, searching for another target. They made it about three blocks before hearing the electric hum of police carts approaching from behind them. Veterans of police shakedowns, both knew instantly, just by the speed they were traveling, that they were going to stop them. Both instinctively looked around for an escape route out of the area—an alley or a maintenance access road that they could run to and make their escape. There were none in easy reach. It seemed that these cops knew what they were doing, not making their approach until their quarry was well out in the open.

"Oh shit," Matt said, resigned. He was very nervous. They had been defacing corporate buildings after all, an act that would have gained them prison time not too long before. Was it possible that the rumors that they had heard about the cops looking the other way about such things were wrong? It sure seemed so since they were about to stop them.

"Just be static," Jeff said as the two carts pulled to a stop behind them. "Maybe we can talk our way out of this shit."

The four doors of the two carts clanked open and four helmeted, armored Eden police officers stepped out, all of them slipping their tanners into their belts. The cop closest to them—the name badge on his armor identified him as Broward—took two steps towards them. Like any ghetto inhabitants worth their salt, Jeff and Matt pretended not to notice them and kept walking.

"Hold up a second there, you two," Broward said, taking a few more steps closer, his entire body braced to run after them if they tried to make a break for it.

They stopped and turned to face them, tough but neutral expressions upon their face. Both kept their hands at their sides, well clear of the holstered guns they carried under their shirts. Broward looked them up and down and then stepped even closer, his own hand resting on the butt of his tanner. His entourage followed behind him, spreading out a bit to provide cover.

"What are you two doing out here tonight?" Broward asked them.

"Nothin," they both muttered, giving the standard ghetto answer to such an inquiry.

"Nothing huh?" he said, looking from one to the other. "We got a report that a couple of guys were going around the neighborhood spray-painting things on buildings. You wouldn't happen to know anything about that, would you?"

"No," Matt said, shaking his head.

"Haven't seen nothin like that," Jeff said.

"Really now?" Broward said. "The report identified these people as gang member looking types, very out of place in this part of town. They're reported to have Capitalist tattoos on their arms, kind of like the ones you two are sporting."

Knowing that they were caught, both Jeff and Matt simply shrugged. What else was there to do? In a minute they would be taken into custody and hauled down to the booking area for processing. It was something that both had gone through several times before, although never for crimes against corporations.

"What's that all over your hands?" Broward asked them next.

They looked at their hands, seeing that they were obviously splattered with paint residue. "I was painting some furniture earlier," Matt said sarcastically. "I forgot to wash up."

"Me too," Jeff put in. "Water don't run too good in the Heights buildings. You know how it is."

"Yeah," Broward said, nodding his head a little. "I heard that about them buildings. So, what are you two doing in this part of town? Just taking a little walk to enjoy the night?"

"That's right," Jeff said.

"We like the night," said Matt.

The cop continued to look them up and down for a moment, his blue eyes piercing. Finally, he nodded, as if satisfied. "Good enough then," he said. "I guess you've explained yourselves."

"Couldn't be our guys," one of the other cops said.

"Nope," said another. "Just some furniture painters out for a walk in the commercial district. Our mistake."

"Huh?" Matt said, confused, wondering what sort of game they were playing.

Apparently, they were not playing a game however. "You two have yourselves a nice night," Broward told them. "We apologize for the inconvenience. And if you see any gang member types going around and painting graffiti on corporate buildings, you give us call, okay?"

"Yes," said one of the others. "That's certainly a crime that we need to stamp out."

"Umm... sure..." Matt said, thinking that this was the most bizarre experience he had ever had. "We'll uh... do that."

Broward gave them a little two-fingered salute. With that, all four of them walked back to their patrol carts, their tanners clanking, and got inside. A moment later they were driving off, their taillights fading quickly with distance.

"Holy shit," Jeff said, watching them go. "Did that really just happen?"

"I think it did," Matt agreed blankly, still unable to believe that they were still standing there after being pretty much caught red handed. They hadn't even scanned them! They hadn't even asked them to lay derm on a screen for identification!

They stood there for more than two minutes, looking at the empty street, their brains trying to convince them that they had just hallucinated the entire episode. "Well," Matt finally said, "shall we carry on?"

"I guess so," Jeff said.

They began to walk again, looking for their next target.

*****

Stanley Clinton had been the director of the Federal Law Enforcement Bureau for nearly ten years. As such, he was accustomed to occasionally briefing the WestHem executive council—that group of nine elected representatives that had replaced the single-person presidency shortly after World War III—on various security issues. Never however, had he dreaded a briefing as much as this one.

He had flown from the rooftop of the FLEB building in downtown Denver, the WestHem capital city, in his private, computer operated VTOL craft, landing after a ten-minute flight on the restricted back lawn of the capital building itself. From there, he had been escorted inside of the 220 story triangular high-rise, the tallest building on planet earth, and up to the 218th floor, where the executive briefing room was located.

The briefing room was not very large, but it was opulently furnished with genuine oak tables and chairs and top of the line Internet screens equipped with the very best encryption gear available. The window on the western exposure looked out upon the snow capped peaks of the Rocky Mountains, which were starkly visible in the clear air. Denver had once been one of the smoggiest cities in the nation but smog was now a thing of the distant past thanks to fusion power and hydrogen burning engines.

Only two of the executive council members were present for Clinton's briefing. John Calvato, who represented to eastern North American district of WestHem, and, at three-quarters of the way through his second six-year term, the senior member. As such, he carried more power than the other members and was accorded with the title *Chief Executive Councilperson*. Like all council members, he was tall, physically attractive, and a good actor for the Internet cameras. He was also a third generation billionaire, something that was an unofficial requirement for the highest office. His chief sponsors on the election circuit were AgriCorp, who owned six of the nine members, and CompWest, WestHem's primary computer software developer.

The other member present for the briefing was Loretta Williams, a first termer in her early fifties. She was one of the junior members, but was the elected councilperson that was supposedly representing Mars (as well as Ganymede and the Pacific Islands of Earth) although she had only been there once and had never been a resident. She too was owned lock, stock, and barrel by AgriCorp and the other food production corporations, having received more than a billion dollars in campaign contributions and other handouts from them over the years of her career. It was

Williams who would present the official federal government face to the growing crisis on Mars. Already she had been on Internet multiple times stating, in no uncertain terms, that Laura Whiting was a corrupt, possibly mentally ill person and that the WestHem government would not now and never would in the future consider negotiating independence with the Martians. "That planet is a part of this great nation," she had been quoted as saying. "It is WestHem that colonized and built that planet and it is WestHem business interests that have paid for everything that is present there. Mars is a part of our union, as much a part as Cuba and Argentina and Ganymede, and they always will be."

That was the official WestHem line on the Martian situation, a line that the corporations who had put the politicians where they were insisted upon. It was a line that Clinton and the sixteen thousand FLEB agents under his command would uphold to the death. It was a line that the big three were feeding the people on Earth and were attempting to feed the people on Mars.

"Welcome, Mr. Clinton," Williams said with an accommodating smile as he entered the room and closed the door behind him. "How was your trip over?"

"It was fine, Madam Councilperson," he said with a slight smile. "The air was very still today, hardly any turbulence to speak of. And the secret service was particularly fast about clearance for landing."

"That's nice to hear," she said. "Sometimes they are a bit too diligent in their duties. Won't you sit down?"

He sat down. Williams exchanged a few more pleasantries with him, most having to do with his family and his office. She then congratulated him on his ongoing campaign against the scourge of software piracy and illegal music file duplication. Since being appointed as director, convictions for those most heinous crimes had increased by more than eighteen percent, as had the prison terms handed out for them. Through this all, Calvato simply sat in place, a frowning, irritated expression upon his face, his brown eyes boring into the FLEB director.

"Now then," Williams said once the preliminaries were taken care of, "about this Laura Whiting situation."

"Yes Ma'am," Clinton said with a nod.

"I don't believe I have to tell you that some very important people are becoming increasingly upset about her continued presence in that capital building. It has been more than four months now since she showed us just what kind of person she was; four months and she is still in office, still riling up those greenies into a fury, and still getting on the Internet twice a week shouting about independence. Can you explain this, Mr. Clinton? Because frankly, we on the council and some of our more important constituents are starting to wonder if perhaps a new FLEB director would be able to handle things more efficiently."

"I understand their concern," Clinton said without hesitation. "And I understand how it may seem that we in the bureau are not doing our jobs. To tell you the truth, I never imagined that it would take this long to make Laura Whiting go away, but she has proven to be very crafty to this point. Obviously, this little independence game is something that she has been planning for years. And her manipulation of the Martian people, well that is quite simply an ability that we had not factored into our equations. What we have on Mars right now is the unsavory reality that the elected representatives of the planet are actually ignoring those who have sponsored them and instead are responding to the demands of the common people."

"That is unacceptable," Calvato said, speaking for the first time. "Having the ignorant greenies making the decisions on that planet is putting at risk trillions of dollars in investments."

"We understand that, sir," Clinton said. "And believe me when I say that we are working as hard as we can to reverse this before it gets any further. As I said, the problem is that Whiting has managed to anticipate and neutralize all of our traditional means of removing a troublesome politician." He then went on to explain everything that had been attempted so far: the criminal investigations of bribery, the media smear campaign, even the assassination plot, and how they had all failed. Williams and Calvato did not seem terribly impressed with his explanations.

"All that we've heard here are excuses," Williams told him. "What we need is action, and quickly. The problem has now spread beyond Laura Whiting. The greenies themselves are on the verge of getting out of control. We have reports that they are distributing fliers on apartment doors about independence, that they are spray-painting epitaphs on corporate buildings. How long will it be until they start rioting in the streets? How long will it be before they start doing more damage to corporate property than mere graffiti? I can even foresee them trying to arrange some sort of general strike or something like that. I don't have to tell you what that could do to the profits of the various WestHem interests on that planet."

"No Ma'am, you don't," he said humbly.

"You need to start cracking down on those greenies," Williams said. "I expect you to continue working on the Whiting problem, which is the root of the matter after all, but these greenies need to have the fear of God put in them, they need to be shown that following and responding to such an obvious madwoman is not in their best interests."

"Crack down on the greenies, Ma'am?" he asked slowly, knowing instinctively that this was a very bad idea and also knowing that neither Williams nor anyone else on the council had been the one to come up with it. No, cracking down sounded like the sort of thing that corporate heads such as Steve Carlson of AgriCorp would come up with. To a man used to operating a huge business and corrupting politicians, this would seem the logical course to follow when people were not doing as they were told. After all, it worked with middle management and blue-collar workers didn't it? It worked with politicians (except for Laura Whiting and the Martian planetary legislature) didn't it? Why wouldn't it work with common people? With vermin? And if the idea had come from the corporate heads, the executive council would not be swayed from this course. Being swayed from a direct order by Carlson or his companions would mean that they risked be cracked down upon.

"You heard me correctly," Williams told him. "We want your agents on Mars to let those greenies know, in no uncertain terms, that these acts of defiance against our business interests will not be tolerated. We want them thrown in jail and held there!"

"We've tried that," Clinton said. "The problem is that graffiti and so forth are crimes against the planet, not the federal government. This puts them under the jurisdiction of the planetary criminal justice system: the local police and the local judges. These people are all greenies. And while we'd always considered the judges and lawyers and police chiefs to be... well... reliable, it seems that we were wrong about that. They are simply not taking action against these crimes. I have even received reports that police officers have caught the perpetrators red-handed and just let them go. We are having the same problems with assaults against the managers and officers of the corporations."

"If they're not federal crimes, then you *make* them federal crimes," Williams told him. "You call it terrorism or treason or whatever you want, but you have your agents on Mars start making some arrests. Get the word out on that planet that the feds are now involved in this fight and you get it out quickly, with action. If you start hauling these radical elements off and extraditing them to Earth for trial, I guarantee you that those greenies will think twice about being so vocal or so artistic."

"These are extreme times," Calvato said. "And extreme measures are called for."

"Yes sir, yes Ma'am," Clinton replied, not showing the dread he was feeling at these orders.

"We expect this to be done immediately," Williams said. "And remember, the removal of Laura Whiting is still the highest of your priorities. Get rid of her by whatever means is necessary. Whatever means! If you do not, we'll be getting rid of you."

"Yes Ma'am," he said.

The meeting went on for a while longer—closing pleasantries were required by protocol after all—but that was really what had needed to be said. Soon, Clinton was escorted from the building and back out to his VTOL on the lawn.

"Enjoy your flight, sir," the secret service agent that had been his escort told him as he climbed into the cockpit of the aircraft.

"Right," he said sourly, closing the canopy and settling into his seat. He strapped in and then put his finger to the computer screen below the windshield.

The computer analyzed his fingerprint and, after concluding that he was an authorized user of the craft, lit up with the opening display. "Good afternoon, Director Clinton," it told him politely. "Awaiting command."

"Flight mode," he told it. "Destination: FLEB building, Denver."

"Warm up sequence beginning," it replied, the hydrogen turbine engines mounted on the wings immediately flaring to life with a hum. The propellers, which were currently in the take-off/landing position, facing upward, began to turn. Clinton felt cool air from the ventilation system blowing on his face.

He sat back in his seat and tried to relax while the computer sent the aircraft through a preflight systems and hardware check and obtained authorization for take-off from the Secret Service air traffic computer system. The authorization was given after only a two-minute wait and the engines wound up to high RPMs for take-off. The aircraft lifted into the sky a moment later, rising slowly to an altitude of one thousand meters above the ground before the engines tilted forward, changing the angle of the propellers and imparting forward flight. Guided by detailed mapping software and an extensive system of global positioning satellites, it darted and banked over the downtown Denver area, automatically avoiding other such aircraft and finally settling down to a soft landing on the roof of the FLEB building five minutes later.

Clinton climbed out and made his way to a secured, private elevator. Two minutes later he was back in his office, loosening his tie and staring at his computer screen. He had one of his staff bring him a stiff bourbon and coke and then called up his communications software.

"This will be a priority message for Corban Hayes, director of Martian field operations."

"Record when ready," the machine told him.

He began to talk, laying out a set of instructions for his underling that were very much against his better judgment.

*****

Two days later, in Eden, Lisa and Brian were working a patrol shift in the downtown area. Their call volume had been much lower over the past month than they were accustomed to and those calls that they did go to seemed to be less violent and less sordid. Once there, they had found themselves being subjected to an increasingly dwindling amount of physical and verbal abuse by the welfare class citizens that they dealt with. Though both were hardened, cynical veterans of patrol services, they could think of no other explanation for the drop in crime and abuse than Laura Whiting and her speeches. It seemed that the vermin were taking her words to heart.

"It's eerie in a way," Lisa said as they drove slowly down the daylight streets of the ghetto section of downtown. "Nobody's flipping us off, nobody's grabbing their crotch, nobody's throwing empty Fruity bottles at us. What's the planet come to?"

"They don't love us anymore," Brian said, watching the throngs of vermin that were hanging out on every planter box, in front of every public housing building. They were all doing the usual vermin things—drinking Fruity, smoking from marijuana pipes, watching porno shows on their PCs—but most of them were completely ignoring the passing police cart. A few even waved at them, something that had been so unusual as to be unheard of not long before. As Lisa had said, it was eerie in a way. It was like everyone had been given some sort of happy gas.

"Incoming call," said the dash-mounted computer, which was linked to the dispatch system via cellular technology. A second later, rows of text appeared on the screen, describing their latest assignment.

"What is it?" asked Lisa, who was behind the wheel.

"A request to assist a FLEB team on a takedown," he said.

"A FLEB team?" Lisa said in disgust. Assisting FLEB agents in apprehension of federal criminals was not a common thing, but it was not exactly uncommon either. "Those assholes? What do they got this time? Another bunch of software pirates?"

"It doesn't say," he told her, reading through the rest of it. "The staging location is over at 101st and Broadway. They sent over Delta-53 and Bravo-56 as well."

"Three patrol units to help take down someone?" Lisa said, shaking her head a little. "That's a lot of guns for a software pirate."

"Big waste of our time if you ask me," he replied, pushing the acknowledge button on the terminal. "Why can't those federal fucks take care of their own pick-ups?"

"They need someone to tell them how to do it, don't they?" she replied, making both of them chuckle. It was a well known fact that the FLEB agents, though sworn law enforcement officers and despite a tough guy reputation garnered by Internet shows, were severely lacking when it came to street sense and tactical matters. It was said in Martian law enforcement circles that the average FLEB agent couldn't find Phobos with a telescope and a tracking computer.

The trip to 101st and Broadway took about five minutes. When they arrived there, they found two black FLEB vans parked outside in a truck-loading zone behind a low rent apartment complex. The FLEB vans were electric panel trucks with the emblem of their agency stenciled on the sides. Both Lisa and Brian were amused to see that someone had spray-painted FREE MARS on the side of one of them in bright red paint. Standing outside of the vans were ten agents, all of them dressed in heavy Kevlar armor gear and carrying M-24 rifles. They looked a little like accountants playing dress up for a Halloween party. One of them walked over to the police cart as it parked, approaching on the passenger side.

"What's up?" Brian asked, opening his door but not stepping out.

"Special agent Walker," the man introduced himself. He was in his late forties and spoke with a heavy Earthling accent. "I'm in charge of this strike team today."

"Static," Brian answered, deliberately thickening his own Martian accent. "What's the deal? Got some software pirates or something you need to take down?"

"No," he said with a shake of the head. "Not pirates. Terrorists."

Brian shared a look of puzzlement with Lisa. "Terrorists?" he asked. "What kind of terrorists?"

"A whole group of them," he said. "Violent Martian separatists. We have information that they're planning to plant explosives near federal installations here on the planet."

"Explosives?" Lisa asked incredulously. "Where the hell would vermin get explosives?"

"That's what we're going to find out," Walker assured them. "Our information is that there are at least six of them up there, maybe more. They may be armed."

"Everybody's armed on Mars," Brian said. "This is a WestHem colony. Home of the right to bear arms, remember?"

"Right," Walker said. "That's why we wanted you locals here with us. We just want the back-up in case we need it. We'll move in as soon as the other two units get here."

Brian and Lisa shared another look. "Uh... just what sort of information do you have that leads you to believe there are terrorists up there?" Lisa asked.

"Sorry," Walker told her. "That's confidential. Anyway, they're up on the 93rd floor of the building here, apartment 9312. We have a door breach and the plan is to just go in and strike and then get out. Be sure to grab your M-24s when we go up."

"Do we have a warrant for all of this?" Brian asked.

"Yes, we do," he told them. "A federal magistrate signed one out less than an hour ago."

"A *federal* warrant huh?" Lisa said.

"That's right," Walker told her. "Is there a problem with that? If so, we can always contact your watch commander to rectify it."

She scowled at his thinly veiled threat. "It's your show, Mr. Walker," she said, reaching under her seat and unclipping her M-24 from its holder.

The other two patrol units arrived a few minutes later and, after they were briefed on the plan of action, everyone headed into the building. It was a typical public housing building and the lobby was full of the usual assortment of unemployed people sipping from Fruity bottles and smoking out. They all gave curious looks to the armed squad of feds and police officers but kept their distance. Walker, leading the parade, walked to the bank of elevators in the rear.

"Okay," he said to everyone. "Half of you take the left elevator and half of you take the right. Don't let any riders in as you go up and we'll assemble up on the 93rd. My maps show that 9312 is sixty meters to the south of the elevator bank. Any questions?"

None of the feds had any, but Lisa did. "Excuse me," she said. "I have a suggestion."

"What is it, officer?" he asked somewhat impatiently.

"Well, it's somewhat traditional in a case like this for everyone to assemble on the floor *above* where the target apartment is and then walk down the closest staircase. That way, you see, if your suspects have a lookout or just happen to be outside at that particular moment, they don't notice you gathering for the strike."

Walker considered that for a moment. "You know," he said brightly, "that's a good idea. Let's do it."

"Christ," Lisa mumbled to herself, resisting the urge to roll her eyes back. Her good idea was basic police academy training.

They did it, all of them riding up to 94 in two shifts. Once up there, they went to the back emergency staircase and down a flight. They passed several people in the halls and on the staircase itself, all of them giving an extremely wide berth to the group of armed and armored men and women.

Walker opened the staircase door on 93 and, after a quick, careless look, waved everyone forward into a hallway that was lined with gang graffiti and anti-Earthling sentiments. They all walked along behind him, their weapons clanking, their boots squeaking, until they reached the doorway labeled 9312. Walker and two of his men then prepared to breach the door.

"Look at these morons," Lisa said softly, without moving her lips. Her throat microphone transmitted her words only to the police officers in the group. "They're standing in front of the freakin door while they do that."

"What do they teach them in FLEB academy?" replied Scott James, one of the other real cops. "You'd think for a two year academy they'd be a little smarter than that."

"They're college educated you know," Brian put in. "I guess all of that higher learning pushes out the common sense."

While the cops all laughed among themselves about the sad tactical performance they were witnessing, Walker placed the door breach module against the power box of the door. The door breach was a device that sent out a strong but brief electromagnetic pulse, causing disruption of the locking mechanism on cheap automatic doors. It worked it's magic now and the door slid open about half an inch, just enough for another agent to put a crowbar into the gap. He began to pry, forcing the door the rest of the way open. Had the inhabitants of the apartment been armed and willing to, they could have easily gunned down several of the FLEB people since they were standing directly in the doorway instead of off to the side of it like real cops. But they were allowed to get away with it in this instance. With guns raised, the FLEB squad rushed inside, all of them screaming at the residents to get down but all of them using different phrases.

"Fucking morons," Lisa said again as she and Brian and the rest of the Eden police officers went through the doorway behind them, M-24s raised in the firing position.

The apartment was a two bedroom with a relatively large living room area. Some old furniture, all of it threadbare and falling apart, all of it undoubtedly from the welfare store or from a rent-to-own shop, was arranged symmetrically on the cheap carpet. On the table next to an Internet terminal was a commercial grade hard-copy printer that could churn out twenty to thirty sheets of hemp paper per minute. Pamphlets, presumably that had come out of the printer, were stacked everywhere, most of them in stacks of a hundred or so and fastened with rubber bands. On the front of them were the words: MARTIAN INDEPENDENCE – NOT JUST A DREAM!

The inhabitants of the apartment—two men and two women, all of them dressed in faded cheap shorts and shirts—were grabbed by their hair or clothing and shoved to the carpet by the FLEB agents. They were thrown roughly down and had steel-toed boots placed against their necks while other agents held the barrels of M-24s to their heads. They were all screaming and yelling, pleading with the black-outfitted agents to tell them what was going on.

"Shut the fuck up, greenie slime," Walker yelled at them, raising his boot and kicking one of the women in the side hard enough to make her gasp out her air.

Brian, Lisa, and the others looked on in shock at the treatment. Though they were no fans of vermin, and though they were all of the opinion that they were forced to be too gentle with those they arrested, the unprovoked violence that the FLEB agents were utilizing was appalling to them. What had these people done to deserve this?

"Get 'em cuffed up," Walker ordered his people. "I want them downstairs in the van right away."

The agents applied their cuffs to the various wrists and cinched them down brutally tight, causing actual bleeding in one of the men.

"Walker," Brian said, after witnessing this, "don't you think you're being a little rough here?"

Walker gave him a seething glare. "I am in charge of this operation," he replied. "I do not recall asking you for advice in how to handle my prisoners. If it's a little too much for you to take, you can just go back downstairs."

Brian glared back but said nothing. Soon Walker returned to his task.

The four men and women, all of them moaning and grunting, all of them still asking what they had done, were jerked rudely to their feet and pushed towards the doorway. Six of the FLEB agents went with them and led them down the hallway. This left Walker and three of his agents in addition to Brian, Lisa, and the others. The agents fanned out through the two bedrooms and the kitchen where they began dumping drawers out and upturning beds.

"You locals are dismissed now," Walker said to Brian. "Thanks for your help."

"What the hell is going on here?" Brian demanded. "Are you trying to tell me that those people were terrorists?"

"I'm not trying to tell you anything," Walker said. "They are charged with plotting to attack a federal building. They will be extradited to Earth for trial."

"Extradited to Earth?" Lisa said. "Why the hell would you do that? There's a federal court right here in Eden."

"It is felt that Martian jurors might not be... well... exactly impartial," Walker said. "Considering the recent events on this planet, it has been decided that all federal prisoners will be tried in Denver or Sau Paulo."

"Unbelievable," said one of the other cops, a six-year veteran of patrol services. "What kind of trial are they going to get on Earth?"

"A fair one," Walker said. "It's the WestHem way."

"And just where is the evidence that they were planning a bombing?" Brian asked. "All I see here are a bunch of leaflets about Martian independence. Those are protected under the first amendment of the WestHem constitution, are they not?"

"There will be evidence here somewhere," Walker assured them. "They'll have it on their computer files or in their bedroom. There will be something."

"This is not right," Lisa said. "What the hell are you feds trying to pull here?"

"We're not pulling anything," Walker said sternly. "We're just trying to keep some greenie vermin in line. You're cops, aren't you? Why the hell are you taking up for these slimebags? I'd think you'd be glad to get them off the streets."

"You thought wrong," Brian said. "They weren't doing anything but printing up fliers. What evidence did you have against them? What information did you use to get your warrant?"

"As I said before, that is not your concern. You folks are dismissed. Thank you for your assistance."

"Walker," Lisa started. "I think..."

"Don't think," he interrupted. "It doesn't suit your... *species*. You're dismissed. Leave my crime scene immediately or I'll have you charged with interference with a federal investigation."

*****

Lieutenant Margaret Duran was sitting behind a desk in the downtown substation, going over some reports that had been filed by her watch the previous shift. She was smoking a cigarette and sipping out of a bottle of water. Soft music issued from the speakers of her Internet terminal. She was in a good mood, as she had been prone to lately, and she hummed along with the melody as she worked. As a veteran watch commander, she was accustomed to dealing with some very sticky issues, both with the troops that she commanded and with the administrative cops that commanded her. Her position was somewhat of a buffer between the management of the police department and the labor that actually performed the work. Strife had always been present between these two groups as the working cops tried to do their jobs with what they'd been given and the captains and deputy chiefs tried to worship the gods of public opinion. But lately, since the push towards Martian independence had really started to take form, things had mellowed between these two groups quite a bit. Management was suddenly not as prone to making new, ever oppressive policies designed to break the backs of the working cops and keep them in line. And the cops were not as prone to slovenliness or morale problems as they had been, probably, in part anyway, because they weren't nearly as busy anymore. It was a strange but true phenomenon that crime had actually dropped significantly since the Whiting inauguration and the defeat of the impeachment movement. Could it be that for the first time, the Martian people were experiencing hope? Duran sometimes wondered if that was the case, and, as cynical and hardened as twenty-five years of Eden law enforcement had made her, she really could not come up with any other explanation.

"Incoming communication from four-delta-five-nine," her computer terminal suddenly spoke up, relaying a message from the dispatch computer. "Would you like to accept?"

Unit 4-D-59. That was Wong and Haggerty, two of her better cops. She took a moment to wonder why they would bypass their sergeant in the chain of command with whatever problem they had. It was a minor breach in protocol that possibly bespoke of a situation that they didn't think he could deal with on his own. Her happy mood faded just a tad. She had a pretty good idea of what the problem might be. Already some rumors from other parts of the department had filtered her way. "Put them on screen," she told the computer with a sigh.

Haggerty's face appeared a moment later, his eyes showing troublesome concern. "Sorry to bother you, el-tee," he said, "but there's something that I think we should talk to you about."

"No problem," she said. "What's up?"

"It might be better," he suggested, "if we could meet face to face. I don't really want to put it out on the airwaves. No hurry, just if you get a chance to get out on the streets this shift..."

"I'll be right out," she told him, knowing that it was best not to put requests like that off. "All I was doing was looking over these atrocities you people call reports anyway. How about 35th Street and 6th Avenue, in the loading area of the Schuyler building? That's where the night shift cops like to hide and sleep, isn't it?"

Brian chuckled a little. "I wouldn't know anything about that, lieutenant," he said. "But I know the place. We'll be there in about ten minutes."

Duran saved her work on the computer and then stood up from her chair and stretched for a moment, relieving some of the pain in her aching back. She walked to the corner of the office and picked up her armor vest, slipping it over her shoulders and fastening it into place. She then donned her helmet, which had her rank emblem stenciled on the front of it, and activated her exterior radio link. "This is watch commander 5-alpha," she told the dispatch computer through the link. "I'll be out in the field for a bit."

"Watch commander 5-alpha out in the field," the computer acknowledged.

A short walk brought her to the cart parking area of the building. She climbed into the non-descript cart that was assigned to the lieutenants of the downtown district and drove out through the secured gate that guarded access to the building. She wound her way through the crowded downtown streets and, five minutes later, pulled into the wide unloading zone behind the Schuyler building. The patrol cart belonging to Wong and Haggerty was already there waiting for her. She pulled up next to them and rolled down her window. "Hi, guys," she greeted, lifting the visor on her helmet.

"Thanks for coming, el-tee," Haggerty said, flipping his own visor up. "We're really sorry to bother you and all."

"Don't sweat it," she said. "It's what they pay me the big bucks for. So, what's the problem?"

"Well," Haggerty told her, seemingly unsure how to describe his dilemma, "we just got done with an assist call for some FLEB agents."

"FLEB agents huh?" she said, her suspicions about what this had to do with effectively confirmed.

"A whole shitload of FLEB agents," Wong said. "Ten of them."

"And let me guess," she said. "This was not to go pick up a couple of music or software pirates, was it?"

"No," Haggerty said. "It wasn't." He then went on to describe the experience that they had had in the public housing building.

Duran listened intently and with growing alarm as she was told of the brutality that the FLEB agents had employed in the takedown of the suspected "terrorists". Kicking arrestees in the head? Calling them greenies? Cinching the cuffs down tight enough to cause bleeding? In this world ruled by lawyers and their abuse of force lawsuits, these were shocking actions indeed, events that would have led to a prison sentence had an Eden cop performed them.

"But the violence was just one thing," Wong said when Haggerty was done. "Those people weren't doing anything illegal! All they were doing was printing up pamphlets to distribute on people's doors. The same kind I got on my door the other day! There were no explosives in there, hell, I didn't even see any guns."

"And you never saw the warrant that they had?" Duran asked them.

"They wouldn't discuss it," said Haggerty. "Every time we asked them about their evidence or their warrant, they told us it wasn't our concern. Finally, they threatened us with arrest if we didn't clear out of there. When we got back downstairs the people that they'd arrested were already gone."

"Have those people lost their freaking minds?" Wong asked. "How could they do something like that? How can they get away with it?"

Duran sighed. "You're not the only ones that have had this problem," she told them.

"No?" Wong asked, raising her eyebrows.

"I haven't heard anything solid yet, but I've heard rumors that a few other watch commanders throughout the city had some similar meetings with their patrol teams and have been told similar tales. It seems that the FLEB is cracking down on the more vocal anti-Earthling elements."

"What are we going to do about it?" Haggerty demanded. "Lieutenant, I don't ever want to go on one of those raids again. I mean, I never liked helping those pricks take down someone who copied software on their computer, but at least *that* is against the law. This was something that's protected by the fucking constitution. And vermin or not, those people did not deserve to be treated like that."

Duran sighed. "If this would've happened a few months ago," she said, "I would've been forced to tell you that you were stuck. But times have changed in the last few months, haven't they?"

"They sure have," Haggerty agreed. "And it looks like those corporate pricks are sending their pet thugs after because of it."

"That's my take on it," she said. "So, here's what I'm going to do. I'm going to give you permission to refuse to take part in any FLEB assistance call if they will not show you the warrant and the writ they used to obtain it. If they do show it to you and it looks funky, you have continued permission to refuse to participate."

Haggerty and Wong looked at her wide-eyed. She understood the source of her awe. She had just taken it upon herself to make a broad reaching decision about cooperation with the FLEB. Again, this was something that she wouldn't have dreamed of before the Laura Whiting inauguration. But as she had told her subordinates, times were different now. She suspected that her decision would be backed up by her captain and by the deputy chief above him. She suspected that she might even be applauded for making it.

"Do you have a problem with my orders?" she asked them, hiding a smile.

"No, lieutenant," Wong said. "Not at all."

"Good," she said. "I'll have it shipped to all the patrol units on my watch as well. Report any incidents with FLEB agents to me immediately. In the meantime, I guess I should go arrange a meeting with Deputy Chief Durham, shouldn't I?"

*****

All over the planet that day, teams of FLEB agents fanned out and made arrests of people they called terrorists. They went out in teams of five or ten, in one or two black vans, always with armor and automatic weapons, and usually with teams of unsuspecting local police along as back-up. They breached door after door in welfare and working class apartment buildings alike, throwing to the ground those they found inside and hauling them away to local FLEB offices. In most cases the "terrorists" that they arrested were those that had been printing pamphlets or who had been the organizers of the recall drives that had threatened the legislature. In each case the warrants used were from the local federal magistrate instead of a superior court judge and in each case the writ that was used to obtain the warrant was not shown to any assisting police officers.

The evening news channels all featured the sweeps as their top stories. This included both the big three Internet channels and the MarsGroup channels, although their respective takes on the subject were somewhat different. On the big three stations, the newscasters would announce how the diligent and overworked FLEB agents of the various cities had wrapped up a complex and far-reaching terrorist conspiracy investigation by arresting hundreds of alleged terrorists in a coordinated sweep. Video clips would be shown in which scruffy, unshaven Martians were being led out of housing buildings and placed in the FLEB vans with others. Agents were interviewed from each head office and they would describe the "terrorist writings" and "other, more dangerous items" they had uncovered in their search. They described intricate plots that these terrorists were engaged in to blow up federal buildings, spaceports, even the Martian capital itself. The implication was that

Laura Whiting and a few of her consorts were behind these groups. While it was true that not very many Martians watched these broadcasts (or believed them if they did), they were beamed to Earth and viewed by the WestHem citizens there. On Earth, the reaction was blind outrage that radical Martians were getting away with such things.

On the MarsGroup stations however, the reports were a little different. Outraged Martian reporters went on camera to inform the public that innocent citizens executing their constitutional right to free speech and assembly were being dragged away by federal agents. Police officers that had been present at the raids were interviewed (in all cases with the blessings of their department brass) and they described the brutality they had observed as well as the lack of any tangible evidence. A senior reporter on the most popular of the MarsGroup channels demanded of the Earthlings to disclose the evidence that the arrestees were being held under. "Let's see the warrants," she demanded. "Let's see the writs that brought forth those warrants. And most important of all, let's see the evidence against these people that justifies their extradition from our planet!" Laura Whiting herself appeared in a special segment demanding much the same answers from federal authorities. She described the FLEB as "fascist SS troops" bent on destroying the separatist movement that was underway. "They're trying to intimidate you, fellow Martians," she warned the people. "They're trying to intimidate you into dropping this great cause. Don't let them be successful."

By the time the sun set over the Martian cities that night, the populace was in a state of near rebellion. This state was intensified the next morning when MarsGroup shots of the arrestees being marched onto surface to orbit ships bound for Triad and eventually Earth were aired. At ten o'clock Eden time, Chief Robert Daniels of the Eden Police Department gave a press conference in which he announced that his department would immediately cease cooperation with the Federal Law Enforcement Bureau. "We will offer no further assistance in the rounding up of what seems to be innocent Martian civilians. We will provide no back-up, no tactical advice, no computer searches, nothing, unless they can provide our administration with detailed arrest writs and proper warrants." By eleven o'clock that morning, three other police departments, including the New Pittsburgh police, had made similar announcements. By noon, all of them had.

This did not stop the FLEB from conducting more raids however. By the end of office hours Eden time, more than sixty more Martians had been taken from their homes and shuttled off to federal holding cells, all of them charged with inciting terrorism or conspiracy to commit terrorism. Most of these incidents were reported upon by MarsGroup stations, fueling the fire even more.

But the biggest event, the one that truly pushed the Martian people over the edge, occurred the following day in New Pittsburgh. A team of ten FLEB agents went to a welfare housing building on the east side of that city and breached an apartment door where six men and women were printing up some admittedly radical pamphlets calling for acts of violence against FLEB "storm troopers". These six people, members of a newly formed group that called themselves the Free Mars Society, saw their door being forced open and knew what it meant. They elected not to go quietly. Using the cheap handguns that nearly every ghetto inhabitant carried, they opened fire the moment the FLEB agents came through the door, aiming for the head and taking down two of them with shots to the face. The remaining FLEB force opened up with their M-24s, spraying bullets throughout the apartment and killing everyone, including a small child asleep in a crib.

The incident might have gone unnoticed or uncommented upon except for the fact that a MarsGroup reporter team had just happened to be in the neighborhood and had spotted the FLEB van parked outside of the building. The reporters and their camera managed to make it up to the apartment in question and get shots of the interior broadcast to their office before the remaining FLEB members took them into custody on incitement charges and smashed their equipment. The clip was played over and over again on the various MarsGroup channels, several times every hour. It was downloaded from MarsGroup Internet sites and emailed all around the planet. By the time the dinner hour fell, nearly everyone on Mars had seen it. When the Martian people saw the bullet riddled corpses of their fellow citizens and the black-suited and armored FLEB agents standing over them with their weapons, chaos erupted.

This chaos was fanned into fury that night by than Laura Whiting during her regular speech.

"These people are Nazis!" she yelled into the camera, her eyes blazing. "They come storming into private homes with automatic weapons, waving warrants that are shaky at best, and they act surprised when the people take up arms against them? While I do not advocate shooting it out with these FLEB thugs if they should happen to choose your apartment to raid, in truth, what is the option? Our people are being hauled off of their planet to Earth where they will be crucified in staged trials and sentenced to life in some shithole Earthling federal prison. I certainly understand why our citizens in New Pittsburgh, who were doing nothing more than executing their constitutional rights, elected to choose violence to combat this."

It was less than an hour after Whiting's broadcast that a riot erupted at the New Pittsburgh federal building in the downtown portion of that city. Hundreds of angry Martians, welfare and working class alike, gathered at all of the entrances and lay siege to the structure. They fired guns at the entrances, putting countless holes in the tempered plexiglass and badly damaging three of the doors. They painted profane words on the walls and doors—epitaphs that made EARTHLINGS GO HOME seem like a term of endearment. They smashed all of the security cameras and threw bottles of Fruity and AgriCorp juice, littering the entryways with broken glass.

They managed to get into the back lot of the building where they overturned and smashed six of the black vans that had been used to carry strike teams. Through it all, the terrified federal agents and employees barricaded themselves inside, the agents armed with M-24s but knowing that they would not be able to gun down everyone who tried to get them if the crowd somehow managed to make it inside.

The New Pittsburgh Police Department finally broke the riot up after more than two hours of desperate calls for assistance from inside the building. The NPPD officers fired no shots, used no tear gas, and made no threats to the crowd. They simply told them that enough was enough and asked them to give it a rest for the night. Surprisingly enough, the crowd complied, all of them throwing a few last bottles or firing a few last bullets and then wandering away towards the tram stations or their housing complexes. No arrests were made or even attempted and the federal employees actually witnessed some of the rioters shaking hands with the police officers.

Director Hayes, hearing of the event, placed an angry call to the chief of the NPPD, demanding an explanation for the delayed response of his officers and the lack of any arrests. The chief shrugged off the inquiry with a flippant remark and then disconnected him. Subsequent calls were not put through.

When the crowd began to gather outside the building on the next night, the FLEB agents reacted a little differently. This time they were expecting the rioters and they had brought in extra troops and weapons for the occasion. Forty agents, all of them in full gear and armed with M-24s, pushed out the doorway of the building once the crowd of Martians began to swell and surround them. They ordered them to disperse, pointing their weapons as they shouted this. The Martians held their ground and began to lob bottles and other debris, bouncing them off of helmets and armored vests and knocking several of the agents to their knees. No one ever knew who fired the first shot but, within seconds, the clattering of automatic weapons filled the air and Martians began to drop to the ground, blood flying from their bodies, heads exploding into brains and chunks of skull as the high velocity rounds ripped into them. The surviving rioters ran blindly away in a panic, a few of them returning fire with their handguns, but none of them causing a lethal wound. Soon, the streets were filled with New Pittsburgh police carts and dip-hoe carts, their crews horrified by the carnage that had resulted. The media, both MarsGroup and the big three, soon followed. The final toll would be 43 Martians killed and 34 wounded.

Laura Whiting made a special address the next morning, demanding an independent investigation into the incident. It was a request that was all but ignored by both the big three media giants and the FLEB themselves. Two days later, the FLEB office placed the blame for the shooting on the Martian rioters and the New Pittsburgh Police Department. No suspensions or disciplinary actions against any

FLEB agents occurred, a fact that was leaked to MarsGroup reporters by Martian clerical staff who worked for the FLEB. Within hours of the ruling, the entire planet knew about it.

The following day, the Martian people expressed their displeasure. The first incident occurred in New Pittsburgh, which was quickly becoming the focal point of much of the anti-fed movement. Two FLEB agents on a routine stakeout of a suspected "terrorist haven" were dragged from their van by an angry mob of Martian welfare class. They had their helmets and armor ripped from their bodies and they were beaten with their own firearms so severely that both were comatose when the police finally broke up the crowd. Though neither would die from their injuries, both would be medically retired because of the incident. No arrests were ever made.

A few hours later, in Libby on the equatorial plain, an entire ten-person team of agents about to conduct a strike were mobbed by a similar crowd as they waited for the elevators to arrive to take them up to their target. In this case, two of the agents were killed, shot through the head by their own weapons, and six were beaten badly enough to require hospitalization. Again, no arrests were made by the responding police officers.

Throughout that day and the next, many other, less severe incidents took place in all of the Martian cities as FLEB agents went out to their assignments and angry Martians reacted to the slaughter in New Pittsburgh. These incidents would send several agents to local hospitals and result in the deaths of three Martians. But the biggest incident of retaliation took place three days after the New Pittsburgh Slaughter—as it was being called—in Eden.

*****

"Incoming multiple agency response call," the dispatch computer said in its calm, cool, collected voice. A second later, rows of text appeared on the screen.

"What is it?" asked Lisa, who was behind the wheel of the cart on this day. It had been another slow shift and she was ready for a little action to break up the monotony. A multiple agency response meant that something big was going down.

"34th Street and 7th Avenue," Brian told her, reading from the screen. "Heavy smoke in the streets. Multiple calls from citizens, and the fire suppression systems have been activated at that intersection. Some of the call-ins seem to think a vehicle of some sort is burning."

"A vehicle huh?" Lisa said, turning the cart around and flipping on the emergency lights. "That could be nasty if it's a delivery truck carrying chemicals or something."

"Yep," Brian agreed, reaching under his seat and pulling out his gas mask.

In the enclosed environment of the Martian cities, fire was treated with considerably more respect than it was on Earth. On Mars, there was no outside to go to when things started to burn and the smoke had no natural way to escape from the area. Visibility would quickly be obliterated as smoke built up under the glass roof and people blocks away could easily be choked to death on noxious fumes if they were trapped in the vicinity. Though automatic fire suppression sprinklers were every twenty meters on the streets and every five meters in every building, they were good only for extinguishing minor blazes in the earliest stages of development. Major blazes, as this one seemed to be, based on the dispatch information, required the use of high-pressure water hoses and lots of manpower. For this reason, all public safety employees, the police included, were trained in firefighting and dispatched in large numbers whenever such an incident occurred.

"Holy shit," Brian said as they approached the area. "I guess something's burning all right." Though they were still six blocks away, a haze of black smoke was quickly accumulating up along the ceiling. It grew into a thick fog further down the street. Hundreds of people, many of them coughing and with soot on their faces, were rushing out of the area, making it difficult for Lisa to navigate the cart through them. "Computer," he asked, "are any units on scene yet?"

"Negative," the computer replied. "I'm showing you as the closest so far. The next-in unit should be DPHS unit Delta-7. They are currently at 53rd Street and 7th Avenue."

"Copy, thanks," Brian said. He turned to Lisa. "We'd better get our masks and goggles on. This shit is gonna get thick in a minute."

"Right," she agreed, reaching down and picking up her own mask.

They covered their faces with the gas masks, which were capable of filtering out all but oxygen and nitrogen from the environment. They then pulled their combat goggles down over their eyes, setting them for infrared enhancement, which would allow them to see through the smoke. It was fortunate that they did this because within seconds the smoke became so thick that visibility would have been impossible. The streets however, were now mostly empty of citizens. Martians knew their fire drills well, having been taught since birth that it was imperative to get into a nearby building in the event of a blaze on the street. Buildings in the vicinity were automatically sealed off and imparted with air pressure greater than the street level to keep the smoke out.

A block away from the incident, the actual flames became visible as a roaring red pyre in the infrared spectrum. Brian and Lisa could vaguely make out the source as a vehicle of some sort, possibly a panel truck. Their computer informed them that the heat was building up and that it was safe to go no further without protection. Lisa stopped the cart and they got out, going around to the back of it to remove their suppression suits, which were essentially coveralls made of bright yellow, synthetic, fire-proof material that did not conduct heat very well. As they put them on, Brian contacted the dispatch computer again. "Who's in command of this incident?" he asked.

"Battalion Chief 9 of DPHS," the computer told him. "She is still several kilometers away."

"Copy," Brian said, sliding his arms into the sleeves. "Battalion 9, this is EPD four-delta-five-nine."

"Go ahead, delta-five-nine," said the husky voice of the chief.

"We're on scene about a block out," he updated her. "It looks like a fully involved vehicle of some sort. Heavy smoke for four blocks in every direction and high heat in the vicinity. All of the citizens are off the streets as far as I can see. I recommend that when you get enough units close enough to fight it, we shut down the blast doors for a five block radius and start ventilating."

"Copy that, delta-five-nine," she said. "Will do."

"We're suiting up now," he told her next. "We'll move in and try to get some water on it."

They finished donning their suits, zipping them completely over their helmets and faces, leaving only enough room for their masks and goggles to peak out. "You ready?" Lisa asked Brian.

"I'm ready," he replied. "Let's do it."

They began to trot in the direction of the blaze, their combat goggles allowing them to see through the choking smoke, their suits protecting them from the heat. The blaze grew brighter and brighter as they approached and the shape of the object burning grew increasingly distinct.

"That looks like a fuckin FLEB van," Lisa observed.

"Sure does," Brian agreed, noting that it actually seemed to be melting from the intense heat. "And somehow, I don't think that fire is accidental."

They split up when they reached the intersection, each of them heading for one of the four "fire stations" that were located at every intersection of streets. The fire stations were locked cabinets in which one hundred meters of six centimeter fire hose was stored, hooked up to a high capacity hydrant. Dip-hoe carts all carried extra hose in case the one hundred meters was not enough to reach a particular incident. In this case however, the burning van was less than thirty meters away from two of the stations.

Brian reached his station first. He looked at the number printed on it and then talked to the dispatch computer. "Computer," he told it. "Unlock fire station 34-7-2."

The computer quickly analyzed his voice pattern and concluded that he had authorization to order such a thing. A second later there was a click and the mechanism slid open. Inside of the compartment, the hemp hose was wrapped around a large reel, a large nozzle resting on top of it. Brian grabbed the nozzle and put it over his shoulder. He began to walk towards the fire, the hose unreeling behind him as he pulled. Across the street, Lisa had reached her station and was doing the same.

When he got within ten meters of the blaze, his patrol computer warned him that the heat was becoming too intense for safety. He stopped. "Computer," he said. "Charge up my hose."

The computer complied, opening the main valve on his station and allowing water to rush forth into the hemp. The flat hose on the street suddenly ballooned up as it was filled, the various twists and turns jumping up and down and then resettling. When the water reached the nozzle, the weight of the hose against his shoulder suddenly quadrupled. Brian brought the nozzle down against his chest and then opened it, allowing a powerful stream of water to blast out towards the burning van. The sheer force of it tried to knock him off his feet but he braced himself tightly, just as he always had in the training classes, and kept the stream on the flames. Slowly, he began to move in.

His stream of water was joined by Lisa's less than a minute later. Although there was no negligible effect at first, their streams were soon joined by others as the first dip-hoe team arrived and activated the other two stations at the intersection. The smoke billowed even thicker for a few moments as the battalion chief ordered the blast doors shut around them to contain it. But a few moments later, it began to dramatically thin as exhaust ports in the roof were opened up, allowing it to escape into the Martian atmosphere. Ventilation engines in the enclosed areas then kicked into overdrive, blasting fresh air into the area as fast as it was being sucked out by the pressure difference.

Once four water streams were concentrated upon it, the blaze was knocked down in less than five minutes, revealing that the vehicle was indeed a FLEB van, although now a partially melted and grotesquely distorted one. It was when Brian, Lisa, and the other cops and dip-hoes moved in to inspect the interior of the van that they made the shocking discovery that it was still occupied. Ten bodies were inside, all of them little more than grinning, blackened skeletons with melted helmets on their heads and charred body armor over their ribs. Their weapons, which were mostly plastic with steel barrels, were melted lumps in their laps or on the floor.

"Christ," Brian said, glad that he still had his mask on. He could imagine what the smell would be like in there. "What do you think did this?"

"A Molotov cocktail," replied one of the dip-hoes, an old, crusty one that looked like he had at least twenty years on the job. "I've seen them used before during the riots of '28. A little pressurized hydrogen in a Fruity bottle, a simple igniter designed to fire on impact, and you have yourself a hell of a fire."

"Where the hell do they get pressurized hydrogen?" Lisa asked, unable to take her eyes off of the charred bodies.

"Contacts in the agricultural industry," the dip-hoe replied. "The same place they get the chemicals for making dust."

This theory was strengthened by the finding of a large chunk of concrete, blackened but still intact, resting between the front seats of the van.

"Look at that," the old dip-hoe said, pointing it out. "I bet they threw that concrete through first, shattering the window, and then followed it up a second or two later with the Molotov." He smiled a little, seemingly impressed by this. "Pretty smart," he said. "Two simple ballistic throws and you've got ten feds charbroiled. Guess they won't be taking down any pamphlet makers anymore, will they?"

"Or gunning down any protesters in front of their office," one of the other dip-hoes put in.

Brian and Lisa both stared at the blackened corpses for a moment, both knowing that they should feel outraged at the murder of fellow law enforcement officers, both feeling guilt that they didn't. After all, these feds had undoubtedly been on their way to yet another illegal raid upon Martian civilians when the attack occurred. When you came right down to it, shouldn't they expect this sort of thing considering the way they had been operating lately?

"Ten less Earthlings we have to worry about now," Brian said, stepping back away from the van.

"You got that right," Lisa agreed.

Once the smoke was evacuated from the area, the blast doors on the perimeter were opened back up and an all-clear signal was given to the surrounding buildings. From every lobby, curious Martians and a few scattered Earthlings came pouring out to resume their business. Human nature being what it always had been, most of them maneuvered themselves so they could pass as closely as possible to the burned-out van. A few were even able to catch bare glimpses of the charred corpses inside. The Martians that witnessed this all went away grinning.

Lieutenant Duran and the DPH Battalion Chief showed up at the same time. While the BC went about the task of arranging a fire investigation, Duran rounded up all of the cops on scene. "All right people," she told them with a sigh. "It looks like we got ourselves a multiple homicide investigation to handle here."

"Question, lieutenant?" said Sam Stanislaus, a five-year police officer.

"What is it Sam?" she asked.

"Is it really considered a homicide if the victims are a bunch of fed fucks?" he asked with a smile. "I mean, shouldn't we think of it as more of a public assistance?"

"Or defense of life," another cop put in. "They were probably on their way to jack some poor slobs printing pamphlets."

Everyone had a laugh over this, Duran included. When it died down she said: "While I'm inclined to agree with you, we still have to go through the motions here. So, Haggarty, Wong, Stanislaus, and Ventner, start picking through this crowd and see if you can find any witnesses."

"Oh right, lieutenant," Brian said. "I'm sure that our fellow Martians here will be glad to provide statements about who killed these poor feds. How many statements should we get? Is twenty enough or should we go for thirty?"

This produced another round of laughter. "Just go through the motions, will you?" Duran asked them. "Even shithead feds deserve the same sort of jerk-off treatment that we give to welfare class homicides, don't they?"

Everyone was forced to agree that this might be true. Brian, Lisa, and the other two fanned out through the crowd, asking if anyone had seen anything and each recording "I didn't see nothing" more than a hundred times for the report.

Just as the forensics unit showed up to begin combing the van and its contents for evidence, three more FLEB vans arrived on the scene. They parked less than ten meters away from the crime scene and fully armed and armored agents poured out of their doors, all of them rushing over to the burned van and looking inside, their expressions horror at what they saw. The cops, dip-hoes, and civilians all watched this spectacle as it occurred, more than a few of them making snide remarks. The man in charge of the team, a high-ranking agent by the name of Don Mitchell, found Lieutenant Duran soon after having his worst fears confirmed.

"Any arrests made?" he asked her, glaring at the jeering crowd of Martians.

"Nope," she said. "Nobody saw anything. At least that's their story."

"Somebody saw it happen," he said, taking an angry step towards her. "Some piece of shit greenie can't throw a goddamn chunk of concrete and an incendiary device through the window of one of my vans in broad daylight without someone seeing it. I want some witnesses and I want them now!"

Duran stared at him levelly. "I'll thank you to take a step back from me and lower your tone," she told him sternly. "I don't give a shit who you are, I will not be addressed in that manner."

"Ten of my men are dead!" he yelled, not stepping back. "How dare you..."

Four of the Eden police officers stepped forward, their hands resting on their tanners. "The lieutenant said to step back," one of them told Mitchell menacingly.

"I'd advise you to do as they say," Duran said lightly. "As you've noted, tempers are a little short among us greenies lately, especially when feds are involved."

"Are you threatening me?" he asked her, his face turning red beneath his helmet.

"Take it for what you will," she told him. "But step back and lower your voice when you address me and we'll get along a lot better."

He took a step backwards, to the delight of the crowd watching. He did not, however, lower his voice much. "My men are taking over this investigation," he said. "We're assuming federal authority under the WestHem code."

Duran smiled. "Static," she said. "It's all yours." She keyed her radio up. "All units on the 34th street incident, turn your reports over to me and resume patrol. Our federal friends are going to handle this investigation by themselves."

Mitchell was somewhat taken aback by how easily she gave it up. "What is this?" he asked her.

"You think we want to stand around here smelling dead fed if we don't have to?" Duran asked him. "Have fun with the investigation. I know you folks have lots of experience with this sort of thing, don't you?"

The sarcasm in her voice was quite evident. Mitchell knew, as well as Duran and all of the other cops, that the federal officers were real good at tracking down copyright violators and computer hackers but, despite the Internet shows lauding them, were a little short on actual crime experience. "Well," he said slowly, backpedaling a bit, "we *will* need to use your forensics unit, of course."

"Put your request in through Chief Daniel's office," Duran told him. "But until he tells me otherwise, the forensic unit pulls out as well. And I have a pretty good idea what the chief is going to say."

"Now wait a minute," Mitchell said. "Maybe we're getting off on the wrong foot here..."

"We'll turn over everything we've gathered to this point to you," she said. "Have fun. Hope you find your man."

Five minutes later, all of the information was downloaded to the FLEB investigation computers and the Eden police officers, every last one of them, cleared the scene and went about their routine duties. When Chief Daniels was asked to dispatch a forensics team to assist in the investigation thirty minutes later, the request was denied without explanation.

*****

Three hours later, in Denver, FLEB director Stanley Clinton was briefing executive council member Loretta Williams on the firebomb attack on Mars. Word had reached

Earth via the big three Internet news stations long before it arrived through official channels. TRAGEDY ON MARS, it was being called, a name which was certainly not the catchiest the media had ever come up with, but which did convey the emotion that the Earthlings were feeling about the loss of ten FLEB agents quite well. The briefing was not a face-to-face one, as it were. Instead, they were accomplishing their meeting via secure Internet transmission from his office to hers.

"We have nothing," he told her, shaking his head angrily. "The Eden police chief has refused to allow our agents the use of their forensics unit or their manpower and the greenies... well, I don't think I have to tell you how much cooperation we're getting out of them. Hayes told me that three of the agents trying to question the crowd outside of that building were physically attacked."

"Why didn't they haul some of those greenies in for questioning anyway?" Williams demanded. "If nothing else, it would've at least shown those savages a thing or two about cooperation."

Clinton carefully kept his expression neutral, despite the disgust he felt at having to explain the basics to this high-browed politician. "Things are already quite volatile on that planet," he said slowly. "I believe that the commander on scene was afraid of forcing another confrontation."

"Forcing another confrontation?" she asked. "What is he, a coward? Did you not just tell me that there were thirty armed agents on the scene? Surely thirty agents could handle any trouble that a crowd of greenies could throw at them."

"Yes," he agreed, letting his composure slip just a bit. "They could have handled it the way they did in New Pittsburgh during the riot."

Williams did not seem to catch his drift however. "Exactly," she said. "That's what we need more of on that planet. It's brutal, that's true, but by God, those agents firing into the crowd dispersed them, did it not?"

"It did," he said quietly. "And I've also had more than ten requests for psychological counseling as a result of it too. That's not to mention that the shooting in New Pittsburgh is probably what precipitated the firebombing of our agents this morning."

"Common terrorists," Williams almost spat. "If you can't catch the ones directly responsible, you simply need to crack down harder on everyone else. You, as a career law enforcement officer, should know that, Clinton. Why do I have to call you up and tell you your job?"

He tried once again. "With all due respect, ma'am," he said, "I will continue to follow your orders, of course, but it is my belief that this process of cracking down on the common Martians is causing much more trouble than it's preventing. Every arrest that we make adds fuel to Laura Whiting's fire. Every confrontation between our agents and the greenies infuriates them more and makes them bolder. We've lost the support of the local police departments and the local criminal justice system. My people are not able to walk the streets there anymore."

"They're not paid to walk the streets," she said firmly. "They're paid to keep that planet under control and to protect our business interests. The crackdowns will continue."

"Yes ma'am," he said dejectedly.

"Now let's discuss Laura Whiting herself, shall we? Have you made any progress in her removal?"

"Not exactly," he said, casting his eyes downward.

"Not exactly?" she said. "Clinton, that is not an acceptable answer."

"Ma'am," he explained, "you have to understand that we've looked into every aspect of her life over the past two months. There is simply nothing that we can legally use to file criminal charges against her. We've leaked everything that we've been doing to the big three of course, and they've done a marvelous job of spreading innuendo and half-truths about her all over the screens, but when it comes down to legalities, Whiting has covered herself very well."

"Then make something up," Williams said.

"Ma'am?" he said, genuinely shocked at the suggestion.

"You heard me," she said. "Make up some charges. Get a grand jury here on Earth to indict her on them and issue an arrest warrant. Extradite her back here to Denver for trial. I assure you that the attorney general will cooperate with you."

"Begging your pardon, ma'am," he said, "but I don't think that's a very good idea."

"Why not?" she responded. "Isn't that what you're doing with all of those greenies that you've hauled off the street down there?"

"Well, not exactly," he said. "They were in possession of certain written materials and so forth that could *technically* be referred to as terrorist writings or incitements. It is a weak justification I will admit, but it is a justification. As far as Whiting goes however, there is nothing like those writings on her computer and her speeches, while they could be said to be inciting the terrorism that's going on, well... I don't think that would stand up in the grand jury room."

"Then you need to come up with something that *will* stand up in the grand jury room."

"Ma'am," he tried one more time, "if we haul Laura Whiting off of Mars with a flimsy excuse, the greenies are going to go insane. There's no telling what they might do. I think a general strike would be the least damaging course of action that we could expect. Open revolt might be the worst."

Williams shook her head in disgust as she listened to these words. "A general strike?" she asked. "You must be joking. Unemployment is twenty-five percent on Mars. You can't have a general strike with that kind of rate. And as for open revolt?

Surely you can't be serious about that. We have a fast action division of WestHem marines stationed on that planet. You don't really think that those greenies would try anything with them there, do you?"

"As unlikely or hopeless as it seems," Clinton said, "I still think that it's a possibility. There could be much bloodshed and disruption of production."

"It won't happen," Williams assured him. "Now do as I say. Get your man on Mars working on something you can feed to a federal grand jury here and then have the attorney general's office pick that grand jury very carefully. I want her indicted by the end of the month, Clinton. I want her on a ship bound for Earth within twenty-four hours of the indictment being issued. And I want her rotting in a federal prison within six months. Do you understand me?"

"Yes ma'am," he said, suppressing a sigh. "I understand."

She signed off a moment later. A minute after that he was composing a secure email to Corban Hayes on Mars.

*****

One fortunate aspect of the recent troubles between the corporations and the Martians had to do with the recent AgriCorp/Interplanetary Food merger. With public opinion being so volatile and unpredictable lately, AgriCorp upper management, showing rare wisdom, had decided to put off the scheduled "mass reduction in force" that it had planned as a result of the merger. Though they still had every intention of laying off more than sixteen thousand people once things settled back down (as they had every confidence things eventually would), fears of more riots or possible boycotts of AgriCorp products compelled them to keep everyone onboard for now.

Because of this decision Lon Fargo, greenhouse maintenance technician of eight years service, was able to remain duly employed for the time being, although with a rather large hammer hanging over his head. As such, he was entitled to remain an active member of the Martian Planetary Guard, where he retained his sergeant rank in the special forces division. Saturday afternoon found him at his training rotation out at the MPG base with the rest of his platoon.

Over the last three months they had trained out in the wastelands almost every rotation, honing and refining their techniques on interdicting and destroying advancing APCs. Their mission this week, however, was something different, something strange. And, contrary to normal operating procedure, their reasons for practicing such an unorthodox maneuver had not been explained to them. They had, in fact, been told not to discuss it with anyone outside of the company.

The entire platoon was inside the back corridors of the base, the long halls and hallways where the weapons and ammunition were stored. This was a tightly secured area and everyone except the special forces platoons practicing their new maneuvers had been cleared out for the day. In addition, the steel doors that separated sections of the hallway and the actual storage rooms themselves had been locked in the open position and large sheets of four-centimeter steel that had been shipped all the way from New Pittsburgh had been bolted into the doorways in their place. The task of the special forces teams on this day was to breach these simulated doorways and clear the rooms beyond them of "enemy" troops, which were being played by other special forces platoons and squads.

"What the hell are we doing this for, John?" Lon asked the platoon commander, Lieutenant Yee. "I mean, it's kind of fun and all, ripping down doors with primacord charges, but what's the point? Our whole mission is to prevent EastHem troops from getting out of the wastelands in the first place. If we ever get to the point where we have to clear them out of the buildings, the war is lost anyway."

"It's orders from Colonel Bright himself," Yee said, not for the first time that day. "Now quit asking about it and just do it."

Lon shrugged and went about the task of readying his squad for the next breach, which was to be their responsibility. The target in this case was the door to one of the processed food storage rooms just off the main hallway. The steel that was serving as the door stood between them and the room and the resistance inside could be heavy, light, or non-existent. They would not know until they made entry. "Gavin," he ordered, "get the charge up there on that door."

"Right, sarge," Gavin said, approaching carefully. Primacord was a shaped high explosive charge designed to cut through rock or steel. It was actually a length of black cord that directed an intense, though compact explosion when activated. He unrolled three meters of it from the five hundred meter supply that Horishito was carrying on his back and stuck it to the door, starting at the floor level and moving up to near the top and then back down to the floor again on the other side. When exploded, this would cut a one and a half by one meter hole in the steel, allowing both a firing port and an entry point to the room. He set a detonator into the end of the cord and then backed away.

"Matza," Lon told the young man on the SAW. "Get in position. Hose down the interior once we blow it. Make sure there's nobody with a line of fire on us."

"Right, sarge," Matza said, putting the weapon down on its bipod on the floor and lying down with it. He trained it directly towards the primacord loop.

"Everybody else," he said, hefting his weapon and flicking off the safety, "get to the sides. We go in fast and low once Matza clears the corridor for us. You know the drill."

They knew the drill. They formed up against the wall on either side of the doorway, their weapons ready, their combat goggles active and in targeting mode. Since they were inside, all of them were dressed in Kevlar armor instead of biosuits. They had additional Kevlar protecting their legs and necks to keep from being injured by the helium filled training rounds.

"Fargo to Yee," Lon said over the command circuit, "we're ready for action."

"Copy," said Yee, who was holding back in the rear with the rest of the platoon. "Breach and enter whenever you're ready. I'll have 2nd squad guard the corridor. The rest of us will follow you in."

"Right," Lon said. He looked over at Gavin, who held the detonator. "Do it," he told him.

Gavin pushed the button, firing the primacord. There was a bright flash of light and a sharp crack that echoed up and down the corridor. The cord sliced through the steel of the door as easily as a knife through butter, sending the section that had been outlined flying into the room.

Matza, on the SAW, was the first to see that there were troops in the room. They looked surprised at the explosion but they were reacting quickly, the ones in his view turning to put weapons on him. He squeezed the trigger on the SAW and sent bursts of training rounds at them, raking his fire from one group to the other. They stopped in place as they were hit and sat down, their weapons on their laps, their arms rubbing the areas where they had been struck. "Clear!" he yelled, once everyone in his view was either down or under cover.

"Go!" Lon yelled, and one by one his men dove through the doorway, flinging their bodies to the ground and training their weapons about the room. Almost immediately they found targets and began to shoot. The crackle of gunfire was shockingly loud in the enclosed room and quickly grew to an intensity that made conversation almost impossible. Lon himself was the fourth person through the doorway, his sector of responsibility the west wall of the room. Even as he was diving for the ground, he identified a target—Steve Jefferson, the sergeant from 3rd platoon—bringing a weapon to bear on him. Jefferson fired at him just as he rolled away, his rounds exploding into water next to him. Lon managed to put his targeting reticle on Jefferson's chest a half second later. He squeezed off a three-round burst, feeling the weapon kick in his hand. The rounds splashed into Jefferson's chest armor, knocking him out of action. He immediately began to scan for other targets but saw nothing but "dead" ones. He was somewhat dismayed to see that the status report in the upper right hand corner of his goggle view was showing that four members of his squad had been killed by enemy gunfire.

"Entry made," Lon barked into the radio to Yee. "Doorway is secure."

"Coming up," Yee returned.

A moment later the rest of the platoon came rushing through the hole in the door. They began to fan out through the rest of the large storage room, probing behind shelves of food stocks. Every few seconds there were bursts of fire as more enemy were encountered.

Within three minutes the entire room, including the back doorway, was secure. The cost however, was a little high. Had it been a real engagement, Yee's 2nd platoon would have lost eight men to the enemy's guns.

"We need to do better than that," Yee said once it was over. "Eight casualties is unacceptable."

"We just need more practice," Lon said, clearing his weapon now that session was over.

"I'll tell you what the problem was," said Jefferson, who had been resurrected from the dead and who had come over to shake the hand of the man who had killed him.

"What?" asked Yee.

"Your doorway was too small," he said. "Only one of you could come through at a time. That made it way too easy for us to pick you off as you entered. It also gave us too much time to go get into firing positions in the shelves while you were clearing the entrance. You lost some of the speed and surprise element because of the doorway bottleneck."

"So maybe a little more primacord on the doors then?" Lon asked.

"That might do it," Jefferson told him. "I think the key to this maneuver is getting two people through the door at a time. Think about it. That would double the take-down speed."

"Interesting," Yee said. "But what about…"

As the members of the opposing teams got together to talk about what had happened, none of them paid much attention to the security cameras that kept vigil over the room. They were all under the impression that the cameras had been deactivated for the duration of the mission. They were wrong.

*****

In the base control room, Colonel Bright was sitting at a chair with General Jackson and Laura Whiting herself. They had just watched the entire mock engagement on the video screens. Jackson did not seem particularly pleased by what he had witnessed.

"Casualties were a little high on the attacking team's part," he told Bright. "Granted, the OPFOR in this case knew they were coming and were probably psychologically prepared for them at least, but still... I'd like to see them pull their entries off a little smoother than that. If they don't, we're gonna have some serious losses up on Triad when the time comes."

Bright was in his late forties and had been with the MPG for ten years. Before joining his planet's service, he had served with distinction in the WestHem marines as part of their special forces division, although, being a greenie, his rank had never risen to higher than corporal. He was a skilled tactician and had honed the guerilla warfare arm of the MPG into a highly disciplined, highly trained point during his tenure, turning it from little more than a harassing force to one of the most potent weapons in the MPG arsenal. "This is the first day that they've worked on door breaches," he said in defense of his men. "It's only natural that they're a little rusty on the technique. They're improving. And look at what they're doing now. They're discussing ways that they can improve their entries. The OPFOR is giving them tips on it."

"That is somewhat reassuring," Jackson agreed. "And you'll excuse me if I sound overly critical. It's just that things are reaching a head here pretty soon. Now that someone fried a bunch of feds, we're gonna start seeing more action from them and their efforts against Laura are going to double, if not triple."

Laura, who had been watching the exercise in awe, nodded. "I fear we have less than six weeks left," she told Bright. "Once the Earthlings make the critical step for us, I'm going to have to ask those men to go into battle for me. Now General Jackson assures me that they'll follow my orders now..."

"Oh, you bet your ass they will," Jackson said. "After all of those speeches, after all the shit those Earthlings have put us through, they'll go to hell and back for you now, Laura."

"And that's exactly why I'm concerned," she said. "I don't want them dying unnecessarily. I realize casualties are going to a part of what's coming, but I want them as minimal for our people as possible."

"They'll be drilled incessantly in these breaching techniques for as long as we have the time to drill them," Bright said. "The same thing is going on in New Pittsburgh and the other cities where I have my people stationed. They'll be ready."

"Let's hope so, Colonel," Laura said worriedly. "Let's hope so. Because if these special forces troops of yours cannot accomplish their mission in the first hours, everything will be lost."

CHAPTER FOUR

The Jupiter System
June 1, 2186

The *WSS Mermaid*, an *Owl*-Class, stealth attack ship, cruised silently and unseen in an elongated polar orbit around Ganymede. Her twin fusion engines were both at idle, allowing the ship to drift along without emitting any heat. Her extensive array of passive sensors kept watch on the space around them for any sign of intruders, particularly EastHem stealth attack ships trying to gather intelligence. *Mermaid* was ninety meters in length with a beam of ten meters. She crewed sixty. Though she was not particularly impressive to look at and though she was downright uncomfortable to serve in, she and her sister ships were among the most sophisticated and expensive machines ever built by mankind. They and their EastHem counterparts, the Henry's, possessed an ability that no other spacecraft could; the ability to move and work in space undetected by the sensors of other spacecraft.

Large spacecraft such as the California Class super dreadnoughts, or the tankers that moved hydrogen from the Jupiter system about the solar system, or even the smaller naval support vessels that carried extra supplies and fuel, were impossible to conceal from an enemy. The problem was not the radar signatures of such monsters. Radar absorbent alloys were commonplace and easily manufactured and were, in fact, used to build most of the planetary military craft of WestHem, EastHem, and the MPG. In large interplanetary spacecraft, however, there was little point in using radar absorbent alloys since the ships in question could be detected at much greater range without the use of radar at all. Passive infrared sensors could pick up and identify a California class in its acceleration cycle from more than half a million kilometers away simply by reading the heat signature from the fusion engines. And when the California was not in its acceleration cycle, when it was simply barreling through empty space between planets awaiting turn-around and orbital deceleration, there were radio signals and forward looking radar beams (used to probe ahead for potentially lethal meteors or other space debris in their path) being constantly emitted, things that were quite easy to home in on with passive electromagnetic sensors. And even if a California were to shut all of its radar, navigation, and radio equipment off— something that never happened, but which theoretically could—they would still emit enough heat and radiation to be detected from one hundred thousand kilometers distance. A California crewed more than four thousand people, employed full inertial damping and artificial gravity, and required tremendous amounts of electrical power just to maintain basic functions. All of this added up to heat and electromagnetic radiation being produced. Large ships simply could not move stealthily through space, no matter what measures they took.

 A stealth attack ship, on the other hand, was not a very large vessel and could move about without being noticed. This class of ships *was* constructed of radar absorbent material that was angled in various places to ensure that even the miniscule amount of radar energy that did get reflected back was reflected in the wrong direction. On top of the layer of radar absorbent alloy was another specially made alloy, several inches thick, which inhibited the absorption of heat, both from inside of the ship itself and from external sources, such as solar radiation. The engine and waste heat generated by the people and the electronics inside of the vessel was radiated into a pressurized space between the inner and outer hulls and was then carefully dumped off in controlled bursts through a series of exhaust ports. When underway, a stealth ship used the minimum power possible for acceleration and deceleration and did not vent their plasma directly out of the exhaust ports as regular ships did, instead, sending it through a cooling cycle first. Since artificial gravity generators and the inertial dampers that were a byproduct of them created significant heat, they were not used or in fact even installed, forcing the crews to endure long voyages in minimal gravity (when under acceleration or deceleration) or no gravity at all. Active sensors, including meteor detecting radar sweeps, were not utilized on typical missions, making the possibility of running into an errant piece of space junk while at suicidal velocity a very real possibility. All of these measures, while making for cramped, uncomfortable, and often dangerous duty, made Owls and Henry's nearly invisible out in space. An Owl class, which was touted as being the best of the two superpowers' (of course the EastHem navy said that the Henry was really the best), could drift to within a few hundred kilometers of a London class super dreadnought or one of its fighters without being detected by either passive or active systems.

 Mermaid had been on her patrol station for a month and was only awaiting the arrival of relief before setting course for her home base: Triad Naval Base in orbit around Mars. It had been an uneventful cruise, with only routine contacts of

EastHem military and civilian vessels logged. The crew was getting quite antsy after two months away from their families (and in fact, any women at all) and the comforting standard gravity of Triad. Their hair was long and unkempt since there was no one onboard who knew how to cut it. Their faces were pale and slightly sunken from the lack of sunlight and gravity. Their clothing—shorts and T-shirts with their rank and last name printed upon them—were horribly faded and, in most cases, much looser in fit than they had been at the start of the voyage. Tempers had been rather heated lately and fights often broke out between enlisted men over such things as whose turn it was to use the bathing room or who had arrived at the relief tube first.

Because of the lack of gravity generators aboard, the *Mermaid*, like all Owls and Henry's, was oriented inside to up and down instead of to fore and aft like gravitated spacecraft. It was as if the entire ship was a small building, standing upright, with the torpedo storage and launching rooms making up the top deck and the engine rooms making up the bottom. Access between the decks was accomplished through small hatches. During periods of drifting, personnel simply floated from one level to the other, as if swimming underwater. During acceleration and deceleration however, up to a quarter of a G of gravity was imported to the ship, allowing people to stand solidly on the floor and forcing them to use small ladders to move between decks. The bridge was located just below the torpedo access rooms. It was a small, cramped area, only four meters by six, with five main stations in addition to the captain's and executive officer's chairs. Computer terminals were mounted into a semi-circular console with ergonomically designed seats before each. The captain and the executive officer sat just behind this console, just in front of the security hatch that led down to the next level. There were no windows on the bridge, or anywhere else on the ship for that matter. Cameras and sensors gave all of the input that was needed to run and navigate the ship.

Spacer first class Brett Ingram sat at the tracking and acquisition station on the bridge. Since the vessel was currently at drift and in zero G, he was strapped securely into his chair with a Velcro lap restraint. His coffee cup, which was sealed shut and imparted with a small amount of air pressure, had a magnet on the bottom to keep it in place. The display station before him was holographic, allowing a three-dimensional map of the surrounding space to be generated, with the *Mermaid's* position as the exact center. The map showed dozens of small dots of varying color and size, most of them moving slowly in one direction or another. These dots represented the contacts that he was tracking with the passive sensors and the ship's computer system. All of the known contacts had a small designator superimposed next to them, identifying their status. One labeled S-7 for instance, was a Standard Fuel hydrogen tanker making its way from Standard City to Triad. It was coded dark green, as were all WestHem civilian contacts. About six thousand kilometers above and two thousand kilometers to the right of S-7—about two centimeters on the map—was S-9, a California Class warship in a high equatorial orbit of Ganymede. It was coded blue, as were all WestHem military contacts. Light green meant EastHem civilian ships and there were four of those—all hydrogen tankers making their way to Earth from Callisto—near the far edge of the map. Red was the color that symbolized EastHem military contacts. There were two of those in *Mermaid's* field of detection, one, a London Class warship escorting the tankers, and the other an anti-stealth ship escorting the London. Yellow represented contacts that had not been identified as of yet. There were none of those on his display at the moment, but Ingram thought that maybe that was about to change. A flickering on his computer screen next to the display was starting to alert his senses.

"Con, detection," he said to Lieutenant Commander Braxton, the executive officer of the *Mermaid*. Braxton was sitting in the captain's chair at the moment since Commander Hoffman, the captain, was currently asleep in his quarters. "I'm picking up some errant readings on a bearing of 148 mark 70."

Braxton looked at the detection tech with an unmasked measure of annoyance. "Errant readings?" he asked. "What the hell is that supposed to mean? Do you have a contact or don't you?"

"Unsure, sir," Ingram replied, his voice neutral. As a ten-year enlisted man with Martian ancestry, he knew not to allow emotion into his tone when addressing Earthling officers, especially pricks like Braxton, who thought Martians were good for cooking meals and scrubbing dishes but not much else. "I'm getting some flickers in the high infrared spectrum. They've been coming and going for about two minutes now. I can't seem to get a lock on it."

"Flickers?" Braxton said, using his hand to call up a duplicate of Ingram's screen on his own terminal. He stared at it for a moment. "I don't see anything."

"Wait for a minute, sir," Ingram said, staring intently at the spot. Finally, the slight flare of white, less than a pinpoint, flashed for half of a second or so and then disappeared. "There," he said to Braxton. "Did you see it?"

"That?" Braxton scoffed. "That's what you're calling an errant reading? That was probably nothing but a vapor formation from a urine dump that some ship performed twenty years ago." The other members of the bridge crew, every last one of them Earthlings, snickered at his comment.

"Maybe, sir," Ingram agreed dutifully, ignoring the snickers, "but it *is* in the same spectrum as a Henry's maneuvering thruster. I recommend that we swing around and try to get a fix on it, just to be sure."

"And risk being detected from our own thrusters?" Braxton asked sarcastically. "I don't think so."

Ingram looked at the XO, a man who was three years younger than him and had two years less time in Owl's, but who, because of institutional prejudice against those of extraterrestrial birth, had been able to attend the WestHem Naval Academy at Triad and would one day soon command one while Brett was stuck forever at spacer first. "Sir," he said, "I really think that this might be a legitimate contact."

"Do you now?" he asked, smiling the smile of condescension. "And what makes you think that?"

"I don't know exactly, sir," he said. "Mostly instinct I guess. And..."

"Instinct?" Braxton said, barking out a laugh, as if the thought that a Martian developing instinct was the most ridiculous thing he'd ever heard of. "You look at a floating pile of old piss vapor from the Jupiter War and you see a Henry in it? That's what you call instinct? Tell me something, Ingram. Do you see Henry's when you use the relief tube too? What do you see when you take a shit? London classes?"

"Sir," he tried again, "this flickering is right in the orbital plain that a Henry captain would use to observe our operations on Ganymede. It's basically the same inclination that *we* use when we spy on Callisto. When you couple that with the spectrum being the same as that of a Henry's maneuvering thrusters, the index of suspicion raises up. If I could get my array more focused in that direction I might be able to..."

"Your opinion has been noted, Ingram," he interrupted coldly. "And it's been filed for what it's worth. Carry on."

"Yes sir," Ingram said, his voice still neutral. He went back to watching his screen.

"And why don't you pay more attention to the 0 mark 180 area?" Braxton suggested. "That's where the *Dolphin* is going to be coming from. If they detect us before we get them, the captain's gonna have your ass." It was an age-old competition between Owl crews relieving each other on station to see who could detect whom first. The losing crew owed beers and bong hits to the winners the first time they found themselves in port together.

"I'm watching it, sir," Ingram told him. "No sign yet."

"If I have to buy that asshole Stinson on *Dolphin* a bong hit, I'm gonna take it out of your ass, greenie, you hear me?"

"I hear you, sir," he said, suppressing a sigh.

Dolphin did not show up over the next two hours, but several more times Ingram saw the flickering in the low infrared spectrum, each time from a slightly different bearing. He continued to watch that area closely, looking for anything else that might give a hint towards what was out there. Eventually, just as the captain came floating in from his quarters to take the con, he got it. The tiniest flash of blue, indicating a lower level in the spectrum, appeared just beside the white for a moment. It quickly faded away and did not reappear, but it had been there, he was sure of it. "Con, detection," he said again. "I'm getting more flickers in the lower spectrums from 151 mark 70."

"Another puddle of piss, Ingram?" Braxton said with a sigh. "I thought I told you to give that a rest. You're supposed to be looking for *Dolphin*."

"What's this?" asked the captain, who was still hovering in the air next to the command chair. "Flickers in the lower spectrum?"

"Ingram is getting heat shine off of a damn urine dump or something and trying to convince us that he sees a Henry out there," Braxton explained.

"That bearing places it in the high orbital plain," the captain said. "Are you sure..."

"Stan, I looked at it when he first reported it," Braxton said. "It's nothing."

"Sir," Ingram said, looking directly at the captain, who, though he was as prejudiced against those of Martian birth as any other Earthling, could at least admit that they were occasionally useful for something, "I just got a reading in the lower spectrum. That's the same spectrum as a Henry venting waste heat. I really think we should maneuver to bring the sensors to bear."

The captain looked from his XO to his greenie detection tech for a moment. Finally, he pushed off of the chair and floated gracefully across the bridge to hover just over Ingram's shoulder. "Show me what you got," he told him.

"Stan," Braxton said, rolling his eyes upward, "there aren't any Henry's out there. I told you, I looked at his contact when he first reported it. It's nothing. *Dolphin* is going to be here any minute now and I for one don't want to pay for any buds back at Triad."

"Let me just take a look," the captain told him soothingly. "You're probably right, but I'd like to just see what we're dealing with here. Ingram's not too bad at this technician shit." He considered for a moment. "For a greenie anyway."

Ingram let the insult slide off his back. It was something that he had a lot of experience with. He pointed to the screen where the tiny flicks of white were still occasionally showing themselves. He then had the computer replay the brief episode of blue. The captain watched all of this carefully, scowling as he absorbed it.

"Hmm," the captain said. "My green friend, it's probably nothing more than a few scraps of metal from an ancient booster or something, but it's definitely worth a closer look." He looked up at the other stations on the bridge. "Helm, roll us to 331 mark 70. Keep those thrusters at absolute minimum. Assume there's a Henry out there until we prove otherwise."

"Aye sir," the young helmsman responded, his fingers going to the controls.

While Braxton shook his head in disgust at the lack of attention being paid to the approach lane of the *Dolphin*, the maneuvering thrusters on the outside of the ship fired with minute blasts of burned hydrogen gas, slowly rolling the ship around on its axis so that the sensor arrays could point towards the contact.

"331mark 70, sir," the helmsman reported a minute later. "Holding steady."

"Thank you, helm," the captain said, still looking over Ingram's shoulder at the display. "Well, Ingram?" he asked. "Where's your contact now?"

"Focusing, sir," he replied, adjusting the gain on his terminal. After a moment, his efforts paid off. A few light blue lines appeared.

"Well, look at that," the captain said wonderingly.

"What is it?" Braxton asked.

"Solid contact in the low infrared spectrum," Ingram reported. "Just a hint, but there."

Braxton switched his display over to get a duplicate view. He frowned at what he was seeing. "That's not very much of a hit," he said. "It could just be a sensor anomaly."

"It's the same spectrum as a Henry's hot spot near the plasma outlets," Ingram said.

"And it's definitely enough of a hit to investigate. Helm, get ready to move us a little. Let's see if we can get a range on this thing."

"Yes, sir," the helmsman said.

"Ingram, designate a contact for that thing and put it on the big screen."

"Yes, sir," he said, his fingers moving over his terminal. "We'll call it Sierra 21. It's now on the screen as an unknown, bearing only contact."

The captain pushed off of Ingram's chair and drifted back over to his own. "I've got the con," he told Braxton, hovering above him as the XO unstrapped himself and floated over to his own chair. Once he seated himself and strapped in, he turned on the ship's intercom system. "All personnel," he said, his voice being amplified throughout the ship. "General quarters, prepare for acceleration and contact prosecution."

The general quarters alarm blared and, on all decks, men dropped what they were doing and stowed any loose items that were in their vicinity. Kitchen crews put away their knives and forks and pressure cookers. Cleaning crews (all of whom were Martians) stowed their rags and spray bottles. Everyone on board reached into small fanny packs that they wore around their waists and pulled out emergency decompression suits, which they unfolded and slipped on. In the event of a hull breach, these suits would automatically inflate and allow the person to survive for a short time in the vacuum that would result. Once in their suits, everyone propelled themselves as quickly as possible to their GQ station. The engine crewmen all assumed their stations in the reactor room. The torpedo room crews passed through a security access hatch and into the room where *Mermaid*'s twelve thermonuclear torpedoes were stored. Two additional crewmen floated up to the bridge and assumed secondary terminals where they could control the four eighty-millimeter anti-ship lasers and the two ten-millimeter anti-torpedo/fighter lasers.

"All stations report manned and ready, captain," Braxton said three minutes after general quarters had been called.

"Very good," he replied, obviously a little perturbed about the slow response, but keeping it to himself. "Helm," he said, "sound acceleration alarm and initiate a point one zero G burn. Heading 100 mark 50."

"Aye aye, sir," the helmsman said, activated his maneuvering thrusters and sounding the acceleration alarm. Once the ship was pointed in the proper direction—a task that the computer oversaw rather than the human instructing it—the main engines began their burn. It was, of course, not actually a *burn* since the method of propulsion was a fusion reaction acting against a propellant of liquid hydrogen, but the term, which was as old as spaceflight itself, remained in use.

Fusion engines did not produce significant acceleration. Their advantage over chemical rockets was not how fast they could burn but how long they could burn. Fusion power allowed a ship to build up velocity over a period of hours, gently pushing it faster and faster. Even a California class warship, which sported the most powerful engines of anything spaceborne, could accelerate at no more than one half of standard gravity. For an Owl, which had to cloak and cool the plasma exhaust to keep from being counter detected, the maximum acceleration was one quarter of a G. At one tenth of a G, there was just enough gravity produced for the personnel on board to feel the slightest downward push against their chairs. Slowly, ever so slowly, the stealth ship moved higher in its orbit and began to ease closer to the contact they were prosecuting; hopefully without giving away their own location.

For more than an hour they built up velocity. Ingram continued to track the elusive flickers of blue and occasional white in the infrared spectrum, comparing different bearings from different locations, the contact gradually firming up into a solid reading. "I'm starting to get enough for a range estimate, sir," he announced.

"Give it to me," the captain replied.

"This is tentative, but we're looking at six to eight thousand kilometers in a standard Ganymede semi-polar orbit. Also, I've got enough readings from the various spectrums to confirm that it's a spacecraft and not a random piece of metal."

"Sounds good, Ingram," he said. "Weapons control, start working on a solution."

Of course, they would not really fire at the ship even if it were identified as being an EastHem Henry. Though there was a cold war going on, it had not been hot since the Jupiter War armistice was signed. And though the Henry, if that's what it was, was violating WestHem space by being within one hundred thousand kilometers of Ganymede, this was actually a fairly common violation, something that both sides did with frequency. If they were able to catch them there, the report would be forwarded to Rear Admiral Cirby, the commander-in-chief of far space command, or CINCFARSPACECOM, back on Earth. A formal protest would be lodged at the

EastHem embassy and the EastHem government would be embarrassed and forced to apologize. It was something that had happened on both side many times before.

It took another hour before *Mermaid* had moved close enough to get a firm lock on their target. By then, the fusion drives had been shut down, allowing the ship to drift once again and therefore reduce the possibility of counter detection. Once Ingram had multiple spectrum analysis of the target, he was able to positively identify it. The blue of the spectrum near the plasma outlets, the white of the thrusters when they fired, the darker blue of the occasional waste heat dump, and the very low-end readings everywhere else, all added up to one thing.

"I'm gonna call a positive ID on this, captain," Ingram announced. "It's definitely a Henry class stealth attack ship. Range is solid at eight hundred kilometers, velocity is standard orbital for Ganymede."

"Are you sure it's not the *Dolphin* playing games with us?" Braxton asked snootily. "An Owl and a Henry can be remarkably similar on the displays you know. And we *are* expecting *Dolphin* to show up at any time."

"It's not *Dolphin*," Ingram said tonelessly. "It's not one of ours. I've detected more than a few Owls during exercises. Our heat vents and our exhaust ports are both in a different spectrum."

"Mark it on the display," the captain said. "Fire control, do you have a solution?"

"On the mark, sir," the fire control technician said. "We're too close for torpedoes, but we could really pound the shit out of them with the lasers if we wanted to."

"Good enough," he said. "Keep them locked up. I'm gonna make a little call to SCNB and report our discovery." He turned to Ingram. "God help you if you're wrong about this, greenie."

"I'm not wrong, sir," Ingram assured him.

He wasn't wrong. The captain sent an encrypted message to Standard City Naval Base by means of a pulsed laser burst aimed directly at their receiver. Ten minutes later, a flight of six A-12 attack ships, each armed with high intensity, rapid charging lasers and two thermonuclear torpedoes, roared out of the base and up into the high orbit. Ingram and the rest of the bridge crew were able to see them as bright white plumes on the display. The tracking crew of the Henry was undoubtedly able to see them as well, and had to know that they meant the jig was up. Within minutes, the A-12s went active with their sensors, probing the area with radar beams and infrared energy, searching for the hidden intruder. It didn't take them long to find it once they knew where to look. Ingram, who was scanning all of the emissions in the area, was able to pick up the guard frequency transmission from the control room of SCNB. With the captain's permission, he put it on the screen.

"Attention EastHem vessel in orbit around Ganymede," said Admiral John Cates, commander of the base, his weathered face stern and unforgiving. "You are illegally in WestHem space. Identify yourself immediately and state your intentions or you will be fired upon."

The captain of the Henry, knowing he was caught, did as he was told. A moment later a young, German featured face appeared on the screen. When he spoke, his words were thick with an EastHem accent. "This is Commander Mark Beil of the *ESS Granite*," he said. "It would seem that we've made a minor navigational error and strayed into your space. We offer our sincere apologies. We will, naturally, vacate the area at best speed immediately."

"And we will, naturally, escort you back to international space," Cates said. "You have five minutes to start heading that direction."

"My apologies again, Admiral," Beil said, offering a small salute. With that, he signed off.

Of course, everyone knew that Beil and the *Granite* had not simply strayed into WestHem space. They had been spying, something that stealth attack ships were uniquely suited for. But diplomacy was delicate between the two superpowers and the game was played this way. Granite lit up its engines four minutes later and began to accelerate to escape velocity. The A-12s, their active sensors still pounding the invader with energy, turned and matched velocities to follow. Ingram and the rest of the *Mermaid* bridge crew watched the departure on the tactical display, Ingram recording every second of energy being radiated from *Granite's* engines for later intelligence reports.

"Secure from general quarters," the captain told Braxton, unzipping his pressure suit.

"Right," Braxton responded. He repeated the order over the ship's intercom system.

"Sir," said the communications technician from his console. "I have a hail from SCNB."

"Put it on the screen," the captain told him.

"Aye, sir."

A moment later the face of Admiral Cates was back on the screen, his features much friendlier now. "Commander Hoffman," he greeted the captain warmly. "I just wanted to tell you that you did an excellent job locating that Henry. Thanks to you, our EastHem friends will have a lot of explaining to do at the next summit conference."

"It was nothing, sir," the captain replied modestly. "I was just doing my job."

"Well, let me assure you that you did your job very well," he said. "I'm going to recommend you for an official accommodation. How does that sound?"

"That sounds just fine," the captain shot back at him. "Thank you very much, sir."

They signed off a minute later. The captain never once mentioned his bridge crew or his greenie detection technician as being deserving of praise. After all, a captain was responsible for everything that happened on the ship, wasn't he?

*****

Two hours later, Ingram was lying on his rack in one of the berthing rooms. It was a small room, one of four crammed onto that particular deck, and there were five other racks, stacked three high on each wall, in the room with his. Since they were just above the starboard engine room, the noise and vibration from the fusion drive hummed loudly and imparted an unpleasant thrumming to the walls. There were only six Martians on *Mermaid*'s crew and strangely enough, all six of them were housed in this room, although four were currently at duty stations and absent at the moment. Steve Sugiyoto, a cook's assistant (which meant that he washed the dishes and cut the food into portions) was lying in his underwear on his own rack directly underneath Ingram. Since *Dolphin* had arrived and relieved them, *Mermaid* was currently under maximum acceleration, just starting the long trip back to Triad Naval Base. As such, neither man needed the Velcro straps to hold them onto their racks. The acceleration of the ship imparted them with one tenth of their natural weight. In Ingram's case this was a whopping eight kilograms, just enough to keep him firmly on the floor or whatever ever surface he put himself upon.

"That's total bullshit, Brett," said Sugiyoto from beneath him, his voice low, almost a whisper. "I heard what went down up on that bridge. You were the one that found that fuckin Henry and you were the one that had to beg the old man to prosecute it. Where the hell does he get off takin all the credit for it?"

"It's the way of the solar system, Sugi," Ingram sighed, stretching out a little. As the senior Martian on the crew, there was an unwritten rule that he was responsible for keeping the other Martians in line

"Yeah," he said bitterly. "Fuck the greenies over every chance you get. That's the way of the solar system all right. That's why I'm trained in fusion engineering and they got me working in the kitchen."

"Shit, Sugi," Ingram told him with a laugh, "this is what... your second cruise on the great *Mermaid*?"

"That's right," he said.

"You ain't seen shit as far as fuckin over greenies goes then," he told him. "Wait until you get ten years on these things like I have and then you can bitch to me about greenie fucking. I was a trained computer systems operator and analyst when I went on my first cruise. And do you know what they had me doing?"

"What's that?"

"The fucking laundry," he told him. "I spent my first year of space duty down in the goddamn laundry room washing the shit stains out of those Earthling's shorts. My second year, I was graduated to the kitchen detail. My third year, they finally trusted me to start working in the torpedo room as a lifter. It took me six years and twelve cruises before they finally put me on the bridge where I belong. If I were an Earthling, I'd be at least a lieutenant commander by now. I'd be at least an XO on one of these tubs and probably in line for a command. Instead, I'm a damn spacer first, just two grades higher then you are, and if I somehow make it another ten years in this place, I'll retire as a spacer first."

Sugiyoto shook his head angrily. "That's depressing," he said. "Why do we put up with this shit? Why have you stayed here so long?"

"It beats being vermin doesn't it?" Ingram said. "What else can I do? There ain't much call for a detection tech in the civilian market now, is there? Even if there were, the Earthlings wouldn't hire no greenie to do it."

They laid in silence for a few minutes, each of them contemplating their second-class citizen status. It was Sugiyoto that brought up the subject of Laura Whiting, asking if there had been any more news heard.

"All I hear is what the bridge crew has to say about it," Ingram told him. "And all they watch to get their information is big three stations. They all seem to think that she should be thrown in prison for inciting terrorism."

"No way to get MarsGroup stations out here?"

"Not these days," Ingram said. "Before all of this shit hit the fan, we used to be able to catch MarsGroup in the enlisted lounge. The Earthlings would make fun of us for watching it, but they'd at least let us keep it on for a while sometimes. Now though, I wouldn't let anyone catch you trying to watch it. I wouldn't even talk about it. Things are bad enough as is without making them more suspicious of us."

They talked a little more about the sad state of Martian affairs in an Earthling ruled solar system. Finally, tiring of that subject, they drifted off to sleep, both trying to catch as much as possible before their next watch. As they snored in the miniscule gravity, the ship kept pushing them faster and faster towards home.

*****

"More trouble?" Laura Whiting asked General Jackson as he entered her office early Tuesday morning. It was not really a question. On Mars these days, there was always more trouble. The question was how bad the trouble was this time.

Jackson was dressed in his standard day uniform of red shorts and a white T-shirt. He nodded solemnly as he helped himself to a cup of coffee from the dispenser next to her desk. "I just got word," he told her. "There was another mass shooting of civilians by FLEB agents. This time up on Triad. They're still sorting through the mess up there as we speak, but preliminary reports are sixteen dead, twice that many wounded."

"Jesus," she said, shaking her head and feeling mixed emotions. On the one hand, she knew that she had set the stage for these confrontations and had put the wheels in motion. She had done that deliberately, with the hope of inciting the rebellion that was now about to boil over. But she had not counted on the price that was being paid in blood. "What happened?"

"There was an attempt to block the transfer of the Martians that were rounded up in yesterday's sweeps," he said. The day before, in response to the firebombing of their van and their agents, the FLEB had performed a planet wide sweep of all of the cities, rounding up and arresting more than two hundred Martian separatists.

"An organized protest?" Laura asked.

"Pretty much," he said. "It was the Triad chapter of the Martian Retirement Club that staged it. They tried to block the prisoners from being placed on the trains to TNB. About four to five hundred people put themselves in front of the access tunnels on the main loading platform. The agents fired on them almost immediately, which made everyone scatter, and then they rushed the prisoners onto the trains. They left the scene before any of the Triad authorities showed up. When the cops and the dip-hoes arrived, there wasn't a single FLEB agent there."

"Bastards," Laura said, shocked.

"There was a news team there covering the protest when it happened. The whole thing was caught on MarsGroup cameras. It should be on the news now if you want to watch it."

She nodded and instructed her computer to turn on MarsGroup primary. The screen flickered to life and a live shot of the main access platform to Triad Naval Base was shown. The loading platform was a wide, open area enclosed by the thick plexiglass and steel walls that made up the edge of the orbiting city. It was here where personnel were cleared through security and loaded onto one of the trains that transported them through one of four one-kilometer tram tunnels that connected the city to the huge base. Except for flying in in a spacecraft of some sort, these tunnels were the only way to get to TNB. The platform was usually an orderly place, swept clean and scrubbed daily by enlisted spacers from the base and guarded by armed military police. Now, it was the scene of chaos as the camera panned from place to place, showing dozens of Triad police officers and dip-hoes sorting through masses of bloody bodies lying on the ground.

"Most of the more seriously wounded have already been taken away by health and safety personnel," a shocked MarsGroup reporter was voicing over. "What you see here are the more lightly wounded and the dead, who are being sorted out for transport or relocation to the temporary morgue on the Triad end of the platform. As you can see from these shots, many of the protesters that were gunned down by the FLEB agents were elderly, since those over age sixty make up the majority of the civilian population of Triad. Reports from the Triad police state that none of the protesters were found to be armed. Most of them, as you can see, were carrying protests signs only." The signs in question could be seen lying next to many of the screaming or deathly silent protestors. The motto: FREE OUR PEOPLE! was the most prevalent, although there were a few others. Bullet holes could plainly be seen in a few of the signs.

"Kevin," she said, feeling tears forming in her eyes. "My God! What are we doing here?"

"I know how you feel," he said, sitting down next to her and putting a comforting arm around her shoulders. "These were old people. Grandmothers and grandfathers trying to pick up our fight for us. They were gunned down like dogs."

"And *we* caused this, Kevin," she said. "We knew that the FLEB would crack down on people! We counted on it to further our cause!"

"We did not cause this, Laura," he told her firmly. "Nor could we have predicted that things would come to this."

"People are dying because I've challenged the Earthlings and riled up the Martians! They're dying! They're being gunned down in the streets, hauled away to Earth prisons! Don't tell me we didn't cause this! My whole intent was to make things intolerable for the people so that they would support a revolt!"

"And that is what's happening," Jackson said. "This incident will come close to breaking the camel's back I would think. But *you* did not make those FLEB agents fire on citizens. You did not order the FLEB agents to crack down and haul anyone off. All that you did was force the Earthlings to behave in a way that you knew they were capable of when threatened. You provided the threat, Laura, they provided the violence, and unfortunately, this is the only way we have to get our people to follow us."

"It's manipulative," she said. "I'm pushing them around like chess pieces in order to further my goals."

"Not your goals Laura, *our* goals. The goals of the Martians. What we've set in motion is a necessary evil in order to achieve freedom. You had to make the Earthlings step over the line. You had to break the chain of tolerance that has kept us subservient for generations. It was the only way."

"That doesn't make me feel any better," she said. "And it doesn't help me sleep at night."

"And you wouldn't be the person you are if it didn't bother you," he said. "I'm sure you feel like you're as manipulative and soulless as a corporate manager, but you're not. You have a conscience, Laura and it's no surprise that yours is being dinged by what is going on here. But try to keep the big picture in mind. We're doing the right thing."

She sighed, her eyes still watching the horrifying scenes from Triad on the monitor. The camera was showing a man of about eighty. He had two bullet holes in his forehead and a puddle of brains and blood beneath him. His eyes were wide open and staring, an expression of shock and horror forever frozen upon his face. "I'm trying," she said. "It gets harder every day, but I'm trying."

"MarsGroup will be calling soon, trying to get a statement from you," he told her gently.

"I'll be ready," she said.

"Good." He gave her one more brief hug of comfort and then released her. "Keep the faith, Laura," he said. "My contacts on Earth tell me that a grand jury is being assembled in Denver. They seem to think it may be for you."

"How much longer will it take if it is?" she asked.

"A week or so to assemble and investigate the jury members," he said. "Another two weeks or so to present whatever evidence they whipped up. I'd say that within a month they'll come looking to take you out of here. Can you hold out that long?"

"I can hold out forever," she said. "The question is, will the people hold out that long?"

*****

Laura gave a scathing statement to the MarsGroup channels less than an hour later. She called for an immediate independent investigation into the events on Triad and the arrest and trial of the FLEB agents that had fired on the protestors. "Those people are common murderers," she said, her words being transmitted all over the planet. "They fired without provocation on an unarmed, peaceful protest against their fascist tactics. They belong in prison for what they did and if there is any justice in this solar system—something that seems more and more doubtful every day—they will be put there."

The big three media channels downplayed the incident as much as they could. Though they were competing corporations, all three reported the story virtually the same way. Their take on the matter was that a violent group of protestors attempted to free a band of hardened terrorists that were being extradited to Earth for trial. In the ensuing scuffle the "besieged" FLEB agents were "forced" to fire their weapons to protect themselves and prevent the escape of violent criminals. It was reported that "a few" people were killed or injured in the fracas. No video clips or interviews were shown and the entire segment carried less than a thousand lines of text on the print sites, less than thirty seconds of coverage on the video sites.

That evening, at 6:00 PM New Pittsburgh time, Laura Whiting gave one of her speeches. The primary topic was the Second Martian Massacre (that phrase had already achieved proper noun status among the Martians) and what she felt the reaction to it should be.

"It's easy," she told the Martian people, ninety-six percent of whom we're recorded as watching, "to blame the FLEB and their agents for what has happened on this planet over the past few weeks. After all, it is they who we see snatching our people out of their homes at gunpoint. It is they who are seen marching them onto Triad Naval Base for extradition to Earth. It is they who are gunning us down like rabid dogs when we protest their actions. But try, fellow Martians, to remember that FLEB tactics and responses are only the enforcement arm of the opposition against us. Somebody is commanding the FLEB to act in the way that they are and I think we all know who those somebodies are. They are not the executive council back in Denver, although I'm sure that's where the official orders originated. No, these orders came from the corporate boardrooms back on Earth, by the very people who are threatened the most by our drive for independence and autonomy.

"We've been over this before in previous speeches that I have given. I have explained to you all how these corporations and their CEOs are really the ones who rule WestHem. They rule with their money and the absolute power of corruption that it wields. They are motivated by greed and self-interest and the quest for ever increasing power. Sure, the FLEB agents are cracking down on us and cracking down hard, but they are doing it on the indirect orders of Steve Carlson of AgriCorp, Brent Holland of IPC computers, Roger Fairling of MarsTrans, and a hundred other CEOs— the men and women who control ninety-eight percent of WestHem's wealth. These people have blocked our attempts at negotiation for independence with the WestHem government and they remain our true enemy in this fight."

She looked into the camera, her expression anger. "I believe that it is time we stop throwing ourselves at the FLEB agents. That is doing nothing but getting people killed and wounded. I believe that we should attack the real enemy and attack them in a way that hurts them badly: their pocketbook. I'm asking all Martian citizens that work for an Earth-based corporation to band together in a general strike starting next Monday, four days from now, and lasting until the following Friday. That means *everybody* that works in any way for any business that is owned at any level by Earthlings, with the exception of hospital personnel and commuter transportation personnel.

"I know that I'm asking a lot of you, particularly those in the blue-collar class. You will not be paid for the days that you miss and you will be risking your very jobs by taking this drastic action. However, if everyone sticks together, if everyone does what I ask, unity will provide the protection you need, just as it did for the legislature when they were pressured to impeach me. A general strike of this scale will hurt these corporate Earthlings very badly even if it were just one day. If it is carried out for an entire week, it will be devastating to their productivity and their profit margin. My staff reports that they will lose more than sixty billion dollars of raw profit from being shut down for a week. This, my fellow Martians, is a language that they will understand. I propose that you undertake this general strike for one five-day period and then, if these corporations do not allow negotiations for our independence to commence, that we extend it to a two week period, and then a three week period, as long as it takes before they agree to listen to our demands and bargain in good faith for our freedom. And believe me, they will be forced to listen to us. A halt of productivity is something that they will not be able to tolerate or absorb.

"Fellow Martians, let this be our most potent weapon against the greed that is ruling us. Undertake this general strike on Monday and deliver a staggering blow to the very heart of that which controls us. You have stood beside me before when the corporations tried to expel me from my position. I ask you now to take the unity that you showed then a step further. Pass the word to everyone. General strike against the corporations! General strike for freedom and self-destiny! Show those Earthlings what we are capable of! United we stand, fellow Martians! Remain united and we will not fall!"

*****

Lieutenant Eric Callahan was a ten-year member of the WestHem Marine Corps. He was thirty-three years old and a native of Dallas in the Texas subsection of the state of North-Southern on the North American landmass. A dark-haired Caucasian of American descent, he was handsome and superbly fit in a physical sense. He commanded the 3rd platoon of the 2nd Battalion of the 314th armored cavalry regiment stationed in Salta, Argentina sector, a mountainous, hellish part of the Earth snugged right up against the towering peaks of the Andes.

Salta, a small city of only two million, was at the center of the thickest concentration of Argentine nationalists in the northern portion of the troubled province. In the mountains to the west of the city were thousands of pockets of poorly armed and trained rebels that were willing to die in their cause to usurp WestHem rule, which, since the end of World War III, they had never accepted as being legal. The mission of the marines from Foxx Barracks, just outside the city, was not keeping Salta itself secure and under control—that was the job of the army—but to patrol and keep secure the perimeter and the outskirts. Platoon strength units regularly forged into the high mountains to seek out the pockets of rebels and eliminate or capture them. It was this mission that Callahan and the forty men under his command were undertaking now as they marched up through the foothills to the higher peaks above.

It was mid-autumn in Earth's southern hemisphere and, as such, it was the beginning of the rainy season. A constant drizzle fell from the leaden sky above, the drops little more than a mist, but steady enough and thick enough to require the camouflage rain gear. Callahan was marching near the center of the formation, his M-24 held at ready, his heavy combat boots squelching wetly through the mud and pine needles of the terrain. He, like all of the men, wore a Kevlar helmet upon his head and a pair of combat goggles upon his face. Thick Kevlar armor, heavier even than that which police officers wore, adorned his chest and upper abdomen. The armor was covered by web gear that contained a combat computer, several fragmentation grenades, and extra sixty round magazines for his rifle. He had no rank markings of any kind upon him and had instructed his men not to salute him or give any other indication that he was the man in charge lest the rebels single him out for a sniper's bullet. The targeting reticle of his combat goggles bobbed up and down with each step that he took, the range display changing constantly as different features were crossed by it. Less than two hundred meters to the right of the platoon was a paved road leading higher up into the mountains, but Callahan was far too experienced to do anything as stupid as lead his men along a predictable route. Though the rebels, as a fighting force, were almost hopelessly outmatched by the marines, there was no sense in sending out open invitations for an ambush.

"Hammy," he said into his command radio link, his words being transmitted via a throat microphone to his four squad leaders, "spread your guys out a little more, will you? That right flank looks like shit."

"You bet, skipper," Sergeant Hamilton, one of his newer and greener squad sergeants replied back. Hamilton and his squad had been forced upon him a month ago after a long stint in the boredom of Alaska region, which contained the heaviest concentration of military forces in all of WestHem, but which never saw any action of any kind. They seemed like they might make the grade someday, but every last one of them had yet to have his cherry popped, as the term for combat went in the corps.

Callahan watched in semi-satisfaction as Hamilton adjusted the inverse wedge that his squad had been in into something approaching a proper formation. He turned his attention forward again, his eyes sweeping over the towering peaks rising into the mist before them. There were literally thousands of places up there that could potentially contain teams of rebels ready to attack them with ancient weaponry for the sheer harassment value of it. Most of the fighters were the direct descendants of those that had fought the WestHem army and marines during the initial occupation after World War III. They knew these mountains better than anyone else ever could or would and, usually, the first sign that they were there was when the bullets started coming in. From interrogating prisoners of the past, it was well known that an Argentine nationalist considered it a great victory if they could kill one marine for every ten of their own that was lost. They were willing to lose a hundred in order to kill that one though. And often that was just how many it took.

"You ever wonder why we're doing this?" asked Sergeant Mallory, his first sergeant and the second in command of the platoon. His squad was taking rear guard on this particular march and he had maneuvered himself to be next to his commander. He had turned off his radio link so that he could talk freely, without everyone else in his squad listening in.

Callahan flipped off his own link and looked at his closest friend in the corps. "Doing what?" he asked, although he was pretty sure he knew what he was referring to.

"Laying our asses on the line up here in these mountains, chasing these gomers around every damn day." He grunted a little. "I mean, really, what's the damn point of it? We can protect the base and most of the area around it and the gomers aren't really that much of a threat anyway. So, why do it? Why not just let them be up there in their mountains?"

"Because the powers that be think it's a good idea to go kill them," Callahan answered. "They want us to suppress this rebellion and to suppress it firmly, so it doesn't spread to other places, so that those who are fighting it are kept at the lowest level of morale possible. If we didn't go out and slaughter them on a regular basis, pretty soon we'd be elbow deep in gomers. And then where would we be?"

"I suppose," Mallory replied doubtfully, spitting a stream of tobacco juice onto the ground. "When you come right down to it though, I'm forced to wonder what the hell WestHem even wants with this shithole province in the first place. What's here that's valuable? This entire province is nothing but mountains and desert populated by vermin and thieves. Hell, most of them have refused to learn English even. What would we lose if we let these gomers be independent? It's not like they're Mars, which is actually worth something. I say give them their fuckin independence and see how they do with it. Once we stop given them welfare and food shipments, they'll come crawling back to us."

"They're part of the empire," Callahan told him. "And once you let one part of the empire go, the rest will start fighting for it too. Right now, we have Cuba and Argentina wanting to rebel."

"And Mars," Mallory put in. "Don't forget about them."

"And Mars," he allowed, although he obviously had little regard for the way that they were going about it. "Anyway, if WestHem were to grant Argentina or Cuba their freedom, within a year you'd have all of those other provinces that used to be their own countries trying to do the same shit. Can you imagine what it would be like if Brazil or Mexico or Canada tried to break out of the union? Shit, this whole nation would fall apart. We'd have to quadruple the corps and the army just to keep our own people under control."

"I suppose," Mallory said again, wondering why anyone would want out of WestHem. After all, they were the greatest democracy that ever existed. The Internet and the schools always said so.

They marched on, gradually tightening up as they entered the steeper terrain. Point men stared into crevices and around the bases of trees, searching for trip wires or loosely covered pits. Fingers tightened imperceptivity on the stocks of weapons. This was the extreme danger zone, the area where the mountains met the foothills, the area where the Argentines loved to initiate their ambushes since it allowed them to strike at their quarry in relatively open terrain while keeping themselves concealed on the peaks and in the thick vegetation. The platoon was ready for trouble and they were expecting trouble. It wasn't long before they encountered it.

As was almost always the case, the first sign that the rebels were attacking was the flashing of their weapons from the hillsides above. They came from a thick stand of pine trees, bright strobes of orange, at least four distinct rifles firing. A second or two later the bullets came whizzing in. The old M-16s and AK-47s that the rebels used had a very slow rate of fire and a pathetic muzzle velocity compared to the modern M-24s that the marines carried. This meant that the rounds would not actually penetrate the Kevlar armor that the marines wore. As such, the only way that the rebels could score a kill was to hit their targets directly in the face or neck, a task that was quite difficult from a range of nearly five hundred meters without combat computer assistance. The only real hope that rebels had of scoring a good kill was in the first few seconds of the battle, before the marines had a chance to react to the incoming gunfire.

In this case, the experience of the marines prevented any lethal casualties. Once the flashes were spotted, thirty of the forty men dove instantly to the ground, even before the sound of the shots reached them. As bullets came whizzing in, slapping into the mud and zinging into the trees, the only two men left standing were Sergeant Hamilton and a green private, fresh from boot camp, in second squad. Fortunately for them, the rebels had not been aiming at them and they were not struck. And once they realized exactly what was happening, they too managed to get into the mud before the second wave of gunfire came rolling in.

"On the hillside! Ten o'clock!" Callahan barked calmly into his throat microphone. "First and third squad, get some fire on them! Second and fourth, get under cover!"

The marines acted as they had been trained. The front two squads began firing up into the hillside, their M-24s chattering rapidly and spewing expended shells onto the ground, the rounds showing up in goggles as almost solid streams of white. The men carrying the squad automatic weapons quickly set up their guns and added their heavier penetration power to the fight, hosing down the entire tree line for suppression. While they were doing this, the rear squads scrambled along on their bellies to find rocks or trees or mounds of mud to hide behind, therefore improving their positioning. Within a few seconds, they had all found such things and they too began to fire.

Callahan, positioned behind a large pine tree, did not fire his weapon. He kept it by his side and instead concentrated on the big picture around them. He ordered first and third squad to displace and get under better cover. They did so, all of them sliding through the mud, one of them getting hit in the leg by a lucky shot. One of the men crawling in front of him backtracked and dragged him clear. Callahan nodded in satisfaction as he saw this and then frowned as he saw how Hamilton was responding to the situation. He and his entire squad were bunched behind a single fallen log in neat line, all of them shoulder to shoulder. "Hammy!" he yelled at him. "Get your people spread out more! This isn't Alaska, motherfucker! For Christ's sake, if they have an RPG or a mortar, they're gonna take you all out at once."

"Right, skipper," Hamilton said, his voice bordering on the verge of terror.

"Fuckin newbies," Callahan muttered, not bothering to damp his link first. A few bullets came plunking into the mud within a meter of him. He didn't even flinch. He called up the geographic display from his combat computer and a moment later a map of the terrain was superimposed on his view through the combat goggles. The map was extremely detailed and very accurate, composed from years of satellite digitals and radar imagery of this most active hot zone. The location of every one of his men—information that was provided by GPS links on their computers and radio linked to his own—were represented as green dots. The location of the enemy position—which the goggles and the computer had automatically pinpointed based on the infrared signature of their weapons flashes—were represented as a series of red dots. "Computer, secure link with fire support!" he said. "Priority one."

"Priority one link established," his computer told him in his earpiece.

"Who's this?" Callahan asked over the encrypted frequency, not bothering with niceties and knowing that whomever he was talking to would understand.

"Lieutenant Burgess here," said a calm voice. "Is that you, Callahan?"

"It's me, Burger," he answered, using Burgess' nickname. "I'm in contact with a squad sized group of gomers. I need some thirty-meter airburst HE rounds dropped at coordinates 34.17, 41.12."

"On the way," Burgess said.

"Thanks, Burger," he said, edging a little closer to the tree that was providing him with cover. "We'll adjust if need be." He switched back to the command frequency. "We have arty on the way, guys," he told his sergeants. "As soon as they hit, I'll get an air strike rolling."

None of them acknowledged him. They had been trained not to. About twenty seconds later, four 150-millimeter artillery shells came screaming in from the east, their approach marked by distinct, fast-moving white blurs in the infrared spectrum and the low-pitched whistling produced by their passage through the air. They exploded thirty meters above the tree line where the rebels were firing from, showering them with deadly shrapnel. There was no need to adjust fire; the coordinates and the gunnery had been perfect.

"On target!" Callahan told Burgess. "Fire for effect! Pound those motherfuckers!"

"Copy, on target," Burgess responded. "Firing for effect."

A few seconds later, more shells came arcing in over the hills, exploding with fury over the target area. The concussions of the high explosive rounds thundered through the mountains, echoing and re-echoing, hammering into the chests of the marines. The enemy fire came to an abrupt halt.

But Callahan wasn't done yet. He switched his radio to the command frequency and asked for an air strike. The marine aviation unit, which always kept planes in the air and on stand-by during the day, quickly directed a flight of two A-50 light attack planes to the coordinates. Just as the artillery barrage let up, the small, stubby jet aircraft came banking in from the south, their engines screaming horsepower, lethal ordinance hanging from their wing pods. The A-50s had been designed as close support aircraft for anti-tank missions but they worked just fine against the non-armored rebels as well.

"Fast movers coming in," Callahan announced over the command net. "Everyone, get ready for the big bang!"

The aircraft shot less than 400 meters over the top of them and dropped two cluster bombs apiece. For a second it looked as if a mistake had been made, that the bombs had been dropped directly atop of the marines themselves, but, moving at 700 kilometers per hour, they quickly passed over and zeroed in on the hillside. At about 100 meters above the target area the bomb casings split open, raining submunitions down over the tree line. The explosions were a series of sharp cracks and the trees that had been concealing the enemy were suddenly engulfed in flame and smoke, branches and bark flying in all directions.

The aircraft banked sharply to the left and spun around to make another run. Less than a minute later, they were back, dropping another two cluster bombs apiece on the area immediately uphill from the first. More explosions ripped the area and more trees disintegrated under the onslaught. With that, the A-50s banked back around and headed lazily off the way they had come in.

"All right now," Callahan said in satisfaction, looking at the smoking ruins that had been left behind. "That's overkill if I've ever seen it. First and third squad, advance up that hill and check it out. Second and fourth, keep hunkered up and cover them. Move!"

First squad, which was the most experienced of the platoon, quickly jumped to their feet and spread out, forming up into two distinct wedges for the advance. Third squad, which was the newbies, was a little slower on the uptake, most of them plainly reluctant to stick their heads up despite the horrific firestorm that they'd just witnessed in the target area. Still, their training as marines directed they do so and eventually all of them did. Hamilton did a half decent job of forming them up for an uphill advance.

Under the direction of Sergeant Mallory, the two groups moved in, weapons ready for action. They closed in from two different directions on the obliterated tree line while the rest of the platoon kept an eye out to their flanks. Callahan, after checking on the wounded corporal from second squad and ordering a helicopter for him, directed his combat goggles to patch into the combat computer of Private Wesley, who was on the point for the advance. Once the patch was made, Callahan was able to see what Wesley was seeing through his goggles. Though it kept him from seeing what was going on around his own body, he trusted the other marines would keep him safe and warn him of any danger.

"You patched in, skipper?" Mallory asked him a few minutes later, as they entered the kill zone.

"Yeah," he replied, watching without emotion as Wesley looked back and forth. "It looks like we got 'em all right."

And indeed, it did. Scattered everywhere throughout the hillside where the torn shreds of what had once been four Argentine rebels. Smoking arms, legs, pieces of skull and bone fragments were spread among the smoldering tree branches, bark, and mud. It was impossible to tell exactly how many men had been up there by the body parts, but the broken pieces of their rifles were more easily identifiable. Three M-16s and one AK-47, the latter with a burned hand still clutching the stock, were pieced together.

"I'd put that down as four confirmed kills, skipper," Mallory told him on the command net. "You know the gomers would rather die before they leave their weapons behind."

"I agree," he said. "Why don't you check out the area above the target real quick just to make sure they don't have any friends up there. I'm gonna release second squad from cover duty and have them set up an LZ for the dust-off bird."

The area beyond checked clear. By the time the two squads worked their way back down the hill, the wounded man had been loaded onto the medivac helicopter and was on his way to the military hospital in Salta. Callahan noticed that the men of Hamilton's squad, including Hamilton himself, looked a little green. He walked over to them, hefting his unfired weapon onto his shoulder as he went.

"Not very pretty up there, is it?" he asked the squad at large.

The men all kept quiet, their eyes turned downward. Hamilton however, was able to find his voice. "It was quite, uh... impressive what those explosive rounds did to those rebels," he offered weakly.

"That's how we deal with rebels in the corps," Mallory told them. "We respond to any acts of aggression against us with brute force, as much brute force as we can possibly bring down upon them. To do any less would encourage further attacks. Do any of you men have a problem with that?"

"No, sir," they all mumbled, although with a distinct lack of enthusiasm.

"Get used to the Argentina way, newbies," he said. "This is combat. It's not quite what we trained to do against the EastHem fascists, but it's combat nonetheless. We're part of an armored cavalry division, true, but we don't ride around in our APCs and we don't surge in force against enemy armor. Our mission is a little different in this part of the solar system. We fight rebels here. Whining, crawling, sneaking, piece of shit rebels who think they want to be free of WestHem—as if they'd be able to take care of themselves if we allowed it. They're hopelessly misguided fanatics who think nothing of killing themselves just to take you out. This was a small attack, and fortunately, only one of us got hurt. If you learn to be careful out here and learn to get your asses in the mud when the shooting starts, you'll live through your stint in the 314th and someday you'll be able to transfer back to Alaska or Iceland or Texas and look down upon all of the cherries at the bases there. Learn to love these skirmishes out here. Learn to love seeing those Argentine fucks all shredded up by artillery and cluster bombs. Learn to love it because you're gonna get a lot of it out here."

*****

As the weekend fell upon the planet Mars, the general strike call by Laura Whiting once more forced the so-called movers and shakers to abandon their leisure time and spend the days of rest in their towering high-rise offices. What had first been taken as a joke by the top executives of the corporations—the thought that the greenies would actually respond to her ridiculous request—gradually changed into ever-increasing alarm that maybe they really would. Though the big three, acting on the theory that to fail to acknowledge something was to mitigate its existence, remained mostly mute on the subject of the general strike, MarsGroup did not. On every channel, on every web site, in every news publication, the story of Laura Whiting's latest speech and the ramifications of it were the top subject. Interviews with blue-collar workers, all of them vowing to honor her request and asking that others do the same, were printed and aired in every news update. Calculations, all of them made by Martian born auditors and accountants, speculating on just how much revenue a five-day shutdown of Martian productivity would cost the corporations, were printed in exacting detail and downloaded millions of times over. Hard copies of these figures were printed out and posted on union bulletin boards throughout the planet where they were emailed back and forth from person to person so often that they flooded the system and forced it to a near crawl.

To make matters worse, Laura Whiting expanded her normal speech schedule of twice a week and began to make appearances every night. She would repeat the figures compiled by the accountants and repeat her requests for all Martian workers employed by an Earthling corporation to participate. As always, Whiting's speeches were the highest rated broadcasts of all time and the powers that be realized that the Martians were not watching them because they found them amusing.

In an attempt to head off the strike, the corporate heads called a press conference to address the planet on Sunday night. In doing so they took the unusual step of asking for this press conference to be aired on MarsGroup in addition to the normal big three broadcast stations. MarsGroup, more out of a sense of sensationalism than anything else, quickly agreed and sent reporters to the AgriCorp building, where the conference was being staged.

This conference took place in the large briefing room on the 300th floor where corporate training was usually held, a locale with spectacular views of the city and the wastelands in all directions. Representing the corporations was William Smith who, as the titular head of corporate interests on Mars had been elected as the spokesperson in this matter. With him, were the heads of more than thirty other corporations that relied on Martian productivity for profits, everything from transportation to manufacturing to mining to food producers that competed with AgriCorp itself. This group of CEOs stood as a unified force against the rebellion that was sweeping their breadbasket. Dressed in their finest, most expensive business suits, they stood shoulder to shoulder, an impressive gathering for a single purpose.

"We, the leaders of the various business interests that operate on this planet," said Smith in a carefully written speech, "are sympathetic to the problems that are occurring of late in the Martian cities. We have denounced the overzealous tactics displayed by federal officials in regards to indiscriminate gunfire and we are appalled by the deaths that have occurred so far. However, we, the corporations, are not to blame for this. We are only here to provide goods and services to the people of WestHem and to provide jobs for the people of Mars. We must take a firm stance against anyone who threatens our productivity. So, with that in mind, let me make it perfectly clear to the people of Mars who are considering partaking in this illegal and subversive action tomorrow. Anyone who fails to show up for work tomorrow will be dismissed from their duties and will go into our hiring computer as unfit prospects for future consideration. This decree will be enforced uniformly, for both skilled and unskilled workers, for both management positions and general workforce. In short, if you strike, you will be fired and barred from future employment with any corporation represented here for the rest of your life. You will lose all health and lawsuit insurance and other benefits that come with employment. This decree applies not only to AgriCorp, which I myself speak for, but any corporation that is represented here today. We are firm and committed to this action so I will advise you all to think very carefully before you decide not to show up for work in the morning. Production on this planet is vital to the continuation of WestHem and it *will* go on. Must I be forced to remind you that there is a better than twenty-five percent unemployment rate on Mars? If the members of the current working class decide to throw their jobs away in this ridiculous work action requested by Governor Whiting, I'm sure that there are millions of unemployed that would be perfectly willing to join the ranks of the employed to replace you."
    The press conference went on for another hour, though mostly it was the other corporate heads spouting variations of Smith's words. The media computers that monitored such things reported that seventy-four percent of Martian viewers had tuned in to watch the conference initially but that the number had dwindled to less than ten percent by the time it ended. Smith and his acquaintances were unsure how to interpret this data, but eventually they managed to convince themselves that it was good news. They figured that they had made their point quite nicely to the ignorant greenies and congratulated each other on outthinking that bitch Whiting.
    8:00 AM Monday morning dawned first in the cities of Libby and Ore City, which were located in the easternmost populated time zone. Libby was an agricultural city along the equator, the center of the third largest expanse of greenhouse complexes on the planet. Ore City was a mining and manufacturing city located 2100 kilometers due north. As the workday began in these places, less than two percent of the total workforce showed up for their jobs. The public transportation trains ran through their Monday morning routes with hardly any passengers on them. The

teaming high-rise office buildings of their downtowns were virtually deserted of Martian workers. The steel processing plants and the mines remained empty and non-productive. The greenhouses went unworked, their equipment going without maintenance.

Smith and his cohorts listened to reports in disbelief as the red planet turned slowly on its axis, bringing the next set of Martian cities towards the 8:00 hour. Never, in their wildest dreams, in their worst nightmares, did they imagine that so many people would actually put their jobs at risk like that. Their disbelief grew as the scene was repeated every hour as more cities moved themselves into the workday and the vast majority of the Martian workers were not there to help run it. In all, it was estimated that more than ninety-six percent of the total Martian workforce that were employed by Earth-based corporations elected to honor the general strike. Of the four percent that did show up, most of them were simply sent home again since their various occupations could not run without the other workers.

On this Monday, no food was picked or tended or processed or packed for shipping on the planet Mars. No boxes were loaded onto trains for the trip to the spaceports and no ships already loaded took off for Triad for distribution. No iron ore was pulled from the ground or processed into steel. No bartenders showed up to work in corporate pubs and no checkers or clerks showed up to sell things in corporate owned grocery or supply stores. Even the big three media conglomerates themselves were forced to virtually shut down much of their Martian operations as their cameramen and computer technicians—men and women that they had thought loyal despite their heritage—abandoned their equipment and went home. Mars and nearly everything on it ground to a halt, strangling profits for the day and, despite the savings in salary outlay enjoyed by the lack of workers to pay, cost every Earth-based corporation, large and small, billions of dollars.

Encouraged by the response to her words, Laura Whiting congratulated the Martian people that night during her speech and continued to encourage them to follow through for the entire week. Smith and company gave another speech that night, this one directed at the welfare class. He invited them to several locations in each city to sign up for job training to replace the unskilled workers that were on strike. It was a fairly good gamble that they made but, unfortunately, it was a losing one. Less than two hundred people planetwide showed up for his job seminars on Tuesday morning and all of them were sent away in disgust when their numbers were realized. As for participation in the strike, nearly ninety-nine percent of the workforce stayed home on this day.

For the rest of the workweek this went on. Smith would beg and threaten the Martians at night on Internet addresses with what would happen if they continued to defy their employers and the next day his words would go unheeded and no one would show up for work. Back on Earth, the stock market actually went into a free fall as food stocks and manufactured goods were virtually cut off at the knees. Pharmaceutical supplies, of which Mars manufactured greater than eighty percent for all of WestHem, dropped to an alarming level for certain brands in a shortage that would reverberate for weeks across the solar system.

When Saturday dawned on Mars, the first general strike officially came to an end. The first workers to return to their jobs were those who worked weekends: the maintenance techs and the service personnel, less than six percent of the grand total. They found their work backed up beyond belief but still waiting for them. No reports of dismissals were reported from any portion of the planet. The same occurred when the rest of the workforce returned the following Monday. Once again, the commuter trains were full of Martians heading to their jobs and the various industries were able to staff themselves and get some work done. No one was fired or disciplined, they were simply told to get back to work.

"The first strike was a rousing success," Laura Whiting told the planet that night on MarsGroup. "I'm sure you've all noticed your various employers trying to pretend it was no big deal, that they all enjoyed their little vacations, but believe me, you folks hurt them badly. I congratulate you on your unprecedented unity. But this is only the beginning. This is only a taste of what we are really capable of. We must now follow up our actions with demands. Please allow me the liberty of making these demands for you. Since the corporations now know that their workers are capable of crippling them, we must demand that they open negotiations with us within the week for a peaceful transfer of assets and recognized autonomy for our planet. If they do not, then we must initiate another general strike fourteen days from now, this time for two weeks."

*****

Corban Hayes was a man who looked ten years older than he had just a few months before. The stress of trying to keep a handle on the Laura Whiting situation while forcing his underlings to participate in a crackdown of citizens not seen since the beginning of World War III were taking their toll on him. He had already been treated by his private physician for a bleeding ulcer and irritable bowel syndrome, afflictions he had never been bothered with before. His face was now gaunt and drawn, streaked with age lines that had not been there at the beginning of this miserable year. And now, one of the worst fears of all had just come to pass. A general strike had occurred on the planet, a strike that had shut down everything and everyone and had come on *his* watch. And that bitch Whiting was already trying to arrange another, even longer one. He could almost feel his head rolling across the table.

The door to his office slid open late Tuesday afternoon to reveal Don Mitchell, one of his senior field agents, the man who had led the New Pittsburgh portion of the crackdown. Mitchell was not a very bright person and certainly was not the best-qualified agent for the position that he held, but, in the world of the FLEB bureaucracy, which was WestHem politics at its finest, that factor was not often considered when promotions and assignments were handed out. Walker was well-connected and had the ear of Director Clinton himself since he was married to Clinton's daughter, thus he would more than likely be the man to replace Hayes when he (Hayes) was eventually reassigned to some shithole office management job in South America or Greenland.

"You called for me, Corban?" Mitchell asked him, using Hayes' first name when hardly anyone else would dare to.

Hayes let it slide, as he almost always did. "Yes, Don," he told him, waving him to a seat. "It's about the Laura Whiting investigation."

Mitchell smiled predatorily. The Whiting case had been handed to him once the Eden crackdown got up and rolling. He and a team of fourteen agents had been working twelve-hour days on it ever since the order from Clinton had come in. "We're pretty close to having an airtight case file drawn up," he said. "It's a lot easier to build a case when you don't have to worry about things like real evidence." He seemed to find this deliciously funny.

Hayes on the other hand, did not. He had at first been unable to believe his ears when the order to draw up false charges against Whiting had come across his terminal on the secure link. Though he had bent the law to his liking many, many times in his career, he had never been asked before to actually make up charges and back them up with falsified evidence. And in such an important, potentially explosive case at that! He strongly suspected that Clinton and those controlling him were forcing him to pull the pin on a hand grenade. Nevertheless, he had followed orders. It was all that he knew how to do. "I've just received a communiqué from Director Clinton himself," he told Mitchell.

"Ah, my good father in law," Mitchell said affectionately. "What did he have to say?"

"Nothing very good," he said. "It seems that the various business interests of Earth and the executive council are rather upset about the little strike we just had. They are even more upset at the prospect of another, even longer one. The picking of the grand jury in Denver is being fast-tracked even faster and they are quite eager to have the complete case file against Whiting so they can get her out before she has a chance to get another strike organized. How close to finished are you?"

"We're just drawing up the final documents now," he said. "You know? Making them look all nice and official, cross-referencing a few of our sources. We could probably have it done in another three days if we rushed."

"Rush even faster," Hayes told him. "Even if it means that it's not quite as pretty looking or complete. Clinton wants the entire file transmitted to him within twenty-four hours."

"Twenty-four hours?" Mitchell said doubtfully.

"That's what your father in law tells me," he confirmed. "And as you know, what he says goes. Now get your people together, get some coffee brewing, hell, go buy some dust from one of the vermin if you need to, but have that report finished by 0900 tomorrow."

"We will," he said.

*****

Two days later, in Denver, Nora Hathaway, the WestHem attorney general, was reviewing the Whiting file from her office atop the Department of Justice building. She was a portly woman of sixty-two years, an appointee of the last administration that had managed to hang on due to her astute political savvy. She scanned through the hundreds of pages of evidentiary documents, getting a thorough read on just what the charges against Whiting were going to consist of and how good of a job the FLEB agents had done "gathering" the evidence. Once she had the basics of it down, she put in a call to FLEB director Clinton on her terminal.

"What do you think?" he asked her once his face appeared. "I've been going over the file since I received it on this end and it looks pretty solid to me."

"I like it," Hathaway said. "The charges themselves are beyond reproach. Solicitation of bribery from corporate officials, incitement of terrorism, trafficking in explosives. It couldn't get much better, especially after all of the media publicity that Whiting's been getting here on Earth."

"My feelings exactly," Clinton replied. "For once this year, my agents on Mars actually did something right."

"It would seem so," she said. "But I do foresee some future problems with this."

"Such as?"

"Such as the trial," she replied. "This file will be enough to get her indicted on the charges, but once we put her on trial, we'll have to come up with some corroborating witnesses for these statements in here. How are you going to do that?"

"Several of the corporations involved have volunteered their services in that regard," he told her. "For instance, Smith at AgriCorp will have a few of his lobbyists testify on our behalf that Whiting asked for bribes from them and threatened them if they did not produce them. The names on the statements are of the actual people involved. And as for the terrorism charges, well, those statements are from... non-people I guess we could say."

"You mean they're completely fabricated by your agents," said Hathaway, who did not enjoy mincing words when she did not have to.

"Well... yes," he admitted. "But in any case, our contacts at InfoServe, the biggest of the big three, have promised to supply us with actors who will pretend to be these people we interviewed at the trial. We'll make a big production out of them, tell the solar system how they'd been caught red-handed and gave up Whiting for a plea bargain, have them testify, and then we'll pretend to sentence them to prison. The pay-off for them will be a billion dollars apiece and new identities when it's over."

"A lot of money," she observed. "Who's paying for it?"

"The coalition of corporations that are fighting against Whiting will pay for half," he told her. "The federal government will pick up the other half. Of course, it's possible that some *accidents* might be arranged for these people instead. It is awfully dangerous to let them walk around after a production like that."

"That would seem the wiser course," she said.

"In any case, the important thing is the now. We need to get Whiting out of office and on a ship to Earth before the next general strike. We'll have plenty of time to worry about the trial later. I'm sure we'll be able to delay and put off the proceedings for at least four years. You know how our justice system works."

"Yes, God love it," she agreed. "I have more good news for you as well. Our grand jury selection is now complete."

"Is it?" he asked, delighted. Of course, the grand jury did not know that it was being convened to investigate the Laura Whiting matter, they thought they were just another routine body being pulled together to serve for a year and investigate whatever federal matters came up in the course of that time. "How's the composition?"

"We have twelve of the biggest morons in Denver sitting on that panel," she told him. "Each one of them has been following the Whiting story on the big three and have only received input from those sources. Not one of them has any contact with anyone who lives on Mars or ever has. They'll believe anything our prosecutor tells them."

"Beautiful," Clinton said, pleased with this news.

"I've already called my two top prosecutors up here. They'll be going over the file in less than an hour. It's Thursday now, so I'll have them work the entire weekend on it. The grand jury will convene for the first time this Monday morning. We'll zip them through an abbreviated orientation in the morning and then start hitting them with the Whiting matter after lunch."

"And how long will it take once it's started?" Clinton wanted to know.

"Shouldn't take too long," she said. "I'll have them present the worst of the evidence quickly. I'd say two days should do it and we'll have that indictment."

"Wednesday then," Clinton said, nodding, a happy smile upon his face. Soon this entire Laura Whiting mess would be but a memory. "I'll be eagerly awaiting it."

*****

Hathaway's prediction of two days turned out to be an accurate one. The Denver federal grand jury, which consisted of seven women and five men, were horrified at the crimes that Laura Whiting, current governor of Mars, was accused of participating in. The evidence that they were presented, coupled with the extensive media coverage of the events that all had been following of late, prompted them to issue a six-page indictment against her on six distinct federal charges, all of which carried lengthy prison sentences if the accused was found guilty.

The two prosecuting attorneys who had presented the case thanked the grand jury for their time and then dismissed them, reminding all that they had agreed to serve for a year and could be called up again. The twelve members left the federal courthouse and went about their business, all of them proud to have served and eagerly awaiting their next assignment, blissfully unaware that the justice system had no intention of ever using them again. They had served their purpose.

The text of their indictment was on Hathaway's terminal before the first of the jury members were even able to board a commuter train for their homes. She quickly read it over and then sent it on to Clinton's office via a secure landline. Clinton read it over ten minutes later and then composed a voice mail giving instructions for Hayes.

"Take her into custody tomorrow morning," he told his subordinate. "Take enough teams with you to ensure that she will not be liberated from you by her security forces or pissed off greenie civilians. The most important thing to remember is that she be taken alive and unharmed. I don't want a single hair on her head to be damaged, nor a single piece of her clothing rumpled. If she were to be hurt or killed during the arrest, we would have hell to pay among those Martians. She is not to become a martyr, do you understand?"

When he finished the voice mail he attached a certified copy of the arrest indictment to it and then told the computer to send it on the secure channel to the

FLEB headquarters in New Pittsburgh. The documents and his mail were digitized, encrypted, and then sent through the WestHem Internet system to a communications satellite in geosynchronous orbit over the coast of Brazil. Since the main communications computer knew that direct communication with the planet Mars was now impossible thanks to the sun being directly in the path, the signal was sent across the solar system to another communications satellite in orbit around Ganymede. It took forty-eight minutes for it to arrive there at which point it was rerouted and sent to another satellite in orbit around Mars. This leg of the trip only took eighteen minutes. And so, one hour and six minutes after being sent, the message and the indictment arrived at the terminal of Corban Hayes.

Hayes watched the email message and then looked over the indictment very carefully. He had a very bad feeling about what he was being asked to do, but nevertheless, he began to make the arrangements to carry it out. He called Mitchell and several other of his top agents into his office and told them the news. All of them were delighted that the greenie bitch was finally going to go down. They went over the basic plan to take her into custody the next morning.

"We need to make sure that we tip the big three first thing in the morning so they'll have cameras and reporters there to watch us taking her away," Hayes told them. "However, if we tip them too early, they'll start asking questions before we want them too. Those media people are helpful but they're also very annoying at times. So, until tomorrow, nobody says a word to anyone about the indictment. This is top secret stuff, okay?"

Everyone agreed to keep it under their hats for the time being. They were dismissed so they could start drawing up their plans and, naturally, the secret leaked within ten minutes to some of the civilian staff. An agent named Skeller, who was trying to penetrate the pants of a young secretary named Darla, was the first to spill the beans. Darla asked him in her flirtatious way just what the big meeting had been all about. Since Darla was an Earthling and very loyal to the FLEB, he didn't see any harm in telling her. "We have an indictment for Whiting," he whispered in her ear. "We're gonna take her into custody tomorrow morning and send her back to Earth for trial."

Darla quickly told another Earthling secretary the good news and that secretary quickly told another. It wasn't very long until the word reached the ears of a Martian receptionist down in the front lobby of the building.

Lisa Vaughn was a fourth generation Martian who worked in the FLEB office because it was the only job that she had ever been able to get and the only thing that kept her from vermin status. She hated Earthlings, particularly the federal variety that were her bosses, but she endured this miserable employment in order to keep her child from growing up in the ghetto. Her ex-husband, the man who had fathered her one legally allowed child, was already vermin, having lost his job in a merger of two computer software companies two years before, so he was of no help to her. If she had had any other prospect of employment over the years, she would have gladly taken it. But, since jobs were few and far between, she had stayed on and, some months before, a man from the MPG intelligence division had recruited her to report to him various information about the daily operations of the agency. She was, in short, a Martian spy. She received no money or anything else in exchange for the information she passed on. She did it only out of sheer loyalty to her heritage and out of sheer hatred of the Earthlings that worked in this building; Earthlings that treated her as a piece of furniture at best and with open hostility at worst. How many times had agents or civilian staff come into the building and called her a greenie to her face? How many times had they excluded her from their gossip circles, from their after-work parties or gatherings? How many times had she heard them mocking her Martian accent as they talked about her? It had not taken terribly much for the handsome MPG lieutenant to convince her to pass a few things on to him.

It was as she was in the lobby level staff restroom that she first heard about the indictment of Laura Whiting and the plan to take her into custody the next morning. Lisa had been in one of the toilet stalls, relieving her bladder of the coffee she had consumed, when two female secretaries for the piracy section of the office had entered to reapply their make-up after their lunch break. For more than five minutes she sat there silently, listening to them flippantly discuss how "that greenie bitch" Whiting was finally going to get what was coming to her.

"I *told* you she was involved in all of the terrorism going on in this place," one said to the other.

"I never had any doubt about it," the other responded. "You say they're going to take her tomorrow morning?"

"First thing," she agreed. "At least that's what I heard from..."

Soon the two women finished their work and left the room. Lisa waited another three minutes before getting up and returning to her desk. She had been briefed to keep her ears out for just such talk and to report it as quickly as possible. Of course, she could not use the main terminal on her desk to make the notification. That would be madness even though the message would seem innocent on the surface. Instead she unclipped her PC from her waist and flipped open the small screen.

"Call Gina Hawkins," she told it, referring to one of the names in her address files. To anyone overhearing her or homing in on her conversation with electronic devices, it would seem she was doing nothing more than conducting a personal call during business hours, something that was against the rules but fairly commonplace. No one would know that she had no friend named Gina Hawkins or that the number she was using to get hold of her was actually a relay station for MPG intelligence.

A pleasant faced female appeared on her screen a moment later. "Hi, this is Gina," she said in a thick Martian accent. "I'm not able to answer your call at the moment. Please leave your name and number and I'll get right back to you."

"Hi, Gina," she said into it lightly. "This is Lisa Vaughn. I just wanted to see if you were interested in going out to O'Riley's tonight after work. Give me a call back if it sounds good. If not, maybe I can stop by your apartment tomorrow morning on the way to work. I have to pick up that blouse I let you borrow. See ya."

With that, she clicked off and put her PC back on her waist. She returned to her duties. At the relay station the computer terminal that took her call identified the code phrase—"Hi Gina, this is Lisa Vaughn"—and automatically sent a copy of the message through several other relay stations. Two minutes later, it arrived at the desk of Major Tim Sprinkle, head of MPG intelligence. He took one look at Lisa's message and knew, just by the words it was composed of, that an indictment for Laura Whiting had been received at the FLEB office and that agents were going to attempt to pick her up the next morning. Within seconds he was on the terminal to General Jackson.

*****

Laura knew that push had come to shove when Jackson entered her office an hour later. She could tell just by looking at his face. "The indictment?" she asked him, half-fearing it, half welcoming it.

"It was issued by the grand jury earlier today in Denver," he confirmed. "I have some sources on Earth that were able to confirm this for me. Six counts, all of them high federal felonies. Just like you predicted."

She offered a weak smile, feeling her stomach knotting up. "It's not that hard to put yourself into the corporate mindset," she said. "I left them with no other option short of actually negotiating our independence. And we know they would never do that. An indictment and a quick removal probably seems like a brilliant solution to them."

"It's brilliant all right," he said. "They'll be giving us the final catalyst that we need tomorrow morning."

"That's when they're coming to get me?" she asked, impressed as always with the quality of Jackson's information.

"We have a source inside the FLEB building," he told her, nodding. "We got a message from her not too long ago. She confirms that the indictment has been received and tells us that they're planning to take you tomorrow morning."

"Does she know how many agents? How many guns?" Laura asked.

"We don't know at this time," he said. "All we have at the moment from her is a code phrase telling us that it's going down. One of our intelligence teams will meet with her tonight to try for a better debrief. In the meantime, it's time we initiated the first stage of operation Red Grab. The first elements need to get rolling as soon as possible if they're going to be in position in time."

"The special forces soldiers," she said. It was not a question. She knew almost as much about the details of operation Red Grab as Jackson himself.

"Right, I need you to give me a governor's order activating them. I'll put the call out and get them on the transports to Triad. When the time comes, they'll be ready to move."

"Will they do it?" she asked pointedly. "We'll be asking them to commit treason and murder. Have things gone far enough so that they'll do it?"

"Time will tell," Jackson told her. "I think that they probably will, but we won't know until we ask them."

"If they can't complete their portion of Red Grab," she told him, "then we might as well just surrender tomorrow."

"I know," he said. "Believe me, I know."

"But remember my conditions," she warned.

"Everyone is a volunteer for this," he recited. "All of the soldiers will be briefed on what the mission is and what the stakes are. They will all be given the opportunity to back out without recourse if they wish. No trickery or lies will be employed to get them to complete their portion of the mission."

"Right," she said. "I know it probably makes things harder for you, Kevin, but no matter how this turns out in the end, I don't want to go down in history as being the woman that tricked people into fighting for her cause. If they're not willing to fight for our freedom, then I guess it's not worth having, is it?"

"That's the truth, Laura," he said. "And I wouldn't have it any other way."

"Good."

"But from this point on, you don't leave this building until it's over," he said. "The capital is now your home. I don't want to take the chance that our information is wrong. If they grab you at your apartment tonight, then everything will collapse."

She did not particularly like the idea of remaining in the capital for another two days or so but she understood Jackson's reasons. "I'll stay here," she said. "I'll order in a pizza tonight."

"Good," he said. "And I'll brief your security platoon in that it's time to act. When the FLEB comes to take you, they'll be ready."

*****

Lon Fargo was behind the wheel of his maintenance truck, his partner Brent by his side. They were on their way to one of the soybean greenhouses to fix a broken fan unit on the environmental supply system. As always, they were passing through other greenhouses in order to get to the one they were after, driving their lift truck along the maintenance roads along the walls. This greenhouse was one that grew rice, one of the staples of the AgriCorp productivity. Stretching off to the far wall were acres and acres of neatly engineered rice paddies, all of them green and glimmering with an approaching harvest. Brent, who was smoking a cigarette on the passenger seat, was bitching about the loss of a week's pay that the general strike had imposed upon him.

"I'm telling you, man," he whined, "I don't know what I'm gonna do if we have to go through another two weeks of that shit. I mean, as it is I was barely able to make my rent payment and still pay for enough groceries to get us through until next time."

"Maybe if you cut down on the buds you smoke you'll be able to absorb it better," suggested Lon, who had also felt the sting of losing half his pay for the pay period, but who was proud to endure it.

"Heretic!" Brent accused. "What kind of man are you? Cut down on my buds? That's uncivilized!"

"These are trying times," Lon said, rolling down his window to ventilate the smoke from his partner's cigarette. "Just be sure to follow through the next time Whiting asks us to strike. The only way we're gonna beat those fucks is to hit them in the wallet."

"Shit, I know that," Brent said defensively. "I wasn't saying I was gonna cross the line or anything. I'm just saying that it's a bitch going without a week's pay. It'll be a bigger bitch to go without two weeks."

"No matter how much of a bitch it is to you, it's five times as much of a bitch to them. Remember, nothing moves, nothing happens, no money gets made when we strike. That hurts 'em bad."

"Yeah yeah," Brent said, taking an especially long drag. "I just wish they'd give us a little more time to recover before the next strike comes."

Lon was about to answer him—something to the effect of how his recovery time was also their recovery time—when his PC began to buzz on his belt, indicating an incoming communication. He unclipped it and opened up the screen, which was showing the communications software and the incoming call information. He expected to see that Barb, the girl that he had been seeing over the past week, was calling to chat with him. Had that been the case, he intended to send the communication to his mail system. Barb was becoming too clingy lately and he had no desire to talk with her just now. Instead of Barb's number however, he saw that it was the MPG headquarters communication system. "What the hell?" he muttered.

"Who is it?" Brent asked. "Is it that crotch you been slamming?"

"No," he said.

"Too bad," Brent offered, grinning lasciviously. "She's a pretty tasty looking piece."

"Answer," Lon told his computer, ignoring his partner.

The screen changed showing the face of Captain Mike Queen, commanding officer of the Eden special forces battalion. It was not a live shot, but rather a prerecorded message. "All special forces members," his image said. "We have a special training exercise today beginning as soon as everyone can be assembled. Report immediately to your duty station. This is an official call up. It is very important that *all* members attend this session. All employers are expected to honor time-off requests. I repeat..." He repeated.

"A call up?" Brent, who had been listening in, asked. "What kind of shit is that? They're calling you up for training?"

"They've done it a couple of times in the past," he said, puzzled, "although usually it's for a multi-company drill on the weekend. I don't ever remember them doing it on a weekday before."

"You can't just leave work," Brent said.

"I have to," he said. "I can't refuse a call-up. That's part of the MPG code."

"What's Pittman gonna say about that?" Brent asked, referring to their supervisor.

"I guess he can take it up with Governor Whiting if he doesn't like it," he told him, stopping the truck and starting the process of turning it around. "She's the one that put in the constitutional amendment about release from work duties."

Pittman, one of the lowest level managers in the entire AgriCorp chain of command, certainly did not like it a bit that one of his people was skipping off for MPG training in the middle of the day. Though Pittman was a Martian by birth, he had been one of the one percent that had not participated in the general strike, apparently feeling that his bosses higher up the ladder would respect him for this and not eliminate his position when the cuts finally came. Whether or not that was the case still remained to be seen, since AgriCorp was still waiting for things to settle down before proceeding with their eliminations. One thing that had resulted from his lack of participation however, was that he was now universally despised by all those he supervised instead of being merely disliked, which had been the case before the strike.

"You can't just leave in the middle of the goddamn day because the freakin' MPG is holding some sort of training session," he said from behind his cheap metal desk in the dispatch office. "Get your ass back out there and finish your assignment."

"Sorry, Pitt," Lon told him, shaking his head without a trace of regret. "This is an official call-up. I'm not allowed to disregard it and you're not allowed to discipline me for responding to it. It's the law."

"I don't think the law applies to training," he replied. "It's meant for an invasion of the planet by EastHem."

"The constitution doesn't say that," Lon told him. "All it says is that you are expected to honor an official call-up of forces. I've been given an official call-up and I'm leaving. I won't let the door slide shut on me on the way out."

"Fargo, I'm warning you," he said sternly. "You are not to leave early for this. If you do, don't bother coming back."

Lon was not impressed with his words. "You don't have the authority to fire me, Pitt," he told him. "Don't even pretend that you do. You're just a greenie like me, although apparently you forgot that back during the strike. All you can do is compose a disciplinary notice for me and recommend that I get fired, but middle management is the one who makes that decision and I hardly think that they'll go up against a constitutional issue for something as petty as this. So, find someone else to fix that fan unit and I'll see you tomorrow. Bye now."

He walked through the door, letting it slide shut behind him. Pittman was too astonished and too angry to even make a parting reply. Instead he started yelling at Brent, who had been hiding a chuckle the entire time.

Lon, knowing that he had a spare uniform in his locker at the MPG base, didn't even bother going home first. He left the AgriCorp maintenance building and made his way to the nearest commuter train station. He walked up the stairway and, coming to the gates that guarded access to the platform, used a fund transfer port in the back of his PC to transfer the cost of the fare to the MarsTrans bank account. The gate then slid open, allowing him access.

A train arrived six minutes later, only four minutes behind schedule, and he climbed aboard, finding a seat near the back among a few elderly Martians and a few gang member types that were probably delivering dust chemicals back to the ghetto. The commuter trains ran atop the street level roof and the train itself, which rode on a magnetic track, cruised along at 45 kilometers per hour, jerking to a halt every few minutes and then, after passengers embarked or disembarked, powered up again for the next leg. Buildings flashed past and turns were negotiated at high speed. None of the motion being produced was felt by Lon or any of the other passengers thanks to the inertial damping system. If you closed your eyes, it felt as if you were standing still. When they reached a hub station ten minutes later, Lon disembarked that train and waited another ten minutes for another one. When it arrived, he climbed aboard and rode it to the station nearest the MPG base.

Since it had taken him quite a while to come in from the greenhouse he'd been traveling through, Lon was the last of his squad to arrive. The rest of his team were gathered in the platoon's briefing room, all of them looking a little confused and gossiping among themselves as to what the meaning of the call-up was and what form the "special training" would take. Lieutenant Yee, whose presence on the base had been confirmed by other members, was conspicuously absent at the moment, probably in an officer's briefing.

Lon was inundated with questions from his men and from the other sergeants in the room, as if he were in possession of some information that they didn't have. "I don't know," he told them all. "I've never heard of them calling us up for special training on a weekday before. Nobody told me shit."

They waited. A few more stragglers from the platoon came into the room and starting the entire round of questioning and speculation over again. All forty men did show up however, many with tales of unhappy supervisors or managers.

Finally, Lieutenant Yee arrived. Since the MPG was light on military formality, no one stood up or saluted him, but they did all quiet down respectfully to await his orders.

"Okay, people," Yee said slowly, "here's the deal. I just received a briefing from Captain Armand and he wanted me to tell you all that we are not really here for a training mission. That was just a ruse to keep WestHem authorities from taking alarm at our call up. The real reason we have been called up is because of possible action up on Triad. I was not told much more than that. All I know is that it is not just the Eden area company, it is the entire battalion. All of us are going to be moved as quickly as possible up to Triad for a possible active service in defense of Mars."

There were some amazed stares at his words. The *entire* special forces battalion? That was four companies of troops, one from each of the four key surface cities thought most likely to be attacked. At 160 soldiers per company, that added up to 640 men! Never before had the entire battalion been called together for a single mission. Special forces worked in small teams employing hit and run tactics. And just what kind of active service were they talking about? Was there a threat from an EastHem invasion force? If so, why were only the special forces teams being called to arms? It didn't make any sense. It was the marines' responsibility to protect Triad and the naval base if an attack occurred. They had an entire division stationed at their barracks and enough surface to orbit craft to move more than a thousand men up at a time. The only surface to orbit transports the Eden area MPG troops possessed were two old C-8 lifters from the Jupiter War era, lifters that could carry only 150 troops at a time. Since each round trip to Triad and back would take three hours, it would be nine hours before everyone could even get up there.

Yee waited for the babble of voices to quiet down. "That's all that I know at the moment, people," he told them. "We're being called up and shipped up to Triad for an unknown purpose. Governor Whiting herself signed the order making it so. If any of you do not wish to participate in this, it is your right under our charter to back out. I was also assured that everyone will be given this opportunity again if the mission that we are being considered for gets a green light. Anyone who wishes to leave, please get up and do so right now. You will be held at the base until the completion or cancellation of the mission and then you will be allowed to return to regular duties. Any takers?"

Not a single person stood up. Lon didn't know for sure what everyone else was thinking, but his curiosity was certainly piqued. He was definitely in for the long haul.

"I didn't think that there would be," Yee said with a smile. "But I did have to ask. All right, let's talk about load outs, shall we? Our load outs will be full interior armor and combat goggles with regular ammunition, not training rounds. Each squad will equip itself with four M-24s with grenade launchers and thirty smart frags per weapon. The SAW men will each draw four thousand rounds of ammunition for their weapons, the riflemen one thousand rounds. In addition, each squad will carry no less than four hundred meters of primacord for door breaching. Biosuits will not be needed but everyone is to draw a gas mask and wear their heavy boots. Don't worry about food packs but do get some canteens. I'm told that you'll need them. Does everyone understand the load out?"

Everyone understood the requirements of it.

"Let's get moving then," Yee told them. "We're going to start loading onto the C-8s in the order we get equipped. I don't want my platoon sucking hind tit here, so let's make it fast."

It took the better part of an hour for the entire company to draw their weapons and ammunition and get suited up. They talked among themselves as they went through this process, all of them speculating on just what it was they were going to be asked to do. A large majority seemed to feel that a secret EastHem invasion force was going to try to make landings of some sort at either the naval base or the Triad commercial spaceport. After all, Mars and Earth were at opposite sides of the sun and Jupiter was situated relatively close to Mars at the moment. This was the planetary configuration that had long been feared as the ripest for such an attack since EastHem ships would legitimately be in the area. As for why the MPG special forces would be the ones to repel such an invasion, it was felt that this was because the intelligence that had uncovered the plot had come from the MPG instead of the CIA or FLEB. Perhaps WestHem authorities had disregarded the information forcing General Jackson to act alone. That would be just like those WestHem pricks. All of this sounded plausible enough that soon it was regarded as the official rumor. There were only a few dissenting opinions, a few of which actually suggested the *real* reason for the deployment, although they would not know it for some time. Everyone, no matter what their opinion of the coming conflict, felt a sharp edge of nervousness and anticipation however. Though the MPG trained obsessively, it had never seen actual combat before and only a few of the special forces troops had done any time in the WestHem army or marines. Of those that had, only three had seen actual shooting in Argentina or Cuba. Now, the prospect of actual fighting, the possibility of delivering or receiving death was upon them.

Once weapons were drawn, the company was moved to a rarely used loading terminal that led to the outside. One of the C-8s that the MPG possessed was docked with the terminal just outside the taxiway entrance. The C-8, like all Martian based surface to orbit craft, was essentially a reinforced terrestrial aircraft fuselage without the wings or tail. On the ground, in the loading position, it rested horizontally upon landing gear that folded out from the bottom. The two pilots were clearly visible through the windscreen going through their pre-launch checks. The bottom of the fuselage was covered with a layer of heat resistant material that was able to withstand the inferno of atmospheric reentry and the aft end was fitted with two rocket outlets capable of propelling the craft to orbital speed. Only the front third of the spacecraft was capable of carrying passengers or cargo. The rear two-thirds were taken up by the engine components and the tanks of liquid hydrogen and liquid oxygen that fueled them. The outside of the craft was painted as were all MPG equipment: in the shades of red camouflage scheme.

The passenger seats had been removed from the spacecraft in order to create more room. Though it wouldn't be a very comfortable flight, the entire company of 160 people and their equipment were able to fit into one C-8. Lon and his squad were among the first to embark. Since the C-8 was at idle and its artificial gravity field was operating, there had been no period of lightening. Lon found himself sitting near one of the windows, his weapon resting against his shoulder, his pack pushing against the wall behind him, two of his men pushing at him from either side. His legs began to ache almost immediately from the cramped position. He, like the rest of the company, kept his thoughts mostly silent as the doors were sealed up and the spacecraft began to move away from the building.

They rolled out across the sandy taxiways, out to the very far reaches of the outside base area, where the thrust from the rocket engines would not cause any damage. The trip took nearly twenty minutes, but finally, they arrived at the launch platform, a hydraulically operated lift built into the ground. The spacecraft positioned itself carefully and there was a clank as the magnetic arms locked onto them, holding them firmly into place. Soon the lift moved into action, tilting the aircraft upward to the optimum launch angle of seventy degrees. Watching out the window, Lon was able to see the ground tilting away from them, but he felt no pull of gravity towards the rear of the spacecraft. The artificial gravity field kept everyone oriented to the inside of the spacecraft instead of to the planetary surface outside. He could have, if he'd wished, stood up and walked around normally, just as if he was on level ground.

"Take-off in ten seconds," the pilot announced over the intercom. He then began a countdown. When he reached zero, the roar of the engines could be heard reverberating throughout the ship. There was a slight sense of vibration but nothing else as they left the ground and streaked into the sky on a fountain of orange rocket exhaust. Though they were accelerating at more than three times the force of standard gravity, no one was pushed backwards and no one had to brace themselves. That was the inertial damping system at work.

Lon continued to watch out the window as the ground receded beneath them. Within two minutes they were more than twenty thousand meters above Eden and he could see the high rises and the agricultural greenhouses spread out beneath like a relief map. He tried to pick out the MPG base that they had launched from, and might have been able to after a moment's study had they not rolled to a different attitude, obscuring his view.

Within five minutes of launch they were clear of the atmosphere and moving at orbital velocity. The main engines of the C-8 shut off for the moment and the maneuvering thrusters kicked on, angling them upward. When the proper attitude had been reached, the main engines fired up again, although only at half power, so they could be forced into a higher orbit for the rendezvous with the orbiting city. Triad was in geosynchronous orbit over the opposite hemisphere. In order to reach it, a spacecraft had to climb to an altitude of 17,000 kilometers, which, when at orbital speed, would perpetually keep it over the same point on the surface. The flight computers in the cockpit did all of this orbital maneuvering and positioning. A mere man could conceivably figure all of this out with paper and a pencil and a slide rule, but it might take him several weeks to do so.

The majority of the trip was spent coasting along in the high orbit, slowly catching up with their target. From Lon's perspective near the window, he never saw Triad approaching at all. There was only the blackness of space, the brilliance of the stars, and the nothingness that was the night side of Mars far below. Finally, ninety minutes after launch, the maneuvering thrusters fired again, slowing their approach. Lon saw the lights of a few other spacecraft in the distance, none close enough or clear enough for him to identify, and then, suddenly, there was the outline of Triad before him.

Orbiting space cities were engineering marvels, truly the culmination of all that man had learned about construction and space flight. More than just a space station where cargo was loaded and unloaded, Triad was home to more than 600,000 people and contained all of the amenities that any modern city had to offer. There was a level that could be referred to as a main street level. It contained parks, duck ponds, even a golf course and a football stadium. It was crisscrossed with a grid pattern of streets where pedestrians could walk or ride the trams from one place to another. It was on the main level, where the spaceport was attached, that huge tanker ships and cargo ships bound for Jupiter or Earth could dock, that passengers could load and unload for trips to Earth or down to the Martian planetary surface. Large food and steel carriers launched from Mars, much bigger versions of the C-8 that Lon was now flying in, would transfer their cargo to the larger, interplanetary ships. Huge hydrogen carriers from Ganymede would disgorge liquid hydrogen and methane into storage tanks. This busy spaceport, which employed over thirty thousand, was Triad's main reason for existence.

Like other Martian cities, Triad construction took advantage of vertical space instead of horizontal. But in orbit, vertical space went two ways instead of one. From the main street level, huge building rose both up and down. There were office buildings of course, and apartment buildings (virtually no one on Mars or above it owned a domicile) where people lived. The more expensive and exclusive buildings tended to be near the edges of the station while the low-rent and public housing buildings where the lower class and the hundred thousand some-odd unemployed lived, were in the center. The farther away from street level you got, the more the apartment would cost you. The most exclusive buildings, both offices and apartments, were on the outside, below street level, since these tended to have beautiful views of Mars hovering far below.

From his perspective in the spacecraft window, Lon was able to see the most exclusive of these buildings stretching both above and below him, their lighted windows glittering majestically against the blackness. At the street level, he could see the tiny figures of people moving to and fro through the glass roof. They went busily about their business, for despite the fact that it was midnight below on the Martian surface, that distinction meant nothing on Triad, which followed New Pittsburgh time as its standard.

They traveled along the edge of the city for some minutes as the maneuvering thrusters fired from various parts of the ship, slowing them and easing them into an invisible travel corridor. Lon had only been to Triad once before, when he was a child, and he stared wide-eyed out the window as they passed different sections of it. Soon they came drifting up to a docking port that protruded out from the MPG space guard base. There was more thruster activity as they eased into position and then there was a solid clank as the mating took place.

"Welcome to Triad," the pilot told them over the intercom. "Docking is complete and we'll be opening the doors in about one minute."

The cramped and weary men of the Eden company pulled themselves to their feet and prepared to disembark. Lon had to stretch and flex his legs for a moment to restore circulation to them. He was not the only one performing this maneuver.

"Okay, guys," said Captain Armand, commanding officer of the Eden company, "I know it wasn't exactly a first-class flight, but we're here now. Let's get ourselves off of this thing in an orderly fashion so they can go to New Pittsburgh and pick up another company. Form up by platoon on the other side and we'll take you to the staging area."

The doors opened up and, one by one, they marched through the docking port and into the main cargo receiving point for the base. Shipping containers were stacked against three of the walls and electric forklifts cruised back and forth, moving them from one place to another or stacking them on electric carts for transport to other parts of the base. The men and women driving the forklifts or unpacking the containers paid no attention to the arrival of the special forces team.

The front wall of the room was fitted with large windows that looked out on space and the docked C-8. The men formed up in front of this window, making four lines of forty soldiers apiece. They had to scrunch a little closer than one arm's length apart in order to accomplish this without hitting the walls on either side. As soon as everyone was settled, Armand waved at them to follow and began walking towards the far end of the room. They trailed behind him, keeping somewhat in formation but not actually marching. The MPG did not march since their philosophy dictated that their precious training time be spent learning something useful instead of how to walk from one place to another in a way that looked aesthetically pleasing.

Armand led them through a series of dank hallways and into a hanger complex full of parked F-20 fighters. These circular space fighters were sitting atop their ground wheels in neat lines, lethal laser cannons protruding from turrets on the front, their canopies open in the alert position. Several of them were undergoing maintenance by spacecraft mechanics in coveralls. A few of the mechanics looked up at the formation as it marched through their hanger and then went back to what they were doing, seemingly uninterested. On the spaceward wall of the hanger were a series of airlocks that the fighters could pass through to be launched. All of the doors were securely closed and locked and marked with yellow danger lines on the floor.

A set of doorways at the far end of the hanger led them to another hanger, this one empty and abandoned looking. Though the floor looked as if it had recently been cleaned and mopped, all of the parking areas were devoid of spacecraft and the airlocks had a layer of dust on the doors. When the last man was in the hanger, Armand brought them to a halt and then walked over to the door and issued a command to the computer terminal that guarded it. The doors all slid shut with a clank that echoed back and forth several times.

"All right, guys," he said to his company. "This is it. We'll be staging in this room for the immediate future. Everyone find yourself a place to call your own and get settled in. Blankets and pillows will be brought in later and we'll be having our meals brought to us here. There are bathrooms at the far end through those doors, but other than that, no one is to leave this room. There is to be no communication out of here and to enforce this rule, the cellular antennas have all been shut down so your PCs won't work."

The men broke ranks and began looking for a favorable piece of the floor to camp out in. They settled in for a long wait. Through the remainder of that day, the rest of the special forces battalion was transported up and marched to the hanger to join them. By 8:00 PM, Eden time, all 640 men were present and accounted for. They waited, unsure what their purpose in being there was but anxious to get on with it anyway.

*****

The WestHem marine intelligence unit, which was quartered at the barracks in Eden and attached to the fast reaction division, had noted that a number of Martian Planetary Guard soldiers were transported up to Triad. They could hardly have failed to note it since the unusual event of a C-8 surface to orbit craft taking off from the various bases around the planet had clearly been seen by tens of thousands of people. The Major in charge of the unit simply filed the information away in his computer, not really giving it a second thought. After all, who cared what the pretend soldiers were doing? He never bothered to try finding out just how many soldiers had been taken up there or what they were equipped with or what their purpose might have been. By the time he went to bed that night, he'd forgotten all about the information. He would remember it the next day however, once it was too late.

The FLEB agents, who tried to monitor everything the greenies did these days, noted the same thing. The information was passed all the way up to Corban Hayes himself, who simply shrugged and disregarded it. He was anxious about the Laura Whiting takedown scheduled for the next morning and wondered why his underlings had even bothered to bring the movement of MPG troops to his attention. So they shipped some people up to Triad? Who cared? It never occurred to him that there might be a connection between this information and the Laura Whiting matter. It would be a matter that he would later deeply regret ignoring.

There was a group of people that *did* take notice of the troop movement and that did find it very interesting in light of recent events on Mars. That group was the EastHem Office of Military Intelligence, or OMI, which operated out of a guarded building in the EastHem capital city of London. The OMI was receiving the take from a Henry that was currently in high orbit over Mars, its sensors peering down at all that orbited the red planet. They too had seen the liftoff of a C-8 lifter from all four of the key Martian cities and had tracked it each time to the space guard base at

Triad. In addition to this, they had intercepted the call up message earlier that day asking for all special forces teams to report to their duty stations. It did not take a rocket scientist to figure out that the MPG had just moved 640 of its most highly trained soldiers to a staging location at its spaceborne base. When analysts evaluated the data back in London, the correct conclusion was almost immediately drawn.

It is interesting to note that the OMI and the EastHem government they served had much greater knowledge of and respect for the MPG than the WestHem government that it was a part of. After all, it was the OMI's job to evaluate the opposition in the event that they ever decided to invade Mars. Ever since the MPGs first fledgling days as a group, Henry's had been spying on their maneuvers and listening in on their transmissions when they could. Operatives on the planet itself, some under diplomatic cover, some illegal spies posing as Earthlings or Martians, had gathered everything they could on the composition of forces and the tactics they employed. There was a file on General Jackson and all of the other commanding officers complete with detailed biographies and up to date photographs. The OMI admired Jackson tremendously and knew that if they ever tried to take Mars from WestHem, that he and his troops would give them quite a rough time of it.

The OMI had been following closely the recent events on Mars, both by monitoring the media transmissions and by observing from stealth ships in orbit. With the cool analysis that came with not being involved, they had long since figured out where Laura Whiting and General Jackson were heading.

"What do you think?" the head of the covert intelligence division asked his boss when the information was confirmed.

"Let me get this straight," asked the deputy director as he looked the data over. "You're saying that the MPG moved their *entire* special forces division up to Triad today?"

"That's correct," he said. "We have about as absolute of a confirmation as we're going to get on that one. Three different sources. We intercepted the call up order as it was put out, three of our operatives were able to observe known members of these teams entering their bases this afternoon, and the asset we have in orbit was able to observe a lifter moving from the four key bases and docking at the Triad MPG base."

"And in Denver?"

"The information is not as solid but it's still high on the scale," he said. "It seems that a federal indictment and arrest warrant were issued by a grand jury accusing Laura Whiting of various crimes. One of our operatives there was able to actually talk to one of those members. It seemed that this young woman, who was not very smart I understand, did not take her oath of secrecy very seriously."

"And do we have any idea if the MPG knows about this arrest warrant?"

"We have no way of knowing for sure," he said, "but I can't believe that they wouldn't. Jackson, as you know, has a pretty impressive array of agents, both on Earth and Mars, including civilian workers in the FLEB building itself. He keeps his ear to the ground and his job is made a lot easier by the contempt that the WestHem people have for him and his organization."

"So, you're saying that if a warrant was issued and transmitted to Earth, Jackson and Whiting would most likely know about it?"

"Correct."

The deputy director smiled. "My friend," he said. "I think that food is going to become a bit cheaper in EastHem in the near future."

"Shall we wake the executive council with this data?"

"I think we should. And I think that we're in for a jolly good show on Mars tomorrow morning."

CHAPTER FIVE

New Pittsburgh, Mars
June 8, 2186

Don Mitchell, son-in-law of Director Clinton, was given the honor of leading the takedown team that would take Laura Whiting into custody. He and his team gathered at the main FLEB office at 0700 that Thursday morning. There were forty of them, including himself, and he divided them up into teams of ten, each of which was assigned a leader. He then briefed them on their mission, an act that did not carry the dramatic punch he had hoped for since every last one of the men had already heard through the grapevine what they were going to be doing that day. Still, those that weren't in the official loop pretended to be surprised when they heard the news, so some of the flair was maintained.

He distributed diagrams of the Martian capital building to each of the team leaders, assigning them positions to take up when the time came. "Team B," he said. "You will be guarding the rear of the building in case she tries to flee. Team C, you'll be covering the front. Team D, you will split into two elements and cover the side entrances of the building in case she tries to come out that way. Team A, which I will be personally leading, will enter the building itself for the takedown. You outside teams, in addition to sealing the building from her premature exit, you will also be keeping the streets clear of greenies. Since we have a federal warrant, I don't expect any resistance from the MPG troops that guard Whiting, but I would expect resistance from any greenies that happen to see us leading her away. So, keep a sharp eye out for that."

"How sure are you that the MPG troops won't resist?" one of the men asked at that point.

"The MPG are technically part of the WestHem armed services," Mitchell responded. "They won't be happy that we've come for her, but I seriously doubt that they would disregard a federal warrant for her arrest. If any of them *does* resist in any way, he or she is to be immediately placed under arrest for obstructing a federal officer."

Everyone seemed satisfied with this and the subject was dropped. The briefing went on for another twenty minutes and then the men were dismissed to go suit up. They retired to the locker room and donned their raid gear. Heavy Kevlar armor vests were put over their torsos and black helmets with FLEB stenciled in white were put upon their heads. They strapped on their weapons belts, which contained their 4mm pistols as well as extra rifle ammunition and handcuffs. Steel-toed combat boots were put on their feet. The picture was completed by the addition of M-24 assault rifles loaded with sixty round magazines. Because it had never been thought necessary in the environment within which they operated, they had no combat goggles. Aiming would have to be by the old-fashioned method if a battle occurred and tactical displays and mapping software would have to be looked at on their PCs.

Once suited up, they walked out to the building's parking area and boarded four of the black panel vans. The vans all had multiple dents and scratches from rocks and bottles thrown by angry Martians over the past several months. There were places where the paint had been scraped off and reapplied to cover anti-fed and anti-Earthling graffiti. And, since the incident of the Molotov cocktail a few weeks before, all of them now had metal bars across the windshields to keep a repeat of that incident from happening.

With Mitchell and his team in the lead van, they pulled out of the parking area and onto the busy street that was teeming with Martians on their way to work. They turned right and started heading for the capital building thirty blocks away. The Martians, as always, were deliberately slow getting out of their way and many of them raised their middle fingers or grabbed their crotches in contempt. Spit flew whenever the van passed close enough for someone to hit it and several times there were thumps as cans or bottles slammed into the sides.

Most of the people on the street had no idea where the federal vans were going or what they were doing. But a few people did, and they were on their PCs to other people before the vans were even out of sight of the office.

*****

General Jackson was waiting in Laura's office with her when his PC buzzed, indicating a high priority message. He unclipped it from his belt and flipped the screen up, seeing the face of Major Sprinkle, head of intelligence. "Talk to me, Tim," he said.

"Four vans just left the FLEB office five minutes ago," he said. "They're heading your way. We didn't get a good look, but it's probably safe to assume that they're coming in platoon strength."

"Any chance that they're just heading out for their normal raids?" Jackson asked.

"There's always that chance," Sprinkle replied, "but they don't typically head out to normal raids with that many troops. Even the biggest takedowns they do usually only require half that much. Also, this deployment fits with the information we received yesterday. My guess is that this is it."

"That's my guess as well," Jackson said, feeling his heartbeat pick up a few notches. "Keep your assets in place until we know for sure. If it is them, things are gonna get real busy in a hurry on this planet. If it's not, we'll just have to wait some more."

"Right," he said. "Continuing to observe. Keep me updated."

"You'll be one of the first to know," Jackson promised. He signed off and put his PC on the desk.

"They're on their way?" asked Laura, who was looking a little haggard this morning due to the fact that she was living on less than an hour's worth of sleep.

"It looks like it," he told her, picking up a combat computer and fitting the microphone and earpiece into place. "And we're ready for them. They won't get anywhere near you."

She nodded, chewing her lip a little nervously. She had always known that Martian resentment towards their corporate masters was something that would not need much fuel to whip into a frenzy. That frenzy had been achieved. But now, in order for them to support an open revolt against those masters, they needed a single, outrageous act to rally behind. The various massacres and mass arrests that had been taking place all over the planet were outrageous of course but, strangely enough, they could not provide quite enough impetus to compel them to act. Something else was needed, something that would unite everyone behind the cause.

The corporate Earthlings, in their glorious predictability, were now providing that something. They were attempting to forcibly remove her from office with trumped-up charges, charges that most of the Martian people, with their cultural intelligence and common sense, would recognize for what they were. The moment was now at hand. Everything—her entire career, her entire life—had all come down to this day. It was time for the most dangerous game to begin.

Jackson realized what the stakes were as well. The plan for the next twenty-four hours was something he had come up with years before in its base form and had been modified and remodified dozens of times since. It was now time to see if it was going to work. He instructed the combat computer to patch him in with Lieutenant Warren of Whiting's security detail. The computer complied, taking less than a second to do so.

"Warren here, General," he said, his voice calm and professional.

"It looks like they're on their way, Mike," Jackson told him. "Intelligence reports four vans moving in, probable platoon strength. More than likely they will not all come inside."

"Both the inside and the outside teams are in place and ready," Warren said. "We should be able to handle them easily."

"Remember," Jackson warned, "get a look at the warrant and the indictment before you do anything. If they don't have it with them, don't let them in."

"Understood," he said.

Laura listened to all this with interest, part of her knowing her security platoon was one of the best in the business, but part of her worrying that the FLEB agents might get in anyway. "How many men do we have around the building?" she asked Jackson once he signed off the transmission.

"One hundred and twenty," he told her. "Warren and his regular platoon are covering the lobby and they'll take the agents that come inside. We also have two platoons of the regular infantry that we quietly called up last night along with the special forces guys. They were briefed in on what was happening early this morning and they've been placed under Warren's command for the duration of this operation. They're hidden in the adjacent planetary office buildings. They'll take the FLEB guys that deploy to guard the exits."

"Did any of them have a problem with their orders?" she wanted to know.

"Not a single one," he said. "In fact, they all seemed rather enthusiastic about them. You're in good hands. This is what I've been training these guys for all these years." He turned Laura's computer terminal towards him. "May I?" he asked her.

"By all means," she said.

"Computer," he said to it, "get me building operations."

"Building operations coming on line," it said.

The screen cleared and, a moment later, a scruffy, unshaven face appeared. A look of annoyance at being interrupted was upon this face until he got a good look at the person calling. "General Jackson," he said, surprised. "What can I do for you?"

"You can shut down the blast doors on all floors except the lobby level," Jackson told him. "Do it immediately. And shut down the elevators as well. Let anyone who is on them get off at the next floor—as long as that floor is not the lobby—and then don't let them go anywhere else."

The maintenance supervisor looked a little taken aback with this request. That was understandable since it was a very unusual one. "Sir?" he asked. "Are you sure that you..."

"I'm positive," Jackson cut in. "Do it now. I want all the workers in this building to stay right where they are. No one is to leave their floors or their immediate area until further notice."

He swallowed a little, trying to process this information. "May I ask why, sir?" he finally blurted. A legitimate question.

"A security threat against the governor," Jackson told him. "There may be some action down in the lobby and I don't want any bystanders blundering into it. I don't have time to explain any further. Now get it done, man, before it's too late."

"Right away, General," he said, signing off.

Less than a minute later, the blast door warning alarm sounded from out in the hallway and the solid steel doors, which were spaced every twenty meters on every floor and were designed to hold in air pressure and everything else, came clanging down. The 6400 planetary government employees, including the legislature and the lieutenant governor, were now trapped in their offices.

*****

The four black FLEB vans pulled up in front of the main entrance to the capital building three minutes later, parking in a neat line. Their doors slid open and the armed agents jumped out, their weapons in their hands. Quickly they spread out. One of the teams took up position directly across the street, pushing their way through the throng of curious Martians that had stopped along their way to see what was going on. Three of the pedestrians were shoved with gun butts before the rest decided that this was not a particularly healthy place to be at the moment. They moved off down the street, most shouting angry and profane words at the FLEB agents as they went. Two of the other teams moved off in different directions. One began trotting around the block to take up position in the rear, the other split up and headed for the side entrances. All forty of them were in contact with tactical radio sets.

"Remember," said Mitchell to everyone on the radio frequency, "she gets taken alive and unharmed at all costs."

No one answered him, but all heard him.

Once everyone was deployed, that left only Mitchell and his nine team members standing before the entrance to the building. They pulled together into a tight bunch and then, following behind their leader, headed for the doorway.

The main entrance to the capital building featured two heavy duty sliding doors that were capable of withstanding a direct hit from a heavy machinegun bullet or a close explosion of significant magnitude. An MPG guard dressed in full armor and with an M-24 slung over his shoulder was manning the security booth right between the two doors. He was protected by a layer of the same glass from both the lobby side and the street side and was able to talk to people only through a series of tiny holes in this glass at face level.

Mitchell walked towards him. He noted that the guard was a lieutenant, a rather higher rank than you would expect to see manning a security booth, but he dismissed this as an irrelevancy, figuring that the MPG guard detail was probably short staffed. After all, what kind of moron would want to guard that greenie bitch in the first place? He also noted that he was dressed in full battle gear, something that he never recalled seeing in his past visits to this place. Usually they were dressed in shorts and a T-shirt with nothing more than a sidearm strapped to their sides. Was there any meaning to this? He thought about it for about a tenth of a second and finally concluded that there wasn't. The greenie—whose name stencil on his armor identified him as WARREN—probably didn't get to wear his armor very often and was taking his stint on booth duty as an excuse to do so.

Warren looked at him expressionlessly as Mitchell stopped in front of the voice holes. "Can I help you?" he asked politely, as if he were a normal citizen asking about tours of the building or an appointment with a legislature representative and not a fully armed FLEB agent holding an assault rifle and leading a team of nine others.

This, at the very least, should have put Mitchell on edge. It didn't. "FLEB," he said simply, with a certain amount of arrogance in his voice. He flipped open a leather case that displayed his federal credentials. "We need immediate access to Governor Whiting's office."

"Oh?" said Warren, raising his eyebrows a tad, only glancing at the shiny badge being shown to him. "I'm afraid that's not possible at the moment."

"Make it possible," Mitchell told him, removing the indictment and the arrest warrant. They were printed in large script on the finest hemp paper available. "I have a federal indictment and an arrest warrant ordering me to take her into custody."

"An indictment and an arrest warrant, huh?" Warren asked, still with no hint of surprise or alarm in his voice. "This sounds rather serious. May I take a look at them?"

Mitchell considered threatening him with obstruction for a moment but finally decided it would be easier to just do as he was asked. Besides, that way the greenie would get to see the official proof of the downfall of his governor. Maybe that would put the expression of fear that he craved upon his face. He slid them through the small slot at the bottom of the glass.

Lieutenant Warren picked them up and looked at them, reading through each document carefully, word for word. Neither Mitchell nor any of his men saw him keying the transmission button on his radio pack three times, sending out a pre-arranged, encrypted signal to the other members of the platoon and General Jackson upstairs. It took him more than two minutes to get through everything. Once he was finished he looked up, his expression still carefully polite and neutral. "Well Agent uh..."

"Mitchell," he provided, more than a little testily.

"Agent Mitchell. Things do seem to be in order here. This is an official indictment and an official arrest warrant for Governor Whiting."

"I'm glad you agree," he said. "Now are you going to buzz us into the building or are we going to have to force our way in?"

"No need for threats," Warren told him. He placed his hands upon a panel on his computer screen and the glass doors slid open. "Come on in. I'll call for the elevator for you."

Mitchell had the vague thought that things were going just a little too easily. It was a thought that he should have listened to. Instead, excited at the thought of getting this over quickly, he dismissed it. He took a quick glance behind him, seeing that the media vans from the big three, responding to the tip that had been given to them less than an hour ago, were pulling up and positioning themselves across the street. That was good. Soon they would film him leading that troublemaking bitch out in handcuffs. He waved his men forward and into the lobby of the capital building, moving past Warren's security booth and onto the simple Martian red carpet that covered the lobby floor.

The lobby was a huge area, stretching from one end of the building to the other. It was decorated as one might expect a seat of government's lobby to be. Ornate sculptures were located in many places along the walls. Decorative planters and even a working wishing well with benches around it were in the center. It was actually quite a nice place and one that workers in the building and tourists enjoyed lounging about in to eat their lunch or rest their feet. At the moment however, the entire area was completely deserted except for Lieutenant Warren. Or at least, that was how it seemed to the FLEB agents as they trooped inside.

Mitchell had never been a soldier before, and he wasn't even really a cop with a cop's instincts. He noted the lack of people in the lobby and it did strike him as a bit odd for the beginning of a workday, but this failed to trigger any danger signals within him. He never considered for a moment that all of the planters and sculptures, all of the benches and information booths, were ideal places to hide security troops that did not wish to be seen.

The glass doors slid shut behind them, latching with a clank of steel mechanisms coming together.

Mitchell turned to Warren. "Keep those doors open," he told him. He wanted his men outside to be able to enter the building in a hurry if it became necessary. He didn't know that it was already necessary.

"I'm afraid not, Agent Mitchell," Warren said, smiling now. "You are now sealed into the lobby. Your men outside will be shortly taken into custody. You and all of your men will now put your rifles down on the floor and then throw your sidearms down there with them."

"What?" Mitchell said, his face scrunching into an expression of annoyance. "Listen to me, greenie. I don't know what you think you're trying to pull here, but I'll advise you that attempting to interfere with a federal arrest is a crime punishable..."

"I'm not *attempting* to interfere," Warren told him. "I *have* interfered. You will not be taking Governor Whiting anywhere. You are surrounded on all sides by my security forces, all of whom are veterans of the special forces division. You will put your weapons on the ground and prepare to be taken into custody, or you will be fired upon."

Mitchell took a moment to digest these words and then keyed up his radio. "All teams," he said into his microphone. "We need some assistance in here! We're getting resistance from..."

"Your radios are being jammed," Warren said matter-of-factly. "We have dampers set up all around the edges of the lobby and set to your frequency."

Mitchell wanted to disbelieve his words, but the lack of response on the channel kept him from doing so. He looked around, seeing the stunned, nervous faces of his men. He didn't know what to do. He had never been faced with a situation such as this before. He was a federal agent! People feared him. They didn't attempt to take him hostage. The very idea was absurd!

"There is no need for this to come to violence," Warren told him. "Drop your weapons and surrender. You will be held here in the capital for the duration of this little crisis and you will be treated well. If you don't, however, my men will be forced to take you down by force. Go the easy way, Mitchell. Let's keep this thing civilized."

It might have ended peacefully. Mitchell was just about to order his men to do as they were told, knowing that the guard would probably not be bluffing about what he was saying. After all, he had looked into Whiting's security force himself when he'd been examining the possibilities of arranging an assassination. But special agent Brackford, the youngest member of the team, had other thoughts on the matter. At only twenty-eight years of age and an appointee to the FLEB by virtue of family connections instead of ability, Brackford was known for his short temper and impulsive actions. These were traits which had earned him reprimands in the past and that would now cost him much more than a black mark on his file. Outraged that the greenies would actually *threaten* federal agents carrying out their duties, he took matters into his own hands.

"Fuck you, greenie!" he yelled arrogantly. Before Mitchell could stop him, he raised his M-24 and pointed it at the guard booth. It is doubtful that the shots would have penetrated the glass, but they never got a chance to find out.

Flashes appeared from four different directions accompanied by the harsh popping of M-24s. Brackford's head rocked back and forth as two of the rounds slammed into his helmet, drilling through into his skull. The other two slammed into his chest, penetrating with ease through the Kevlar of his armor vest. He dropped to the carpeted lobby without even firing a shot.

The reaction from the rest of the agents was ill-advised, but instinctive. They raised their weapons and turned towards the flashes they'd seen, opening fire. From all around the lobby, from behind plants, behind staircases, behind counters, gunfire and bright flashes erupted. Bullets streaked across the lobby in both directions, the ones fired from FLEB guns striking the walls and the windows and the solid objects that the MPG troops were using as cover, the ones fired by the security force finding chests and heads and legs. Agents screamed and thumped to the ground as the supersonic rounds ripped into them. Warren had planned his takedown well. There was nowhere for the agents to find cover, nowhere for them to run. Mitchell himself managed to trigger off a single burst towards the staircase before he felt his chest peppered with hammer blows and his feet were suddenly refusing to hold him up. He dropped to the ground, blood now running from his mouth, his eyes looking at the carpet against his face, his mind wondering just what the hell had happened.

*****

"Goddamn it!" Warren yelled, opening his booth door and stepping out into the lobby. His orders had been to take the FLEB agents without gunfire if possible. The young hotheaded agent had made this impossible. Now, all ten of them were laid out on the carpet, only two of them showing any signs of life whatsoever. The Martian red carpet beneath them was soaking up the blood and turning a darker shade.

"Second and third platoon," he said into his radio link as he walked carefully towards the pile of FLEB agents, "we've made contact. Move in and secure the outside forces." Both of the platoon commanders acknowledged his orders. He then asked for a status report on his own men. "Anyone hurt?" he asked the group at large.

None of them answered up, which meant that either all of them were dead or none of them had been hit. Logic favored the latter. "Get down here and secure these idiots," he ordered. "Medics, start sorting through them."

From all around the room, his platoon emerged, all of them dressed in battle gear, all of them pointing their weapons at the FLEB agents.

"Get those weapons secured," he ordered. "Move the dead off towards the back of the room, move the living towards the doors so we can get some dip-hoes in here to pick them up."

"Warren," came Jackson's voice over the link. "What the hell's going on down there? Give me a status report!"

"The lobby is secure, General," Warren told him, watching as his men went to work disarming and securing. "They went the hard way. All ten are down and we're sorting through them right now. All of my people are uninjured. The outside forces should be moving in as we speak."

"Copy that, Warren," Jackson responded, a hint of regret in his voice. "I'm sure it was unavoidable."

"It was," he confirmed.

"Mark this moment, son," he said. "Your platoon has just fired the first shots of the revolution. Let's make sure that they weren't in vain, shall we?"

"Yes sir."

*****

The FLEB agents standing by outside heard the gunfire from the lobby. More than forty M-24 assault rifles firing in fully automatic mode made a considerable amount of noise. They also heard the silence on the airwaves when they tried to contact their companions. Instinctively, the four groups of them rushed to whatever entrance they were guarding to try to lend assistance. In each case, the entrance in question was closed and locked, inaccessible to anyone without a cutting torch or some primacord.

The Internet camera crews, who had set up shop across the street, had heard the gunfire as well and had actually transmitted the entire gun battle live on the air as it unfolded with the assistance of digital zoom and infrared enhancement. Perversely enough, the camera crews and the few people on Mars that were actually watching the big three at the moment (less than three percent of the Martian viewers, the computers would later reveal) knew the fate of the FLEB agents inside the building long before their companions.

It was while the FLEB agents were peering through the thick glass, trying to get a look inside to see what the situation was, that the two MPG platoons swarmed out of their hiding places, weapons ready for action. Each platoon had split into two elements, which gave twenty soldiers to cover each side of the building. The FLEB agents never even heard them coming until it was far too late.

"MPG! Everyone freeze!" yelled the leaders of each element as they positioned themselves behind what cover they could find.

Most of the agents took one look at what they were facing and complied with the order, knowing that to do otherwise would be futile. A few hotheads of the Brackford variety however, did make the mistake of trying to resist capture. On the south side of the building, against the side entrance, a five-year member of the FLEB made what he thought was a quick spin towards the enemy behind him. He made it less than halfway around before five rifles cracked out three-round bursts of high velocity bullets at him. All fifteen shots hit within a half a second of each other, ripping through every major organ in his chest. He collapsed to the ground, a bloody, twisted mess. On the west side, next to the main entrance, another agent, this one a twelve-year veteran, tried diving down to the ground to make himself a smaller target. This he was able to accomplish, but, before he could bring his weapon to bear, nine bullets smashed into his face, exploding his skull into three separate pieces. On the east side of the building, an agent that had once been a corporal in the WestHem army actually managed to turn and get a single shot off. His bullet passed neatly between two MPG members and buried itself in the steel of the building across the street. The unfortunate agent was then plastered by more than sixty rounds as the entire line of infantry troops fired at him.

Any cute ideas that the rest of the agents might have had about resistance or escape disappeared at this point. They threw their weapons to the ground and allowed themselves to be restrained with their own handcuffs. Before their radios were removed however, most of them managed to squeak out pleas for assistance from the main office.

Once disarmed and secured, they were marched inside the nearest entrance where they got a good look at what had become of their fellow agents that had gone in to make the arrest. Seething with hatred, rage, and fear, they were led down a stairway and into the building's basement where they would be placed under guard.

With the outside threat taken care of, the two platoons of infantry pulled inside the building, leaving the street to the astonished crowd of reporters and bystanders.

*****

"The capital is secure," Jackson told Whiting once the status reports had all come in. "Most of the FLEB guys out front surrendered without a fight."

"Most of them?" she asked, sipping from a cup of coffee.

"Most of them," he said. "Three were killed trying to resist. We have no reports of civilian casualties. Of the agents that came inside, seven of them are dead, three quite badly wounded. We've asked for some dip-hoes to pick them up out front of the main doors, but the police aren't letting them through."

"I see," she said wearily. "Are there police out front right now?"

"You know it," he said. "A lot of the FLEB agents outside were able to call for assistance on their radios. Plus, the entire thing was captured on Internet cameras. It would seem that the FLEB tipped the big three to what was going on here. The camera crews arrived at about the same time as the agents themselves."

"Imagine that," she said cynically.

"Yes, big surprise, huh? In any case, the FLEB office called the New Pittsburgh Police Department for assistance with a hostage situation. They've deployed most of the downtown patrol units around the building and they have the SWAT teams on the way. I also have reports from intelligence that forty more FLEB agents in full gear have left their main office and are heading this way."

"I see," she said. "What is our next step?"

"Now, the rest of the infantry that we called up last night will secure the entire area. They were staging at the MPG base and I just gave the order to have them move in. They should be here in less than an hour. We need to get those cops out of there before they arrive."

"I'll talk to Chief Sandoza," she said. "Hopefully it won't be a problem. He's a bureaucrat in every sense of the word, but he's also a Martian. He's supported the reforms that we've initiated so far."

"Do it quick," Jackson said. "The worst thing that could happen to us right now is for there to be gunfire between the MPG and the police. And it's also time to put out the general call-up of forces. We'll need everyone suited up and ready to go as quickly as possible. Those marines at the Eden barracks need to be secured before someone has the bright idea of using them."

"I'll do that right now," she said, putting her coffee down and turning her computer terminal towards her. "Computer," she told it, "initiate order 74-1." 74-1 was the section of the Martian constitution that allowed the governor to call up all Martian Planetary Guard units to active duty to repel an imminent invasion of the planet. It authorized the planetary government to take over the MarsTrans public transportation system to facilitate the movement of soldiers to the MPG base and ordered all employers, under penalty of treason, to release the MPG members from their regular jobs. It was an order that had never been initiated before, not even as a training exercise.

"Order 74-1 is pending," the computer told her, flashing a text of the call up notice upon her screen. "Voice recognition of Whiting, Laura E, Governor of Planet Mars, is confirmed. Please give the authorization code."

Laura rattled off a nine-digit number that she had long since memorized.

"Authorization code is correct," the computer replied. "Please sign the order."

She placed her right index finger on the screen, signing it.

"The order will be initiated," the computer told her.

Within ten seconds, the main MPG database was contacted and the names and PC addresses of every single member were called with a pre-recorded message. At the same time, the MarsTrans office was contacted and given some very unpleasant news. They would have to surrender use of their trains for the next twenty-four hours.

"Okay," Jackson said after watching all of this. "Now get those cops out of here. While you're doing that, I'll get the guys up on Triad moving." With that he left the room for the office next door, where he had his own terminal set up now.

"Computer," Laura said, "get me Chief Sandoza of the New Pittsburgh Police Department. Highest priority."

"You have forty-three callers attempting to reach you at the moment," the computer told her. "Would you like me to list them?"

"No," she said, knowing that most of them were people like Corban Hayes or William Smith. "For the time being, accept no incoming calls."

"Accepting no incoming calls. Contacting Chief Sandoza."

"Thank you," she said, leaning back in her chair and closing her eyes for a moment. Things were moving fast now. Soon they would move even faster.

It took about three minutes before Sandoza came on the line. Laura understood. He probably had a lot on his mind at the moment. His handsome, aristocratic face appeared before her, his eyes stern but confused. "Governor Whiting?" he said. "What the hell is going on over there?"

"Nice to hear from you too, Nick," she said lightly. "I suppose you've caught a small glint of the proceedings here?"

"Governor, to tell you the truth, I simply can't believe what I'm hearing. The FLEB director himself called me up to ask me to mobilize my force and move in on the capital building because your security troops are holding his men and all of the workers inside of the building hostage, including the lieutenant governor and the legislature." He shook his head. "Hostages? Surely there is a mistake going on here. He also said that an indictment has been handed down on you and that you are to be taken into custody. Is this true?"

"It's true, Nick. A federal grand jury in *Denver*..." – she emphasized the name of that city, knowing that most Martians hated the very sound of it – "...has indicted me on corruption charges. FLEB agents came to the capital to arrest me for extradition to Earth. My security team prevented them from doing that."

"Jesus Christ!" he said, shocked.

"Unfortunately, some of the FLEB agents did not surrender peacefully. Ten of them are dead, three badly wounded. The rest of them are in the basement being held under guard. As for the lieutenant governor and the rest of the workers, they are not hostages but they are being kept in their offices to keep them out of harm's way. They'll be allowed to leave as soon as this situation is under control."

"Laura, what in the hell do you think you're doing over there? You've killed federal agents! You've resisted arrest! You'll be given the death penalty!"

"Nick," she said quietly, "I know exactly what I'm doing. I know that right now, your cops are surrounding the capital building at the request of the FLEB, initiating a hostage response. I've known you for a long time and I know that you're a Martian, not an Earthling. I need to ask you something, and I want you to answer me honestly. Do you believe that the indictment against me represents real corruption charges or is it simply a result of WestHem trying to remove a troublesome governor from office?"

He stared back at her, though he was actually staring at a screen in his own office twelve blocks away. "Of course they're not real charges, Laura," he said. "Everyone knows that. But it's a federal indictment. The place to fight it is in court, not in the lobby of the capital. The corruption charges are going to be secondary to...."

"Nick," she interrupted, "I don't think you understand where I'm going with this."

"What do you mean?"

"I'm *not* going to be removed from this building. Events are bigger than a simple hostage situation. This is the opening move in a revolution. I need you to pull your cops out of here."

"I can't do that!" he exclaimed. "We're not talking about refusing to cooperate with a questionable raid on Martian citizens here. We're talking about the illegal seizure of a government building in which deaths have occurred. The deaths of federal law enforcement officers! The law..."

"It's *WestHem* law you're talking about," she interrupted again. "I'm telling you, Nick, I will not be removed from this building. MPG troops are already on the way to secure it and they will follow my orders, at least for the time being. Your cops are all Martians and I don't want them to get hurt. Pull them back. This is not between them and me, it's between the feds and me. Don't let the feds involve your people in this. Your cops are not equipped to deal with army troops and they are not the enemy my people need to be fighting. Pull them back and withdraw your cooperation with the FLEB. You are under planetary control, not federal. I'll take the heat and I'll tell everyone I ordered it."

He stared some more, his brain obviously on overload. Laura knew she had struck several chords with her words, something she had a knack for, something that had brought her as far as she'd come. "What exactly are you planning?" he finally said.

"I can't discuss it right now," she told him. "Like I said, things will be clear in another day and you'll have the opportunity to evaluate my actions along with all of the other Martian citizens. But for now, you're just going to have to trust me. Pull back your people. Keep them on the right side of this thing and let them decide for themselves in the next two days. If you keep them in place here, some of them are going to be killed and that's the last thing in the world I want. Pull them back. I know you're recording this conversation and I take full responsibility for this action. If you have red blood flowing in your veins, you'll do as I ask and give no more assistance to the FLEB."

He bit his lip nervously as he stared at her, a simple Martian politician who had just had the most important decision of his life dumped into his lap. But he was not a dumb man by any means. He was a former street cop who had risen through the ranks to achieve the position he now held. He knew Laura Whiting and he knew what she stood for. "They'll be pulled back," he finally said. "And God help you, Laura."

"God help us all." Laura replied with a grateful smile.

*****

Officers John Williams and Zifford Resinman of the New Pittsburgh PD had been on scene less than ten minutes. They were sixty meters from the main entrance of the capital building, covering behind their police cart. Their M-24 rifles were in their hands, pointing at the doors, the selector switches set on full automatic fire. Their helmets were firmly in place and their combat goggles showed only a glare of the dim Martian sunlight reflecting off of the glass and a strained view of an empty lobby beyond it. Their radios crackled out a hundred different orders and inquiries, adding to the general feeling of confusion that was pervading the scene. All around them were other NPPD police officers deployed in a similar matter. The elite SWAT team had just arrived and was taking up position against the walls of the capital building itself. They had primacord and anti-tank lasers with them for breaching the doors if that became necessary. About a hundred yards down the street, well out of the line of sight of the capital, the FLEB troops had arrived and were milling about behind their vans, talking to Lieutenant Bongwater, who was in charge of the police aspects of the operation.

"Ziff?" asked John over their private tactical link. "What the hell is going on here? Do you really believe that the governor's security troops fired on FLEB agents?"

"Do you really think that they were trying to arrest the governor?" Zifford asked. "If they were, I'm glad they did. Fuck those federal assholes. You know that whatever the charges are, they're bullshit."

"Yep," John agreed. "It'd be just like those pricks to try and indict her on some bogus charge to get rid of her."

Zifford nodded. "Yeah. And if we're hearing right, those are MPG guys inside there. For God's sake, we're part of the MPG. I don't want to shoot any of my own people." This was true. Both men were members of the MPG New Pittsburgh division. Zifford was a tanker. John was a Hummingbird pilot.

"I know the feeling," John said. "Hell, I probably know some of the guys in there. I transport the special forces out to their staging areas every weekend. That's where all the fucking VIP security guys come from." He shook his head. "It can't end this way. I hope they don't force us to stand here and help them take her away."

"I don't think I could be a part of that," Zifford said. "I really don't."

At that moment their PCs both began to vibrate, indicating incoming calls. They both reached for them, taking care to keep their rifles aimed at the building with one hand as they did so. Around them, a few of the other cops that were deployed were doing the same thing, thus clueing them in to what they were going to see when they answered. Both flipped open their screens and saw that the MPG main headquarters was the calling party.

"They're calling us up," Zifford said slowly, a hint of fear in his voice.

John looked at him and looked around at the others. "Answer," he told his PC.

The face of General Jackson himself appeared before him. "This is General Jackson and this message is for all active members of the Martian Planetary Guard," his image said. "This is a general call-up of forces for an imminent threat to the planet. MarsTrans trains are being cleared as we speak. Make your way as quickly as possible to your duty stations and you will be given a briefing and deployment orders at that time. This is not, I repeat, this is *not* a drill."

"Holy shit," John said.

"Is this because of the feds?" Zifford asked softly. "Is it the feds, or is it an EastHem attack?"

John looked over at the gathering of FLEB officers. They were standing in a large group, their apparent leader apart from them and talking to Bongwater. He seemed upset about something. "I think it's the feds," he said softly. "Coming right now, while they're trying to take Governor Whiting away? What else could it be?"

"Whiting is going to ask us to fight for her," Zifford said. "She's going to ask us to fight against WestHem."

John nodded. "I think you're right."

They contemplated that thought for a moment, both of them letting their attention lapse from the section of the building they were supposed to be watching.

"Will you do it?" Zifford finally asked.

He nodded. "If it means making us free... I'll do it."

"So will I," Zifford said.

All around them similar conversations were going on. The consensus seemed to be the same in every instance.

*****

Lieutenant Glory Bongwater was as confused as the rest of them, though her information was a little bit better. She stood before an Internet screen at the command post, a block away from the main entrance to the capital. Beside her was Special Agent Waxford, the highest-ranking FLEB agent left from the field office besides Corban Hayes himself. Waxford knew exactly what he wanted done, but otherwise didn't know his ass from a hole in the ground. Bongwater detested him immensely and longed to slam the butt of her pistol across his mouth.

"When can your people rush the building?" he demanded of Bongwater. "I have agents in there, some of them wounded."

"I know that," she said for the fifth time. "We're following our standard hostage situation procedures. We've contacted General Jackson inside and we'll work to try to end this thing peacefully. We only rush the building when we're given no other option."

"My wounded might die in there while we're waiting!" Waxford yelled. "Don't you understand that?"

"Jackson offered to let the dip-hoes take the wounded away," she reminded him. "It's you who ordered that that not be done, remember?"

"I don't want to give them more hostages!" he said. "You can't let a bunch of dip-hoes go running up to the door to take people away. They'll be shot down!"

"It would be our SWAT team that approached the doorway," Bongwater said. "And I believe they would be safe. Those are MPG troops in there holding that building, not criminals. They wouldn't fire on them."

"They fired on our agents, didn't they?" he countered.

Bongwater took a deep breath, fighting to control herself. "Perhaps that is because they figured that your men represented a danger to Governor Whiting," she said. "Perhaps they felt that your warrant and your indictment were fabricated."

"Ridiculous," he spat. "You don't actually believe that, do you?"

She held his gaze. "What I believe doesn't really matter now, does it? My point is that we can safely remove your wounded and get them assistance if you'll allow it. I was once a member of the MPG myself. They won't fire on us for doing that."

"Request denied," he said icily. "You just start formulating a plan to charge that building. I want this situation brought under control within the hour."

"And I want there to be peace in the solar system," Bongwater said. "But we don't usually get what we want now, do we? If your agents want to rush the building, that's fine. Go rushing in. We'll even lend you the primacord and the AT lasers. But as long as my people are involved in this thing, we do it my way. And my way is to negotiate with the people in the building to try to end this peacefully."

"Maybe I should talk to your superior about this," he said in a threatening tone.

Bongwater knew an empty threat when she heard one. "Maybe you should," she returned.

Waxford muttered something under his breath and then stormed away, back to the crowd of agents that were standing around in their armor, waiting for someone to tell them what to do.

"Goddamn FLEB fucks," Bongwater said to herself.

She looked down at her command computer, which had been set up on the hood of her cart. It showed a schematic of the building and the location of all the friendly forces. There were more than eighty police officers, not including the SWAT team, now deployed around the building. That was still somewhat less than the 120 to 150 MPG troops that were rumored to be inside the capital. And the MPG were better trained and better equipped as well. No, even if she did feel that a crime of some type had been committed, something that she had serious doubts about, she never would have ordered her forces to go head to head with those kinds of numbers.

"Priority communication from Deputy Chief Winston," her terminal suddenly spoke up. "Would you like to answer?"

"On screen," she told it.

The screen flashed briefly over to the communications software main screen and then was just as quickly replaced by the middle-aged face of Winston, a twenty-two year veteran and, until the Laura Whiting reforms had taken place, one of the brownest nosed people that the department employed. "Bongwater," he said. "Are you with any FLEB people right now?"

"No," she told her. "My friend Waxford has gone off to stew somewhere. What's up? Any news?"

"Big news," Winston told her. "Direct from Chief Sandoza himself."

He began to speak, giving a series of orders. Bongwater smiled in satisfaction as she heard them. "I'm happy to comply," she said. "Thanks, chief."

"My pleasure," Winston said and signed off.

Bongwater looked over to the crowd of FLEB agents and got Waxford's attention. He came trotting over.

"What is it?" he asked, seeing the smile on her face and assuming it was good news for his team. "Did Jackson decide to give up?"

"No, even better news than that," she said. "We're pulling out. You're now on your own."

He looked at her, confused. "What do you mean?"

"I mean I've just received orders to cease cooperation with the FLEB. I'm pulling my cops out of here and breaking down the perimeter."

"You can't do that!" he yelled loud enough for everyone within thirty meters to hear.

"I can and I will," she said. "Direct orders from Chief Sandoza. Pull back and resume routine duties. Do not interfere with operations at the capital and do not respond to any calls for assistance from FLEB personnel. You're gonna have to take this building by yourself."

Veins began to poke out on Waxford's head as he heard this. "What kind of shit is..."

"It's the kind of shit that's a direct order from the Chief," Bongwater told him calmly. "And it's an order I'm happy to obey. Have fun fighting your way in, Waxford."

"I have federal authority," he told her. "I *demand* you follow my orders! If you don't, you'll stand trial in federal court for..."

"You have no authority over me or my people," she said. "This is a federal matter and we're local law enforcement. Cooperation with the feds is simply a courtesy and it's just been revoked." She turned to her Internet terminal. "Command channel."

"Command channel activated." The computer replied.

"This is Lieutenant Bongwater," she said. "All New Pittsburgh Police Department personnel on the capital building perimeter will immediately demobilize on orders from Chief Sandoza. Return to previous patrol assignments. SWAT personnel return to training stations. No further assistance will be given to federal personnel including calls for assistance in the future. All members of the force that are MPG members are hereby released from duty to respond to their military assignments. I repeat, all New Pittsburgh Police Department personnel...

*****

In the governor's office, Jackson turned to Laura. "All NPPD personnel have pulled back and returned to their routine duties. All we have out front now in terms of opposition are about forty FLEB people, damn near the entire compliment for New Pittsburgh"

Laura sighed in relief. "Thank you Chief Sandoza," she proclaimed. "That certainly makes this next step a little easier, doesn't it?"

"Indeed," he replied, raising his pocket computer to his face. "Get me Major Dealerman."

*****

The 2nd Battalion of the 8th armored infantry regiment had been called up as part of the initial preliminary forces the day before. Major Dealerman had been initially very confused by the "special training" order that had brought him and the 836 troops under his command to the base in the middle of a weekday, both because he knew that special training of that sort was unheard of and because only his battalion had been requested. Upon arrival at the base however, he had been briefed in by General Jackson himself over a secure Internet line and told the *real* reason for the call-up.

"The feds have a warrant for Governor Whiting's arrest," he'd been told. "They're going to try to take her into custody tomorrow morning."

Dealerman had been shocked by this news and more than a little outraged as well, but he'd still had no idea what that had to do with he and his battalion. He'd said as much and Jackson had then laid the biggest shock of his life upon him.

"We're going to fight them," Jackson said. "The security force at the capitol building is going to capture the agents that arrive to arrest her. They're capable of securing the building itself and preventing her arrest, but we're going to need additional troops to secure the outside and the surrounding blocks."

"You're ordering me to do this?" he'd asked, just for clarity. "To engage WestHem federal officers?"

"I'm *asking* you to do this," Jackson corrected. "The MPG is a volunteer outfit. If you don't want to do it, we'll find someone else. The same applies to your men. If you accept this assignment, I expect you to brief your command in advance and give all of them the opportunity to decline."

"I understand," he'd said.

"Then you'll do it?"

"I'll do it," he'd said without hesitation. "Tell me the plan."

The plan had started the night before with the briefing by Dealerman. He had been honest with his men about the ramifications of their actions and, unsurprisingly, not a single member of the 1st of the 6th had elected to forgo participation. They were ready to do or die for Mars.

Charlie company had been separated out the night before for a couple of different tasks that had to do with the capital itself. Two of the platoons had been moved to the capital in the early morning hours and placed under Warren's command. It was they who had hidden in adjoining buildings and taken the outside FLEB agents. The other half of this company was performing its mission now. Since 0700, the eighty men that consisted of third and fourth platoon had been mounted in their APCs awaiting their movement orders. These orders had come and the movement was now under way.

The column of eight APCs clunked noisily through the streets of Eden, working their way towards downtown, their treads riding over a surface that they were never meant to be upon. Pedestrians, most of whom had no idea what was going on, scrambled to make way for the monstrous machines as they passed, staring in confused awe at the heavy weapons and the helmeted, goggled heads of the commanders. The ground rumbled beneath and long after the armor had passed the vibration and noise could still be heard and felt.

Lieutenant Presley, a ten-year member of the MPG infantry, was sitting in the commander's seat in the third APC from the front, far enough forward that he could see what was going on, but far enough back so he wouldn't be easily identified and taken out by the opposition. Not that the opposition in this case had much of a chance at that. He kept his hand resting upon the butt of the 4mm machine gun mounted just outside of his port and his eyes upon the tactical display that showing through his combat goggles.

"Presley," a voice said in his earpiece, which was tuned to the command channel. "Dealerman here. Do you copy?"

"Go ahead, Major," Presley replied.

"I just got word from Jackson," Dealerman told him. "The New Pittsburgh Police Department have pulled back. Opposition is now only about forty feds equipped with light weapons. Move in and secure a perimeter for two blocks around the capital building, including the two tram stations. Hold until relieved or ordered to withdraw. Weapons free but a little tight. Don't smoke them unless they ask for it."

"Yes sir," Presley told him without hesitation. He was a building maintenance technician in his civilian life and had spent his entire working career being looked down upon by rich corporate Earthlings in the Kendall-Brackely building. He was ready and willing to take the planet away from such people and proud to be involved in the first conflict. He switched to the tactical channel he used to command his men. "All right, guys," he told them. "NPPD has pulled back. All we have opposing us at the objective are about forty feds with light weapons. We're going to secure a radius of two blocks centered on the capital. Fourth platoon, break off at 23rd street and maneuver around to the south side. Come back down to 5th at 18th street. We'll hold back over here and then box them in when you're in position. ROE is weapons free but a little tight."

"Copy that," said Lieutenant Carmichael, commander of that platoon. "Let's go kick some fed ass."

*****

The FLEB agents had redeployed their vans to the corners of the building and were using it as cover to watch the building from. Others were crouched behind the decorative planters that lined the middle of the street, their faces scared, their weapons trembling in their hands. Waxford, hiding behind the furthest van from the front of the building, was on the communications channel talking to a shocked and horrified Corban Hayes back at the main FLEB building. He had just given a report on the unbelievable events and they were still trying to figure out what their next move should be.

"We only have twenty more sworn agents in New Pittsburgh," Hayes told him. "That's not even enough to provide security for our own building, let alone take the capital building and free our captured men."

"How about the other cities?" Waxford asked. "We have almost a hundred agents up on Triad. How soon can you get them on a surface to orbit and get them down here?"

"Not for at least three hours," Hayes replied. "I'll get them started though, and I'll have fifty from Eden and Proctor get on one of the inter-city trains."

"Jesus, what a fuck-up," Waxford almost cried. "I knew we should have sent more agents for this arrest."

"They'll regret this sorely," Hayes assured him. "Have your men hold the perimeter until reinforcements arrive. Shoot anyone who tries to come out of that building. I'll try to call that prick Sandoza back and threaten him with some more federal statutes. Maybe I can get him to send those greenie cops back to help end this thing. If we shut off power and utilities to that building we can flush them out in a matter of hours."

"What about the MPG call up?" he asked. "What's the deal with that?"

"We've been hearing that over here as well," Hayes said. "I don't know what that's all about or if it's related. I've got Benson over at the Eden office looking into that one. It's probably just some sort of false alarm or a training mission."

At that moment, the clanking of treads reached Waxford's ears for the first time. It swelled up from the north and the south simultaneously and grew louder by the second. The agents in their position all began to look around, searching out the source.

"Waxford," Hayes said, noticing that his underling seemed suddenly preoccupied. "What's going on? Are they trying to break out?"

"We have armored vehicles moving our way," he said softly, feeling fear gripping him.

"What?"

"A lot of them," he said. "Coming from both directions."

"Armored vehicles?" Hayes demanded. "What kind of armored vehicles? Tanks, APCs, what? Those things can't move inside of the city!"

"You might want to tell them that," Waxford said as the first of them came into view from around the corner three blocks away. Three others followed it. From the other direction, behind him, four more appeared. He recognized them as WestHem ET-40 armored personnel carriers. They were painted in the shades of red camouflage scheme and the Martian flag flew proudly from the communications antennas of each one. They spread out of their formation almost as soon as they became visible and took up positions on adjacent corners, hiding the bulk of their bodies behind the corner of buildings, their sixty-millimeter guns as well as their twenty millimeters pointing directly at the FLEB positions.

"Waxford!" Hayes yelled. "What the hell is going on?"

"I don't think that the MPG call-up was a coincidence," Waxford said softly.

As the terrified FLEB agents watched in horror, the ramps of the APCs swung open and out climbed heavily armed troops who immediately fanned out and took up firing positions, each squad of ten equipped with a light machine gun, three grenade launchers, and ten rifles. Weapons were trained upon them and they felt themselves start to sweat, could almost feel the targeting reticles from the MPG combat computers resting upon their foreheads.

Waxford, as leader of the FLEB agents, was perhaps the most horrified. He did not know what to do. In all of his training and experience, he'd never been faced with a problem like this before. He'd never even conceived of such a thing. He was a federal officer! People were supposed to fear and respect him! There weren't supposed to surround him with armored vehicles and automatic weapons!

His Internet screen lit up before him, showing him the face of a greenie in combat goggles and a helmet. "Agent Waxford," the greenie addressed him politely. "I am Lieutenant Presley of the Martian Planetary Guard. Can you hear me?"

Waxford stared at the screen, wondering how the greenies had gotten access to his terminal. The communications frequency that they were using was supposed to be secure. It occurred to him for the first time that maybe they had been underestimating the greenies a little bit. "Yes," he finally replied.

"You are surrounded by two platoons of MPG troops with light and heavy weapons. You do not have a chance of defeating them. You will order your men to disable all of their weapons and then walk to the center of the street and drop them in a pile. They will then lie down and await being taken into custody. This is your first and final offer. If you do not do as I say in the next sixty seconds, our troops will open fire upon you and move in. I will reiterate the fact that you do not have a chance of defeating them. Do you understand me, Agent Waxford?"

He licked his lips nervously, his body trembling with adrenaline as he surveyed the massive firepower that was arrayed against him and his men.

"Agent Waxford," Presley said firmly. "Do you understand my conditions?"

"I do," Waxford said, near tears. "We will do as you ask."

"You have fifty seconds."

Waxford issued the order. "All FLEB agents. We have been betrayed and we are in the face of overwhelming opposition. Disable your weapons immediately and take them to the middle of the street. Drop them there and then lie down. Do this now or we will be fired upon. We will be taken into custody by the greenies. God help us all, but there will be a reckoning for them and there will be justice."

One by one the agents did as they were told. Waxford waited until all of them were prone on the street and then he too disabled his weapons and joined them. He was crying with humiliation and rage as he lay on his stomach.

*****

Since very few Martians were actually watching the big three channels, most of them missed the live shots of the capture of the first elements. But word and rumor traveled fast and, within twenty minutes of the first shots being fired, nearly everyone on the planet had tuned in and was watching the subsequent events unfold live and in surround sound. MarsGroup quickly sent its own reporters to the scene and, by the time that the New Pittsburgh Police Department members pulled out of the perimeter, the Martians were able to switch to those channels and therefore not have to listen to the syrupy commentary about the poor FLEB agents and the evil acts that had been committed by the rogue governor.

For the most part, the emotion the Martians displayed was one of shock and anger at what was going on. They were shocked that the feds and the WestHem corporations would attempt such a blatantly obvious scheme to rid themselves of Whiting, and angry that they thought they would be allowed to get away with it quietly. Most Martians cheered when the final confrontation took place between the newly activated MPG units and the handful of feds that had been left to guard the building on their own. Once the feds were led away in handcuffs, hustled inside the buildings to join their companions, the big three reporters began focusing on how the "hostage crisis" (as they called it) was going to be resolved. Some suggested that the marines from the Eden barracks would be activated and used to liberate the building, others suggested a mass gathering of the remaining federal agents on the planet. None of them entertained the thought that Laura Whiting would not be eventually taken into custody for her crimes. The very idea was inconceivable to them. The big three completely ignored the activation of the MPG and only mentioned the take-over of the public transportation system as an aside. On the MarsGroup channels however, speculation immediately turned to the obvious connection of the general call up of MPG forces.

"There has never been a general call-up in the entire history of the MPG," one MarsGroup commentator pointed out soberly. "This is only supposed to happen when there is an imminent threat to the security of the planet, such as an EastHem invasion. Now, since we see no signs of an EastHem invasion and there have been no reports of such a thing occurring, I'm forced to conclude that the deployment is in response to the attempted forcible removal of Governor Whiting from the capital building. As to just what Governor Whiting and General Jackson are going to utilize these troops for, well, only time will tell."

Neither she nor any other MarsGroup reporter bothered speculating as to what the future mission of the MPG might be. As a general rule, the MarsGroup stations did not present unconfirmed speculations as news even though the big three had no moral problems doing so.

One thing that nobody needed to speculate about was the fact that the call-up was quickly in high gear. In every city on the planet, the part-time soldiers of the MPG left their jobs and made their way to the nearest public transportation station where they found MarsTrans trains waiting for them, each one full of other MPG members on their way to their bases. Most of those summoned were following the news closely on their PCs and strongly suspected that the reason for their activation had nothing to do with EastHem and everything to do with WestHem. They went anyway, many of them excited at the thought of defending their governor from being kidnapped and whisked away, anxious to fight for Mars and all it stood for.

*****

Corban Hayes was frantic as he watched the live feed on his Internet terminal and listened to reports coming over his communications terminal. He still could not believe that the MPG had actually interfered in the arrest of Whiting and that they had captured the majority of his agents. And now the entire compliment of MPG members was being called to active duty. They were even now making their way to their bases all across the planet for God knew what purpose. What in the hell was Jackson going to do with them? He wasn't actually going to try something so mad as to take control of the planet, was he? To do so would be beyond asinine.

Whatever they were going to be doing, it was his job to get things back under control. He was the ranking federal officer on the planet and, since communications with superiors back on Earth took more than three hours to accomplish, he was the man on the spot. His first step was to call Greg Jones, CEO of MarsTrans, to see if could slow down the deployment of troops.

"I can't," Jones told him, his face pale and scared.

"What the hell do you mean you can't?" Hayes nearly yelled at him. "Those commuter trains are yours, aren't they? Shut them down! Stop them in place! Do whatever you have to, but don't let them carry those men to the MPG bases where they'll pick up arms against us!"

"You don't understand," he replied, sounding somewhat indignant at the thought of a mere civil servant talking to him like this. "Once Whiting gave order 74-1, our command and control computers for the system were rendered useless and control was passed to the capital building. It's part of the plan for war deployment."

"What?" Hayes said. "What freakin' moron came up with that?"

"It's been in place ever since the inception of the MPG," he explained. "Part of the War Powers Act. There's nothing that I or my people can do, short of actually sabotaging the hardware of the train system, that will stop them from running."

"Christ," Hayes said, shaking his head in disgust. "You'd better get your programmers working on this thing. Do whatever you can without actually damaging the system, but get those trains shut down."

"I'll try," he said doubtfully, "but there is one little problem with that."

"What's that?"

"Almost all of my engineers and programmers are greenies," he said. "And the greenies all support what's going on. How helpful do you think they're likely to be stopping this deployment?"

Hayes hadn't thought about that. "Just do what you can," he said and then broke the communications leak. He buried his head in his hands for a moment, reluctantly concluding that he would probably not be able to stop the MPG deployments the easy way. "Get me General Jackson of the MPG online," he told the computer next. "Highest priority."

"Attempting," the computer told him.

He smoked a cigarette and continued to watch the Internet coverage while he waited. Everything was still quiet at the capitol building. Armored MPG troops could be seen setting up barricades and clearing out all of the pedestrians within the perimeter that they had established. Dip-hoe carts were being allowed through to bring out his wounded agents but, as of yet, none had emerged. He spared a moment to wonder if any of those shot would live and then put it out of his mind as an irrelevancy.

"General Jackson is not taking calls right now," his computer told him. "Priority push attempts were ignored. Would you like to access his vid mail system to leave a message?"

"No, I would not like to access his vid mail system and leave a message," he returned sarcastically. He then remembered that he was talking to a computer and took a deep breath. "Just keep trying to access him," he said. "In the meantime, get me the general in charge of the marine barracks. What the hell is his name?"

"General Norman Sega is currently the commander of the WestHem marine expeditionary unit on Planet Mars," the computer replied. "Is that who you wish to speak to?"

"Yes," he said. "Get him online. Highest priority."

*****

General Sega, unlike many of his peers in the higher ranks of the corps, was actually assigned to his position because of his military knowledge and experience and not because of family or political connections. That was how it had always been with the commander of the fast reaction division since the powers that be recognized that this division, more so than any other in the corps, needed to be ably led since it would more than likely be the first to contact the enemy in the event of war. That, and the fact that no one who had any political or family connections *wanted* to be assigned for an extended stint on Mars, guaranteed the efficiency of command.

Fifty-six years old and as fit as he had been at twenty, Sega had served numerous tours in Argentina, Cuba, and other trouble spots around Earth before being placed in charge of a battalion during the Jupiter War. Though his battalion, like all others in that troubled conflict, had been thrown forcibly off Callisto by the dug-in EastHem marines, it had suffered the least amount of casualties of any comparable unit in the conflict and had inflicted the most damage on the defending EastHem forces. Sega's career had been a slow climb uphill ever since. Not politically savvy, he had always been kept out of high-profile assignments for fear of offending sponsors or the public and placed in commands where actual work and training needed to be done. As a colonel, he had commanded the unpopular Northern Argentina brigade, the unit that had, for the past fifteen years, seen more combat than any other unit in the corps. From there, he had received his first star and done a tour in charge of the troops on Cuba, which saw the second highest level of action. His second star had led to his current assignment and the promise of virtual banishment on Mars. He had gone as far as his connection-less status would allow him.

He, like most of the other inhabitants of the red planet, had been watching the events on the Internet channels as they unfolded. At first, he had been pleasantly amused by the resistance the MPG troops had offered at the capital, chuckling as they took the feds into custody. As a professional soldier of the highest caliber, he had little respect for the part-time soldiers of the MPG or the man who led them. It had been his opinion that the hostage crisis would be over by dinnertime, with Whiting either on a ship to Earth or dead, all of her supporters in the MPG under arrest and awaiting trial on federal charges. But when the news that a general call-up of MPG forces had been issued reached him through his intelligence chief, his opinion quickly changed to one of excitement. This excitement grew when he saw the camera shots of the MPG soldiers deploying around the capital building in their APCs. The excitement came not because he had any ill-will towards the federal officers that had been killed or captured—on the contrary, he had the greatest sympathy for them (at least that's what he would say in public)—but because the problem on Mars was no longer something that the federal officers would be able to take care of by themselves. In short, it would take real soldiers with real guns to take back the capital and enforce the federal warrant against that traitor Whiting. And that meant his marines would finally get to see some action. Granted, it would probably be brief action, over in a matter of hours, a day at the most, but action was action and something that any soldier longed for. Here would be a chance to get some much-needed publicity for his forgotten division.

While the MPG platoons around the capital building were still securing the area, Sega had already been on his office terminal, telling his colonels to tell their majors to tell their captains to start arming up and getting ready for deployment. It had already occurred to him that the quickest, easiest way to diffuse the situation would be to have his marines march on the MPG base itself and capture it, cutting the incoming Eden reservists off from their weapon and ammunition supply. That would not prevent them from deploying in the other three principal cities of Mars, but it would deny them of their most powerful division and sap the morale from those that were left.

"How much longer until your men are ready to move?" he asked Colonel Westley, the commander of his best brigade.

"Fifteen more minutes, General," Westley told him over the Internet terminal. "The boys are suited up in their indoor armor and they're loading their weapons up right now."

"Good enough," Sega said. "I want that base captured as soon as possible. The more greenies that are allowed to reach it, the more problems we're going to have if they decide to fight us."

"Will they fight, sir?" Westley asked hesitantly. "They have an awful lot of armor over at that base. And until our boys can get some of our equipment down from TNB, we won't have anything to battle armor with."

"We won't be bringing anything down from TNB," Sega said, as if speaking to a six year old. "And don't worry about those greenies hitting us with their armor. Chances are, they'll surrender as soon as they see us heading their way. And even if they don't, they haven't had enough time to deploy any of their APCs or tanks yet. It takes time to gear those things up."

"Yes, General," Westley said.

"Incoming communication from Director Corban Hayes of the Federal Law Enforcement Bureau," his computer terminal suddenly spoke up. "Would you like to accept?"

Sega smiled. Here was the communication he had been waiting for, the one that would give him the authority to unleash his men upon the greenies. "On screen," he said.

Hayes appeared on the terminal, his hair somewhat in disarray, his eyes showing a great deal of strain. "General Sega," he said, nodding respectfully. "Thank you for receiving my call."

"Of course, Director," Sega said graciously. He had never actually met Hayes before, either in person or online. Federal agents and military commanders did not usually run in the same circles. "What can I do for you? I assume this has something to do with the events at the capitol building?"

"That's correct," Hayes said. "As I'm sure you're aware, elements of the MPG have fired upon my men as they attempted to serve an arrest warrant on Laura Whiting."

"I've been watching on Internet," Sega said. "My sympathies for your men."

Hayes waved his hand dismissively at the mention of his men. "The perpetrators will be brought to justice, I can assure you of that," he said. "At the moment, however, I'm reading some alarming intelligence about the remainder of the MPG."

"You mean the call-up?" Sega said. "Yes, we've been monitoring that from here as well."

"Then you know that greenies are streaming onto those bases from all over the planet," he said. "They're hopping onto MarsTrans trains and being taken there and they'll be loading their guns and firing up their tanks pretty soon. I fear that they may have reacted a little strongly to the arrest warrant for their governor and that they might be... well... contemplating serious action."

"A revolt," Sega said, not mincing words. "You're afraid they're planning to attempt a capture of the planet or something equally foolish."

"That's correct," he said. "And while the FLEB has the investigative authority in this instance, this unfortunate turn of events has left us woefully short of firepower to prevent such a thing. We need to stop these greenies before they hurt someone or before they cut into productivity of the various businesses that operate on this planet. Hell, I wouldn't put it past them to attempt some act of terrorism against the agricultural fields or something like that. They need to be stopped from deploying."

"I've already anticipated your request," Sega told him. "I have my entire division gearing up for duty as we speak. I'll deploy an entire brigade to the Eden MPG base within thirty minutes."

"I see," Hayes said, a little confused. "And a brigade is?"

Sega gave him a look of contempt. "I take it you've never served in the armed forces before?"

"Well... no," he said with a shrug.

"A brigade is four battalions of combat troops," he explained. "About 2500 men."

"That's a lot," Hayes said uneasily.

"Better too much than too little," Sega responded. "My guess is that the greenies will give it up as soon as they see us marching on them. In any case, once the MPG base and Eden itself is secured, I'll get the rest of my men to the other three cities where the MPG is deploying. I'll send a brigade to New Pittsburgh, one to Libby, and one to Proctor."

"How will you do that?"

"We'll load them on our C-12 transports and put them into orbit," Sega said. "We have enough lifter craft to move the entire division up to our ships in less than twenty-four hours. Instead of putting them on the ships though, I'll just have them de-orbit and land at the other three cities. We can capture the spaceports and use them as operations bases from there. My guess is we'll have this entire planet, including the Capital Building, secure and under control in forty-eight hours."

Hayes nodded wisely, obviously pleased with the efficient self-confidence of the general. "It sounds good, General," he said. "You do whatever needs to be done. There is one concern I have about your men however. You have a number of greenies in your division, do you not?"

"About one thousand total," he confirmed. "Most of them are in support positions. I've already ordered my MPs to remove them from their units and place them under house arrest."

"Very good," Hayes said, smiling for the first time. "Once that base is secured, I'd like them all turned over to the FLEB so they can be held until this crisis is over."

"It will be done," Sega assured him. "Now if you'll excuse me, I have a base to capture. I'll get back to you once it's in our hands." He looked at his watch. "Should be less than an hour I'd imagine."

"Thank you general," he said. "And good luck."

"We don't need any luck," he scoffed. "We're WestHem marines."

*****

General Jackson was still at his command post in the capital building, monitoring the various operations that were taking place around the planet. The entire operation was at its most vulnerable right now since the bulk of the MPG members were still in transit to the bases. His greatest worry was the security of the Eden MPG base, which stood less than two kilometers from ten thousand WestHem marines. His worry was increased by a call from Sprinkle.

"What's up, Jack?" he asked, seeing the intelligence chief's face on his computer screen.

"The marines are moving a little faster than we thought they would," Sprinkle told him. "I just got a call from a few of my contacts that are part of the fast reaction division. They say that all of the Martians have been rounded up and are being held in their dorms, but that the rest of the troops are gearing up for deployment. Estimates are that they'll be on the move within fifteen minutes or so."

"Great," Jackson said with a sigh. He looked at his tactical display and switched the view to a map of the military corner of Eden. Macarthur Avenue was the street that gave access to both the MPG base and the marine barracks. The barracks had two pedestrian entrances, which were located two blocks apart, and a wider, delivery truck entrance in between. He only had one single platoon of infantry troops to cover all three of those entrances. Forty men with small arms, light machine guns, and a few grenade launchers to hold back God knew how many marines who would be trying to egress from those doorways. They would be able to hold them for a little while by virtue of the fact that the marines would have to exit from a narrow corridor. Eventually however, the MPG would be as overwhelmed as the fabled Snoqualmie defenders back in World War III, that single American battalion that had tried to keep an entire Chinese army from descending out of the Cascade Mountains onto the plains of Washington. The Snoqualmie defenders had ultimately failed in their task, more than three-quarters of their number killed while buying the WestHem alliance no more than eighteen hours of time. Jackson had no intention of allowing the Macarthur Avenue defenders to share this same fate. He needed more troops there and he needed them now.

"Get me General Zoloft," he told his communications terminal.

Zoloft was the commander of the Eden division. Like all of the high commanders of the MPG, Zoloft had been briefed in on the plot to eventually seize the planet from WestHem some years before. He was an outstanding leader and an enthusiastic supporter of the plot. He came online within seconds of his hail. "Zoloft here, General," he said.

"How many troops do we have on the base, not including those in Dealerman's command?" Jackson asked him.

Zoloft consulted another screen for a moment. "About two hundred have arrived," he said. "Not all of them are combat troops however. Probably about half are admin and support people."

"Get them armed up and moving towards the marine barracks entrances," Jackson told him. "The marines are going to be trying a breakout any minute now."

"You mean the combat troops only?" he asked.

"Negative," Jackson replied. "I mean *everyone*. Get them guns, form them up into squads, and send them out there."

"But, Kevin," Zoloft protested, "a lot of those troops are women. Surely you don't mean to..."

"They've been through basic training, haven't they?" Jackson interrupted. "Get them armed and on the move. Right now."

"Yes sir," Zoloft said.

"Be sure to let them know what they're up against and that they will be in fact rebelling against WestHem, but get those that will go out there. And we'll need some armor on those entrances as well. As soon as you get some APC crews ready, get their vehicles moving. Send them out through the main entrance like we did Dealerman's people that went to the capital. Those entrances have got to be covered."

"Working on it now, Kevin," Zoloft said, signing off.

*****

Lisa Wong was one of the female soldiers that were hastily assembled into a makeshift squad of infantry. Since the downtown area where she worked as a police officer was fairly close geographically to the MPG base, she and her partner Brian had been among the first to arrive. She had quickly suited up in the spare shorts and T-shirt that she carried in her locker and had been on her way to report to her duty station—the main administration office where she worked as a materials supply clerk—when her PC had gone off with an emergency tone.

"All available MPG personnel," announced General Zoloft, the base commander, "report immediately at best possible speed to the armory for combat load out. This means *all* personnel, regardless of sex or assignment. We need you over here, people, so let's move it!"

He repeated the message but, by the time he was three words into it, Lisa had disconnected from the transmission and was sprinting through the hallways of the base towards the armory. His message had sounded urgent and the fact that he was asking for non-combat volunteers spoke volumes about the desperation of the situation. The materials allotment unit would just have to do without her for a while.

As she ran, others kept pace with her. Men, other women, some people still in civilian clothing, all trekked along, pushing through doors and making their way to a single destination. When they arrived there, huffing and puffing from the exertion, a group of supply personnel were hastily handing out weapons and equipment while an infantry lieutenant was forming them up into groups.

Lisa made her way to the front and was handed a helmet, a set of combat goggles, a radio pack, an M-24 rifle and five 100 round magazines. "You're C squad, part of Sergeant Jan's platoon over there," the lieutenant told her.

"Where are we going?" she asked, fumbling with all of the gear.

"Your sergeant will explain it in a moment," he said impatiently, his tone telling her that there was no time for questions. "Get outfitted and loaded up."

"What about armor?" she asked.

"No time for it," he told her, turning and grabbing another set of equipment for the man behind her.

She carried her equipment over to where a tough looking sergeant was standing with about twenty other people. There was a mix of men and women, a few of whom she recognized as being admin personnel, most she had never seen before. Sergeant Jan was dividing them up into squads and placing those few people he had that were part of the combat arm as the leaders.

"You," he said, pointing at Lisa and reading her name from her shirt, "Corporal Wong. Get that weapon loaded and those extra mags stowed. You'll be in second squad under private Zink's command. Your radio frequency for squad operations is 7-C. Got it?"

"Got it," she replied, feeling overwhelmed and more than a little confused. Just what the hell was going on here anyway? Nevertheless, she put her helmet on her head and attached her throat microphone just above her shirt. The radio pack—a small plastic transmitter about half the size of her PC—she tuned to bank 7, channel C and attached to her waist. Though her entire career with the MPG had been spent as an office worker, she knew how to run the radio as well as any of the most hardened combat troops. Likewise, she was familiar with her weapon, combat goggles, and other gear as well, and not just because of her job with the Eden Police Department. Ever since the earliest days of the MPG, General Jackson had made it a part of the training requirements that *every* member, no matter what their rank or assignment, qualify as expert with the combat gear at least twice a year. Though he had been derided many times in the Earthling media for this alleged waste of money, he had stuck to his guns and now, at what seemed a critical moment, all of that training and expense seemed to be paying off. She, as well as the other non-combat soldiers in her understrength platoon, were ready for action in less than five minutes, with weapons loaded and calibrated to the goggles.

"All right, folks," Jan said, looking them over. "Looks like we're ready to roll. I don't have time for any inspirational speeches or extended briefings, so I'll give it to you straight. The MPG is in the process of capturing Eden and the entire planet of Mars from WestHem control. What we are doing is an act of treason. Right now, we have some combat troops that are trying to pen the WestHem marines inside of their base to keep them from opposing our capture. They're going to need help badly in a few minutes. We'll probably be forced to fire on some of those marines in order to prevent them from breaking out. This will be seen as premeditated murder by WestHem authorities. Anyone who does not wish to participate in this action, put your weapons down and step to the rear."

There was a stunned silence for a moment as everyone comprehended what they were being told. Lisa had to run it through her circuits a few times to get it to clear. Capturing Eden? Capturing the entire planet Mars? Firing on WestHem marines? She waited for the punch line, concluding that it had to be a joke of some sort. No punch line came however. Jan was apparently serious. "Holy shit," she muttered, feeling a strange surge of fear and determination running through her. If there was going to be a fight to free Mars, she was going to be a part of it. She did not drop her weapon. Neither did anyone else.

"All right then," Jan said, smiling. "1st reserve platoon. Let's move it out! Triple time!" With that he turned and began jogging towards the door. His platoon of twenty-five men and women fell in behind him.

*****

Lieutenant Rod Espinoza, a four-year member of the MPG, had been given the dubious honor of leading the Macarthur Avenue defenders. A simple platoon leader whose civilian job was head of security at a small office building, he rose to the occasion quite nicely despite his lack of previous combat experience and his usual reliance on his company commander for guidance. He had divided his forty troops into three sections. One squad was covering the south pedestrian entrance, one was covering the north, and two were covering the larger truck terminal in between. On the orders of Major Dealerman, these squads had held back, out of sight of the marine MP positions that guarded each entrance platform. Though they had aroused the curiosity of many a pedestrian walking by their shadowed forms—and more than one off-duty marine—the guards in their booths remained oblivious to their presence. That was about to change.

"Espinoza," Major Dealerman's voice told him over the command link, "move your people in and secure the platforms. Take those guards out without gunfire if possible. Disarm them and send them back into the base."

"Copy," he said simply.

"Information is that the marines are going to try a breakout within a few minutes. Once the platforms are secure, pull back to covering positions and get ready to drive them back in. Weapons are free, wartime rules of engagement are in effect."

"I understand, Major," he said assuredly, hiding the worry he felt. "What about reinforcements?" he asked. "We're pretty heavy on ammo, but we're not gonna last long if they're determined."

"Reinforcements are on the way," Dealerman told him. "We've scrapped together some mixed units of combatants and non-combatants. Put them to use as you see fit, but use them. They're all trained in weapons and tactics."

"Yes, sir," he said a little dubiously.

"We'll get you some armor out there as soon as it's available. Don't let those marines out of that base. The entire operation depends on keeping them penned."

"I understand," he said.

As soon as the transmission ended, he began giving orders to his squad leaders. Less than thirty seconds later, his men began to move in.

The pedestrian stations were not terribly busy at this time of the day but still, there were upwards of fifty people, most of them working their way through the security checkpoints, at each one. At the truck entrance things were a little better. Since delivery trucks were a phenomenon of the night on Mars, this platform was virtually deserted. Each one of the stations was guarded by a four-man team of military police, each of whom was armed with a sidearm and an M-24 without combat goggle enhancement. Their command posts were glass-encased booths equipped with computer terminals and communications gear.

When the MPG troops stormed the stations, the squad leaders shouting at everyone to get down, one of the MPs at the north station reached for his rifle out of instinct. He was pummeled by rifle fire and dropped like a rock. The rest of the guards at that particular station, seeing this, immediately threw their hands up in surrender. At the other stations, all of the guards surrendered peacefully once they saw what they were up against.

"Civilians and non-uniformed personnel," shouted the squad leaders at each place, "off the platform and out of the area, right now! Move it!"

They moved it, rushing in a near panic down Macarthur Avenue and disappearing out of sight. The MPs were quickly disarmed and pointed in the direction of the base. "Get in there and stay in there," they were told. "Tell your commanders that we have the entrances guarded and that anyone trying to get out will be fired upon."

The MPs wasted no time in sprinting through the gates and down the entrance corridor. All three groups of them reached the main avenue of the base at approximately the same time. It was only the three that had guarded the north entrance, the entrance closest to the MPG base, that encountered marines massing for a march.

Colonel Frank Forrest was the commander in charge of the brigade that Sega had tasked with capturing the MPG base. He and most of his men were assembled on the exercise lawn undergoing final weapons checks and radio calibration prior to marching out. The men were in neat, precise military rows on the green grass, lined up by platoon and squad. Sergeants and lieutenants circulated among them, making last minute inspections and giving inspirational speeches. When the three MPs, stripped of their weapons and red-faced with terror, came bursting into the columns, they were very nearly shot by more than one startled soldier.

"What the fuck is going on here?" an angry sergeant screamed at the three men. "Corporal," he told the highest ranking of them, "you'd better have a goddamn good explanation for this!"

"Sir," he said breathlessly, coming to a partial state of attention, "greenies just stormed our checkpoint! They took our guns and sent us back in here!"

"Greenies?" the sergeant yelled. "What the fuck are you talking about, boy?"

He managed to spit out the story in a coherent fashion, coherent enough that the sergeant immediately brought him to his lieutenant where the story was repeated. From there they went to the captain of that particular company and from there, to the Major that commanded the battalion. Ten minutes after the storming of the guard posts, the three MPs were finally led before Colonel Forrest himself, by which point they had calmed enough to tell their tale without stuttering or repeating themselves.

"How many of them were there?" Forrest asked, only a little worried at the thought of armed greenies at his point of egress.

"Twenty or thirty," they all agreed, their minds wildly exaggerating their memories.

Forrest nodded. "And they were armed with M-24s?"

"Yes sir," the corporal told him, unaware that the troops with the SAWs had held back in cover positions during the charge.

"And they shot one of your men?"

"Yes sir," he said. "They blew Bill damn near in half... for no reason."

Forrest's face scrunched into an expression of anger. "Goddamn greenies," he spat. "They're nothing more than terrorists!" He turned to his majors and captains, who were gathered near him. "Get on the com link and find out about the other checkpoints," he told them. "If they captured one, they probably captured them all."

It took less than five minutes to confirm that all three checkpoints had in fact fallen to MPG troops. In the other two instances the estimations of the troop strength were the same as that offered by the first: about twenty troops armed with M-24s.

"We need to push out of here right now," Forrest told his subordinates, "before they are able to move enough troops in to really be an annoyance to us." He looked at Major Starr, commander of his first battalion. "Starr," he told him, "get your recon elements moving and recapture the checkpoint that our young corporal and his friends came from. Once it's secure, we'll move the rest of the brigade out to our main objective and send the rest of your battalion to go capture the other two positions."

"Yes, sir," Starr said, hiding the dejection in his voice. He had wanted to be a part of the main thrust into the MPG base. But orders were orders. He trotted off towards his men, talking on his command link as he went. Within five minutes they were moving towards the exit corridor, his recon platoon breaking trail.

Meanwhile, back at the checkpoint in question, the MPG squad that was guarding it had pulled back to positions of cover on Macarthur Avenue. They kneeled behind the cement planter that lined the middle of the street, their weapons trained on the entrance, their combat goggles down and set for infrared enhancement. The young private that operated the squad automatic weapon was in the center of the formation, his field of fire such that he could sweep the entire corridor from one side to the other. Four extra drums of ammunition, each containing 600 rounds, were stacked neatly next to his leg.

The marine recon platoon, its members among the most highly trained in the corps, didn't make it within one hundred meters of the Macarthur side of the access corridor. Though they were moving along the walls, making themselves as small of targets as possible, there was simply nothing to use for cover or concealment and they were spotted almost as soon as they started heading for their objective.

Espinoza ordered the SAW gunner to fire a few bursts down the middle of the corridor on the theory that this would drive them back without having to kill any of them. It was a hopeful thought but one that didn't quite pan out. The private unleashed twenty rounds, the gun barking loudly, the rounds flying at high velocity right between the two elements of the platoon. Instead of retreating however, they began firing back, simultaneously pushing forward.

"Fucking idiots," Espinoza said in disgust as rounds began to slam into the concrete around them and whiz over their head. "Open fire," he told his men. "Take them out."

It was far too easy, sickeningly so. The private on the SAW swept it back and forth, moving his reticle across the figures of the marines while firing controlled bursts. The other squad members opened up with their M-24s, putting their own bursts on the men who were diving to get out of the way of the automatic weapons fire. The forty marines were pummeled with bullets, their bodies twisting and turning and dropping to the ground, every last one of them dead or dying in the space of twenty seconds. Not a single MPG soldier was hit during the exchange.

"Good job, guys," Espinoza told them as the last echoes of the gunfire faded away. The fact that they had just killed WestHem soldiers, that they had just actively partaken in a revolution, seemed to hang in the air.

Nobody said anything in reply.

"Let's do an ammo check," Espinoza said. "They'll be back soon and there'll be a lot more of them."

*****

Starr, waiting safely back on the base, had watched the entire thing through his combat goggles by patching into the platoon commander's goggles. Never having been in actual combat before, he was horrified at the speed and violence with which forty of his men had just perished. He had, in fact, been holding his breath throughout the entire episode.

"Starr, report!" screamed the voice of Colonel Forrest in his radio link. "What the hell was all of that shooting?"

"Sir," he said slowly, his voice strangely calm despite the adrenaline surging through him, "the greenies fired on the recon platoon. They're down."

"All of them?" Forrest said in disbelief.

"All of them," he confirmed.

"Jesus fucking Christ," Forrest said. "How many guns do they got out there now?"

"It looked like no more than fifteen to me," Starr told him. "They're behind the planter on Macarthur Avenue, situated directly across from the entrance."

There was silence on the link for a moment. Finally, Forrest came back on. "We need to take that position immediately," he said. "You had an eyeball on it. Suggestions?"

Starr put the thought of his dead men as far back in his mind as he could and thought through the problem for a moment. "Let me throw a company-strength assault at them," he suggested. "I'll put all of the men with grenade launchers on their 24s up front and have them blast that greenie position as soon as they're in range. It's simply a question of throwing enough men at them to overwhelm their defenses."

"Do it," Forrest told him after only a moment's thought. "And do it quickly. If they reinforce that position, they'll be able to keep us from exiting this way. If they do that, we'll have to put on our biosuits and take that base from the wasteland side. I don't have to tell you that that would be a damn sight more difficult."

"I'll have them moving within five minutes, sir," Starr promised.

*****

Unfortunately for the marines, five minutes was just a little too long. While they were still regrouping and getting the grenadiers adjusted to the front ranks, the makeshift platoon that had been formed back at the MPG base trotted up Macarthur Avenue and reported for duty. Espinoza put them to immediate use.

"Send five of your people to the north pedestrian entrance to reinforce them," he told Sergeant Jan. "The rest of you, take up position behind this planter with us. Spread out as much as you can, but keep your guns massed on that corridor. ROE is weapons free. They're probably going to hit us with at least company-strength on the next assault and we need to engage them as soon as they come into view."

Lisa, carrying her M-24 and feeling naked without any armor on her chest, took up position about two thirds of the way to the right of center. She gazed down the long corridor, seeing the bodies of those marines that had died in the first breakout attempt. The sight of those corpses, of the blood running slowly towards the drains along the walls, brought home to her the reality of what she was getting herself involved in. "Jesus," she muttered, shuddering a little. She was participating in a *rebellion* against WestHem, a rebellion in which men had been shot and killed.

"You all right, Wong?" a young private from the armor maintenance section asked her. His eyes looked terrified but determined.

"Fine," she said, giving him a shaky smile. "Let's kick some Earthling ass, shall we?"

"Fuckin A," he replied, gripping his weapon a little tighter.

The attack began a few moments later. From far down the corridor, the figures of twenty, then thirty, then fifty men suddenly swarmed forward, keeping low and moving fast, the outlines of their weapons clearly visible.

"Enemy to the front," Espinoza's voice barked over the command channel. "Open fire!"

Guns began to crack from all around her and, from the center of the column, the SAW barked to life, sending streaks of bullets into the marines. They began to drop, but more of them surged forward. Lisa put her targeting reticle on a figure, centering it over his chest, and pulled the trigger. The weapon jerked in her hand, exploding three rounds out of its barrel, and the figure fell forward, his weapon dropping beneath him. Without pausing to reflect that she had just killed a man, she put her reticle on another and repeated the motion.

Suddenly, all along the line of marines, there were bright flashes, much brighter than the individual weapons signatures, and what appeared in the infrared spectrum to be large red blobs streaked at high speed towards them.

"Grenades," a voice barked on the radio frequency. "Cover!"

Lisa, along with everyone else, ducked quickly down behind the planter, hiding her head from view. Less than a second later, the grenades exploded in the air directly above them, directed to do so by the combat computers of the marines that had fired them. The noise was tremendous, a series of harsh cracks that overwhelmed the eardrums and made the ears ring. The concussion from the displaced air slammed into them, driving the air out of their lungs. Shrapnel rained down, chipping off the cement of the planter, shredding into trees that grew from it, and striking several people. Lisa felt a piece gouge through her lower leg, stitching a burning across her calf. As her ears cleared a little from the concussions, she heard several people yelling that they were hit and calling for a medic. She moved her leg, found that it still worked, and did not add her voice to the chorus. Instead, she put her head back up and found another target.

The firing from the line of MPG troops picked up again and the marines rushing down the tunnel began to fall once more. By now, many of the marines were firing back, sending a hail of high velocity bullets towards them and trying to force their heads down so they could advance. The tree trunks were peppered with bullets, most flying right through and exiting out the other side. More slammed into the concrete barrier, breaking large chunks of it off and hurling them over the top of their heads. A few of these bullets found their marks. The young private next to

Lisa was struck directly in the head, the bullet drilling a neat hole through the front of his helmet and exploding out the back of it in a spray of shattered Kevlar, blood, and brains. He slumped forward lifelessly, his rifle falling from his hands. Lisa ignored this the best she could and continued firing, dropping any marine that she saw moving.

Another volley of grenades came flying at them and this time not everyone ducked in time. The detonations slammed into the line and the private operating the SAW had his face and neck shredded to pieces by the shrapnel. He flew backwards, spraying blood out of his wounds, dragging his weapon down with him. From around them, more screams of "I'm hit" sounded out.

"Resume firing!" Espinoza yelled frantically, spraying an extended burst with his own weapon. "They're moving in!"

Lisa popped back up, switching her M-24 to full automatic fire. She put her reticle on a group of four marines that were rushing forward and squeezed the trigger, raking it over them. They spun and fell, crashing to the ground.

"Shimmy," Espinoza yelled to Corporal Shimamoto, one of his regular men, "take over the SAW and start putting some fire on these fucks!"

Shimamoto pried the squad automatic weapon from the private's dead hands and put it on its tripod atop the planter. Not wasting the time it would take to calibrate his combat goggles to it, he simply began to fire, aiming by sight and ripping into the advancing marines once again.

This, combined with the supporting fire from the riflemen and the absolute horror that they had just endured, finally broke the marines. None of them, not even the most experienced veterans of Argentina or Cuba, had ever encountered or even imagined combat as deadly as this was becoming. Bullets were flying everywhere, pinging off of the walls of the corridor and ripping through their lines like some supernatural force. Men were torn in half by the sustained bursts from the SAW. Their heads were blown to pieces by the shots from the M-24s. Blood was flowing freely on the floor of the corridor, more than an inch thick in some places, it was being splashed all over them, obscuring their combat goggles and making their feet slip. And the bodies absolutely littered the ground, some screaming in pain, some deathly silent. And, as they got closer to the exit of the corridor, the fire grew exponentially more intense and accurate. There was no official call to retreat, but as the entire front rank of what remained of the company was mowed down by the renewed vigor of the MPG outside, retreat is what occurred. Men turned tail and ran, heading back for the safety of the base as fast as they could, many leaving their weapons behind them.

"They're retreating," someone told Espinoza as they saw the mad push back towards the far end of the corridor.

"Keep firing," Espinoza ordered. "Keep the pressure on them until they're out of sight."

And so, the marines suffered the additional horror of being shot in the back as they ran away, a fact that pushed them even further over the edge of panic. When the battered, terrified survivors rushed out of the far end of the corridor, bullets still chasing after them, only 52 of the original 160 were still on their feet.

"Cease fire, cease fire!" Espinoza commanded once the last of them had disappeared.

The guns fell silent after a few last isolated pops, and the haze of gun smoke that was hanging over the planter began to slowly dissipate. The ground around them was covered with ejected shell casings, chips of concrete and wood, and rivulets of blood. The moans of several wounded could be heard.

"Ammo check," Espinoza said. "Everyone, make sure your weapon has a fresh mag in it. We don't know when they'll be back or with how many. Let's assume they're gonna hit us again in the next five minutes with battalion strength." He looked over at private Stinson, a DPHS employee in civilian life and the only medic in the bunch. "Stinson, start checking these people. I'll see what I can do about getting some dip-hoes in here to take away the wounded."

"Right," Stinson said, immediately heading for the private lying next to Lisa. He took one look at him and shook his head sadly. "Not much to do here," he said, seeing the shattered skull and the dull, dead eyes. He turned towards Lisa, spying the wound on her leg. "You're gonna need that fused back together," he told her, reaching in his pack and pulling out some gauze bandages.

Lisa looked down at her leg for the first time and saw that a five-centimeter chunk of it had been neatly ripped open by the grenade shrapnel. Blood was oozing from the wound and onto the ground.

"Can you move your foot and your toes?" Stinson asked her hurriedly.

She moved them, seeing with gratification that everything still worked. "I'm all right," she told him. "Go work on the others."

He handed her the gauze. "Wrap that up to stop the bleeding," he told her. "We'll get you off the line as soon as we can."

"I don't need to get off the line," she told him. "I'm staying until we're relieved."

He nodded, giving her a smile, and then headed down the line until he reached the next wounded person. In all, the total was three dead and four wounded. Not too bad considering that they'd been fighting a force more than five times their size.

*****

Captain Starr, who had been leading from the rear as any competent company commander, was one of the survivors of the failed assault on Macarthur Avenue. Unfortunately, he no longer had much of a company to command since three of his four lieutenants and twelve of his sixteen squad leaders, not to mention a good portion of his enlisted men, were dead on the entrance corridor floor, riddled with MPG bullets. Starr and his remaining men were moved to the rear and a fresh company, this one commanded by Captain Freely, a hardened veteran of the Cuban campaigns, was brought forward.

"Alpha company was hit hard," Freely told his men as they fidgeted in their ranks thirty meters from the front of the corridor entrance. "But we need to go back in there and take that position before the greenies get a chance to reinforce it. We need to do this so we can clear them off of Macarthur Avenue and take that base and so that we can get Alpha company's wounded out of there, understand?"

"Yes sir," they all dutifully replied, though with a distinct lack of enthusiasm. They had all seen the result of the previous attacks.

"I know that nobody wants to do this," Freely said. "It's a very poor tactical situation since we are forced down a narrow path right into the teeth of the enemy. We can't outflank them and we have little or nothing in the way of cover or concealment for our advance. Unfortunately, it has to be done and this is the best time that we're going to get to do it, while they're still reeling from our first two attacks and while they're probably low on ammunition. So, let's get it done. Those of you with grenade launchers, I want you massed in the front. We're going to put sustained grenade fire on that greenie position as we advance. Half of you fire, half of you hold back. While the first half reloads, the second half will then fire. That way, there should be minimum time where the greenies are able to put their heads up and oppose us. Once we clear that front entrance, surround those fucks and put them down. No mercy!"

"No mercy!" the marines yelled back, this time with more emotion.

"Let's move it out," Freely said.

They moved it out, not knowing, as Starr hadn't before them, that the situation outside of the corridor had already changed. Two tank crews and one APC crew, all from different units of the division, had gotten their machines fired up and were led through the larger corridors of the base to the main entrance. These three pieces of heavy armor then clanked their way out onto Macarthur Avenue, past the commuter tram station where fresh loads of troops were disembarking the trains, and down to the first of the marine base entrances. Espinoza, nearly gushing in gratitude at the sight of them, quickly commandeered one of the tanks to reinforce his own embattled position. The other tank and the APC, he sent further down the avenue to reinforce the other positions in case the marines attempted a break-out through one of them.

There was no place to really conceal the tank since the center planter that the soldiers were kneeling behind was only a meter high, but there were also no working anti-tank weapons available to the marines on their base. All they had were low-yield training weapons, their real equipment safely tucked away inside of the landing ships at Triad Naval Base. This, in effect, made the armored vehicle invulnerable to being destroyed or displaced, able to put impenetrable, horrendous fire upon the enemy with complete impunity.

In a way, it was perhaps fortunate for Captain Freely's company that the armor arrived when it did. Like the use of atomic weapons had done at the end of World War II, it was likely that the display of such overwhelming force created an abandonment of aggressive intentions before they could be fully implemented. The moment that the marines entered the corridor and began to set up the first of their grenade launches, the tank crew spotted them on their infrared equipped monitoring equipment. A single 80mm high explosive shell had been loaded into the long gun and aimed down the corridor. The gunner had already calculated the range to the end of the corridor and had adjusted the elevation of the barrel appropriately. As soon as he saw the marines forming up and preparing to fire, he put his hand on the firing button.

"Computer," he told the tank's firing computer, "set for airburst at 200 meters."

"Range set," the computer instantly replied.

Before the first volley of grenades could even be launched in their direction, he pushed the fire button and the gun roared, blasting the shell out of the barrel at a speed of more than three kilometers per second. When it reached precisely 200 meters from its point of origin, it exploded, spraying razor sharp shrapnel out in an expanding cone. The grenadiers and the other marines entering the corridor behind them never knew what hit them. They were sliced to pieces, their bodies literally torn apart from the force of the blast and the steel of the shell. In an instant, more than thirty men died in a spray of blood and shredded body parts.

"They got a fuckin tank down there!" shouted a squad leader in horror as he saw the men erased from existence. He had been just around the corner from the corridor entrance, just about to step through to join the charge when the explosion had hit. He shuddered uncontrollably as he thought of the fate he'd almost shared in.

No further shots were required. Though Captain Freely and Colonel Forrest and General Sega all agreed that to attempt further breaches of the exit corridors were futile, it is unlikely that they would have convinced any of the marines to take another crack at even if they'd ordered them. Marines like to follow orders and will often fling themselves carelessly into overwhelming danger at a superior officer's whim, but they are not suicidal.

"Leave a few platoons near each entrance to keep the greenies from moving onto the base," Sega ordered Colonel Forrest. "We're not going to be able to go out that way."

"Yes sir," Forrest said, fuming at the losses he'd had inflicted upon his men by a relatively small number of greenies.

"Start getting everyone else in biosuits," Sega said. "We'll take the division out through the airlocks and move overland to the MPG base from there."

"I'll get right on it," Forrest said.

CHAPTER SIX

Triad, Mars
June 8, 2186

There were no Internet terminals set up in the abandoned hanger the special forces soldiers were being housed in at the Triad MPG base and, though every last one of them had a PC that was capable of monitoring Internet channels, the signals had all been damped for security reasons. So it came to pass, that the 640 men who were slated to strike the first real blow to the Earthlings were the least informed about events on the planet.

They had been fed well during their stay there. Dinner the previous night had consisted of steak and baked potatoes cooked in the base mess hall. Breakfast that morning had been scrambled eggs and pancakes prepared by the morning shift mess staff. All had eaten voraciously despite the nagging knowledge that some unspecified, possibly dangerous mission was awaiting them.

"When the hell are they going to tell us something?" Horishito demanded of Lon about an hour after breakfast. Lon's squad was leaning against the far wall of the hanger, very near the front doorway, their weapons and packs resting beside them.

"When they have something to tell," Lon replied automatically, though he too was growing impatient and bored.

Several of his men had brought decks of cards along with them and an impromptu poker game was being waged. In the absence of Internet access to facilitate betting, they were forced to revert to the old-fashioned technique of using poker chips to represent money. In this case, the chips were actually paper clips that had been bent in specific formations to represent different denominations.

Lon was just about to go get himself dealt in for a few hands when the door to the opposing hanger suddenly slid open and Colonel Bright entered the room. Even at the age of 56, Bright was still an imposing presence, able to outrun and outgun a good number of his younger soldiers in the training fields. He was a stickler for training standards and quite a hard-ass when it came to admission to his elite corps. It was well known that he personally gave final approval on all inductees into the cadre.

Nobody stood up or came to attention when Bright entered the room of course—it just wasn't done in the MPG—but everyone immediately stopped what they were doing and looked up at him as he walked to the front of the room and took up position near a podium that had been set up earlier. A microphone sat on the podium and he tapped it a few times, confirming that it was live. He then began to speak, his voice gruff and self-assured.

"Good morning, men," he told them. "I know it sounds very cliché to say so, but I know you've all been wondering just what you've been brought here for. For security reasons, I've been forced to be very vague with you in regards to the call-up and your deployment. The time for being vague is now over, however. Let me begin by explaining to you all what has been happening on the surface over the last few hours and from there I'll get to the mission that I'm going to ask you to perform." He paused, his eyes tracking over the collection of soldiers. "Last night, in Denver, a federal grand jury consisting entirely of WestHem civilians and hearing evidence presented only by the federal attorney general's office, voted to indict Governor Whiting on charges of corruption and misuse of office and several other things."

Some angry uproar erupted from the crowd. Lon heard several utterings of profanity echoing off the hanger walls.

Bright waited patiently for them to quiet down and then continued. "This morning, in New Pittsburgh, a group of forty FLEB agents, all of them armed with automatic weapons, attempted to serve this warrant at the capitol building and take Governor Whiting into custody. Their intent was to extradite her to Earth for trial and imprisonment, therefore leaving the Lieutenant Governor in control of the executive branch of our planetary government." He gazed out, seeming to lock eyes with everyone at once. "The capital security team—which, as I'm sure you are all aware, is made up of MPG special forces soldiers—fired upon the FLEB agents and prevented them from completing their mission."

Now there was shocked silence in the room as every man tried to contemplate the ramifications of Bright's words. *Fired* on federal agents? *Prevented* them from completing their mission?

"The attempt to take our governor into custody on these trumped-up charges was unsuccessful," Bright told them. "All of the FLEB agents participating in the raid were killed or captured. The New Pittsburgh police department has been ordered to stay out of the situation by their chief. When the second wave of FLEB agents showed up at the capital, they too were taken into custody by regular infantry troops from the New Pittsburgh area division. At this moment, the capital building and two blocks around it is secured and being guarded by MPG soldiers. Governor Whiting has issued an order for the rest of the MPG to mobilize for deployment. As we speak, several platoons of our soldiers are fighting a battle with WestHem marines at the main gates to the Eden marine barracks. Their intent is to keep the WestHem soldiers from exiting the base and impeding MPG operations on the surface."

He let that sink in for a moment and then went on. "Gentlemen, you're all Martians. You have all grown up on this planet under the rule of WestHem and you know what their system has done to us. We are second-class citizens on our own planet. I won't try to duplicate the speeches of Governor Whiting here today because I'm just not up to the task. But I know that all of you have been listening to her words and that most of you agree with what she has been saying. It is time for us to break free of WestHem by whatever means necessary. I want none of you to make any mistake about the gravity of the situation that I have just described to you down on the surface. Our troops have fired upon federal officers, killing several of them. We have defied federal orders to hand over Governor Whiting to them. Our planetary guard troops have initiated firefights with WestHem marines and are using armored vehicles to keep them in check. What has happened today is nothing more nor less than the opening move in an armed revolt by the Planet Mars against the Western Hemispheric Alliance. It is a bid for independence from WestHem by force of arms. A revolution. And I'm about to ask you men here to play a part in it."

Without giving them time to think too deeply, he continued. "Now, I've been your commanding officer for a long time now. I like to think that I'm the type of CO that makes himself available to his troops. I visit all of the commands regularly and I know most of you by name and by face. I've heard you talk to each other around the dorms and out on the training field. I've seen you all enraptured by Governor Whiting's words when she speaks on Internet. I've heard you rant about those 'fucking Earthlings' and about how Mars needs to be free. I've heard you cuss the name of WestHem and the bastard capitalist corporations that rule our lives."

He stared at his crowd, his expression now challenging. "Well, gentlemen, guess what? The vehicle for that change you all want has arrived and you have the opportunity to be it. A plan has been in place for this day for several years now and the day has come to put it into action. If you really want Mars to be free, if you really want to break the bonds of WestHem rule, the time has come to shit or get off the pot. I'm about to ask you men to go into combat against WestHem soldiers, against the institution that rules us. I'm about to ask you to commit high treason, the penalty for which is life imprisonment on Earth."

"If any or even all of you does not wish to do this, you are free to stand and leave the room right now. I have orders direct from Governor Whiting herself that I am not to compel a single soldier to do my bidding. This is a voluntary assignment from this point on and that means more than one thing. If you commit to my plan, you will be doing so of your own free will and you will not have the excuse that you were simply following orders. If we lose, you will most likely suffer the fate I just explained. If we win, you will be heroes for the rest of Martian history.

"If any of you chooses not to be a part of this, I will be disappointed, I will label you as a hypocrite, unwilling to put his money where his mouth is, but you will be allowed to leave this room and go about your lives. You will, of course, be held until the operation is complete, but you have my word and the word of Governor Whiting that you will not be persecuted in any way.

"So..." He looked at his men, wondering if any would fold. A large part of him feared that all 640 would stand as one and move to the door. "Those who do not wish to participate, please stand and exit the room at the back right now."

Not a single soldier stood up. The chant started somewhere in the middle of the room and quickly spread. "Free Mars, free Mars, free Mars!"

Before long the entire room, Colonel Bright included, was shouting it at the top of their lungs.

*****

The *Mermaid* had docked at Triad Naval base two hours before, after its long deployment to the Jupiter system. Though the majority of the crew had been released for three days of shore duty at Triad, Spacer first class Brett Ingram was not among them. He was in charge of a work detail tasked with unloading the unused food supplies left over from the deployment and returning them to the main Owl supply area. It was somewhat insulting work for a skilled computer technician but, after nine years in the WestHem navy, he was quite used to insulting behavior from his superiors. When Lieutenant Commander Braxton had been faced with the task of forming an unload detail, he'd picked the six Martians out of the entire crew to form it, seeming to pick at random but, out of forty-eight enlisted men it was quite a large coincidence that only those of Martian heritage had been chosen.

This was all status quo on the good old *Mermaid* of the good old WestHem Navy, but today it was particularly irritating because Brett and the members of his detail were burning to monitor the news broadcasts regarding the situation on the surface. Could what they were hearing possibly be true? Had they really indicted Laura Whiting? Had her forces really fired on federal agents? And now new reports were coming in as well, reports about some sort of battle at the entrance to the WestHem marine base. Were MPG troops engaging the marines? What kind of madness was going on down there?

Every compartment on the ship had an Internet terminal in it and, since they were docked, they were patched into the base Internet system. They didn't dare turn any of these screens onto anything other than a music station however, nor did they dare monitor things on their PCs. There were security personnel on board the *Mermaid* too and, as Martians, it would be unwise to show much interest in the goings on down on the surface.

"Do you really think that Whiting is holding the capital building hostage?" asked Spacer third class Fairfield, a young African-descended man in his first year of naval service. He was still young enough and dumb enough to take visible offense at his treatment by his Earthling shipmates. If he didn't get it under control right quick, he would find himself tossed out of the Navy and virtually unemployable before too much longer. Brett had already had a few talks with him about this.

"It sounds pretty wild, doesn't it?" Brett replied, careful to keep his voice down. They were descending the ladder from the galley area, carrying the last of the eggs from the supply room, which was connected to the spaceport dock by its own airlock door. Since they were docked, the *Mermaid* was connected to the base gravity generators and therefore under normal gravitation.

"It's sounds fuckin' crazy." Fairfield told him. "Can you believe those Earthling motherfuckers? Arresting Whiting? Just because…."

"Hush, Fairfield," Brett barked sharply, looking around nervously at the supply room which, thankfully, only contained one security person at the moment, and he was on the other corner watching two men pack up milk and powdered juice packages. "Remember where we are. Remember the talk we had. Be static."

"Yes sir," Ingram, his face scowling, nodded. "It's just that…"

"Shhhh," Jeff reiterated. "We'll talk later, once we get out of this ship. We'll go get ourselves a drink, okay?"

"Yes sir," he repeated, handing over a carton of eggs, which Jeff carried silently over to the pile by the airlock.

They continued to work, unaware that they would not be going to any bars for quite some time.

*****

The Triad Primary control building was near the center of the city, in the worst neighborhood. It rose thirty stories above the street level and was surrounded on all sides by high-rise, low income housing complexes. The street level here was a dangerous place full of intoxicant shops, pawnshops, and massage parlors. The walls and even the ceilings were covered with graffiti of all sizes, colors, and sentiments, most of it illiterate, much of it anti-Earthling in nature. Each housing entrance lobby was a gathering place of the residents here. Most of them were unemployed and living off of the meager allowances of the welfare system. They sat out in front of their buildings hour after hour, day after day, smoking cigarettes of tobacco and marijuana and drinking Fruity. Crime was high in the neighborhood and, before the Whiting reforms of the past few months, there had been multiple incidents of control personnel being assaulted or robbed of valuables, enough incidents so that the Triad Police made a habit of hanging around the building at shift change time and escorting the workers to the tram station two blocks over.

The entrance to the building was much like the capital. Two guards armed with body armor and sidearms controlled access from behind a bulletproof layer of glass. The guards were watching an Internet screen and keeping half an eye on the pedestrian traffic walking back and forth in front of them. Currently the lobby was empty and there was not much going on. Shift change would not be for another three hours.

The channel they were watching was a MarsGroup channel. A live news broadcast was in progress from in front of the capital building. Nothing had changed there in the last hour. MPG troops could be seen in force out front and patrolling the perimeter. Pedestrians stayed well away from the goings on. Every once in a while, they would clip to other shots; the FLEB building in New Pittsburgh, which was now under a similar guard; and the city jail, where it was believed that the FLEB agents had been taken. In Eden, news teams were reported to be heading for the entrance to the WestHem marine barracks where it was said that some sort of battle was going on.

"Governor Whiting," said a pretty female reporter of Asian descent, "has yet to make a statement of any kind in regards to the startling chain of events that has occurred today. It is unknown just where this will all lead. Speculation remains high that the only course of action that Whiting will be able to use is to give herself up to the WestHem authorities on a variety of charges, which now include murder. Like all Martians I find myself...."

"This shit is getting way out of hand," said Roger Ire, the first guard, to his partner. Like most Martians watching the events unfold, he was in a state of shock and disbelief. "What's gonna happen to Whiting? They're gonna execute her when they finally get their hands on her."

"I'm not sure that they're *going* to get their hands on her," Julie Woo replied nervously. "This is starting to look more and more like... well..."

"What?" he asked.

"Like a rebellion," she said, saying the words that she had been thinking for the past hour. They sounded strange on her lips.

"A rebellion?" he asked, astounded and scared. "What kind of shit are you talking?"

"Think about it," she said softly. "The feds come to take Whiting into custody and the MPG fires on them. A few minutes later a whole group of MPG just appears out of the woodwork and secures the entire capital. There's a general call-up of forces and now there are more MPG troops shooting it out with marines at the barracks. What does that all spell to you?"

Hearing her logic spoken out loud, he had a hard time coming up with another explanation. "Damn," he said slowly. "Can we do that?"

"You mean legally?" she asked, looking at him as if he were a dumbass. "I'm pretty sure that WestHem considers it illegal to rebel against them."

"No," he said, pushing at her with his hand, "I mean physically. Do we have the manpower and the weapons to take this planet for ourselves?"

"I don't know," she said. "What if they ask you to fight?"

He thought about that for a minute. "I'd do it," he said. "Just give me a gun and I'm out there with them."

"Me too," she said.

Their chance to participate in the revolution came sooner than they thought. Their Internet screen changed from the news broadcast to the face of their supervisor. His expression was strange, a mixture of shock and excitement. "Julie, Roger," he barked at them, much too loudly. "There is a platoon of MPG troops heading your way. They are accompanying a Colonel. Let them into the building when they get here."

Julie and Roger looked at each other silently for a moment. What the hell was this about? MPG troops on Triad?

"Do you understand?" their supervisor asked.

"Yes," Roger finally replied. "What is this about? What are..."

"I don't have time to explain right now," he answered, which they correctly interpreted as 'I don't know'. "These are orders direct from Sanchez herself. Let them in when they get there and direct them to the VIP elevator."

"Right," Julie nodded.

"And let me know when they're on the way up."

*****

They emerged out of the train platform and marched down the stairway. The stairwell was crowded with dangerous looking thugs hanging out, some of them undoubtedly waiting for fresh robbery victims. The thugs exited quickly as they saw forty MPG soldiers wearing tactical helmets and carrying M-24s out before them. Whatever was going on, they were certainly not going to mess with a platoon of soldiers in any way.

The troops formed a loose diamond formation after leaving the stairwell and began marching down the street towards the control building. A Triad Police officer who was talking to a young gang member about some outstanding warrants for theft saw them approaching and stared in disbelief. She had never seen anything like this before on the streets of Triad. What did it mean? She let the young man go about his business and walked up to the soldier on the point. The platoon halted before her and all eyes turned to her.

"What's going on here?" she asked a little nervously. Events at the capital and at the marine barracks had not escaped her attention and she could not help but draw the conclusion that they were related to this.

The soldier on point said nothing. Instead, a tall man, unarmed but wearing the rank of colonel, approached her from the center of the formation. He stared at her, looking at her nametag on her right breast. "Officer Smith," he addressed her, "I'm Colonel Bright of the Martian Planetary Guard. We have been mobilized at the command of Governor Whiting and we are on our way to secure the control building."

"The control building?" she asked incredulously.

"The control building," he said levelly. "We have a mission to accomplish there. Is it your intention to try and stop us?"

"No, of course not, Colonel, but...."

"We are in haste, Officer Smith." Bright told her. "Things will become clear to you very quickly. Free Mars," he hailed using a greeting that had become commonplace since Whiting's inauguration.

"Free Mars," she replied back, smiling.

The soldier on point gave a signal and the platoon moved out again. Smith stepped aside, allowing them unimpeded passage. Bright stood until the center of the formation caught up with him and then he began to march once again.

Three minutes later, they were at the entrance of the control building. Lieutenant Nguyen, the platoon commander, approached the two glass encased guards and identified himself. The guards opened the doors without question, just as he'd been assured they would. He began barking orders.

"First squad, accompany Colonel Bright upstairs. Second and third squads, secure the outside of the building, fourth squad, come with me for inside security. Weapons tight, people, until told otherwise. Under no circumstances are you to fire on any Martians and that includes cops. If the feds show up, normal rules of engagement apply, self-defense only unless they try to breach the building."

His four squad sergeants affirmed his orders and the soldiers began moving quickly to their destinations.

"Will the elevators take us where we need to go?" Colonel Bright asked Julie.

She seemed awed at his presence but answered quickly, "Yes, Colonel. We have orders to let you immediately up."

"Thank you." He began walking towards the elevators. His squad followed behind him

The elevator doors opened before them and the eleven men crowded inside. The elevator, like all of Triad, was under the influence of the artificial gravity system and the inertial damper. The elevator shot upwards towards the thirtieth floor of the building, the only indication that they were rising the changing numbers on the display. When it reached 30, the doors slid open to a small foyer tastefully decorated with modern art and couches. The carpet on the floor was threadbare but presentable. A uniformed guard stood before them.

"Colonel Bright?" he asked politely.

"That's me," Bright said, stepping forward and out of the elevator.

"Follow me, sir," the guard replied. "I have orders to take you to Mr. Sanchez and the main control room."

They were led down a long hallway and around two corners before coming to a steel security door. A computer terminal with a fingerprint analyzer was installed in the door. It was supposed to only allow access to authorized personnel. The guard placed his hand on the pad and the door slid open, revealing the large control room.

The control room was a crowded, busy place. Forty people were sitting at computer terminals monitoring all aspects of the orbiting city. They looked up as the doors opened, almost to a person. A tall Hispanic man walked over to Colonel Bright as his escorts crowded into the room and took up positions near the walls and windows. The two men appraised each other silently for a moment. Frank Sanchez, the watch commander of this shift, had been recruited for his part in the mission back in the planning stages. His counterparts on the other shifts had likewise been recruited. In this building, in this very room, was the key to success of their mission.

"Colonel Bright," Sanchez said loudly, loud enough for everyone to hear. "Welcome to the main control room. It is my honor to turn this facility over to the MPG in the interests of a free Mars."

There was a gasp from the assembled controllers, none of whom knew why Bright and his men were here. It was a shocked gasp but not an unhappy one.

"Thank you, Mr. Sanchez," Bright replied. He turned to the controllers. When he'd recruited Sanchez, he'd made sure that Sanchez would never allow anything other than a second-generation Martian to work in this room. He didn't figure he would have any trouble with these people. "Ladies and Gentlemen, I am Colonel Bright of the Martian Planetary Guard. You have all heard of the events at the capitol building and in Eden, I'm sure, so I will spare you the details of that. Let me say to you now that Mars is in the midst of a rebellion against WestHem rule. As I speak, the MPG troops that Governor Whiting called up earlier today are making motions to secure the planet from WestHem forces. They will be successful as long as we can keep the WestHem marines trapped on their base. However, the entire thing will be useless without a single key element that involves this room."

He peered at their faces, wondering how they would react to what he next had to say. "You are all Martians in here. Mr. Sanchez saw to that a long time ago. You know what WestHem rule has done to this planet. The time has come to put a stop to it. I need your help, people. You are the operators that control this orbiting city and the future of our rebellion now depends on the next two hours. I will ask you to act in the interest of Mars and Martian freedom. If you do not wish to participate, you may stand up and be counted. You will be removed from the room and held until the forthcoming operation is complete and then you will be released. You will not be persecuted in any way for failing to assist and you will have the same opportunity to evaluate Governor Whiting's actions tomorrow. We will not compel a single person to participate. This is a voluntary revolution, people. So, what do you say? Does anyone wish to stand?"

There was some murmuring but everyone remained in his or her seats. Colonel Bright smiled.

"I thank you," he announced. "Shortly we will begin." He turned his head to Sanchez. "Fred, have all voice and text communications from this building been halted?"

"They have, Colonel," Sanchez said with a nod. It had been done in fact, before the MPG had even entered the building. Secrecy was now paramount and they could not take the chance of word about what they were doing leaking out to the wrong ears.

"Good," Bright answered. He keyed up his communications link. "Get me Major Shaw."

"Shaw here," replied his second-in-command, who was with the bulk of the special forces battalion and who would lead the attack.

"We are in position," Bright told him simply. "Are you ready to execute?"

"We are," Shaw replied. "Standing by for the go signal."

"Copy," Bright nodded. "Initiating now. Have the men stand to."

"Standing to," Shaw said, signing off.

Bright turned to Sanchez once more. For security reasons Sanchez, though a part of the conspiracy, did not know what Bright intended to do in the control building. He had simply supplied schematics, access, and promised to assist in any way possible once the time came to enact the plan. Bright sat before an empty Internet screen and called up the schematics he was looking for. "Mr. Sanchez, will you have your people shut down electric power and the trams in section 48-63, 64, and 65?"

Sanchez turned to controller in charge of electric service for those sectors. He ordered the shutdown and then did the same for the master tram controller. He saw immediately what Bright was doing and wondered how he had never managed to guess it before.

Triad Naval Base was not actually a part of Triad. It orbited two kilometers away from the edge of the city, far enough away so that the risk of the main city being accidentally struck by off-course naval vessels was at a minimum. But TNB and Triad were not completely independent of each other. When viewed from above, the two large structures seemed to be connected by three tiny hairs that stretched out from the west side of Triad to the east side of TNB. These hairs were actually steel tunnels through which freight trams and passenger trams carried people and supplies back and forth. They were the only way to move back and forth between the two places without boarding a space ship.

The sections that Bright had just ordered powered down were the ones that adjoined the connectors for Triad Naval Base. Although the trams that ran from Triad to the naval base were security controlled and separate from the rest of the city's system, and although TNB had its own internal power supply that could not be controlled from Triad's control building, the power that ran the trams themselves came from Triad's power grid. With a simple command, the trams came to a halt at the Triad end of the station. The interiors went dark as night, darker even, and the plan was under way.

"Shaw," Bright spoke into communication link.

"Yes, Colonel?"

"Everything's ready. Execute immediately."

"Executing."

He turned back to his screen and consulted the diagrams for a moment. "Sanchez, please open access hatches 3127 through 3150."

"Access hatches?" Sanchez asked, surprised. These were manholes in the street level that allowed access to the tunnels below the street. The tunnels carried sewage pipes, fresh water pipes, electrical and Internet lines. Were Bright's men down in the tunnels? It was absolutely brilliant.

"Yes, Mr. Sanchez. Open them now please."

"Carla," Sanchez said to the proper technician. "Open access hatches 3127 through 3150."

"Yes sir," Carla said, speaking to her terminal. "Hatches are open."

"And now," Bright said, "please cut power and Internet to section 29-50."

"The FLEB office," Sanchez said, repeating the command to another tech.

When this was done, the waiting began.

*****

They had marched for nearly six kilometers through the musty, smelly underworld of Triad. It was a dark, damp, crowded place, narrow and confined. Rats lived down there, as well as entire species of bugs and spiders. Their combat goggles allowed them to see in what otherwise would have been complete darkness. Each member of each squad had a map of the complex as well as a map of Triad Naval Base and of their individual objectives programmed into their combat computers. The maps could be superimposed into their goggles allowing the image to seemingly float in the air before them. Each platoon of forty men was equipped with six hundred meters of primacord and the detonation equipment. They fanned out in the tunnels when they reached the staging point, every platoon going to a certain ladder beneath a certain access hatch.

Lon and his squad, who were assigned to second platoon, bravo company, took up position beneath hatch number 3140, which was directly below the southern passenger tram entrance to the naval base. "Okay, guys," he told his men as they waited, "we're gonna be less than sixty meters from the guard positions when we come up. The lights will be out and there will be a lot of confused civilians on the platform, so be careful. If we have to shoot, be sure you have a positive ID on your target and be cognizant of where your stray rounds are going to be heading."

The execute command was given. Fifteen seconds later, the access hatches slid open, directed to do so by the control room five kilometers away. Men began to climb as fast as they could, hefting themselves up the steel ladders in a controlled manner, separated from each other by a space of only two rungs. From twenty-three hatches, armored and armed men began pouring into the streets of Triad near the tram station that led to the Naval base.

The streets above were in chaos. People were huddled everywhere in corners and on the streets in fear of the pitch blackness that had suddenly engulfed them. Power outages were not unheard of in Triad, but they never lasted more than five seconds or so, the amount of time it took for some computer to route a supply around whatever damaged area had caused the failure. In the buildings around them, elevators would be stopped, electric doors would be jammed shut, people would be in panic. It was a pity to do this to fellow Martians, but it was needed.

The troops pouring from the access hatches formed into their squads and platoons as they emerged and handed up their heavier weaponry and their equipment packs. They began to move to their first objectives: the entrances to the tram tunnels that led to Triad Naval Base.

The main force, which consisted of two companies, headed for the primary personnel tunnel, since it would lead them to the main foyer of the base and drop them close to the vital control room. Another single company headed for the northern tunnel, which was a secondary entrance for ship crews and dock personnel. The last company of the battalion took the south tunnel, which was a freight tunnel though which fuel, supplies, and other staples entered the base after being shipped from the Triad civilian docks. It was this entrance where the first contact between MPG and Navy military police took place.

The freight loading platform was large and was staffed with a squad of MPs whose job it was to check each incoming train for infiltrators, bombs, or anything else. The MPs were no less confused than the civilians. They had no combat goggles, so they were as blind as everyone else in this section of Triad. Their Internet screens had gone dark and they were trying to reach someone on the base over their back-up radio frequency, which did not rely on Internet cables, when the sounds of many feet and clanking armor appeared all around them.

"WestHem MPs!" boomed a voice from an amplifier. "You are surrounded by MPG troops! Surrender immediately or you will be fired upon. Drop your weapons to the ground, walk to the center of the platform, and lay down!"

Sergeant Broker was the twenty-three-year-old MP in charge of the five-man squad. He heard the voice just as he'd succeeded in getting through to the Naval Base MP barracks inside the main gate. He had heard the number of feet clomping around on the platform and knew that he held a useless position. His people were blind and horribly outnumbered. The greenies would have combat goggles on and probably had beads drawn on all five of them.

"Do what they say, guys," he commanded, his voice shaky with fear. "Do it now."

"Broker!" A voice replied from his radio channel. "What is going on there? Did you say the lights were out? I have reports from the main gate and the secondary of the same thing."

"This is Broker," he said. "My position is under attack from a large number of greenie troops. I am surrendering to them."

"Broker!" the voice yelled. "What did you say?"

He had time for no more. He left the link open so that they would at least be able to hear what was going on. He then walked to the center of the street with his hands in the air, moving gingerly in the darkness. His men did the same. They were quickly handcuffed with plastic ties and left lying on their bellies for the moment. The south gate had fallen without a shot being fired.

At the main gate platform, things went a little differently. The MPs were more numerous and more confused by the unusually lengthy darkness. There were also many more civilian and military people standing by the security checkpoints, awaiting access to a train that was now stopped in the tunnel. When the MPG troops rushed onto the platform, their commander yelled through the intercom for everyone to get down immediately.

The commanding MP was talking on his radio at that very moment.

"Lieutenant Beal," barked the confused voice of Lieutenant Smack back at the barracks. "I've just received a report that the main freight access platform is under attack by greenie troops. Expect trouble at your position, take up defensive positions."

"Greenie troops? But..." It was then that the announcement to get down boomed across them.

Beal was young and inexperienced at his job, only recently having been promoted to officer. He had no idea how many troops the MPG was throwing at him and did not consider the fact that they would have the advantage of sight on their side.

"We're under attack by the greenies," he yelled at his men. "Defensive positions, now!"

His men scrambled in the darkness, training their M-24s outward, unable to see a thing, but able to hear the stomp of steel-toed boots and the clank of raising weapons. There were screams from the civilians trapped on the platform, the cries of children.

"MPs!" The voice boomed once more. "You are surrounded and your position is hopeless. Drop your weapons and move to the center..."

It happened fast and was over in seconds. One of the MPs unleashed a blast from his M-24 at the general direction of the voice. The bullets arced out and hit several civilians, putting them on the ground. Fortunately, most of the civilians had taken the first piece of advice and gotten down. The other MPs opened fire also, Beal included. The darkness was filled with the thunder of automatic weapons and the nightmare strobe-light effect of the flashes.

The point platoon of the MPG reacted in less than half a second. Through their goggles, they saw each MP and the flashes emitting from their weapons. They saw the white streaks of the hot shells flying at them. Thirty-six M-24s and four SAWs opened up as one, drowning out the roar of the MPs weapons. The Martian soldiers were trained well, each knowing what their sector of responsibility encompassed. Eight of the fifteen MPs went down with the first bursts. Of the remaining seven, four of them tried to return fire and were cut down with the second burst. The remaining three, one of whom was wounded, threw down their weapons and cried surrender.

"Hold your fire," the platoon lieutenant barked over his command channel. The Martian guns fell silent at once, their thunder replaced by the hysterical cries of the civilian and military personnel that had been caught on the platform between the two groups of soldiers. He flipped on his intercom system again. "Civilians on the platform, remain where you are and do not move! MPs, walk unarmed to the center of the platform and lie down. NOW!"

The remaining MPs stood and, with hands raised, walked towards the center.

*****

"Objective Green is secure," came the voice of Captain Evers, the commander of that section, over the command channel. "We had contact with the MPs and there are wounded enemy and civilians on the platform."

"Copy that," Shaw replied. He was a kilometer away, at the south tunnel with bravo company. "Are any of your men wounded?"

"Negative, sir."

"Get your medics in action once everyone is in the tunnel."

"Yes, sir."

He then addressed all of his company commanders. "Okay Alpha, Bravo, Charlie, and Delta companies," he said. "All tunnel entrances are secured. Move forward now and quickly. Heads up on the other side. The WestHems have been alerted. Weapons free, but use your discretion. There are a lot of civilian and non-combatants in that base."

He received four acknowledgements and the next phase was begun.

At each of the three tunnels leading to Triad Naval Base, the primacord was placed on the security doors that guarded the entrances the trains used. The explosive material formed half ovals two meters wide by three meters high. Detonators were attached. The troops stood back a safe distance from the doorways and the detonators were fired, exploding the cord and blasting neatly through the three-centimeter steel. In all three tunnels, at virtually the same instant, sections of doorway clanged to the ground, allowing entry to the MPG.

The commands to move came and, at each of the three tunnels, nearly two hundred troops rushed forward and through the newly created holes in the doors. A squad of infantry stayed behind at each platform for security and prisoner guarding. At the main entrance, a squad of medics went to work on the wounded civilians and MPs.

The tunnels were two kilometers in length and thirty meters in diameter, each of them with two side-by-side magna tracks. The MPG special forces troops moved rapidly forward at not quite a double-time pace, weapons ready, infra-red enhanced eyes peering forward. Though complete surprise had been hoped for, it had not been achieved. The WestHems knew they were coming and were probably scrambling troops to try to stop them. When they reached the other end of the tunnels, the fun would really start.

*****

Commander Gravely was in command of the Triad Naval Base MPs. He was at his desk in front of his Internet terminal, supposed to be going over some budgetary figures but actually watching the Internet coverage of the events in New Pittsburgh with growing rage. What the hell did those greenies think they were doing? Firing on federal officers. Refusing to honor a valid arrest warrant. Holding all of the workers in the Martian Capital building hostage. There were even rumors that they were engaging WestHem marines down at the barracks entrance. The green bastards had gone too far this time and he relished the thought that the WestHem federal system was soon going to land on them with both feet. And about damn time too.

Things had gotten very bad since that bitch Whiting had been sworn in. What had once been simple animosity between Martians and WestHem had turned into vicious hatred that was often punctuated with violence. The naval personnel on the base were afraid to even go into Triad or down to the Martian surface for fear of being attacked by angry Martians. And now Whiting actually had MPG troops—which were under federal control for Christ's sakes—firing upon FLEB agents and holding hostages. He hoped that when this was all over, they lined every one of those traitorous bastards up against a wall and...

His Internet terminal cleared, showing the face of Lieutenant Smack, the dispatch CO. "Commander," he yelled frantically, his faced flushed. He was obviously excited about something. "We need you in here right now. A serious situation is developing."

He almost asked for information right then, would have if not for the petrified expression on the Lieutenant's face. He acknowledged the request and stood, leaving his office and entering the dispatch center less than thirty seconds later. Five dispatchers sat at computer terminals, Smack included. Normally, their jobs were to take calls from base personnel regarding matters that required an MP response and to route those calls to their available MP units. They weren't doing that now however. On all of their faces were expressions of disbelief mixed with fear.

"What's going on?" he demanded.

"Sir," Smack reported, "five minutes ago we received radio reports from the access tunnel stations on the Triad side. All three reported that the lights and Internet had gone out and not come back on. Shortly after that, the main freight squad leader reported that he was under attack by greenie troops and surrendering his position. We then...."

"What?" Gravely yelled loudly enough to make everyone in the room jump. "Greenie troops? Attacking our MPs? And they *surrendered*?"

"Yes sir," Smack nodded rapidly. "And that's not all. A minute or so later, the main gate on the Triad side reported they were under fire by the MPG. We haven't heard from them since. The north gate then reported they were overwhelmed and surrendering too. While we were trying to figure this out we received breach alarms on all three Triad to TNB tunnel doors."

"The cameras," Gravely barked. "In the tunnels. What do they show?"

"Nothing sir," Smack answered. "The power is out in them. The power supply for the tunnels comes from Triad, not from TNB."

"Those green sons-of-bitches," Gravely proclaimed, now beginning to feel fear himself. He thought for a second, wondering how bad this situation was. Greenie troops were moving through the access tunnels towards the main base. Why? What could they possibly do if they got there? A terrorist attack of some sort? How many of them were there? There couldn't be that many, could there? Where could you hide a large number of troops on Triad after all?

"What should we do, sir?" Smack asked.

"Move all available MPs to the three tunnel access points. Give them weapons free status and tell them that Martian infiltrators may try to break through. Send the bulk of them to the main personnel tunnel. That's right outside here and is the best access to the rest of the base. Alert TIRT and have them deploy with all of the heavy weapons they have." TIRT was the terrorist incident response team, a platoon of specially trained and equipped MPs kept on hand for just such an incident. Well, maybe not *this* sort of incident. No one had ever considered the possibility of an armed number of infiltrators attacking the base through the access tunnels.

"Yes sir," Smack replied, calmer now that someone else was calling the shots. He went to work.

Gravely sat down at an Internet terminal and activated it, giving his authorization code. "This is Commander Gravely," he told the computer. "On my authority, set base to condition Red Zebra. All personnel to GQ stations."

"Order confirmed," the terminal replied. "Initiating condition Red Zebra."

Red Zebra was the code for occupation of the city of Triad by enemy forces. Even during the Jupiter War, it had not been initiated. All over the base, doors between sections buzzed and slammed shut, latching securely and trapping people in their work areas or in hallways between doors. Only MP personnel would be able to get through them and only after their IDs were confirmed both by the security computer and by visualization by command staff. The base was locked down tight as a drum.

"Get me Admiral Rosewood," Gravely told the computer next, referring to the commander of the naval base.

Rosewood was on the screen almost immediately. Obviously, when his door had slammed shut on him, trapping him with his secretary in his office, and when the announcement came over his screen letting him know that his base was now on the highest level of alert it had ever experienced, he became a bit curious as to what was going on. A quick check revealed the source of the order. He could have instantly revoked it, and figured that someone had made a career-ending mistake, but he decided to see what the situation was first.

"Commander Gravely," he said, staring from the screen. "Did you order a condition Red Zebra?"

"Yes sir," Gravely answered. "I did." He then quickly explained the chain of events that led him to do this.

"That's absolutely insane!" Rosewood said after hearing the story. "Are you sure about this?"

"As sure as I can be, sir. I already saw the alarm displays on my screen. Sir, our tunnels have been breached and I have every reason to believe that MPG troops, unknown in number, are in those tunnels for unknown intentions. They do seem to have the ability to breach the doors when they wish." He then explained the steps he had taken so far.

Rosewood seemed deep in a troubled thought. "Gravely," he asked, "what the hell would greenie troops want to attack this base for? Why would they risk the casualties it would produce?"

"I don't know, sir," Gravely answered. "I only responded to the information that...."

"Holy shit," Rosewood interrupted. "The ships in dock!"

"Excuse me, sir?" Gravely didn't see what that had to do with anything.

"Jesus. Mars and Earth are now nearly as far apart as they can get. Whenever that happens, we move a large portion of our ships to Triad in case of trouble with the EastHems during this time. We have fifteen Owls and nine Californias in dock right now, in addition to the pre-positioned container ships and all of the escorts. All of the personnel that man those ships are on this base right now. If they can take the base, they can deny us nearly a third of our naval forces. A third!"

Gravely stared blankly. "You don't really think..." he started.

"Why the hell else would they be attacking us?" Rosewood asked. "Your precautions should be enough to stop them, I hope, but send the TIRT to the dock entrances in case the Martians break out. I'm gonna have the crews report to their ships and scramble the fuck off of this base until this thing is settled. But you need to give me some time to do that and you need to allow ship personnel through the checkpoints. Can you instruct the computers to do that?"

"Yes sir," he replied, "but it'll take a couple of minutes."

"Get moving on it. And call up all off-duty MPs and have them report to either the docks or the gates."

"Yes sir. Should I..."

Alarms blared in the room, making everyone peer at their terminals.

"What the hell was that?" Rosewood asked.

Gravely looked at his screen and paled. "Sir," he told the admiral, "the tunnel doors into the base have just been breached."

"Which one?"

"All of them," he answered, fighting back panic. "At almost the same instant."

"Are your men in place?" Rosewood demanded, catching a little of the panic.

He consulted his screen briefly. "No sir. Most of them are still trying to get through the checkpoints. I have fifty men spread around the three tunnels with the heaviest concentration at the main."

"Shit," Rosewood said. "I hope that's enough."

*****

Like before, most of the action took place at the main entrance. The primacord was detonated and a large hole was blown in the door. The MPG troops were deployed well back from the entrance, backs against the tunnel wall, bodies against the floor. The minute that the door was breached, automatic weapons fire began pouring in from the MPs stationed outside. Most of the shots simply ricocheted harmlessly off of the walls but some of them found their marks in the crowded tunnel. It was inevitable. Cries of "Medic!" began echoing over the tactical net.

The MPG machine gunners opened up, pouring fire through the hole, as did the troops whose M-24s were equipped with grenade launchers. Their fire was marginal at best since they couldn't really see their targets too well, but some of the bullets found their marks and some of the grenades caused injury or death by exploding luckily near a deployed MP. Still, the MPGs knew the same thing that the WestHem marines down in Eden had found out the hard way. They were vulnerable in the tunnel since they were pinned into a narrow corridor. Here, the difference that kept them from being routed out and pushed back to the loading platform was the fact that the doors were not completely missing. There was still solid steel to either side of the hole that had been blasted, allowing cover and a firing position for a limited number of soldiers. Using this small place of safety to best advantage, men were stationed there to keep the approaches clear of MPs. But still, it quickly became clear that an easy break out was simply not in the cards. There were too many MPs out there and, though they didn't have combat goggles or combat computer support, they were able to lay down a field of fire that was accurate and concentrated enough to make a casualty out of anyone who tried to push out. The invasion of the base would not take place as planned right here.

At the south freight tunnel, things were going easier. Once the door was breached, the fire was sporadic and light from the opposition on the other side. They had not had a chance to deploy in any significant numbers. The special forces platoons that made up bravo company pushed forward to the entrance and poured machine gun fire and grenades out into the deployed MPs with much greater accuracy and effect. Squads began to pour through the hole into the freight storage and unloading platform beyond it. Here, the training that they had been engaging in on the inside of the MPG base—training that they had not understood while they were undertaking it—began to make sense and show its effectiveness in the fight. Like a well-oiled machine, man after man passed through the doorway and rolled either to the left or the right, their eyes searching to acquire targets, their hands and arms adjusting their rifles and then firing at muzzle-flashes and moving figures. There were some casualties taken—that was pretty much inevitable—but the sheer speed with which they exited the tunnel kept them to a minimum.

Lon and his men were part of the second group through the door. They spit up into two elements, half moving to the left, half to the right. Lon and the four men with him concentrated their fire on a group of three MPs that were hiding behind an electric forklift and sniping at the men emerging from the tunnel. Lon sent three of his men further right to flank them as he and private Matza on the SAW provided covering fire. The flanking maneuver worked admirably and soon the three MPs were gunned efficiently down with a combination of grenades and automatic weapons fire. From that point on, the tunnel exit was clear and Lon's squad moved off to the right flank to help silence the rest of the opposition. The remaining MPs that they encountered began to throw down their weapons and surrender. Each of them was handcuffed with the plastic ties and put down on the ground.

In all, it took less than ten minutes before the loading platform was secure and a beachhead of sorts was established. Medics were brought forward to care for the wounded Martians and, when the time was found, the wounded MPs as well. Major Shaw, who had been lingering in the rear of the column during the firefight, came forward and surveyed the first section of the Triad Naval Base to come under MPG occupation.

"Good job," he told the men. "Now let's push onward. You know your objectives, so let's go secure them before they have a chance to gear up to a real defensive posture."

They split into two elements and headed for the two large corridors at the far end of the platform, corridors that led further into the bowels of the base. The doors guarding them had slammed shut and locked in response to the Red Zebra condition. Teams went to work putting primacord on them.

Before they had a chance to blow the doors however, Shaw got a vital update on the other elements of the battle. The north freight tunnel, which alpha company was assigned to, had been breached and its entrance station captured with only three killed and four wounded. At Shaw's direction, they too began preparing to move further into the base towards their own objective: the docking complexes and the ships that were at anchor there.

But Charlie and Delta companies, in charge of breaching the main gate in the center, had a different story to tell.

"We're pinned down in the tunnel," Captain Evers, the commander in charge of this force told Shaw over the radio net. In the background, Shaw could hear the chatter of weapons fire and the hollow booms of explosions. "We won't be able to break out without taking heavy casualties. And every minute we wait, more MPs show up."

"How bad are casualties so far?" Shaw asked him.

"Twelve wounded, six dead."

"Hang tight for a few," Shaw ordered. "I'm gonna send you some help. Wait for my order and then initiate the breakout."

"Copy," Evers replied.

Though the situation Evers found himself in was bad, it was not something that had been unanticipated. "Armand!" Shaw barked into the air, not bothering to use the radio since the object of his yell was standing less than ten meters away.

"Sir?" responded Armand, the commander of Bravo company, as he trotted over.

"Break loose a squad with a hundred meters of primacord and one SAW. We need to flank the MPs on the main entrance before Charlie and Delta can break out. Have them go weapons-free by the quickest route and stand by. I'm gonna send a squad from Alpha over to hit the north flank too. Who would be squad leader you're sending?"

Armand thought for a moment. "I'll send the third squad from second platoon," he said. "Sergeant Fargo."

"Good," Shaw said, nodding in approval. He knew Lon personally and was impressed with him. "Get them moving. Fargo will probably be the senior NCO, so he'll be in charge of this makeshift platoon under the direct orders of Captain Evers."

"Yes, sir," Armand replied.

"Send the rest of your company to their objective, but leave another squad here with two SAWs for beachhead security. If this base isn't secured in the next hour, it's never going to be."

"Yes, sir," Armand said, switching his radio frequency.

Lon and his squad were called over and given their new orders. He absorbed the information quickly and then consulted his map of the base to find out the best means of getting to the main pedestrian platform. It took him only a minute or so of study to lock in on a route of travel. "Let's go, people," he told his men. "The sooner we get there, the less Earthlings we'll have to fight."

They made their way across the loading platform to the north side of it, where a small access corridor, its door sealed shut, led along the perimeter of the base. Horishito, one of the two men carrying the large coils of primacord, placed a length of it on this door and then set a detonator in it.

"Third squad, breaching side door now," he announced over the command net. There were quite possibly MPs waiting on the other side of the door and his men pointed their weapons in preparation. Part of the security squad that had already been in position trained theirs too.

"Go ahead, Hoary," Lon told him once everyone was in position.

Horishito blew the door, sending it crashing to the floor. No fire came through hole that had been made and his men advanced slowly and carefully to the sides. They took quick glances through the hole finding no MPs but about ten civilian personnel already lying peacefully on the floor, their hands behind their heads, begging the men that they assumed to be heartless terrorists not to shoot them. Lon and the others dashed into the room and secured it, ordering the civilians through the hole and into the main loading area where they joined those already taken prisoner. They then began to move towards the main tunnel entrance nearly a kilometer away.

*****

Admiral Rosewood had moved to the command post in the main TNB control room. This room was a much larger version of the main control room for Triad since it also was responsible for controlling docking, power, gravitation, and traffic control of the naval vessels in port. Sixty-four controllers worked at computer terminals and monitored security camera displays. They watched in disbelief at the events unfolding around them. Rosewood understood.

He now had a better idea of what he was up against and, as such, he feared for his safety and the security of his base now. Thanks to digital camera images that had been taken before the cameras had been shot out, he knew that he had enemy troops in company strength fanning out from two directions, from two different tunnels into vital parts of the base. The blast doors were presenting no problems for them; they were simply blasting them open with primacord. A third company—at least he assumed it was a company; he had yet to get an image of it—was still pinned down in the main tunnel by the MPs. That wouldn't last long, he feared. He could see squad strength concentrations moving in on the main gate through other tunnels, obviously to flank. He had no MPs to spare to try to stop them. He couldn't even offer more than token resistance to the companies that were moving deeper into the base by the minute. One of them was heading, as he'd initially suspected, directly toward the space docks where access to the 43 docked ships could be had. The TIRT team, as well as about twenty regular MPs, were in position there but, even with the heavy weapons, they would not be able to stand up to a company for very long. His attempt to get the crews to their ships to scramble them had been inspired but useless. It had taken too long and their access was now cut off by the advancing MPG.

He had never felt so out of his element in his life. He was a naval admiral, not a ground combat soldier, and he was ill equipped to deal with this situation. He had sent off a report to Earth, but the length of communications meant that he could expect no reply for nearly three hours. By then the base and all of its ships, all of its highly trained naval personnel, could very well be in Martian hands. That included the pre-positioned container ships with the marine division's equipment on board! If they got their hands on those ships, it would nearly double the MPG's inventory of tanks, artillery, and other heavy weaponry! That simply could not be allowed!

It was the thought of these container ships and the marines they were meant for that gave him a glimmer of hope. There were twelve thousand marines down on the surface of Mars! Twelve thousand marines with M-24s, SAWs, and hundreds of thousands of rounds of ammunition. And there were lifter craft capable of bringing those marines directly to the naval base in a short amount of time.

He turned to the terminal that he was using for communications. "Get me General Sega down at EMB," he said. "Highest priority!"

A few seconds went by and the computer told him, "General Sega is not taking calls at the moment. Would you like his mail server or would you like to..."

"I'd like you to get him on line," Rosewood interrupted. "Go through whoever you have to and tell them that this is a matter of federal security that supersedes whatever he is dealing with down there."

"Attempting to recontact," the computer dutifully told him.

Another minute went by before Sega's face came on the screen, impatience clearly showing. "John," he said, "I hope this is important because we've just been hit by the MPG. I've got a bunch of dead marines over here and a bunch of greenie ass that I'm getting ready to kick. And I'm not gonna take any fuckin names either."

"It's important," Rosewood assured him, dismissing the startling news about the marine base for the moment in light of his own problems. "I'm having some greenie trouble of my own up here. My base is under attack."

This put a sobering expression on Sega's face. "What do you mean?" he asked slowly.

"They hit the access tunnels about fifteen minutes ago," he explained. "Uniformed and armed MPG soldiers, complete with M-24s, squad automatic weapons, combat goggles and combat computers. It looks like they're in battalion strength."

"Jesus fucking Christ," Sega said, paling as he heard this. "How are you holding?"

"Not too well," Rosewood admitted with a certain amount of shame. "They've breached all three of the tunnels on the base side and two of their elements are now moving through the base. We have another element pinned down in the main tunnel, but the greenies have reinforcements in motion to flank my men. I need some help up here. My MPs and my TIRT team are not going to be able to hold for very long."

"Our equipment ships are up there," Sega said. "If the greenies get their hands on those..."

"I have forty-eight front-line naval vessels up here as well," Rosewood interjected. "As well as the crews that operate them. That's nearly a *third* of the WestHem navy. I would say that this problem is one that requires immediate attention. How soon can you get me some marines up here?"

Sega considered for a moment. "I can load a battalion into two C-12s and get them launched in about twenty minutes if I put a rush on the pilots," he said. "Once in flight, it'll take them about ninety minutes to dock with you. Can you hold that long?"

Rosewood looked at his display doubtfully. "I don't know," he said. "We're outnumbered and outgunned by the greenies. I don't even know where the hell they came from or how they got up to Triad without anyone noticing, but there is a shitload of them up here."

Sega now looked a little embarrassed. "Well," he said slowly, "there were reports last night of a large number of MPG troops transporting up to Triad in C-10s."

"What?" Rosewood said, a glare developing on his face. "And nobody thought to mention this to *me*?"

"It was assumed that it was just one of those bizarre training missions that the greenies are always doing," Sega said. "How the hell were we supposed to know they were going to attack TNB?"

"Jesus," Rosewood said, shaking his head. "What a clusterfuck." He didn't dwell on the how of the problem and the assignment of blame for the time being. "Norm," he said, "I'll try to keep those greenies contained, but I really don't know if I'm going to be able to hold until your marines get here. If that company we have pinned in the main tunnel manages to break out, they'll head directly for this command post. If they take it, I won't be able to initiate docking for your transports."

Sega paused, seeming to think for a second. Finally, gingerly, he said, "John, with all due respect, would you mind downloading me a situation schematic? I know that you're above reproach as a naval officer, but what you're dealing with now is more along the lines of my profession. Maybe I can..."

"Norm, the download is on the way. I'll do more than take advice from you, I'll put the defense of this base directly under your control."

"I think that's a good idea. I'm assuming control of TNB defense as of now." He paused again while Rosewood instructed his computer to send a copy of his schematics across. Once it arrived, he spent a few minutes staring at it intently. "John," he said when he came to a decision, "I need you to pull your men out of the dock area and move them to guarding your command post."

"But the ships...." Rosewood started.

"The ships can't leave or do anything without commands from where you sit. The MPG won't be able to do anything with them until they have the command post secured. Trust me. You must keep them from taking that command post at all costs until my marines can dock. That means you put every available man with a weapon in front of and inside of the building. I'll upload a deployment schematic for you as soon as I have it."

"Okay, it'll be done."

*****

Sega's office looked out over the troop assembly area adjacent to the airlock complexes. From his desk, he was able to see the huge, cavernous room that contained the flight area, where his C-12s were sitting idle, and the outside assembly staging. There were ten outdated tanks down there that had nothing but training ammunition to fire, as well as twenty-five outdated APCs with the same problem. The vehicles were being ignored as the brigade he had tasked to take the MPG base—those that were left of it anyway—came out of the locker room one by one in their bulky biosuits. They assembled in their predetermined positions, exactly one arm length apart, their weapons slung over their right shoulders. Soon, they would exit through the airlocks and move overland to the main city, where they would breach a hole in the wall, causing the loss of pressure in that particular section. The blast doors surrounding the section would slam down and the marines would enter. They would then seal the hole that they had entered through, thus retaining the integrity of the section, and re-flood it with air by drilling holes through into the undamaged portions of the city. Once the pressure was equalized, they would blast through another wall and start heading for the base. This was the textbook manner of assaulting a pressurized city or structure, something that had been practiced many times, but that had never actually been attempted in real combat positions, neither by WestHem or EastHem.

Satisfied that the Martian portion of his plans was going forth as scheduled, Sega instructed his computer to get Colonel Summers, commander of his third brigade, on the screen. Summers and his men were currently gearing up in the locker rooms so that they could move out through the interior gates once they were liberated from the greenies.

"Summers here, General," he said once he came on line.

"Summers," Sega said, "there's a bit of a situation going on up at the naval base. I'll need you to break loose one of your battalions to deal with it."

"A situation, sir?"

"Greenies are attacking TNB," Sega said. He then explained the details as quickly as he could.

"Those motherfuckers," Summers said, outraged. "We'll kill them. We'll absolutely murder them, General!"

"I'll be satisfied if you just prevent them from gaining control of the base," Sega told him. "Scrounge up two of our flight crews and start loading your best battalion into those lifters. I want you launching within thirty minutes."

"Yes sir," Summers said, signing off.

Sega gave a quick call to Rosewood to tell him that help would be leaving shortly. Nothing had changed up there. The greenies that had already broken out were still moving through the base, the ones that were pinned down were still stationary, and the ones who were attempting to flank the gate were moving into position.

"Thanks, John," Rosewood told him gratefully. "The shifting of troops from the docks to the control room is underway now. If we can keep those greenies contained in the tunnel for a few more minutes, we might be able to keep them in there indefinitely."

"Yes," Sega said sourly, thinking of the hundreds of casualties he had just suffered under such circumstances. "It's not that hard to do."

He had no sooner signed off from this transmission than two flight crews for the C-12s came rushing out of their ready shack to begin firing up their spacecraft. Ground crewmen followed them out and immediately started the process of hooking starter carts up so that the preflight checks could begin. Sega watched in satisfaction as they went about their work. The sooner his marines got up to Triad, the better chance they would have of safeguarding the pre-positioned equipment. And if they were able to do that, he thought, maybe it would become necessary to bring a few tanks and APCs down for his marines to use in retaking the planet. After all, the MPG were using such things in their defense of Eden. It would probably be prudent to fight fire with fire, as it were.

Optimism flooding through him, Sega's state of mind shifted almost without his realizing it. Instead of worrying *if* he was going to be able to safeguard his equipment, he began speculating just what to do with it *when* it was secured. Surely, he wouldn't need an entire division worth of tanks and APCs, would he? Probably a brigade's worth would be sufficient. That way he could divide them up into four company-sized units and send one to each of the MPG occupied cities. And as for artillery, well, he wouldn't need any of that at all. This would strictly be an indoor conflict, wouldn't it?

As the 640 armed troops slated to head to Mars came marching out of the locker room, their weapons ready, their ammunition and supply backs upon their backs, Sega called up some planning software on his computer and began to formulate just how he was going to retake Eden and the other three cities. As the marines marched up the ramp and crowded into the two surface to orbit craft for the ninety minute trip to Triad, he had the bare beginnings of his plan already formulated.

"General Sega," came Summer's voice over the terminal a few minutes later. "We're loaded up and ready to launch."

Sega glanced at him, giving a little smile. "Very good," he said. "I'm looking at Rosewood's tactical display. The greenies are still moving through the base towards the docks and the housing areas but the main force of them are still pinned in the tunnel. I've ordered all defenders to cover the base control building. There's a good chance the main force of greenies will have broken out of the tunnel by the time you get there, but Rosewood's MPs should hopefully be able to hold them from actually taking control of the place. In any case, it is absolutely vital that you secure that building as quickly as possible. The entire base, not to mention all of the ships at anchor, are controlled from there."

"Understood, General," Summer said. "Can you keep updated schematics of the situation at TNB flowing to me and my men? That would be very useful in letting us know exactly where to land and in what direction to move once we clear the C-12s."

"I'll see to it," he promised. "Now have your pilots get moving. Time's wasting."

"Yes sir," Summer told him, offering a salute before signing off.

While the main assault brigade preparing to march out across the wastelands was still assembling, the first of the giant C-12 lifters released its brakes and powered up its maneuvering thrusters, filling the flight deck with the roar of a hydrogen rocket motor. The brakes were released and the 350-passenger craft began to creep across the floor towards the airlock complex on the far side of the room. The first set of steel doors was standing invitingly open. The C-12 made its way inside and the doors slowly slid shut behind it, sealing it from the rest of the room. The airlock then began its cycle, expelling the majority of the air out into the atmosphere.

*****

Two kilometers away, a ten-man squad of Major Chin's infantry soldiers were huddled inside of a forward defensive trench. The trench was fifty meters long, a meter and a half deep, and had the entire top lined with heavy sandbags filled with dense industrial shavings. The trench had been built more than ten years before as part of the basic line of defense against EastHem invasion. It was but one of more than a thousand such positions in the Eden vicinity alone. The squad had been in their position since being deployed the night before, their mission to help pin the marines inside of their base. They had been staring at the same view all night long and through much of the morning. All were tired but remained alert, especially since the word of what was happening at the main gate of the base inside the city had reached them.

It was one of the privates of this squad, a twenty-one year old junior member of the MPG, that first spotted something different in their area of responsibility. One of the massive airlock doors that led from the interior of the base to the paved flight tarmac was slowly sliding open along its track. "Movement at the airlocks," he reported, gripping his M-24 tighter against him. "Number three lock is opening."

Around him, the other soldiers of his squad stiffened up, peering through the gaps in the sandbags they were nearest to, readying their own weapons. The SAW gunner racked a round into his chamber and gripped the handles of his weapon. The squad sergeant, a twenty-six year old delivery truck driver for an AgriCorp subsidiary company, took a quick look himself just to confirm that what his private had reported was true, and then pointed his own weapon outward.

"Okay, guys," he said, his voice betraying no nervousness. "Looks like the Earthlings are making their move. Get ready to light them up when I give the word. I'll get on the link to command."

As the airlock slowly ground along its track, the sergeant talked to his lieutenant, who was in a trench six hundred meters to the southwest. The lieutenant then talked to his captain, who was in an APC a half a kilometer further west of that. The captain then told the rest of his command and then switched to the artillery channel, telling the three batteries of mobile guns that they had available for their operation to stand by for a mission.

"You know the drill, guys," the captain announced to everyone over the tactical net. "As soon as they start to emerge from the airlock, start putting some fire on them. If they continue to advance, we'll plaster them with arty. If that doesn't drive them back inside, the tanks and the APCs will move up and tear into them."

The Eden MPG forces, for security reasons, had no idea what was going on up on Triad. Therefore, they had no reason to think that the airlock was going to be used as it was intended: to launch a spacecraft. Everyone was braced for the rush of marines to come pouring out of the large doorway, probably in at least battalion strength, possibly in regimental strength.

It was the squad sergeant that was first to identify the true nature of their enemy. Instead of the forms of hundreds of biosuited marines, he saw the sleek shape of a modern C-12 surface to orbit lifter when the door finally opened enough to allow a visual. "That's a fuckin C-12," he yelled in bewilderment. "Hold your fire." He keyed up the command net. "There are no troops in that airlock," he reported. "It's a C-12 lifter. I repeat, a Charlie-one-two surface to orbit lifter is the only thing in that airlock!"

His report was quickly passed up the chain of command and the order to hold fire was quickly passed back down. This took less than thirty seconds to accomplish, during which time the C-12 utilized its rear maneuvering thrusters and began to edge out of the lock towards the launching area a kilometer away.

Major Chin, who was in the base command post, instinctively wanted his tank crews to move in and blow the living crap out of. But then he had second thoughts. The C-12 was undoubtedly full of hydrogen and liquid oxygen, enough to blast it free of the Martian atmosphere and elevate it up to geosynchronous orbit. If the tank rounds or the lasers were to ignite this mixture in just the right way, the resulting explosion would wipe out a good portion of the airlock complex that the craft had emerged from. MPG doctrine was not to cause needless casualties to the enemy, especially not when the base that they occupied might be useful to your own forces after you took it. He quickly contacted General Jackson for instructions.

"A C-12?" Jackson said, frowning a little. He did not, however, seem particularly surprised by this. "Just one?"

"Yes sir," Chin said, looking at his tactical display. "I have no idea what they're hoping to accomplish by launching spacecraft."

"There's a special forces operation taking place on Triad," Jackson said, figuring it was safe enough to let that particular cat out of the bag since it was well underway now. "They're probably trying to get some marines up to reinforce the navy forces up there. We can't allow them to dock."

Major Chin smiled at the information he had just been given. Special forces up on Triad? Naval forces engaged? That could only mean that the MPG was trying to take the naval base and the ships at anchor there. He silently wished them luck and then returned to business. "My tank crews have a bead on it," he told Jackson. "Should we try to take it out without hitting the fuel tanks? We could probably put a few rounds low and take out the gear."

"No," Jackson said, shaking his head. "Too risky. Let it proceed unmolested to the launch pad and lift off. We'll take care of it once it's in the air."

"Yes General," he said.

*****

The C-12 rolled slowly across the tarmac of the exterior base, its occupants completely unaware that hundreds of Martian eyes were peering at it, that dozens of anti-tank lasers were pointed at it, that a battery of artillery guns were tracking it. It was painted in Martian camouflage colors, patterns of red, like all Mars assigned ships, and it was filled to overfull with 340 angry marines packing M-24s, grenade launchers, and SAWs. The marines had been hurriedly briefed on what the situation in Triad was. The greenies were trying to take the base. The greenies! They were outraged by the very thought of this and they were eager to land on the base and kick some green ass. They could also show the navy pukes a thing or two about defense while they were at it.

Five minutes after leaving the airlock, the spacecraft rolled to the launching platform and stopped. The platform latched onto the ship and lifted it to the textbook seventy-degree launch angle. Inside the passenger compartment, the marines sat in continued comfort thanks to the inertial damping system. They felt the thrum as the engines slowly cycled up and then dropped back. They waited, gripping their weapons. In ninety minutes, they would be docked and deploying. The greenies were going to get a little more than they bargained for.

*****

The Eden area regional command building for the MPG was located six kilometers west of the main base in the unsavory neighborhood of Helvetia Heights. Even in times of absolute peace, it was necessary to guard the building with a full platoon of armed MPG soldiers and to escort the workers to and from the tram stations lest they be molested by the gangs that ruled the streets here. On this day however, while the building was rapidly filling with recently called up MPG workers, a full company of infantry had been sent over from the main base and were now deployed around and inside of the building and all the way to the nearest tram station six blocks away. The street thugs were smart enough to keep well clear of the area. The MPG soldiers did not seem to be in a playful mood.

Inside the building, the excitement was electric as word was passed about recent events at the capital and the marine barracks. Rumors flew in all directions. On the sixth floor was an office labeled "REGIONAL AIR DEFENSE". Inside this office were fifteen technicians, many of them women, who were monitoring the airspace in a ten thousand square kilometer range around Eden. Orders had already been sent out to the civilian spaceport to halt all flights to or from Eden until further notice. For the first time since the Jupiter War, there was not a single craft in the air or in transit to or from the surface.

The air defense commander, Robert Vendall, had not been briefed in about the events that were now taking place on the planet but he, like most of the people in the building, had long since glimmered that a revolution was now under way. As such, when he received a very powerful order from General Jackson himself, he did not question it and was proud to be the man to carry it out. He, in fact, had every intention of forcing any man or woman from the room if they hesitated for an instant in following his commands.

"Section four and six," he said into his terminal, speaking to the controllers that manned, or in this case, womanned, the tracking terminals for that particular section of the city. "A C-12 will be launching from EMB in less than five minutes. Charge your lasers and lock onto it as it ascends."

"Yes, sir," came the duel reply. The women spoke commands into their screens.

On the northern fringes of Eden, just outside the city perimeter, two fixed anti-aircraft laser sites came to life. Their covers slid open and the stubby barrels of their

150mm cannons pointed upward. The lasers charged up, an operation that took about fifteen seconds, receiving the power from a cable that ran from Eden's main grid. If this supply were to fail, something that could happen in time of war, each laser had a self-contained hydrogen powered generator beneath it. The barrels swung back and forth restlessly as their human controllers, peering through infrared magnifiers that were attached to the top of the laser and downlinked to their screen, searched for a target.

*****

The pilot of the C-12 received his launch order. He ran the engines up to one hundred percent thrust and the entire craft began to shake as hydrogen was burned and expelled with great force out the back of the craft. It shot quickly up the launch platform and streaked into the red sky. Inside, the marines watched the ground drop rapidly away below them as they flew out over the greenhouse complexes and the frozen wastelands of Mars.

"We're coming to get you, you fuckin greenies," a young corporal yelled out triumphantly.

His call was met by enthusiastic cheers from his comrades.

*****

"I have the C-12," the first controller said calmly. And so, she did. The infrared plume from the spacecraft's engines was glowing brighter than the sun.

"Me too," said her counterpart on the other gun.

"Lock onto them," Vendall ordered.

"I have a lock."

"I have a lock."

The anti-aircraft lasers revolved on their axis, following their targets remorselessly, awaiting their own orders.

"Altitude and range?" Asked Vendall.

"Passing through twelve thousand meters," came the answer. "Sixty kilometers downrange."

"Are they past the edge of the agricultural complexes?"

"Just about."

Vendall nodded, his face expressionless. "Fire."

The two controllers looked at each other for a moment and then at their commander, perhaps wondering if they'd misunderstood him.

"I said fire," he repeated. "Do it now!"

Another brief look passed between the two women but they followed their orders. Two fingers reached down to two buttons and pushed them.

*****

The effect on the C-12 was instantaneous. The quarter second laser pulses burned through the steel of its engine compartment. The delicate thruster engines exploded, sending a rain of steel fragments out in all directions. The spacecraft shuddered violently and began to spin, continuing upward through sheer inertia, but rapidly feeling the effects of the Martian gravity pulling it back down. Inside the passenger compartment, the inertial damper died at once and the marines, none of whom were wearing their safety harnesses, were thrown against each other violently and tossed about the cabin. Unfortunately for them, the cabin had not depressurized from the strike, an act that would have left them mercifully unconscious. The pilot, who *was* wearing his safety harness, tried desperately to power up the maneuvering thrusters, which were used for landings on the surface, but his display was dead and dark, the APU attached to the engines destroyed. He knew it was hopeless, but he kept trying anyway. Out his windscreen the ground, far below him, was spinning madly around.

The C-12 finally reached the limit of its forward momentum and started downward in a ballistic arc, spinning lazily all the way like a pencil that has been tossed by the hand of a child. It took nearly five minutes before the craft met the stony Martian soil eighty kilometers from Eden and smashed itself and everyone in it to oblivion.

*****

Lon and his company were now nearly in position. They had been moving section by section through the perimeter corridor of the base, blasting open the doors with primacord as they came to them. These doors were situated every one hundred meters and were monitored by security cameras up on the walls, cameras that fed directly to the main control building. His men shot out the cameras as they went, knowing that it was a case of closing the barn door after the horse had gotten out, but doing it as a matter of course anyway. At each door they blew, they braced for MPs on the other side. At each one they found nothing except the occasional unarmed military person whom they advised to march back to the main loading area to be taken prisoner.

"People wandering around by themselves might get hurt," Lon advised each of these people. "Announce yourself well before you get to the last door and keep your hands up. I'll let them know you're coming."

All of them did just exactly as they were told, surrendering themselves to the Martians. Lon announced each one's presence to the sergeant in charge of securing the docks and told him to expect them.

At the eighth door they passed, two before their new objective, some MPs were trying to pass through the security point. They made the lethal mistake of firing at the new hole in the door and were cut down in less than two seconds, their bleeding, dead bodies crashing to the steel deck in a heap.

"Idiots," Lon commented, before moving his men forward.

The ninth door revealed a deserted corridor. They moved to the tenth and Lon halted his squad in place. On the other side of that door was the main entrance to TNB, the place where the MPs were pinning down Charlie and Delta in the tunnel. He contacted Captain Evers on the command link.

"Fargo to Evers," he said. "We are in position, awaiting orders."

"Stand by for movement orders," Evers told him. Lon could hear the sound of small weapons fire in the background. "The other reinforcement squad is still moving in. They made contact with a squad of MPs in one of the corridors and this slowed them down a bit."

"Copy that," Lon said.

"I'm sending you a schematic of the known enemy position and strength out there. We're gonna move ASAP because the longer we wait, the more of them show up."

His combat computer beeped with an incoming download. Lon called up the schematic and it superimposed itself over the map of his objective. He could see the layout of the base main entrance area floating before him but now there were symbols representing enemy concentrations. Red marks indicated known positions, yellow marks indicated suspected positions. There were more yellow than red. He ordered his computer to download the information to the rest of his squad. They waited.

*****

General Sega was following the advance of the greenie flanking position on his screen, noting with alarm that they were now both in position. He expected them to move in and hit the defenders with a brutal cross fire any time now. It would be touch and go for the MPs guarding the base entrance and the command post. Only about a quarter of the troops he'd shifted from the dock area were in place and he foresaw heavy casualties on their part when the greenies finally initiated contact. He hoped they could hold for another ninety minutes.

Now that the first ship was in the air and the second was clearing the airlock, he looked out over the assembly area. Almost all of the troops assigned to take the MPG base were now geared up and ready to roll. He expected them to start heading out through the personnel airlocks shortly.

Sega, aside from being a career military man, was also the holder of a master's degree in military history. A part of him analyzed the moves that the Martians had made so far and couldn't help but be impressed. Imagine the MPG pulling off something like the assault on Triad. Imagine them even conceiving of it. Like most Earthlings, he held a low opinion of Martians and their intelligence. After all, where had the majority of Martians originated? They'd come from the ranks of the hopelessly unemployed, the welfare recipients of the Post World War III era. Vermin were their forefathers, hopping on a ship and traversing across the solar system to a godforsaken dirtball in space just to hold a job. It never occurred to him to remember that this was the same manner in which the states of California, Texas, and Alaska had been founded; how the countries of Australia and South Africa had begun. Though a student of history, he'd failed to learn an important lesson from it. He was missing something big, but could not put his finger on it.

The sensation nagged at him as he watched the three columns of red symbols march rapidly forward on his TNB display, pausing for approximately two minutes at each door in the station, the length of time it took for their primacord teams to cut through it. They had assaulted TNB brilliantly in what was obviously a pre-planned and pre-staged invasion. Their intentions were clear: to seize the base and gain control over the ships and personnel on it, denying WestHem of a good portion of their navy. It smacked of a carefully thought out and planned operation. Someone had even entered a counter-plan in the event that one of the attacking companies became trapped in the tunnels. Had whoever planned this not considered the fact that there were twelve thousand armed marines only ninety minutes away in Eden? Surely anyone who planned this operation would have taken that factor into consideration, wouldn't they?

Was there some sort of nasty surprise awaiting his men up in the orbiting city? What sort of plan could be in place to prevent reinforcement? The front of his brain assured him that the Martians had counted on seizing the base so quickly that reinforcements would not have time to arrive. This answer did not feel right however. The Martians were gambling heavily on this operation, which could only be the opening move in a full-blown revolt, a war of independence. They had planned smartly and well so far. They *had* to have some sort of contingency plan to keep reinforcements from taking back the station from them. What was it?

The answer was so obvious and was staring him in the face so closely that he did not see it until the base control tower urgently called him.

"General Sega!" shouted the excited Lieutenant in charge of the tower crew. Even looking at the two-dimensional image on the Internet screen, Sega knew by the man's face that major trouble had just showed its head.

"Yes, Lieutenant?" he asked tonelessly, bracing himself.

"The C-12 has disappeared off of the screen! It's gone, sir! It's fuckin' gone!"

"Lieutenant," Sega replied, feeling dread worming its way into his stomach, "I need you to calm down immediately and give me a short, concise report on whatever the hell you're talking about. Start with what C-12 we're discussing here and work your way forward in chronological order from there. Do you understand me?"

"Yes, sir, I'm sorry, sir!" he barked, seeming to take a deep breath. "The first C-12 full of the marines headed for TNB launched normally six minutes ago. It went up on a normal path until it reached thirteen thousand, six hundred and seventy meters. It was sixty-eight kilometers downrange. The flight path was right on the money, sir and then..." He shook his head. "And then it just disappeared from our screen. The IFF display went dark and it was gone. No distress calls, no nothing. We've been trying to contact it ever since with no result."

"I see," Sega answered, lowering his head a little, knowing now the obvious, stupid mistake he'd just made that had killed 350 men. "I suppose you've contacted Eden tower for assistance?"

"Yes sir," he said, nodding rapidly. "It's SOP. We did it within a minute of losing contact. They said they'd tracked it on infrared for the same amount of time we did and then it just disappeared at the same time we have. They even yelled at us for not filing a flight plan or letting them know we were launching."

That had been on Sega's orders. He hadn't trusted the Martian civilian controllers. He'd been right not to. "I understand, Lieutenant. Have you halted the launch of the second C-12?"

"Of course, sir." he said, and then paled. "Is that okay? I mean we don't know what happened and we have to launch some Hovers to go look for..."

"That's perfect, Lieutenant. Initiate your SAR procedures and continue to hold the remaining C-12 until we find out what's going on."

"Yes sir."

Sega figured he already knew what was going on. The missing piece of the puzzle had just fallen neatly into place. His suspicion was confirmed a minute later.

"I have General Jackson from the Martian Planetary Guard on the line," his computer announced. "It is a highest priority communication attempt. Do you wish to speak to him or would you like me to refer him to the mail server?"

General Jackson, Sega thought sourly. A man he'd held in contempt since his appointment to the leadership of the MPG when it had been formed. A man he'd considered to be no more than a figurehead who knew a few military terms, a has-been soldier in charge of a large group of men and women that were thought to be no more than a speed bump in their role as defenders of Mars. Had he planned all of this? It seemed unlikely. Could he see reason? "Put him on screen."

It took only a second before the dark black face was staring at him. "General Sega," Jackson greeted politely. "Nice to talk to you."

Sega decided to take a stern approach. "Jackson," he demanded, "are your forces responsible for the loss of one of my C-12s a few minutes ago?"

Jackson seemed to smile. "Yes, they are, General. Your reinforcements for Triad Naval Base were shot down by the anti-aircraft lasers that defend the City of Eden. Any further attempts to launch spacecraft or aircraft of any type from that base will be dealt with the same way. I suggest you stand down your troops."

"I have rank over you, General," Sega said. "Your little band of wanna-be soldiers are subservient to federal forces under the constitution. I *order* you to cease all hostilities immediately on Triad and everywhere else. If you refuse my order you will stand trial for..."

"General," Jackson interrupted, shaking his head in amusement, "surely you have figured out what is going on here. Mars is in a state of revolt against WestHem. You are not in command of me, you are an enemy soldier and I'm advising you to halt all flights from your base. If you launch a single vehicle from there, it will be shot down. And before you ask, yes I am well aware of the consequences of my actions."

"Jackson, listen to me," Sega said reasonably, "I need to launch hovers for search and rescue of the downed C-12."

"Not a single vehicle, General," Jackson repeated. "The C-12 was shot down from an altitude of nearly seventeen thousand meters. Eden air defense personnel tracked it all the way in. It came down without power and struck hard. Survivors are out of the question. And as for that cute idea you have about sending your marines out through the airlocks to take my base from the wastelands, forget it. I have a battalion of armored infantry deployed right outside of your base, covering all potential exits. They have heavy artillery support and, in about fifteen more minutes, they'll have air support as well from our Mosquitoes."

"My men outnumber yours," Sega said. "They *will* be coming to take your base."

"Then they will be slaughtered needlessly," Jackson told him. "You have no tanks, no anti-tank weapons, no significant air support. All you have are a bunch of jarheads with guns who will be forced to attack in open ground along predictable avenues of advance. Keep your people inside. Stand down your troops and await further developments. There's nothing you can do to help. We planned things this way, you see."

"Jackson," Sega prophesized. "You'll be executed for this."

Jackson simply shrugged. "Whatever will be will be," he told him. "But that's not your concern. I've given my advice and I suggest you take it. In the meantime, I've got a war to fight." He gave him an ominous grin. "I'll be talking to you soon, General."

With that, he signed off, the image on the screen being replaced by his schematic of Triad once more. Without surprise, he saw that the Martians had broken out of the main tunnel there.

*****

The MPs guarding the main gate had the advantage of knowing exactly where their enemy was, in what numbers they were in, and what their plan most likely was. They knew that two squads and at least one battalion would push towards them from three directions, undoubtedly all at once. For many groups of trained soldiers, this might have been enough despite the numerical and weapon superiority of the enemy. But the MPs were not trained as soldiers, they were trained primarily as a security force for the base, and while General Sega had issued orders on *where* they were to deploy in general, it was up to the on-scene officers to decide where at that spot to put the men. They thought that they had decided well by positioning the troops in groups behind planters, MP carts, and other obstacles facing all of the known egress points of the enemy. This seemed like it would keep the men safe from deadly crossfires. On the surface, the defensive plan looked good. Underneath, it was a deadly mistake.

On a given signal, the two steel doors adjacent to the main gate were breached by primacord charges and came crashing to the steel floor. The MPs opened fire into the holes trying to drive the invaders back in, trying to pin them down as they'd pinned down the main battalion. The MPG troops inside held their rifle fire, returning fire only with short bursts from their SAWs while the men armed with grenade launchers on their M-20s crept forward as far as was safe on their bellies. They marked the position of the flashes and aimed targeting lasers towards the obstacles.

Horishito, one of the grenadiers under Lon's command, was among the first to fire. Bullets pinged all around him and tracers from the friendly SAW behind him streaked less than two feet over his head as he concentrated on the MP cart in the main foyer area where the flashes were emanating from. His body was flooded with adrenaline and he was seriously wondering if he would live through the next two minutes, but he went forward nonetheless. He pointed the targeting laser on his M-24 at the cart and sent it out. The reading flashed before his eyes, seeming to float in the air courtesy of his combat goggles. 93 meters.

He flipped the selector switch on his weapon to the grenade setting. A red targeting reticle appeared in his goggles. He centered it in the air about a meter above the cart.

"Ninety-three meter air burst," he said into his throat microphone, which was set to computer command mode. When his instruction was logged, he spoke a single word and switched it back to communications mode.

"Hoary, taking a shot," he told Lon.

"Weapons are free," Lon replied. "Get the fuckers."

He pushed the fire button on his weapon and it kicked harshly against his right shoulder as the 50mm high explosive fragmentation grenade was shot out of the stubby barrel below the M-24s main barrel. The grenade exploded precisely over the top of the cart and the weapons firing behind it went instantly silent. He inched forward some more, focusing on a planter where another group of flashes was emanating from. He pushed the target laser and began setting up the next shot.

From all three locations where MPG troops were facing the MPs from tunnels or corridor entrances, grenades came flying out, exploding with deadly precision over the top of groups of defenders. The steel shrapnel sliced easily through the armor and helmets of the MPs, killing many outright, horribly wounding others. The sounds of the explosions echoed loudly off of the steel walls, reverberating back and forth with jarring concussions. In between explosions, the air was filled with the chattering of machine guns and the screams of wounded men.

When the firing positions in front of them were knocked out or forced into silence, the MPG troops were at last able to rush out of their hiding holes. The reinforcement squads came first, all at once. They ran into the main foyer area and spread out, diving to the ground and searching for targets. The remaining MPs reacted quickly, shooting at the choke points and hitting a few of the Martians as they exited.

Lon, positioned in the middle of his squad, his own weapon gripped tightly in his hands, saw rounds from the MPs' weapons go flashing within inches of his head, some of them close enough that he could feel the wind of their passage. On his right, Jim Gantry, one of his senior men, suddenly gasped as two high velocity bullets slammed into the top of his head, drilling through his helmet and sending a spray of blood into the air. He slumped forward lifelessly, his weapon dropping from his hands, a puddle of blood forming beneath him. A part of Lon wanted to cry out at the loss of one of his men, one of his *friends*, but his training kept him from reacting. Instead, he simply continued to crawl forward, placing his targeting reticle on the head of an MP and squeezing off a burst. Around him, the rest of his men were doing the same, including his newest member, Matza, who was spraying the MP positions with pinpoint bursts from his SAW, providing covering fire for the advance.

At the entrance of the pedestrian station, the two companies that had been pinned in place for nearly forty minutes now finally were able to attempt a break out. With the defenders of the entrance occupied by the flanking squads, they began to pour out of the tunnel using the same entrance maneuvers that the rest of the teams had. One by one, from each side of the entrance, they hurled themselves outward, diving to the ground and then rolling clear for the next man, firing as they went. They drew some fire from the MPs, of course, some of it quite heavy, and several of their numbers were struck by bullets, but, within thirty seconds, enough of them were out to lay down a vicious blanket of gunfire on the MPs.

Hit from three directions at once, and unable to find anywhere on the entrance platform where they could be safe, even for a second, from bullets smashing into them, the MPs gave up the field very quickly. Those who had not been killed or wounded retreated in disarray towards the main corridor of the base, desperate to get to a place of relative safety. Many were shot down since Evers had given the order to keep the pressure on them. Targeting reticles were placed on their backs and rounds reached out, cutting them to the ground. But the MPG could not get them all. More than twenty made it through the wide door at the far end of the platform before the steel door was shut and locked. Battered and terrified, they were ordered to the control building to help with the last line of defense.

The foyer area, for the first time since the doors had been blown, was now silent of gunshots and explosions. Men were screaming in pain and despair and the air smelled thickly of gunpowder and burned explosives. Expended shell casings were everywhere, marking every point that someone had fired from. The MPG soldiers, weapons trained before them, fanned out through the platform to secure it. For the first time they saw the results of the battle they'd been engaged in. They saw it in graphic detail as they came across dead MPs with their heads torn open and brain matter leaking out, armor ripped apart by steel fragments with intestines, kidneys, livers protruding through the holes. They saw heads blasted apart by high velocity bullets and higher velocity, larger caliber SAW bullets. They saw wounded MPs screaming in pain and fear and they kicked their forgotten weapons away from them. They saw their own comrades dead on the steel deck or wounded by the same weapons they carried. They looked at each other with haunted eyes, the gravity of what they were a part of coming home to them in a big way. Thoughts of shouting "Free Mars" at the MSG base a few hours ago entered some minds. They were hard pressed to believe the ease with which they'd shouted that incantation.

Medics went to work on the wounded, treating the MPG first before they even headed for the worst of the MPs. Captain Evers, himself somewhat shaken by the mayhem that had taken place, did his best to put it aside and immediately issued orders for the attack to continue towards the base control room. Within three minutes of securing the platform, primacord was being placed on the door that the surviving MPs had escaped through.

*****

Admiral Rosewood had watched the entire battle on the security cameras. He was numb with disbelief and fear. He could not believe how quickly his MPs had been overwhelmed and soundly slaughtered by the MPG troops once the break out had occurred. The entire thing had taken less than eight minutes. Only twenty of the ninety-three MPs that had been deployed at the main gate had made it through the corridor at the end of the battle. They were now rushing to join the defense of the control building. He had forty-five MPs already in position there. 115 more, including the elite TIRT team, were moving in from other parts of the base, but their deployment was pitifully slow, hampered by the very security procedures that had been initiated by the Martian attack.

He checked his computer, looking at the time display. The marine reinforcements would arrive in less than an hour now. Would they make it to the control room in time to prevent the MPG from gaining entry?

As if in answer, his Internet screen came to life, showing the face of General Sega. Sega did not look happy at all, in fact, he looked downright miserable. This did little to allay Rosewood's own fear.

"General," Rosewood enquired, "did you see the results of the main gate battle on your display? Those MPG troops killed..."

"I saw it, Admiral," Sega said with a nod, his voice strained. "I'd hoped your MPs would have held longer, but I suppose it doesn't matter now."

"Doesn't matter?" Rosewood exclaimed. "Are you mad? We have to hold until your reinforcements..."

"There will be no reinforcements," Sega said simply.

Rosewood stared in disbelief. "No reinforcements?" he demanded. "What the hell are you talking about, man? Didn't you tell me that they launched and were on the way? Where the hell are they?"

"They were shot down by MPG air defense batteries," Sega told him. "340 of my marines went crashing to the ground from seventeen thousand meters in the sky. That's 340 emails to 340 families that I have to write. General Jackson contacted me right after that and informed me that any other ships launched from my base will also be shot down."

"They can't do that!" Rosewood yelled, outraged.

Sega blinked. His patience was obviously at a minimum. "John, I'm not sure exactly what you mean by that statement. If you mean that it is morally and legally wrong to shoot down WestHem armed forces ships and kill WestHem marines, I agree with you, but as for the Martians abiding by that code, I'm afraid that they've already proved that they don't. If you are referring to the physical possibilities of the greenies doing this, well, I'm afraid they've got the upper hand there too. My barracks is located directly adjacent to Eden and the city is virtually ringed with anti-aircraft lasers of varying caliber. There is no way for me to launch a vehicle of any size without their noticing it and engaging it. In addition, they have my pedestrian access tunnels blocked in by armed troops and armored vehicles, making it impossible to exit into the city to retake it. I intended to move my men overland through the airlocks to seize the base from that direction, but Jackson has assured me that that avenue of escape is covered with infantry, tanks, and artillery. While I have not actually checked out this statement, I find myself inclined to believe Mr. Jackson in this instance. In short, my men are stuck here on this base, as useless to what is going on as a cock on a cow."

Rosewood sat silently for a moment, letting the information he'd just been given sink in. Faintly, even through the steel walls of his building, he could hear gunfire erupting from the street level below as the battle for the control building began.

"What do I do now?" he finally asked. "I have the MPG right outside my building now."

Sega stared levelly at him. "Surrender your forces," he told his naval counterpart.

At first Rosewood was not sure he'd heard him correctly. "Did you say surrender?"

"I did," he repeated. "You have a grand total of about two hundred poorly armed and poorly trained MPs, many of whom are not even in position yet. Pitting this against a battalion of trained infantry soldiers with machine guns and grenade launchers is like sending a boy scout troop to defend South Korea during I-day. Without hope of reinforcements, all you can accomplish is the needless deaths of your MPs. Surrender your men right now, before any more of them are killed."

"And just turn the base over to the.... the greenies? I will *not*!"

"You will!" Sega commanded. "I am the highest ranking WestHem military officer on the Planet Mars. As of now, I'm assuming command of all WestHem forces stationed here and that includes your naval base. I'm giving you a direct order to surrender the base peacefully to the MPG."

"Sega, do you know what you're saying?" Rosewood was outraged and terrified. "A third of the WestHem navy is in dock here right now. You would turn that over to the greenies? You'll be imprisoned for ordering such a thing!"

"We can't win this battle, John," he said, seemingly near tears. "All we can do is get a shitload of our forces killed and give the greenies valuable combat experience in the bargain."

"But what about..."

"John, sit there and think for a minute. What are the greenies going to *do* with all of those ships? They don't have the personnel or the know-how to man them. Are they going to use them against us? Please. And did you think that WestHem is simply going to relinquish the planet to them because their guard force managed to overwhelm the pitiful number of troops that are stationed here." He shook his head firmly. "Mars has enough armor and trained men to hold back a few divisions of EastHem troops for a week or so. Our intelligence estimates have always been that it was doubtful that they could even do that. Do you really think they can stand up against the full fury of the WestHem armed forces when they come to re-occupy this planet? WestHem will send five times the number of men the MPG has and will equip them with five times the armor. Sure, we'll be taken prisoner for about five months or so, the amount of time it will take for WestHem to send over a task force, but believe me Rosewood, there will be a reckoning for this and the greenies are gonna pay a stiff price for fucking with us this way. That cunt Whiting and that nigger motherfucker Jackson are going to have their heads on spikes on top of the capital building in New Pittsburgh. The MPG will be disbanded and its officers will be imprisoned for life, some of them even executed. As the old saying goes, they may have won this battle, but they don't stand a fart's chance in a windstorm in the war."

There was silence as Rosewood considered these points. He found that Sega's words made sense, as much as he was loath to surrender his beloved base to those green traitors. He had to admit that there seemed no other option. Already he was envisioning his testimony before the justice subcommittee that would inevitably follow this heinous act.

"Okay," he said to Sega. "I'll reluctantly surrender."

Sega nodded. "Good. Do it immediately so that not a single soldier is unnecessarily killed or wounded. Send a report off to Earth before the greenies take control of the base and, for God's sake, be sure to disarm and scramble all of the nuclear weapons on your ships." He smiled. "Perhaps we'll see each other in whatever POW camp they send us to."

"Perhaps we will." Rosewood nodded miserably.

*****

General Sega got General Jackson on the computer and told him his intention to surrender the forces on the planet and above it, effective immediately.

"Very wise decision, General," Jackson said amicably. "I must say that I'm relieved. Our intention is to make this transfer of power as bloodless as possible."

"The marines are going to come take this planet back from you," Sega told him. "If you truly want it to be bloodless, then you'll surrender to me immediately before they deploy."

"Why don't you let me worry about the marines?" Jackson said. "In the meantime, we have some shooting to stop, don't we? Things are quiet at the base right now. I'll instruct my troops guarding it to take defensive measures only for the time being. You need to instruct your troops to disable their weapons and put them back in storage. Nobody is to leave. When things stabilize around here, we'll be entering the barracks to take control of it."

"I want my men to be treated as POWs," Sega said. "With all the rights and privileges that come with it. I don't want any of them beaten or killed by your thugs."

"They'll be treated under the Geneva Accords, you have my word on that," Jackson assured him. "In fact, they'll be held right where they're at. EMB will make an excellent POW camp once we get all of the computers and weapons taken out. Now, shall we discuss the situation on Triad? We still have heavy fighting taking place outside the control room. The navy personnel and my men are being needlessly killed as we speak. I'll order my men to hold in place and take defensive measures only. You get Admiral Rosewood to have his men cease fire immediately and disable their weapons."

"It'll be done," Sega said.

He signed off a moment later and then began composing a hasty email video that would be sent to Earth.

*****

No further shots were fired at the Eden Marine Barracks. The MPG troops holding the perimeter continued to build up at each stronghold, just in case Sega's surrender offer was nothing more than a deception, but they kept their weapons down and their lasers uncharged.

Up at Triad Naval Base, things went just a little differently. Thanks to communications difficulties between Rosewood's command center and the MPs that were deployed throughout the base, it took nearly twenty minutes before all of them got the word that the brief war was over. Several skirmishes occurred in the corridors near the housing area and the ship docks resulting in more than fifteen deaths—all of them MPs—and more than thirty wounded—twenty-five of them MPs. At the control room itself, the MPs here were among the last to hear about the cease-fire. Finally, however, after more than twenty of them were shot down, the proper radio frequency was located and the order was given. The word was quickly passed and their guns fell silent one by one. More relieved than anything else, they dropped their weapons and allowed themselves to be taken into custody. They were handcuffed with plastic ties and stripped of their radio gear. The MPG troops then moved to the control room itself.

They did not have to blow open this door with their primacord. Admiral Rosewood opened it for them voluntarily. A platoon from Charlie Company entered the building, their guns ready for action. They didn't need them. Everyone inside was unarmed and sitting peacefully in their chairs, some of them weeping softly in fear or anger, most stoic. Admiral Rosewood was one of the stoic ones.

"You will all be executed for this, you know," he told the troops as they searched everyone, one by one.

"We all have to die sometime, don't we, Admiral," a voice replied. "I'm Captain Evers, the commander of the group that hit this part of the base. You put up a much better defense than we gave you credit for in the planning stages. You should be proud of yourself. You cost me a lot of good men."

Rosewood said nothing. He simply glared at the captain.

Evers was unoffended. He had seen too much in the last hour to be offended by much. He tuned his radio to the command frequency and keyed it up. "Evers here," he said to Colonel Bright, who was still back at the Triad Control Center. "We have the TNB control room secured. We'll start working on gaining control of the security functions."

"Copy," said Bright. "We've restored light and power to the main tunnels. We're offloading all of the passengers on the trains that were trapped at this end and then we'll be sending them back empty to start transferring the wounded. I've got the dip-hoes moving to the platform to help our medics and start transporting them. How many are we talking about from your section?"

"I've got nineteen dead and thirty-three wounded," Evers told him. "We're still getting a count of the MPs but it looks like upwards of seventy dead and almost a hundred wounded."

"Could've been worse I suppose," Bright said with a sigh.

"Yeah," Evers agreed. "We could've lost and had them die for nothing."

*****

Brett Ingram and his group of Martians that were unloading supplies from the *Mermaid* were as surprised as anyone when the security alarms had activated in response to the condition Red Zebra. Still, they had followed the protocol that was established for such an event, which stated that any ship personnel in the immediate vicinity of their vessel at the time of the alarm would return to their vessel and assist in its individual security. They hadn't done much to assist in the security, but those of them that had been in the supply room at the time had come back just seconds before the base computer system automatically closed and locked the docking door, sealing them inside for the duration of the crisis. And so, as the MPG special forces troops were forcing their way through the access tunnels and engaging in battle with the MPs, Brett was sitting on a small chair in the supply room.

Trapped in the ship with he and his offload crew were two security personnel, who's presence was required at all times due to the nuclear warheads on board, and Lieutenant Commander Braxton, the executive officer, who had been overseeing the details of extended docking. They too had been quite confused at first, with the security personnel grumbling about ill-timed drills and Braxton complaining about missing a lunch date with his wife. That confusion came to an end when they scanned through the radio frequencies and happened across the MP force's tactical channel. Upon discovering that Martian troops were invading the base, their grumbling had turned to rage that had quickly been turned upon the six members of the off-load crew. Guns had been pulled and Brett and his people had been ordered into the crew quarters.

"Sit the fuck down there!" Ordered Braxton, pointing at the floor next to the folded-up sleeping racks. "If any one of you green motherfuckers so much as twitches, I'm gonna kill you!"

Braxton kept the two security men with him, putting the three of them between the Martians and the hatch. Their guns remained in their hands while they monitored the developing situation on their com-links. Brett was able to overhear enough information to gather that the MPG had attacked the base in force and were overwhelming the base security teams.

What the hell was the meaning of it? he wondered silently, trying to figure things out. Obviously, the attack was related to the events going on in the capital but what was the purpose of attacking TNB? Whatever it was, he was very fearful as he watched the faces of his captors. They were scared stiff and they were holding guns on them. As reports of company strength incursions moving towards the docks surfaced, they became even more nervous.

Finally came the order for all WestHem forces to surrender.

"Surrender?" Braxton yelled in disbelief. "What the fuck are they talking about? Surrender the base to greenies?"

"What's gonna happen to us now?" one of the security men enquired. "Are the greenies gonna kill us all?"

"What about the ship?" asked the other one. "What about the torpedoes on board?"

Braxton ignored their questions, fixing his eyes on Brett and the others sitting next to him. His gaze was murderous as he raised his pistol and pointed it at them. He began to walk forward.

"Your fuckin' people did this," he said, his finger firmly on the trigger of the gun. "Give me one good reason why I shouldn't kill every fuckin' one of you green bastards!"

To Brett the 3mm hole at the end of the pistol looked as big as the tunnels the MPG had used to infiltrate the base. He swallowed nervously, staring back into the furious madness of Braxton's face.

"Sir," he finally said, fighting to keep his voice calm and reasonable. "We are WestHem naval personnel. We are not MPG members. If you kill us, you'll be committing cold-blooded murder and you'll be court-martialed for it when this is over. Don't do anything rash. We didn't attack the base. We're spacers, just like you are."

"You're fuckin' greenies!" Braxton yelled, stepping closer and training the pistol directly on Brett's forehead. "How dare you say you're just like me! You are lowlife pieces of shit and your people just killed *hundreds* of my people. You fuckin' terrorists!"

"Commander," Brett said, "we may be of Martian descent, but we are WestHem naval personnel. We are not enemy soldiers. We are not terrorists. If you kill us, you will not be a hero, you'll go to prison for the rest of your life. Think this through, sir!"

"Commander," said one of the security men, who looked even more nervous than Brett felt, if that were possible. "He's right. They may be greenies, but they're spacers in our navy. You can't kill them."

"C'mon, commander," The other security man chimed in. "Put the gun down. Think about what you're doing."

Braxton took a deep breath, his hand trembling a little on the barrel of the pistol but not wavering in its aim. "You're the little green prick that's always making me look bad in front of the captain," he said. "I bet you just love what's going on here, don't you? I bet you just love that your terrorist buddies have taken over this base."

"Sir," Brett said, "I'm just as appalled by what's going on as you are." This was not exactly true—he was more confused than appalled—but it seemed that a little white lie was appropriate under the circumstances.

"Yeah, right," Braxton said, but he seemed a little calmer now. Slowly he lowered the gun down, not holstering it, but at least not pointing it at anyone anymore.

Brett let himself exhale a brief sigh of relief, aware that he had come within a bare inch or so of death.

Just then an announcement was paged across the ship's intercom, which had been accessed by the main control computer.

"This is Admiral Rosewood," a voice said. "Greenie troops have attacked this base in large numbers and we have been forced to surrender it to them. All ships in dock will remain sealed for the time being. We will delay allowing the terrorists access to them as long as we can. The highest-ranking officer on each vessel carrying nuclear weapons is ordered to disable those weapons as quickly as possible using the computer scrambling procedure. I repeat, the highest-ranking officer on each vessel carrying nuclear weapons is ordered to disable those weapons as quickly as possible. These weapons must not fall into the hands of the greenies in a state in which they can be detonated. Scramble them immediately! When the greenies do gain access to your ship, you are instructed to surrender peacefully to them and to obey their instructions. Do not attempt to fight or flee them. God help us all in this dark hour."

There was no further from the admiral or anyone else.

Braxton left the six Martians under the watch of the two security personnel and headed up the ladders to the torpedo room. It took him less than ten minutes to permanently destroy the detonation computers on the weapons.

*****

Brian could not believe the day he was having. He had awakened early that morning expecting nothing more than another day on the streets of Eden, answering calls for assistance and taking crime reports. Now, with lunchtime barely passed, he was in a completely different uniform, sitting in the cockpit of a Mosquito, and circling two thousand meters above the MPG deployment area on the edge of the city. His laser cannon was set to wartime charging level and his wing pods were each holding a 1000-kilogram free-fall penetration bomb. Mars was rebelling against WestHem. He still couldn't believe it, was still not quite sure just how he felt about it.

The surrender and cease fire had taken place less than an hour before. Down below, he could see the rows of MPG tanks and APCs that were forming up. The call-up was still underway, but better than seventy percent of the Eden division soldiers had already reported for duty. More than a hundred armored vehicles were now poised and ready for action, their task to march on the marine barracks and gain entry to it. The APCs each contained a squad of heavily armed and bio-suited infantry troops. The tanks would support them at the entrances. Brian and his gunner were but one of more than thirty aircraft that were circling above in tight formations. Their task would be to support the breach from the air, which meant that they would bomb the living shit out of the barracks if any harm came to the troops trying to enter it.

"I feel like a sitting duck up here circling like this," said Colton, his gunner. "Those anti-air emplacements on the edge of the barracks have probably got a lock on us right now. Those are heavy caliber guns. If they hit us, we won't have to worry about ejecting. There won't be anything left to eject."

"There's only four emplacements," Brian said soothingly, although he was a little nervous as well. "They may get four of us but they'll be dead before they can recharge. I don't think even marines are that stupid."

"I think maybe you're giving them too much credit," Colton replied.

They circled in silence for a few more minutes, the engine humming at only a few RPMs above idle, the fuel and oxygen gauges steady. They could stay up nearly five hours at this rate of consumption.

"Where's this all gonna lead, Brian?" Colton said softly, breaking the silence. "Did Whiting just dig herself a hole and pull us in after her?"

Brian made a quick check out the cockpit window, checking the position of the Mosquito on his wing. He then scanned his eyes over his instrument panel, checking the readings. He then returned his eyes forward, looking out at the armor that was assembling below. "She might have," he allowed. "But we all got the speech before we suited up today, didn't we? We all had the opportunity to back out of this thing. If we're going down a hole it's not because she dragged us in. We jumped in after her."

*****

The Martian troops began to move in a few minutes later. From the wasteland side of the marine base, the tanks and APCs rolled across the sand at half speed, their treads kicking up a huge cloud of dust that was slowly blown east by the prevailing winds. The Mosquitoes moved even closer to the base, circling virtually right above it, where they could provide mass bombing and laser fire support if needed. The tanks held back a half a kilometer from the airlocks, their laser cannons charged, their eighty millimeter main guns locked and loaded with high explosive, penetrating shells. The APCs continued on, not coming to a halt until they were less than a hundred meters from the doors of the airlocks. Their ramps swung down and the troops offloaded, quickly forming up into company sized units, their rifles and SAWs ready for action. Slowly they advanced, expecting to be fired upon at any moment.

Their expectations were not met. When they reached the airlocks, the doors slid obediently open, just as had been promised in the surrender agreement. Inside, all of the marines had been removed from the assembly area and the entire section had been decompressed. The troops passed through the airlocks and into this room quickly, fanning out and covering all of the doors. The airlock doors were then shut again and the assembly room was recompressed, a process that took more than twenty minutes. Only then were the doors to the main part of the base finally opened. The troops began to move onto the base to take it under occupation.

At the main entrance on the Macarthur Avenue side, other troops moved down the corridors to enter from here. At the tunnel where the fighting had taken place, they stepped over the corpses of the marines that had fallen in the three breakout attempts.

In all, more than nine hundred MPG infantry soldiers entered the base and took up occupation duties. They found the marines inside to be verbally abusive but otherwise unarmed and docile. They were instructed to return to their dormitories for the time being and they went without question. No shots were fired and the long process of clearing the base of weapons and communication gear began to take place.

At Triad Naval Base, a similar process was underway. Here, the task was complicated by the limited number of soldiers available and the high number of civilian personnel that worked on the base. It was quickly realized that more soldiers were needed and an order went out to both New Pittsburgh and Libby to send a battalion apiece up. The decision was made to hold all personnel exactly where they were until their arrival.

Meanwhile, the deployment of the MPG continued and, by 4:00 that afternoon, 98% of the active members had reported to their duty stations across the planet. Each unit that deployed was told of the circumstances of the call-up and offered the chance to forgo participation in what was going on. A few took the offer, removing their uniforms and going home, but the vast majority stayed and agreed to follow whatever orders they were given.

Movement orders were issued to nearly every combat unit that formed up. In every Martian city, armed and armored soldiers took control of control centers and federal offices. Corban Hayes and the remaining agents were in the New Pittsburgh office when a company of troops rolled up outside in APCs and surrounded the building. Though the agents were armed with automatic weapons, they gave up without a fight when an MPG captain in the city control center shut off their power and utilities. Hayes was reportedly in tears as he was handcuffed and led towards the city jail to stew with the rest of his men.

*****

Laura Whiting was still sitting in her office, high above the streets of New Pittsburgh, her attention divided between two Internet terminals, one of which was showing a MarsGroup station, the other of which was showing a big three station. For once, the two news services shared a common thread: that of confusion. They reported on the fighting that had occurred on Macarthur Avenue in Eden, and the movement of troops and armor outside the two military bases themselves. They also had a few reporters on scene up on Triad near the tram stations, although they had no idea of what had occurred there except that there had been shooting on the platform between MPG soldiers and MPs.

"The only thing we know for sure," the MarsGroup anchor told her audience at the hourly recap, "is that a large scale deployment of the Martian Planetary Guard has taken place and that those soldiers are being used to fight WestHem forces that are stationed on the planet. Heavy fighting was reported at the Macarthur Avenue main entrance to the Eden Marine Barracks, including the use of tanks and armored personnel carriers with heavy weapons. MPG troops in large numbers have been observed entering the base from both the Macarthur Avenue entrances and from the outside airlocks on the planetary surface itself. They did not seem to be under hostile fire as they did this. It is unknown just what their exact intention is, but it would seem that occupation of the base is their goal.

"Meanwhile, other elements of the MPG have taken control of federal buildings, including the FLEB offices, in the cities of Eden, New Pittsburgh, Libby, and Procter. We have tried to interview some of these soldiers, but they have all refused comment on what their exact mission or intentions are. Governor Whiting, who's indictment and arrest warrant are what apparently precipitated all of this activity, has not responded to requests for interviews but she has released an email announcing that she will address the planet tonight at 1900 hours, New Pittsburgh time. We will, of course, carry that address live."

The big three recap was basically the same information, although with a decidedly different slant to it.

Laura sighed as the reporters began rehashing the same information again. Her stomach was knotted and burning from the tension of the day. She took a sip out of her ninth cup of coffee and continued to wait and watch.

Soon Jackson's face appeared on one of her screens. His face was showing the strain of the past few hours as well, but he seemed to be happy nonetheless. "The planet is pretty much secure," he told her.

"Pretty much?" she said.

"We have TNB locked down tight and all of the MPs accounted for. The same goes for EMB. We're in occupation of the base and more than ninety percent of the weapons there are now accounted for. We're going room to room with scanners to find the rest. In the four cities where we have MPG divisions, all of the FLEB and other federal law enforcement have been captured and are accounted for. Now we just need to get some soldiers over to the other cities and take control of them there. I've already sent battalions out on the inter-city trains for that duty."

"Could those agents cause problems for us?" she asked, knowing that each of those offices had around a hundred agents.

"Nothing that's going to put our possession of the planet in jeopardy," he said. "They could put up a fight if they were stupid I suppose, but it'll be an ultimately losing one. We'll have them all secured or dead within twenty-four hours."

She nodded. "Let's hope that it doesn't come to that," she said. "What else has been done?"

"Communications with Earth have been virtually shut down," he said. "We've assumed control of the com-sats and have shut off all outgoing transmissions except media broadcast. Per your orders, they're still allowed to receive signals and email."

"Very good," she said, and then braced herself. "And the casualties?"

"Relatively light," he said, offering a crooked grin. "Since General Sega surrendered all of the WestHem forces once it became apparent that they could not win, we were spared..."

"Numbers, General," she insisted.

He breathed deeply, casting his eyes upon her. "Thirty-three dead, forty-seven wounded," he told her. "Most of them up at TNB from the force that was pinned in the tunnel."

"And the enemy?" she asked next.

"We haven't got a firm count just yet, but we have a rough estimate," he told her. "Including the feds at the capitol building and the marines in the C-12, it looks like about 560 dead, 133 wounded. We also lost two civilians and had three of them wounded when those idiots guarding the passenger platform at TNB opened fire on our troops instead of surrendering. For what it's worth, the numbers are considerably lower than what was predicted for the operation."

She nodded. "I understand. See to it that names are gathered as soon as possible and that the families of those killed are notified immediately after my speech tonight. And as for the WestHem casualties, make sure a full accounting is sent to Earth as soon as possible."

She seemed morose, and this bothered Jackson. It bothered him greatly. After setting all of this in motion, after all the years of planning and scheming, was she now paling due to the casualties sustained in the successful operation? She should be cheering.

"Laura," he said carefully, "we knew we were going to take casualties when we started this thing. Those MPG troops knew when they went in that they might get killed. The all voluntarily went in anyway. They died fighting for Mars. For Mars! Not for some moon that circles around Jupiter that nobody was even using but that our government wanted to deny to EastHem so they could keep selling them fuel. They didn't die in some godforsaken shithole in the southern hemisphere of Earth fighting fanatical nationalists that hate WestHem rule as much as we do. They died for *Mars*, Laura, for this planet, so that we could be free. And while I'm sure they'd rather be alive right now and I'm sure their families feel the same, they died for us and I'm sure they'd be proud of that fact; as should we all."

"I understand all of that, Kevin," she told him. "I also understand that you did everything you could to keep those casualties to a minimum. It's just that..." She paused, trying to figure a way to articulate what she was feeling. "It's just that I sent those people in there and some of them are dead now. Tonight, I'm going to ask for more people to sign up to do the same and, if they agree to do it, we're going to lose some of them too. We face a long, hard struggle against a superior enemy and each one of our soldiers that dies in this conflict is a living, breathing person with a family, with a *life*. I just want to make sure that I never allow myself to forget that, that I never treat them as pawns in a chess game against WestHem. I never want to hear you say the term 'acceptable losses' to me. Never. No loss is acceptable, Kevin. Each one is a tragedy and should be treated as such. If I start accepting the deaths of my soldiers as acceptable or inevitable, I'm no better than the pigs we're fighting. Do you understand?"

"Yes, Governor," he said, finding himself moved by her words. Laura had a gift for that. He remembered himself as a young private in the WestHem marines, stationed in Argentina region and fighting the nationalist guerillas. He remembered his friends dying there, ambushed when alone by the poorly trained and equipped but fanatical Argentines. He remembered the sensation that his superiors simply didn't give a shit whether or not he lived or died. He did not want a single soldier under his command to ever feel like that. "I do understand, perhaps even better than you do yourself."

"Good." She gave him a weak smile. "Please continue your report."

Jackson looked down, consulting some notes he had before him. "We have a preliminary estimate on POWs here. We have captured approximately forty-six thousand WestHem military personnel at the two bases on Mars. Of course, more than eight thousand of those captured at TNB are Martian civilians that worked on the base. They'll be released as soon as they are identified. The rest are sworn members of the WestHem armed forces. Preliminary numbers put the number of *those* that are Martian citizens at approximately eight percent. We've got people working the computers right now and we'll segregate the Martians from the Earthlings when we ID them. As for how many of that eight percent are loyal to Mars?" He shrugged. "Your guess is as good as mine. I like to think it'll be in the upper ninety percent range, but who knows?"

"If it isn't at least in the upper eighties, especially among the navy," Laura opined, "we're in a lot of trouble."

"Well, we'll squeak by, no matter what," Jackson answered optimistically. "Right now, the POWs are still confined to their bases, most of them in their assigned housing units. Processing will start shortly. We'll segregate the Martians and keep them at TNB and then we'll move the bulk of the Earthlings to the compounds we'll be setting up in Libby and Procter. Most of the marines however, will be held right on the barracks grounds where they were stationed. A convenient, pre-positioned POW camp. We'll use the MPG troops that are prison guards in their civilian lives to watch over them; those that aren't vital to combat operations anyway."

"Sounds like a good plan," Laura said approvingly.

"Thank you. I thought of that part myself."

"Any idea whether or not we'll be able to use *Interdiction* as a plan?"

"Matt Belting will be launching to Triad later today. He'll be the man to make the final decision on that, but I don't imagine he'll be able to say until after we vote whether to go ahead with this revolution or not and after he has a preliminary report on the recruits we get with naval experience. I certainly hope we'll be able to pull it off. If we don't, my troops are gonna have quite a fight on their hands when the WestHems finally make their landings here."

"Too much of a fight?" she asked.

He stared at her. "Laura, you know what kind of odds we face even under the best of conditions. WestHem has the power and might to send a whole lot of trouble our way. We need *Interdiction* to go off at least in some capacity or we're going to lose some cities to the marines once they land. That may not lose us the war, but it'll sure make it longer, harder, and deadlier. I've planned my campaign under the assumption that we won't man a single ship or stop a single WestHem transport before it reaches Mars, but my job will be a whole lot easier if *Interdiction* goes forth with at least a small measure of success."

"Then I guess my speech tonight had better be inspiring," she said simply.

"If I know you Laura, and I do, you might even get some of those corporate haunchos to sign up."

*****

Under Whiting's orders, all of the office workers in the capital building were released, including the legislature and Lieutenant Governor Scott Benton. They did not go home as was offered. At Benton's suggestion, the legislature immediately convened a special session and voted to condemn Laura Whiting's actions and to open an investigation into impeachment proceedings for her actions. They added an addendum demanding her immediate removal from office during the course of the investigation. This time, with a clear course of action and with no pause to consider recall campaigns, the vote passed, with only half of those legislative members that had shifted loyalties during the last few months voting against it. The Lieutenant Governor ordered the results of the vote immediately transmitted to her through the secure Internet channels.

Laura did not address them in person, though she did broadcast her reply to them on the big screen in the legislative chambers.

"Sorry, folks," she told them, shaking her head sadly, "I'm afraid I won't be honoring your vote, at least not yet. Things have gone a little far for that."

"It's a constitutional requirement that you honor the vote," Benton, acting as spokesman, told her firmly. "You do not have a choice whether or not to honor it. You will step down immediately and I will take over as Governor."

"Our constitution was put aside when the first shots were fired downstairs," she returned. "I will not stand down unless the Martian people ask me to stand down. No votes from the legislature will be binding until further notice."

"You can't do that," Benton nearly screamed. "You have no authority to disregard a vote. None!"

"Those armed men under my command have given me the authority," she said. "Right now, they are following my orders and they are securing this planet from WestHem interests, of which you Scott, and most of you on the legislature are included in. As Martian citizens, you will have the opportunity to judge my actions and vote upon them in a few days. Until then, this office and the Martian Planetary Guard are in charge of the planet. The legislature is hereby dismissed from office until further notice. You will all vacate the building immediately or I will have the troops remove you."

"We're not leaving," Benton told her. "And we will not allow you to pervert our constitution in this manner. You will step down right now and submit yourself to custody or I will..."

"You will what, Scott?" she asked him. "Have the feds take me into custody? There are no more feds in New Pittsburgh. The MPG is loyal to me and my orders and we have initiated a revolt against WestHem. A *revolt*, do you understand? Revolts are not stopped by votes cast by playthings of the people we are rebelling against. Now I'll tell you one more time, leave the capital building or you will be removed by force."

"We're not leaving," he repeated stubbornly.

She smiled. "Tell that to the soldiers when they come up to remove you then," she said, and then signed off.

Ten minutes later, an entire platoon of armed soldiers entered the legislative chamber. Five minutes after that, the entire legislature and Scott Benton were escorted out of the building at gunpoint.

CHAPTER SEVEN

Planet Mars
June 8, 2186

At 1800 hours, New Pittsburgh time, people all over the planet found an Internet screen and tuned it to the proper channel. Some were gathered around a single screen in the living room of a public housing apartment. Some sat in luxury apartments on the edges of the cities. Many were freshly deployed MPG troops on occupation duties. If they were near a screen, they watched it, if they were not near a screen, they watched their PCs instead.

When the speech began, there was no fanfare beforehand, no commentary by reporters, no speculation as to what was to be said, no spurt of advertising commercials. The image simply blinked on, showing Laura Whiting sitting at her desk dressed in her normal garb, a dark blue T-shirt. Her graying hair was styled but not perfect, her face showed strain with large bags under her eyes. In that instant, the planet held its breath. And then she began to speak.

"Citizens of the Planet Mars," she said, looking easily into the camera as she'd done so many times before. "By now, you undoubtedly know that some rather strange events have been taking place on this planet, most prominently right here at the capitol building. I will now explain in detail what has happened today, what steps I have taken, and what I hope will come next.

"I was elected Governor of this planet by a considerable margin. As I've mentioned in my speeches before, I ran under a false flag, proclaiming my allegiance to WestHem, and particularly certain WestHem corporations. This was done so that I could be put into a position where I could fulfill a life-long dream. My dream was not to rule Mars, but to free it from WestHem control and influence. My goal, as I've told you time and time again, was to bring this about peacefully. I offered many times to negotiate with the WestHem government in Denver and the various corporations that control this planet and its assets. I have done this publicly and in private, pleading with the so-called 'powers-that-be' for a transfer of assets over to Martian control that would allow these corporations to maintain a profit while still allowing us self-rule and self-determination.

"They refused to even consider this. Instead, they committed themselves to removing me from office in order to silence my voice. When their attempts at using legal means failed, they attempted to destroy my reputation with their propaganda arm—also known as the Big Three media corporations. When that failed—which it did only because of the intrinsic intelligence of you, the Martian people—they began resorting to other means, namely, the use of the WestHem federal government and its law enforcement branch.

"Now I know that all of you are aware of how this tactic affected you, the citizens of Mars. They arrested hundreds for doing nothing more than exercising their freedom of speech. They shot down others like dogs. But while they were behaving like Nazis in our streets, stomping on our human rights, violating all we hold sacred, another group of them was working in secret, acting directly against me. They put together federal charges—charges that were completely and totally fabricated—against me as a means of removing me once and for all. As you all have undoubtedly heard during the course of this day, a federal indictment with six separate charges was issued against me yesterday in Denver. This indictment was followed up with an arrest warrant today – a warrant that calls for my extradition to Earth for trial. The charges listed in this indictment are as follows: Abuse of high office, solicitation of bribes, racketeering, gross incompetence of high office, and..." she offered a smile to her viewers, "...my personal favorites, incitement of terrorism and trafficking in explosives."

Her face turned back to serious. "These are six very serious federal charges against me. I refused to recognize the legality of this indictment when it was served and I'll explain why. For one, this indictment was handed down by a grand jury in Denver. Denver! On Earth. The members of this grand jury were not citizens of Mars. They were not my peers. I was never given the opportunity to answer to any of these so-called charges leveled against me. I was never questioned a single time about these charges by any federal officers. Does this sound like a fair and impartial investigation?

"Some might say that an indictment is merely a charge and that if I'm innocent it will be proven in court. I'm sorry, but I just don't see it that way and I believe that most of my fellow citizens don't either. If I were to have gone to Denver and stood trial, I would have been found guilty on all counts by another jury of Denver citizens, after being defended by a *federal* defense attorney. No, this indictment was not a response to criminal activity committed by me. It was meant to be my removal from office.

"I have committed no corrupt acts, I have not abused my office, I've accepted no bribes, and I don't believe I've been incompetent in my duties. I have certainly not incited any terrorism or trafficked in any explosives. So, when federal agents showed up at the capitol building this morning to take me into custody, I refused to go. And I will not go until you, my true peers, tell me that I must go, that the events that took place today must end. As it stands now, I'm guilty of much more than simple corruption. I will now explain what happened today so you can all fully understand what is happening.

"When the agents showed up to arrest me, my security detail was ordered by me to stop them. I will point out that I carefully explained to them that if they thought the indictment should be honored, if they truly thought that I was a corrupt, incompetent governor, then they should *not* follow my orders, that they should allow the feds entrance to the building and assist them in the arrest. I explained to them that failing to follow the feds' orders might expose them to treason charges later on. Not a single one of my detail backed down.

"My detail attempted to take the FLEB agents into custody until such time as the matter of Martian autonomy was hashed out. Unfortunately, the FLEB agents did not surrender peacefully but elected to shoot it out inside the lobby of the capital. My troops returned fire, killing and wounding many of them. Most of the outside detail, as you saw on Internet, were taken peacefully into custody.

"As for the other events at the capital this morning, the reinforcement of the feds, the pull-back of the New Pittsburgh Police Department, the peaceful surrender of the remaining feds, you all saw that on Internet live as it happened. I will not rehash those events right now but I would like to thank Chief Sandoza for pulling his men back at my request. This kept Martian police officers from becoming involved in a firefight with MPG troops and led to the surrender of the federal agents. That is how I was kept from being taken into custody for these fabricated crimes under the guise of this illegal and fabricated indictment.

"But as you know, some other things have taken place on this planet and above during the course of this day, things much more serious than my refusal to surrender to a warrant, things with far-reaching implications for the future of this planet."

She paused for a second, taking a sip from a glass of water that was sitting next to her. She set it down and then looked into the cameras once more. "I have known all along," she said, "that the WestHem powers-that-be would most likely not go along with my plans for a peaceful transition to autonomy. I have hoped for the best but, at the same time, I have prepared for the worst. I have moved forward under the assumption that most of my fellow Martians favor autonomy and are willing to take certain risks for it. As I've said, you will all have opportunity to judge my actions in this regard.

"Many years ago, long before I was elected your governor, in order to assure that when the time came the citizens of Mars would have the means to make ourselves free, I asked my good friend General Jackson of the Martian Planetary Guard to draw up plans for assuming control of this planet from WestHem authorities if it ever became necessary. That plan was code-named Operation Red Grab and today it was put into effect on my orders. Whether or not it was necessary will be up to the Martian citizens to decide and you will be given the power to shut down this operation if you so desire, but let me explain first what steps were taken and where we stand at this moment.

"When word of the coming indictment and arrest reached my office yesterday afternoon, I put the plan into action. The first thing that happened was a call-up of the entire special forces battalion planet wide. These soldiers were transported up to Triad last night and stationed there to wait for confirmation of the indictment and arrest attempt. At the same time, additional MPG combat troops were called up and activated down here in New Pittsburgh and in Eden. Some of these men helped secure the capital this morning, but most of them were stationed outside of the Eden MPG deployment center, where they manned tanks, aircraft, artillery, and infantry positions. They too waited for conformation of the indictment and arrest attempt. When that confirmation came, the special forces battalion, who again, were given the free choice to back down from their task, invaded Triad Naval Base and secured it. As we speak right now, TNB and all of the WestHem naval ships docked there are firmly in our hands. At the same time, the infantry and tank troops outside of Eden moved in to secure the Eden Marine Barracks. That base too is now firmly in our hands, all of its occupants and weapons captured."

She frowned sadly. "Unfortunately, these two bases did not meekly surrender to our troops. Thirty-three of our soldiers lost their lives in the fighting. Forty-seven were wounded. Casualty lists are being formed right now and the families of those soldiers killed and wounded will be notified shortly after my speech tonight.

"These deaths weigh heavy on my soul," she said, seeming to stifle a tear. "I know that is what a politician is supposed to say and I know that they rarely mean it, but please believe that I am speaking these words with the utmost sincerity. Thirty-three young men died while following orders that initiated with me. Thirty-three people with families, children, lives. I will not try to justify their deaths with a lot of patriotic blathering. This was a tragedy and I want you all to know right now and understand that if we follow through with the course of action that I have set into motion today there will be more tragedies like this, some undoubtedly worse, and maybe too many for us to handle."

She stopped, wiping a tear from her face and clearing her throat before continuing. "Once the fighting began at the two bases, I ordered a general mobilization of the entire MPG. My purpose for this action was nothing less than to take control of this planet, to seize it from WestHem in the name of the citizens of Mars. This goal was successful. As of 1520 hours today, the Planet of Mars is firmly in the hands of the MPG."

She took a deep breath. "This is where my actions will stop without further consent from you, the Martian people. Most of you are probably trying to digest what I have just told you. You are saying to yourselves in disbelief 'My God, Mars has rebelled against WestHem'. But that is not what has happened, not yet. Mars has done nothing, I have. I have initiated preliminary actions to secure this planet in the hope that we *will* rebel, that we *will* tell WestHem that we no longer wish to be a part of their corrupt system, that we are going to carve out our own destiny from now on. But I will not, I *cannot* go any further without the consent of the people in whose name I am doing this.

"I've told you several times during the course of this speech that you will have the opportunity to evaluate my actions. I will now explain just what I mean by that. I am calling for a vote on this matter. I will give you two days to think it over and then you may cast your ballots via your Internet terminals starting at 0800 local time on Friday. The question will be simple. Do you wish to declare autonomy from the Federal Alliance of the Western Hemisphere and enforce this declaration by any means available and necessary?

"This is a question that requires a simple yes or no answer. But this yes or no will be the most important you will ever answer in your lives. Your future, your children's future, and your grandchildren's future rides on this vote, so I want you to discuss it with your friends, your families, and then vote how your heart tells you to. Due to the gravity of this decision, I will require more than a two-thirds majority of yes votes before I will consider the measure passed. I will also require greater than ninety percent voter participation before I will consider a yes vote to be binding.

"If the vote is no, either through lack of participation, lack of two-thirds majority, or outright defeat, I will immediately stand down the MPG and release all federal agents and WestHem soldiers. I will turn myself and my conspirators over to federal custody to stand trial on whatever charges they can initiate. Lieutenant Governor Benton will assume the governorship and things, for the most part, will go back to the way they were before. If this is your wish, then vote no. If you do vote no however, you will never again have the right to complain about the unfairness of the WestHem system or the unfairness of their rule.

"But before you vote yes on the matter, I want some hard facts out on the table for you to peruse. To gloss these facts over would be the worst sort of hypocrisy on my part. I want to make sure that each and every one of you knows exactly what a yes will get us into.

"Right now, the timing for a revolt against WestHem could not be better. Mars and Earth are nearly as far apart as they ever get. It will take at least twelve weeks before WestHem can send any troops our way, but believe me when I say that they *will* send them. Mars is worth trillions of dollars to WestHem and is a primary source of food and steel. They will not simply let us go. If we want Mars to be free, we are going to have to fight them for it.

"Will we win?" She gave a cynical smile. "I certainly hope so, but it will not be a cakewalk in any case. No matter what we do, no matter how prepared we are for them, WestHem marines *will* establish orbit around this planet. We do not have sufficient resources or people to prevent that. WestHem marines *will* establish beachheads outside of our cities. We do not have the resources or people to prevent that either.

"'So, we cannot win', some of you may be saying right now. That is not true. In order to take this planet from us, the WestHem marines are going to have to march from their beachheads to our cities and occupy them. Sounds simple? It would be if not for the Martian Planetary Guard. This is exactly the situation the MPG was formed to prevent in the first place. Now you have all seen Internet shows deriding our planetary guard force, proclaiming it to be nothing more than a 'speed bump', good only for holding off an EastHem invasion long enough for 'real' soldiers from WestHem to get here." She smiled. "Well, I believe we can do a little better than that. Under General Jackson's command, the MPG is a highly and specifically trained group with excellent equipment and tactics. Their very reason for existence is to *prevent*, not just hold off, an armed invasion of our planet, and, if WestHem comes in here thinking that they're dealing with a simple speed bump they're going to have a nasty surprise in store for them.

"But as the MPG stands right now, we do not have enough combat personnel for a prolonged combat operation. We need volunteers to sign up for service and, if you vote for rebellion, we need you right away in order to give us time to train you prior to the arrival of the WestHems. If you sign up, you must know that you may die or be horribly wounded in this war. We may, despite all of our preparations, lose this war and you may be arrested and charged with treason if this occurs. I want that to be right up front and in the open.

"We may lose. I cannot, and General Jackson cannot guarantee success. If we lose, we will be subjected to occupation by WestHem soldiers for the foreseeable future. We will be subjected to even greater persecution and prejudice than we already have to deal with. We will never be trusted, never! If you need a graphic example of this, take a look at the fate of the Asian descendants of Earth. A hundred and fifty years ago they initiated and lost World War III. On Earth today, it is still legal to discriminate against Asians, even those whose ancestors were American or Canadian citizens during the war.

"In addition to the tactics of fighting WestHem, we have to worry about one other thing. Fuel. Fuel to run our tanks, our aircraft, our space fighters. This fuel, as you know, comes from Jupiter and is supplied to us by WestHem. It is the one resource that we are not self-sufficient in. If we are to successfully fight WestHem and gain independence, we must secure a fuel supply. Now obviously, WestHem is not going to keep sending fuel ships here. That leaves us with the unappetizing necessity of trading with EastHem for fuel.

"Aside from the distastefulness of doing business with an entity that once bombed our cities and killed our people, this opens up several variables to the equation of independence. For one, I have not yet contacted EastHem and asked if they will assist us; if they will trade fuel for our food surplus. They may refuse. If they do, all is lost. EastHem is going to have to make a decision of its own.

"If EastHem does agree to assist us, WestHem may try to stop them. I don't believe that they will, since this will flash the cold war to a quick heated state, but they might. If they do that, I cannot predict what the long-term consequences will be. Again, this is a chance we'll have to take if the vote is yes.

"So, you can see that our fate is far from certain if you vote yes. If you vote no, you can all go back to your lives in three days. You can continue to work for WestHem masters and continue to be fired at their whim and forced to be quartered in public housing.

"But know this. This is the best and only chance we will ever get to make ourselves free. If we vote no, WestHem will see to it that this opportunity is never repeated. Never. We will spend all of eternity as WestHem subordinates and second-class citizens. We will spend all of eternity as slaves to that corrupt, evil system.

"I urge you all to think very carefully about this decision, to think not just about your own future, but the future of this entire planet and all of your descendants. It is my feeling that we can win this war, that we can throw these greedy, corrupt Earthlings off of our planet and live in a society ruled by common sense and justice. Talk to others and gather information and, most important of all, keep an open mind. Most important of all, you need to vote. For better or for worse, I ask you to give me that ninety percent turnout in this most critical decision.

"In the meantime, I'm declaring a two-day holiday for all except vital services workers. The planet is not under martial law, so you may move about your business as normal and I encourage you to do so. The MPG will remain activated until after the vote and will be patrolling our cities to help the police keep order. Earthlings among us, you are free to move about as you wish as well. It is not my intention to make prisoners of you in this conflict. If the vote is for independence, you will be allowed to leave the planet if you wish if transportation is available.

"That is my speech for the day. I hope I have explained myself sufficiently and I hope that you will head my words. Good night, and think carefully about what I have told you."

*****

Orbiting City of Departure—Geosynchronous Earth orbit.
June 8, 2186

Admiral Tanner Jules was the commander-in-chief of the WestHem navy's Far Space fleet. CINCFARSPACE was his handle. He was the latest in a long line of naval commanders his family had produced, a direct descendant of the first captain of the first space-going warship that WestHem had ever launched. Though he was mainly a bureaucrat these days, he had seen combat as the captain of a California class warship back in the Jupiter War; a ship that had destroyed two EastHem warships before being crippled by a nuclear torpedo from an EastHem stealth attack ship.

He had not been privy to the impending arrest of Governor Whiting on Mars and his day had been filled with routine computer work. He was now at home, with no idea that the worst evening of his life was about to commence.

This really was a pity, because he was engaging in a rather pleasant evening otherwise. His wife was on vacation in Hawaii and he was entertaining a young staff officer that worked in the Far Space Headquarters building at Armstrong Space Force Base, where the space fleet of Earth was based. She was twenty-six years old, blonde, very attractive, and very eager to work her way, as it was, up the Navy bureaucratic ladder. He'd spotted her from almost the instant she'd appeared in her current assignment, but this was the first time he'd managed to get her alone. She seemed more than receptive to what his intentions were.

They were in his residence quarters on the -103rd floor of an exclusive housing building on the outside of Departure. The apartment itself was six hundred square meters, a virtual kingdom aboard a space city. The living room, in which they were currently sitting, featured a large picture window that looked out upon the blue, white Earth floating far below. From the Internet system soft, sensual music was playing and a blazing fire hologram (complete with artificial warmth) was showing in a space specifically designed for it across from the window. The furniture was ultra-modern, comfortable, obviously expensive. Jules was in a genuine silk dressing gown, sipping a glass of white wine. The young staff officer, Lieutenant Megan Riley, was wearing a cocktail dress. She was beaming at him delightfully, making his libido soar.

"More herb, my dear?" he asked, inching a little closer to her.

She giggled. "Maybe a little."

He picked up the slender hose that sat on the table before her, putting it to her lips. The other end of the hose led to a small electric bong that sat on the table. The bong had a cartridge of compressed Martian green marijuana in its chamber, perhaps the finest and most expensive variety commercially available (a product of AgriCorp). She giggled as he pressed the button on the hose and a water-cooled stream of smoke was ejected. After inhaling deeply, he gently pulled the hose from her mouth and put it to his own. A push of the button and his own lungs filled with the sweet, intoxicating smoke. He held it in, staring into her eyes, noting her receptiveness. He put his arm around her and pulled her to him. She came willingly. He knew that when he exhaled the smoke he would kiss her and then the fun would really start, all of the innocent, though politically necessary innuendos cast aside.

The music was suddenly halted, breaking the mood.

"What the hell?" Jules barked, the smoke belching out of him.

"Priority message from Admiral Lucid," the voice of his computer said. "Would you like to answer it or refer it to the mail server?"

He felt his face turning red. What the Christ was this? A priority message? From Lucid? Lucid was the supreme commander of WestHem naval forces—his boss—though he was an idiotic political appointee. He looked at the nearest time display, seeing that it was 2135 hours here in space. That would make it 2035 hours in Denver, long past the time that fat prick should have been gone from his office for the day. What could possibly have come up after office hours that he needed to send a priority message—which Jules was obligated to answer—right now?

He sighed. "Excuse me for one moment, my dear, will you?"

"Of course," she giggled, picking up the marijuana hose again.

As he strolled over to the nearest terminal, he shot a glance out the window. Departure was in geosynchronous orbit over the west coast of South America. From this vantage point, Jules could clearly make out North America. The central portion was in darkness at the moment but free of cloud cover. He could see the tiny blot of light that signified the Denver metropolitan area. He projected a death wish towards it.

"Send the message to terminal two," he spoke into the air.

The computer picked up his voice, performed the normal security check upon it, and then routed the transmission to the living room Internet terminal. The screen filled with the face of Admiral Lucid.

"Hi, Gene," Jules said pleasantly. He was an experienced bureaucrat and allowed no hint of his real feelings in his voice or facial expression. "What's going on?"

"Tanner," Lucid answered, visibly upset. "We've got big problems on Mars."

"Mars?" Jules repeated, alarmed. "Is it EastHem?" In any hot war with EastHem, Mars would most likely be a primary target for attack or invasion.

"No," was the reply. "It's not *that* bad, but it's close, and much more embarrassing for you and me both." He shook his head sadly. "The goddamn greenies have attacked and captured TNB."

"What?" Jules said, his mouth dropping open. The greenies? Triad Naval Base? Attacked it? "How? Who?" he finally asked.

"That's not all they've done," Lucid said. "That bitch Whiting has apparently taken command of the Martian Planetary Guard and they have the entire fucking planet under control. They have possession of *all* of the ships in dock at TNB and all of the personnel that manned them. They have possession of the nuclear torpedoes on the Owls and the Californias as well."

"Gene," he said in disbelief. "That's insane." He had more than 40,000 people stationed at Triad! He had his *entire* far space fleet there except for whatever was deployed at Ganymede. "How could they have done something like that?"

"My understanding is that it was a surprise attack by the MPG, forcing entry through the transportation tunnels and cutting their way in with primacord charges. They overwhelmed the security force in less than an hour. General Sega—a fucking jarhead in charge of the Marines on Mars—took command of all the Martian forces and surrendered them." He shook his head. "Surrendered them! To greenies! Can you believe it? That bastard will be court martialed for *that* little decision, I can tell you that."

Jules paled as a thought occurred to him. "The nuclear torpedoes, Gene, are they still..."

"The security watch crews were able to wipe their programming. It's SOP. I wouldn't think that the greenies would be able to utilize them for anything. But they do still have the physical components."

"Thank God for small favors. But Gene, how could something like this have happened? What the hell are the greenies doing? What could they possibly hope to gain?"

"We don't know, but we need to find out," he said, since the transmissions in which Whiting gave her speech to the planet were still on their way across the emptiness of space. "I need you to address the executive council tomorrow morning at 0800 on what has happened and what we're going to do about it."

"The executive council?" he said, fear shooting through the stoned haze of his mind. "I don't *know* anything about what's happened! How can I brief them? I need someone to brief *me*! And that will take..."

"You need to get dressed immediately and head for Armstrong. A T-7 will take you down to Colorado Springs. I'll have all of the info we've developed so far on a disk waiting for you. You can get yourself briefed in on the way down. Once you're in Colorado Springs, I'll have a room ready for you at VIP quarters. Get on the Internet and start researching from there. You need to have a complete briefing ready for them at 0800 tomorrow, even if you have to stay up all night. Include what happened, how it happened, and what the possibilities are that the greenies can get any of those ships operational."

"Operational?" Jules said, puzzled. "How the hell would they do that? They don't have any naval personnel capable of commanding a warship."

"Don't they?" Lucid asked. "They have a hell of a lot of former WestHem navy spacers living on Mars and carrying Martian citizenship. Many of them work on the food and steel transport ships. Is there any possibility that..."

"No," Jules said firmly, wondering why he had to explain something so basic to a man that was allegedly his superior. "No Martian has ever been placed in command of one of our ships since that idiot Belting back in the Jupiter War. And you know what happened there. I'd say that well over ninety percent of the Martians that have served in the navy never made it past enlisted rank. Sure, some of them may have *observed* command tactics and procedure, but it is simply inconceivable that they would be able to operate a single one of those ships. And even if they could, what would they do with them? The most dangerous things they have are the Owls and those are useless without the torpedoes being active."

Lucid seemed somewhat relieved. "That's good to know." He said. "Be sure to come up with hard statistics to back it up when you brief the executive council. I just got the ass chewing of my life from them a few minutes ago. They are extremely worried about the possibilities of the Martians manning those ships. You'll have complete, top secret Internet retrieval access of course."

Jules shook his head again, still unable to believe what he'd just been told, still waiting for Lucid to tell him this was an elaborate joke. But it wasn't.

"Your T-7 pilot has been told to be ready to depart for Colorado Springs in one hour. See to it that you do not make him late."

"Yes, sir," Jules said.

The face disappeared from the screen, leaving only the time display. From the speakers the soft music returned. He looked across the room at the young lieutenant. He no longer felt stimulated.

*****

Armstrong Space Force Base – Departure

The T-7, and its civilian counterpart, the LX-5, were among the smallest Earth-to-orbital vehicles manufactured. They were less than seventy meters in length, ten wide. Their primary purpose was the transportation of the elite, those that did not care to travel with the masses on standard orbital flights. In the civilian world, the LX-5s were utilized by corporate heads and upper management. In the military world, they were used by executive committee members and high-ranking command staff. They were obscenely luxurious, equipped with plush seats, carpeting, overlarge Internet screens with full access, drink and marijuana delivery systems in each seat, and inertial dampened comfort to keep the occupants unaware of the stringent pitches, dives, and acceleration/deceleration cycles.

Though Admiral Jules was not important enough to rate his own personal T-7, he was important enough to rate the use of one of the spares that were always in waiting at Armstrong for people such as him. He and his two senior staff members boarded at the prescribed time, each grabbing a seat and plugging the briefing disks they'd been provided into the Internet screens before them. Though the craft was capable of carrying another twenty-two passengers in the same comfort as the Admiral and his staff, the pilot, a senior commander, knew that this was the load for the trip. It seemed an awful waste of the precious fuel that had come all the way from Jupiter to be burned, but that was not his concern. He sealed up the craft and was given immediate departure clearance.

The T-7 broke contact with the docking airlock and fired its starboard maneuvering thruster briefly, causing the orbiter to drift away. As it cleared the docking area, the thrusters were fired again, longer this time, pushing it out into the departure corridor. With further bursts of different maneuvering thrusters, the craft spun around so it's main thrusters were facing in the direction of its orbit. This minute maneuvering was the main part of the pilot's job. While he was doing it, the computers calculated all of the factors to bring the craft out of orbit and onto a proper trajectory towards Colorado Springs and a soft landing at the field there.

When the pilot had the craft steady in the corridor, he checked with Armstrong control. They gave him the go-ahead and he gave the computer the go-ahead. There was a brief countdown and the main thrusters fired, initiating the de-orbit burn. From the perspective of the T-7, the spacecraft seemed to streak rapidly away from the orbiting city of Departure, leaving it far behind. In actuality it was Departure that was continuing ahead on its normal orbital path while the T-7 was decelerating at three times the force of gravity. It began to drop towards the Earth and its rendezvous with the atmosphere far below.

Inside the cabin, Admiral Jules did not watch the Earth growing in his window and, thanks to the inertial damper, he was not pressed violently backwards into his seat. He was watching in disbelief as the events of the last eight hours were displayed for him on the screen. He watched the news clips of the shoot-out in New Pittsburgh, he watched the initial reports from TNB as the MPG troops attacked it. He replayed several of these over again, as did his staffers.

Just as he got to the cry for reinforcements from Admiral Rosewood to General Sega, the T-7 cut its engines and spun around once more, presenting its belly to the approaching atmosphere of Earth. It continued to drift downward, pulled by the forces of gravity that were now stronger than its forward momentum. Shortly, the craft entered the atmosphere where friction began the job of decelerating it from orbital velocity to atmospheric flight speed. The view out the side windows disappeared, replaced by steaks of fiery red as the tremendous heat of reentry was bled off.

Normally during reentry flights, Jules would stare out the window at this point, nervously awaiting the reappearance of scenery, which would signify the end of the dangerous friction period. Over the course of history, reentry had accounted for more spacecraft accidents than anything else. Accidents that were invariably fatal to the occupants. A single flaw in the heat shield, the simple result of a simple maintenance oversight, and the spacecraft in question would incinerate itself and everything inside of it. It was said that it usually happened so quickly that the occupants were dead before they even glimmered that something was wrong. Jules would ponder that knowledge while watching the streaks of intense heat outside his window, wondering what it was like to be there one moment and evaporated into ash the next, wondering if what was said was nothing but propaganda designed to make space travelers ride easier, if they actually died in burning agony, their deaths taking minutes.

But on this flight, he paid scant attention to reentry, not even breathing a sigh of relief when it was over and the many cities of Brazil, Venezuela, and Columbia regions could be seen glowing beneath them once more. As the wings deployed, slowing them further, and the T-7 turned northwest, heading across the Caribbean Sea towards North America, Jules continued his perusal of the attack on TNB, expressing guttural profanity but also feeling, very much against his will, a large measure of respect for the author of the attack. They had been caught with their pants down; nothing more, nothing less. But how could they have anticipated something like this? An attack on the base by so-called friendly forces? They had underestimated the MPG. It would not do to make such a mistake again.

*****

WestHem Capital Building—Denver
June 9, 2186

The view was impressive from the large picture window in the executive council briefing room. The window looked east, out over the entire expanse of the thirty-eighth most populous city in WestHem; the sixty-third most populous in the solar system. The tops of innumerable high-rise buildings could be seen stretching away for kilometers in every visible direction. Each roof was dotted with landing pads and parked VTOLS, the transportation system for the elite. It was 0745, just fifteen minutes before the start of the workday, and the little craft could be seen buzzing and circling everywhere like flies, the computer systems that ran them delivering their corporate masters to their offices. Beyond the high rises of downtown were the housing complexes of the upper and then the middle class. Beyond those were the slums, which stretched to the horizon and beyond; thousands of square kilometers of unspeakably dangerous neighborhoods populated by more than eight million unemployed and unemployable. Every major city on the planet had similar ghettos of similar proportion.

Like most employed WestHem citizens, Admiral Jules got the screaming horrors at the mere thought of ever having to live in the squalor of WestHem's ghettos; the fate of those that suddenly had their income removed from them. They were the epitome of lawlessness and chaos. The cops themselves did not enter them in anything less than platoon strength; and even then, they might take casualties. They only reason they did go in was to track down a person responsible for a crime against an employed person or to enforce the stringent breeding laws. Among themselves, the unemployed were free to rape, kill, assault, rob, or even molest each other's children. They were an entity onto themselves with little chance to ever pull themselves free. They were not even counted in the census. As long as they stayed within their boundaries, obeyed the breeding law, and confined their crimes to each other, they were left alone, living on welfare money, free alcohol, free marijuana, free Internet, free substandard housing. He eyed the ghettos nervously from his chair in the briefing room while he awaited the arrival of the rulers of the western hemisphere. The TNB fiasco would be penned as *his* responsibility. Would they dismiss him for it? Remove his pension? Sentence him to live out his life in those ghettos? He vowed he would kill himself long before it came to that.

He was bleary from lack of sleep and his stomach burned from the three strong cups of coffee he'd consumed with his breakfast. He'd been up until well past 0400 researching and preparing his briefing; perhaps the most important briefing he would ever give in his career. He was dressed in his Class A uniform, of course, all of his campaign and service metals neatly in place. Before him, at the large rounded oak table where the guests of the council sat, was an Internet terminal into which he'd already inserted the briefing disk he and his staff had created. At the front of the room, above the elevated seats that the executive council would soon occupy, was a larger screen, onto which his figures and the figures of the other briefers would appear.

Would there be other briefers? he wondered. Currently he and his staff were the only ones in the room besides the secret service team, who stood expressionless at their positions near the doors, the council chairs, and the window. Surely, he would not be the only one called on the carpet for what had happened on Mars.

As if in answer to his question, the door slid open behind him and General Wrath, the commander in chief of the Far Space marines entered. CINCFARMAR was his designation and Jules knew him well, on a first name basis in fact. The far space navy and marines, though full of the traditional animosity that had existed between the navy and the marines since the 1700s, worked closely together and relied upon each other. Wrath and Jules' jobs were closely entwined. The two were professional acquaintances, quite close in that regards, although not exactly friends.

"Richard," Jules greeted, offering a smile and an outstretched arm as the General and his staff entered the room.

Wrath, dressed in his own class-A uniform, little changed since the early twentieth century, shook his hand warmly. "Tanner," he greeted. "I see you're here for the same purpose as me."

Jules nodded his head cynically. "Yes I am. It seems our bosses want a few questions answered about what happened yesterday."

"Those fuckin' greenies," Wrath commented sourly. "Who the hell would have believed they were capable of this? And that bastard Sega." He shook his head. "He'd better hope the greenies kill his ass. Can you imagine? Surrendering all of the forces with barely a fight? He must've been mad."

The men took their seats, Wrath taking the chair next to Jules, Wrath's staff taking the seats on the other side. The marine general inserted his own briefing disk into the Internet terminal before his chair.

"Were you up all night too?" Jules asked, noting the bags under his counterparts' eyes.

Wrath nodded wearily. "This clusterfuck pulled me out of a formal dinner party. Not that *that* was upsetting; I hate those fuckin' things. But I spent the next five hours on a flight from Buenos Aires getting briefed in. We then stayed up all night researching and planning how to take that planet back from the greenies if it comes to that."

"Do you think the greenies will really vote for independence?" Jules asked him. "I mean, Whiting didn't exactly make it sound too hopeful in her speech or anything. She actually told them that they might not win. What kind of propaganda is that?"

Wrath shook his head. "I think they just might," he said. "Greenies are not like Earthlings. They don't think the same way we do. Think about where they came from; the unemployed. They actually like speeches like that, they actually like to fight the odds."

"They can't possibly beat us though," Jules pointed out. "What the hell are they thinking?"

"I don't know," Wrath answered. "She told them in her speech that we would send troops to take the planet back and you can bet your ass that we will. She can't possibly think that their little civilian soldier force and their cute little airplanes are going to stop us when we land a half a million troops with tanks, full hover support, artillery, and APCs on that flying shithole. We'll have them routed and mopped up in two days."

"Maybe she *is* mad," Jules suggested. "Maybe she's trying to go down in Martian history as a martyr; the first woman who ever tried to make Mars free or some shit like that. Who knows what she is thinking, but I've been over the figures time and time again and I can see no conceivable way that they can prevent us from landing and taking that planet back."

"There is no way," Wrath agreed. "But whoever said the greenies were smart?"

The door opened once again and yet another briefer entered. This time it was a man that neither Jules nor Wrath had ever met personally, though both recognized him on sight thanks to his frequent appearances in Internet news clips. It was FLEB director Stanley Clinton. He was dressed in a neat, conservative suit and had bags under his eyes similar to the two military officers'. He had no staff with him, simply walking alone to a seat well away from the military leaders and their staffs, making not so much as a nod of greeting, and sat down. He inserted a disk of his own into a terminal.

Silence prevailed until 0804 when the set of doors near the front of the room slid open, signaling the entry of the council. Everyone in the room quickly stood to attention as the nine men and three women of the council, all dressed in business suits of their own, strode into the room. Their faces were grim as they took their chairs, taking their time making themselves comfortable. Finally, one of them, Loretta Williams, spoke. "You may be seated," she said stiffly.

With a shuffle, everyone resumed their seats.

Williams, as the representative of Mars, was still acting as the spokesperson for the council in this matter. "Begin recording," she told the room computer system. Digital cameras and audio microphones clicked on.

She stared at the assembled group of military officers and the single civilian. Her expression, matching the other council members, was of barely concealed rage. "Gentlemen," she said coldly, "yesterday an unprecedented event took place on the WestHem possession of Mars. An event with such far reaching and cataclysmic implications that, even if the situation is resolved quickly in the next two days, an issue which is doubtful, we will be left unable to predict the long-term consequences." She shook her head angrily. "What in the hell happened here, gentlemen? How in the hell could something like this have been allowed? These are questions that I want you to answer only briefly in as few words as possible before you start explaining to this council how we are going to rectify this situation." She stared at the two military officers in particular. "I trust that we *can* rectify this situation."

"Yes, ma'am," spoke Jules and Wrath in unison.

"I certainly hope so," she said. "I don't need to tell you that the entire WestHem economy is fully dependent upon that little red planet. Ninety-eight percent of our steel comes from there. Forty-six percent of our food, our *food*, comes from there. The profits from that planet account for more than twenty-nine percent of our tax base. And, as if that wasn't bad enough, more than a third of our navy is in dock under Martian control right now. Admiral Jules, I trust you have prepared a side-briefing on the implications of *that*."

"Yes ma'am," Jules answered, grateful that he'd taken the time to do that. He almost had not.

"Very well," Williams said. She turned her gaze to Clinton. "Director," she said, "we've already been over the fact of Laura Whiting's election to high Martian office in the first place time and time again with you. We will skip rehashing that part. But if you will please begin our briefing by explaining how the circumstances of her removal went so badly wrong?"

"Yes, ma'am," Clinton replied, standing and activating his Internet terminal.

He explained the fiasco of the previous day in short, concise statements, occasionally using news clips or transmissions from his disk to illustrate some point. The council listened without interrupting. They knew most of the story anyway. When he finished they had only a few questions.

"How many agents do you have on Mars?" Asked one council member.

"Six hundred and forty-three," Clinton replied. "Of course, twelve of them were killed at the capitol building yesterday."

"Are the whereabouts of all of these agents on Mars accounted for?" was the next question.

"Not officially," he answered. "I know that all ten of my field offices were occupied by Martian troops and that all ten surrendered to them. We can presume that all of the agents in those buildings at that time are in Martian custody. As to the fate of those agents that were either off-duty or out in the field at that time, I have no information, nor even a guess as to how many that might be. Unfortunately though, the number of off-duty agents is probably pretty low. When news of the events in New Pittsburgh reached Director Hayes he mobilized the entire force. Many of them were probably inside the buildings when they were taken."

"In any case did the FLEB offices under attack by the MPG request assistance from the local police departments?" asked Williams.

"Ma'am," Clinton replied, "in *every* case they did and in every case the assistance was refused on orders from the various police chiefs. I have information that in three of the cities; Eden, Dow, and Triad, the mayors attempted to override the orders of the police chiefs in question. The mayors of each Martian city, as you are aware, are subjected to the same scrutiny that legislative and gubernatorial candidates are." By which he meant that the corporations owned them. "In all cases, obviously, the orders were disregarded and no assistance was given. As far as I know, not a single Martian police officer lifted a finger to prevent this revolt from occurring. As to the fate of the mayors and city councils involved; I have no information. I suspect they may have been taken into custody, but we are currently completely out of communication with Mars; even the Internet feed has been severed from their end."

"So, we are no longer receiving Martian Internet transmissions?"

"That is correct; although they are still monitoring our Internet. I ordered that the feed not be cut to Mars on the hope that some of the citizens will be able to access our point of view in this thing; to see the preparations we will be utilizing if they do not surrender themselves. It may assist in having Whiting's proposal voted down."

There were some quiet murmurs among the council at this. Finally, Williams said, "That seems a wise move, Director. You may continue to allow outgoing transmissions. Since you brought up this vote that Whiting has asked for, what would you say the chances are that it will be successful? Also, do you think there is any possibility of fraud in the vote?"

This was a trick question. Voter fraud and false results were a patent impossibility with the current system of ballot casting. It was done on the Internet by social security number and fingerprint identification. The programs that ran the voting were unalterable and would not allow such a thing. But if the vote were to be in favor of revolution, then the WestHem authorities would naturally issue propaganda stating that the election had been rigged and was meaningless. Clinton knew this and knew how he was expected to answer.

"I believe that fraud is the most likely possibility and that we will be unable to trust any election results they send us," he said. "There is no way that Laura Whiting is going to back down now. If the Martians do not vote this measure in—and I don't believe that they are so mad as to do so—then her conspirators will simply change the results to look as if they did." This was a bald-faced lie. He knew it, the council knew it, any thinking person would know it; but it was how the game was played. If the Martians voted down Laura Whiting's proposal, then WestHem would demand that she abide by her promises. But if the Martians actually did vote for independence, then WestHem would claim the election was rigged and demand she surrender. Of course, it didn't matter one way or the other which way they voted. The vote itself did not carry any legal weight under the constitution. But politically, WestHem would never admit that the Martians actually *wanted* to be independent in overwhelming numbers. They would have to portray the vast majority of the Martians as innocent, loyal WestHem civilians caught up in a conspiracy by a few radical elements acting in self-interest.

There were a few more meaningless questions, which Clinton answered to the best of his ability. Williams then said, "Thank you, Director. You are dismissed. I would like your office to begin immediate research and author some recommendations as to who should be prosecuted and charged after this little revolt is over and done. Should we prosecute every police officer? Every MPG soldier? Every citizen that voted for independence? Please be firm in your recommendations, with an eye towards ensuring that our Martian friends never get any cute ideas like this again. I would also like recommendations as to what we should do with those Martian citizens on Earth or Ganymede at the moment. How many such people are there? Should we take them into custody until this is over? Do they represent an espionage or sabotage threat? Can they be used as leverage?"

"Yes, ma'am," Clinton said, standing and gathering his briefing disk. "My staff will get to work on this immediately."

"Fine," she said. "We will expect a briefing on these matters by early next week at the latest."

Once he was out of the room, the council's attention turned to Admiral Jules.

"Admiral Jules," Williams said, staring at him, "you are the *current* commander in chief of WestHem far space naval fleet, correct?"

"Yes ma'am," Jules answered, not caring at all for the way in which she'd emphasized the word 'current'.

"Please enlighten this council on the events that transpired yesterday on Mars. After this we will have many questions for you, I'm sure."

"Yes, ma'am," Jules replied, standing up.

His initial chronology of the attack on TNB took nearly thirty minutes. Like with Director Clinton before him, the council simply stared at him or his presentations on the screen; asking no questions, making no comments. Jules knew how the game was played too. He already sensed who the fall guy in the Martian revolt was going to be, General Sega, and he placed blame heavily upon him.

"That last communications we received from TNB stated that the arming and detonation programs for all of the stored nuclear torpedoes, both onboard the ships in dock and in the storage facilities on base, had been wiped. This will, of course, make it impossible for those weapons to be detonated." He spoke a few commands into the screen before him. "You can see here a complete list of all naval ships that were in dock at Triad during the takeover. You will note that it includes nine California class warships, fifteen Owl class attack ships, and our three pre-positioned container ships full of marine landing equipment and supplies. We are formulating a list of the naval personnel captured there. As for the MPs killed in action; we will not know their identity unless the Martians provide us with that information."

Williams looked at him for a moment and then asked, "Is it your opinion Admiral, that had General Sega *not* ordered the surrender of your MPs, the base might have been saved?"

Again, politics was at work here. He knew that the defense of the base had been hopeless. A few hundred lightly armed naval MPs stood no chance of standing up to a battalion of trained, well equipped special forces soldiers. Had Sega not surrendered them, the base would have fallen in the next thirty minutes anyway, only with more dead MPs to add to the list. But that was not what the council wanted to hear. They wanted the blame shifted off of surprise and overwhelming superiority and onto a single man; a traitorous man. They wanted Sega to be blamed for the loss of Mars. The MPG did not *take* Mars, Sega *gave* it to them. By the time this made it to the Internet, they probably would have "evidence" showing that Sega had been in collusion with the Martians the whole time.

Jules was only too happy to go along with this. He felt a twinge of sorrow for Sega, who had only been doing what he thought was right under the circumstances, but it *did* serve to shift the blame off of him. WestHem could not admit defeat after all. Someone had to be responsible. He suspected that had they not found Sega as a convenient target, he himself would have been cast in the role. He suppressed a shiver as he realized how close he'd come to becoming a federal scapegoat. They would have said that he'd been criminally negligent in his anti-terrorist preparations for TNB. They probably would have manufactured evidence suggesting that multiple warnings had been issued about an imminent attack on the base and that they'd been disregarded.

"Admiral Jules?" Williams, clearly irritated, barked at him.

"My apologies, ma'am," Jules said with a start, realizing that he'd been so lost in his near-demise that he'd forgotten to answer her. "In my opinion, the base would undoubtedly still be in our hands had Sega not surrendered its defenders. At the very worst, the MPG might have eventually taken the base, but we would have been able to scramble all of the ships out of docking; keeping them in our hands."

The council members actually smiled at this statement; reinforcing Jules' belief that it was exactly what they wanted to hear. He breathed a sigh of relief, feeling himself slipping off of the proverbial hook.

"Thank you, Admiral, that is as we'd suspected."

There was a brief conversation between the members for a moment, their words whispered. Finally, Williams said, "Now that we have a good idea *what* happened at TNB, I would like to address our primary concern. Will the Martians be able to man any of those ships they have captured and use them against us?"

"Absolutely not," Jules said firmly, grateful to be speaking what he thought was the truth. He spoke a command to the Internet screen and a row of figures appeared on the main screen. "As you can see here, I have compiled statistics on all Martian citizens with naval experience. This would be, obviously, experience gained in the WestHem navy. The population of Mars, not including WestHem citizens living there, is just over eighty million as you can see. I asked the Internet to give me a count on all Martian citizens, currently living on Mars, that have naval experience and are between the ages of eighteen and sixty years old." He pointed to one of the figures with a laser pointer. "There are twenty-six thousand, four hundred and sixty-two people who meet this category."

"That certainly sounds like enough to man some ships," Williams replied to this. "If your intent is to make us feel better about this, you're doing a poor job."

"Yes, ma'am," Jules nodded, licking his lips nervously. "I know the initial number sounds like a lot, but allow me to explain the other factors involved here. Just to account for the absolute worst scenario, I instructed the computer to assume that all of these Martians are loyal to Mars and will go along with Whiting. Of course, I do not believe that will be the case; I believe that many of these are actually loyal WestHem citizens who will..."

"Admiral," Williams interrupted. "Please save the patriotic bullshit for the Internet cameras and continue your briefing."

Jules jumped as if slapped. "My apologies," he said. He took a deep breath to gather his thoughts and then went on. "Of the twenty-six thousand, four hundred and sixty-two, fourteen thousand, five hundred and eleven are over the age of forty and have not served aboard a ship in more than ten years. The technology involved has changed considerably since then and it is unlikely that those people will be of any help to the Martians. That leaves us with a core group of eleven thousand, nine hundred and fifty-one. Of this group, only nine hundred and twelve have ever served aboard an actual combat ship capable of doing any harm to our forces. Of that nine hundred and twelve, only thirty were ever officers and only sixteen of those were ever officers that had conning responsibilities. Twelve of them on a California, four on an Owl. None of these sixteen except for one—the infamous Lieutenant Commander Matt Belting—has any command experience."

"Belting is still alive?" one of the other council members interjected at this point. "I thought he'd died years ago."

"He's still alive and living in the ghettos of New Pittsburgh. He hasn't held a job of any kind since his release from federal prison five years after the Jupiter War armistice. My guess is that he is an alcoholic or a dust addict that probably doesn't even remember his navy time. In any case, it is quite inconceivable that the greenies could put together enough people to effectively use one of those ships in any manner. And even if they could, they have no pilots capable of operating the F-10s or the A-112s on the Californias, and the nuclear torpedoes they've captured are useless to them. Without the torpedoes, the Owls are useless as anything other than a monitoring platform anyway."

"There is no way they can reprogram those torpedoes?" Williams asked.

"It's impossible," Jules said. "Once the computer that controls the detonator has been wiped, it is impossible to reprogram it. It is nothing more than junk after that."

They seemed satisfied.

"The pre-positioned marine ships," another council member spoke up. "What of those? Will the Martians be able to utilize the equipment inside of them?"

Jules replied, "I think that there is a good possibility that they may not even be able to manage the unloading and transfer of this equipment to the planetary surface. It is quite a complex procedure, after all. The landing craft that contain the equipment must be launched from the Panama class ship itself and then piloted down to the surface. However, I believe it may be prudent..." He cast a glance at his Marine counterpart for a moment, "...and I am actually stepping into General Wrath's briefing here, but in my opinion, I believe in assuming the worst; to assume that they will in fact manage to utilize this equipment."

"Do you agree with that assessment, General?" Williams asked him.

"I have taken into account the faint possibility that they will be able to unload those ships," Wrath replied.

Williams nodded. "Very well." She turned her attention back to Jules. "Do we have any assets in the area at all?" She asked him.

Jules nodded. "Yes, we do, ma'am. We have an Owl that had been returning to TNB from Ganymede at the time of this revolt. They were in their coasting period between acceleration and deceleration burns, about halfway between the two planets. I ordered them to take up position as close to Mars as they could get without detection. That should be close indeed, probably inside of twenty thousand kilometers. They will be on station in less than a week and able to send us data on what the Martians are up to with the ships at TNB. They should also be able to monitor communications. They are low on consumables and on refrigerant for the anti-detection systems but, with rationing, they will hopefully be able to remain on station until our forces can get there. We have other assets in place in the Jupiter system; two California groups and two Owls, but frankly, they are needed there in case of trouble with EastHem; particularly with the loss of our marines and their equipment. I'm quite hesitant to break them loose and I don't see what good they would do anyway."

They nodded. "Any other points that you would like to add, Admiral?"

"Yes, ma'am," Jules said. "As you are probably aware, we have a number of Martian citizens enlisted in the Navy. Nine hundred and forty-six of them are on ships that were not captured by the Martians or on Earth shore stations. I have ordered all of them removed from duty and kept under house arrest for the duration of this crisis and pending a decision on what to do with them."

"Good thinking, Admiral," Williams said. "I want all of them removed from our ships as soon as possible. They are not to be trusted and they are never to be allowed to enlist in our navy again. We will decide later what to do with them when this little revolt is over."

"Would you like my briefing on our naval situation as it stands with the loss of the far space fleet?" Jules asked next.

"Not just now, Admiral," Williams replied. "We'll hear it after General Wrath gives his briefing. You may have to modify your calculations when he tells you what equipment will be needed for the retaking of Mars."

"Yes, ma'am," Jules agreed, not mentioning that he already had anticipated the equipment that his counterpart would need.

General Wrath began his briefing in the same manner. Like Jules, he placed the bulk of the blame on the traitorous General Sega, claiming that his Marines could have easily faced off anything the MPG threw at them. Like Jules, he knew it was a lie; but he knew how to play the game too. He apologized sincerely for allowing such an incompetent traitor to achieve a position such as commander of Martian marine forces. In a particularly dramatic bit, he even proclaimed that he was indirectly responsible and offered his resignation if the council so desired.

"I don't think that will be necessary just yet, General," Williams responded, smiling at him. She seemed quite touched by his offer however. "I would like to hear you plan for regaining control of the planet though."

"Yes, ma'am," Wrath responded. He called up some maps and plans on his screen. "My staff and I worked well into the morning hours on this plan, taking many things into consideration. Chief among them is the avoidance of WestHem casualties during the operation. I have taken the liberty of naming the operation. I would call it 'Martian Hammer'."

The council exchanged pleased glances as they tossed the name around. It had become customary back in the late twentieth century to give a catchy name to military operations; all the better to ensnare public support for it.

"Now, I could undoubtedly retake that planet with one hundred thousand troops complete with hover support, tanks, APCs, and support troops. We are dealing with a poorly trained civilian force after all. But I believe that unacceptable casualties may result." By this he meant more than two hundred or so WestHem soldiers killed. Enough to displease the masses. "So, the plan I have developed, though it may seem a bit excessive, will ensure that minimal WestHem casualties are taken, while at the same time, heavy damage is inflicted upon the MPG. Damage that they will remember for generations if they are so foolish as to not surrender immediately."

"Yes, General," Williams said. "Your proposal please?"

"I propose a force of five hundred thousand marines equipped with massive tank support, heavy hover support, and heavy artillery support hit that planet all at once."

"Five hundred thousand?" Williams said after a moment of disbelieving muttering from the other council members.

"Yes, ma'am," Wrath said enthusiastically. "And I propose that we start assembling this plan today, right after the briefing, with full media coverage. Since you are allowing Internet transmissions to be returned to Mars, there is a good possibility that the Martians may surrender or vote Whiting's proposal down when they see what we are sending their way. If they do not, we will offer them one more chance after we establish orbit, warning them that once the landings take place, we will make unrestricted war upon their planet. I believe that will do the trick if the initial phase does not, but, on the off-chance that they still insist on non-surrender, we will make landings at the following places." He pointed out cities on a map of Mars. "Eden, New Pittsburgh, Dow, Libby, and Procter. We will establish beachheads according to doctrine, three times the distance of artillery range from the nearest enemy position. On Mars, with its thin atmosphere, that means we land three hundred kilometers from each city. We unload our equipment and assemble the tank columns and artillery. We give them one last chance to surrender, and if they don't..." He paused dramatically. "We move in. It's a two-day march across the wastelands from those distances. We send in the hovers ahead of our tanks and pound on their defensive positions. We then move the artillery forward and pound on them some more. If they still insist upon fighting, we roll forward with our tanks and continue the job of destroying them. Four days after landing, we'll have those key cities under our control. They will have no choice but to give up then."

"You said unrestricted warfare, General," Williams asked. "Surely you don't really mean that?"

"Of course not, ma'am," Wrath replied. "We are not EastHem after all. We have to use that planet after we take it back from the Martians. Obviously, we cannot do many of the things that the EastHems would. We cannot shell or bomb the agricultural complexes or the cities themselves. We cannot go after the power reactors. We can only concentrate upon the MPG equipment itself and, in truth, I'd prefer not to destroy too much of that. It is, after all, top of the line military equipment that our future forces on Mars can use. But the Martians won't know this. We need to make them believe that we are willing to destroy that planet before we let them have it. We need to appeal to the common Martian that our fight is *not* against them, but against Whiting and her forces. I believe there's a good chance that we can end this conflict without a shot being fired. But if we can't, we'll outnumber the Martian troops by more than four to one in both personnel and equipment; even assuming the use of our pre-positioned supplies. At worst, I cannot conceive of losing more than a hundred men in this fight or having it take more than a week once we land."

"They have a space guard at Triad," one of the other council members pointed out. "Will they be able to use it against our forces in orbit?"

"I'll refer that particular question to Admiral Jules," Wrath replied. "Fleet defense is more his line of expertise."

"Admiral?" Williams asked.

"No," Jules answered immediately. "Their space guard poses no threat to us as Whiting herself pointed out. Their purpose it to prevent attack upon Triad and upon the communications satellites. The wing that they have there would have to fight its way through our combat space patrol and then through our fleet anti-spacecraft defense systems before they could even get in range to attack any ships. They would have to attack with every ship that they had at once to even hope to get four or five ships in close enough to fire their lasers with any accuracy. These four or five would not be able to do much damage and it would leave Triad undefended except for its fixed laser sites. No military commander, no matter how incompetent, would ever take such a suicidal risk. It's a lesson we learned in the Jupiter War. Fighters and bombers cannot go up against space stations or heavy ships.

"On the other hand, we will not be able to attack Triad for the very same reasons and we will be forced to establish our orbit well away from Triad, preferably on the other side of the planet. The only way to get Triad back is to have it surrender to us."

"Which they will do," Wrath picked up the thread, "once their ground forces are defeated."

"Do we have sufficient forces and equipment readily available to initiate this operation?" was the next question.

"Speaking from the marine standpoint," Wrath said, "I have the equipment readily available from units in training and from supply warehouses throughout WestHem. I propose that we start moving it to Colorado Springs, Edwards, Buenos Aires, and Dallas for transport up to Admiral Jules' ships. As for the men, I can pull them from Argentina, Cuba, Brazil, Hawaii, and Alaska. The army can send in replacement troops in Alaska and as for the rest, I can call up reserves to replace them."

"And the navy?" Williams asked Jules. "Do you have sufficient ships available to transport and defend the operation and still maintain security in the event of a conflict with EastHem?"

Jules consulted some figure before him. "It will be a little overcrowded," he finally said. "And I won't have as many Owls and Californias in defense as I'd like, but I can do it. We can put the troops and their equipment into eighteen Panama class transports. We can escort them with three California groups and four Owls. This will leave us with enough ships to defend Earth and Ganymede in the event of a conflict."

The council seemed satisfied with this. "Operation Martian Hammer it is then," Williams said happily. "We'll have our staff contact the media groups today so we can start pushing it."

*****

Capital Building – New Pittsburgh

The time difference between Denver and Eden was variable, dependent upon the differing rotational periods of the two planets. On Mars, time was kept differently than on Earth in order to account for the slightly longer amount of time it took the latter to rotate once. This was augmented by the long delay in the reception of transmissions. In Denver it was 6:00 PM, nearing the end of a frantic workday. It was 1:24 AM in Eden, the early morning hours after the capture of the planet.

Laura, General Jackson, and several of Jackson's command staff were in the Capital briefing room viewing the Internet news programs from Earth. Though they had expected just what they were seeing in one form or another, it was still infuriating to watch the lies the WestHem media were formulating. The media, in their normal fashion, had turned the Martian revolt into popular entertainment.

Crisis on Mars was the heading flashed on the screen every time that the program returned from an advertising break. The words took up the bulk of the screen and were etched in 3D against a Martian red background. A dramatic flair of trumpets accompanied each flash of this motto. The news reports had initially consisted of rumors only, sketchy reports of fighting between "rogue elements of the MPG" and WestHem forces on the planet. It was reported that Whiting had touched off this fighting when federal forces attempted to take her into custody on corruption charges. There were reports of executions and atrocities committed by these rogue elements. It was even reported that the MPG was running rampant through the streets of the cities, killing those MPG troops that were *not* loyal to Whiting and raping any convenient women that happened to be around.

Finally, WestHem executive council member Williams, her expression sober and concerned (executive council members had to be, above all else, good actors), appeared before the cameras for the first official statement.

"My fellow WestHems," she said, staring into the camera. "By now you have heard reports of some unbelievable events taking place on the WestHem federal colony of Mars. Events that began early this morning, our time, and are continuing as I speak. When these events were first brought to the attention of the council we viewed them, as many of you undoubtedly are doing, with shock and disbelief. Mars, after all, is full of WestHem citizens, innocents for the most part. We expressed shock that such events were even possible in the first place. We did not address you prior to this because we wanted to get as many answers as we could before we passed the facts on. I believe that we now have an accurate summary of all that took place yesterday."

"This should be good," Jackson commented sourly.

"Yesterday afternoon, Denver time, a federal grand jury issued an indictment and an arrest warrant for Martian Governor Laura Whiting. This indictment was handed down after the grand jury heard more than a week's worth of testimony from various sources and examined pages upon pages of computer documentation from Mars. The charges consisted of corruption, incitement of terrorism, graft, trafficking in explosives, and gross incompetence. As you are aware from previous news reports, Governor Whiting has been quite a nightmare for the Planet Mars since her inauguration when she revealed herself to be a radical separatist.

"This woman and her core of followers have managed to intimidate other members of the planetary legislature into not impeaching her. Her conspirators were quite canny in covering their tracks and we were able to produce no proof that this heinous perversion of democracy took place. Under the law, Whiting had to remain in office."

"This is actually pretty amusing," Laura pointed out. "It is sad to think that most of the WestHems will actually believe it."

"If you see it on Internet," Jackson said, "then that's what happened. Right?"

"But our FLEB agents stationed on the planet Mars were not intimidated by Ms. Whiting and her thugs," Williams was saying. "They watched her every move knowing that criminals like Whiting always make mistakes. Well, Whiting made many of them and she was caught at them. A legal indictment was issued, an indictment which Whiting says she will not honor, and our brave, diligent FLEB officers in Eden went to arrest her as they were commanded to do."

She paused, staring into the camera, anger spreading across her face. "Those federal agents were *ambushed* by followers of Whiting as they entered the capital building. We have confirmation that more than ten of them were killed, gunned down by thugs masquerading as soldiers, using the very weapons that our military has provided for planetary defense."

"Notice how she doesn't mention," Jackson said, "that we taxed ourselves to pay for those weapons."

"The whole thing is a production," Laura said. "God forbid they admit that there are discontented people. God forbid they admit that they'll fight to the death for this planet because of money. Oh no. There have to be oppressed people and horrible human rights abuses. Earthlings are so shallow."

They turned their attention back to Williams, who was now talking about the attack on TNB.

"These terrorist criminals entered Triad Naval Base under cover of darkness. They were led by this man." A graphic of Jackson was placed on the screen.

"Hey," Jackson said to the applause of the assembled staffers, "there I am. But what the hell did they do to my face?" The image of Jackson had been worked on by someone. His handsome face had been altered to look evil and scowling. His eyes had been darkened considerably giving him an almost demonic appearance. And the blackness of his flesh had been enhanced, making it appear darker than it really was.

"So-called *General*, Kevin Jackson. The man Laura Whiting appointed as the head of the Martian Planetary Guard. This man, who we believe to be Whiting's chief conspirator, led a group of armed, radical separatists, equipped with MPG weapons, to the gates of Triad Naval Base. They were allowed entrance to the base by this man."

"*Allowed* entrance?" Jackson asked no one in particular. "We blasted our way in."

"Who the hell is that?" asked Whiting. "He's not one of our people."

Jackson looked, his eyes widening in surprise. "That's Sega!" he exclaimed. "The Martian marine commander for the expeditionary force."

"General Ronald Sega," Williams confirmed. "And I am sad to state that this man is not a separatist. He is not even a Martian citizen. He is, or rather was, a highly trusted commanding general in the WestHem marines."

"Holy shit," Jackson said, shaking his head. "They're gonna blame Sega for all of this!"

"This man was in charge of the marine forces on the planet of Mars." Williams said with utmost sincerity. "He was also the highest-ranking military officer on that planet. We now know that he is the worst traitor this great hemisphere has produced since Benedict Arnold in the American Revolutionary War. General Sega apparently provided Kevin Jackson with access codes that allowed him and his thugs entrance to Triad Naval Base. The MPs on the base responded quickly to the intrusion and managed to pin the invaders near the front gate of the base. General Sega, as I mentioned before, was the highest-ranking officer on the planet. He declared an emergency and then sent a message to all WestHem military personnel ordering them to surrender to the Martians. To surrender! To throw down their arms. He stated to the brave commanders leading these MPs at Triad, as well as his very own marines at Eden Marine Barracks, that the situation was hopeless, that fighting on would only get them killed. And these brave soldiers, who lacked the information to make any decision to the contrary, who had no information to tell them that their commander was exaggerating things horribly, did as they were ordered.

"Thanks to General Sega, Martian separatists have taken control of all of our military assets on that planet. We have information that the separatists then marched onto TNB and executed more than a hundred of the MPs that were fighting them!"

"Executed?" Jackson nearly screamed at Williams' image. "You have got to be..."

"Shhh!" Laura hushed him.

"Before communications with the naval base were shut down, we received frantic cries for help and horrid descriptions of these thugs lining up the MPs and spraying them with machine gun fire, of shooting grenades at them. These are atrocities on the magnitude of the Asian Powers during World War III. Worse even. At least the Asian Powers were humane about how they killed prisoners."

"Laura," Jackson said, "are you *sure* we should be allowing this feed out to the entire planet. Some of our people might believe this crap. This could alter the vote."

Laura simply smiled. "On the contrary, Kevin," she said. "I have a little more faith in the intrinsic common-sense of our citizens than that. I believe these broadcasts will do nothing but help our cause."

Jackson was doubtful, but he knew that Laura was almost supernaturally adept at reading the pulse of the citizens. He would trust her judgment over his own.

Williams lies continued. She claimed that General Sega himself had executed scores of marines after the base fell. She claimed there was evidence of a sexual relationship between Sega and Whiting. She claimed that thousands of MPG troops had been shot or imprisoned by the "rogue elements" when they refused to take up arms against WestHem. "It appears now that Generals Jackson and Sega have purged the MPG of all soldiers that have professed allegiance to WestHem," she said. "And unfortunately, all of our soldiers on that planet have been captured. Their fate is unknown and our prayers are with them. Our prayers are also with all of those loyal Martians and WestHems trapped as hostages on that planet by this terrorist take-over."

"Terrorist take-over?" Jackson said in disgust. "Hostages? Shit."

"Did you really expect anything else?" Laura asked him.

"No," he admitted.

"But you can be assured," Williams proclaimed firmly, "that this lawlessness and terror will not be allowed to continue. As we speak, preparations are being made to send a force of WestHem marines to Mars to restore order and to effect the arrest of those responsible for this situation. As you all know, it takes some time to travel to Mars; approximately eight weeks at the current planetary configuration. It will take at least two weeks to assemble the forces and equipment necessary for this operation.

"We on the council realize that this leaves two and a half months for the current situation on Mars to continue. As horrible as that sounds, leaving those poor people under those conditions for that length of time, there is no other option. We will, of course, commence negotiations with Laura Whiting and her cohorts and let them know in no uncertain terms that what they are attempting will not be tolerated and that we will hold them responsible for any lives lost during this period. We will try to convince her to surrender herself and her thugs before our Marines land.

"But if she refuses, then our Marines will land on that planet and forcibly return it to the citizens of Mars and its proper place in the WestHem system. Ms. Whiting," Williams stared meaningfully, "if you are listening, and I suspect you are, then I advise you to stop this madness before it goes any further. If you really care about the Martians, if you have a single ounce of empathy for them, you will stop this dangerous game before our troops arrive.

"Since I doubt that you will do this and, since I have received information that this broadcast may be still visible to the citizens of Mars, it is Whiting's sympathizers that I am now addressing. I'm talking to the men who have, for whatever twisted reason, volunteered to take up arms against WestHem at this evil woman's direction. Drop those arms now, right this minute, before it is too late. We have no wish to land on your planet and kill you; our quarrel is with the leadership you have followed. If you have not killed anyone, if you have simply gone with the crowd out of peer pressure, then you are in no trouble as long as your weapons are dropped by the time our forces land.

"Because, believe me, they *will* land and they *will* take control of the planet. I hope with all of my heart that this is a peaceful process, but if it must be a violent one, you stand absolutely no chance of preventing our reoccupation. None. I do not wish to see a lot of misguided people killed for no reason, so I plead with you, I beg of you, drop your arms. Do it now, today, this very moment, and do not pick them up again. That is the worst path that you could possibly follow."

That was the end of Williams' speech. The news conference continued on with a question and answer period in which the reporters began inquiries into such things as what the name of the operation would be and when bids on the advertising and marketing contract would be accepted.

Laura ordered the computer to reduce the volume. "She got in some good blows there near the end," she was forced to admit. "She must have a hell of a speech writer."

"Do you think anyone will listen to her?" Jackson asked. "Do you think it will change the vote?"

Laura smiled. "Maybe a little," she admitted. "But I still think that our citizens have had quite enough of WestHem and their lies. I think most of them will see right through that speech."

"But what about the threats?" Jackson asked. "Many will believe in that even if they don't believe anything else. It would be ironic indeed if our citizens voted for autonomy and then no one volunteered to fight for it."

Laura stared at him, anger now apparent on her face, anger that had not flared this brightly even during the worst part of Williams' inflammatory speech. "Do you really think that our citizens are *that* shallow?" she asked him coldly. "Do you really think that they would vote for freedom and then ask someone else to fight for it?"

Jackson looked back at her, upset by her anger but unwilling to concede her point. "I certainly hope not, Laura."

*****

Martian Planetary Guard Base Troop Club – Eden

The smell of marijuana smoke hung thickly in the air, overpowering even the odor of alcohol and tobacco smoke. The ventilators in the room struggled to keep up with the outpouring but it was a hopeless task. Scores of off-duty MPG soldiers of all ranks, sexes, and ages were sitting at the bar or at cocktail tables; smoking and drinking the intoxicating substances, unwinding from the stressful twenty-four hours that had just occurred. Even though the bar contained about twice as many MPG members as usual, particularly for a weekday, the absence of any marine personnel was conspicuous and a constant reminder of what had occurred.

The speech that Whiting and Jackson had just witnessed had been played in the club on the large Internet screen above the bar; the sound reproduced perfectly by speakers at every table. During the speech itself, the room had been eerily quiet, the silence broken only by the occasional outraged muttering from a soldier that knew what Williams was saying was a lie. But the final part of her speech, the part addressed to the soldiers in this room, had been met with stony, worried silence.

When the speech ended, conversation erupted everywhere, much of it angry, some of it terrified and hysterical.

At a table near the rear of the room, Lisa Wong and Brian Haggerty sat together. Lisa was taking a thoughtful draw off a bong the server had brought to her. She had paid for the double hit with her debit card; forking over six dollars for it, and was now smoking the last of it. Across from her, Brian was sipping out of a bottle of beer. He'd declined the marijuana, not in the mood for it today. The two partners had coincidentally run into each other at the front door of the club an hour ago and decided to sit together.

"Brian," Lisa said, "you're in a combat branch and I'm only in admin so I want you to give me an honest opinion."

"Okay," Brian agreed, already knowing what she was going to ask.

"Can we win this thing? Can we actually hope to defeat the WestHem marines when they land here? I mean really? I know most of what that WestHem bitch said was bullshit, but she wasn't bullshitting about them sending marines over here to take this planet back from us."

"No," he agreed thoughtfully, "she wasn't. They're gonna send a shitload of them here."

"Are we fighting a hopeless cause here? I don't mind fighting for Mars. In fact, I'd be more than proud to do it. And since Whiting is opening up combat branches for women, I'll volunteer for combat duty." She smiled. "I should be able to get in given my background, don't you think?"

Brian nodded.

"I don't even mind fighting if the odds are way against us. I will gladly take the consequences of losing too. But are there any odds? Is there *any* chance at all we'll win? I don't want to sacrifice myself for no chance at all. I don't want to be a martyr if it's hopeless before we begin."

Brian picked up his beer and took a sip from it. He stared at his partner thoughtfully, thinking of a way to say what was on his mind. "I met General Jackson a few times," he finally said.

"Oh?"

"I did more than just meet him once. We were at a formal party for MPG promotions and I actually got to sit down and talk to him for a while. He's a very smart man. You can tell that just from a few minutes of talking to him."

"What did you talk about?" Lisa asked, suspecting that whatever they talked about had bearing on her questions.

"Military history," Brian replied. "You know I never got much further than tech school. I'm not one of the elite that was allowed into our university system. But I have studied quite a bit of military history on my own. Do you know what General Jackson's degree is in?"

"Military history," she answered. "Any MPG member knows that."

"That's right," he said. "Military history is his passion. In the fifteen-minute conversation I had with him I could see that he was more than an expert on the subject. He is *the* authority on it. And do you know what particular wars interested him the most?"

"What?"

"There were three of them that fascinated him. Three that he told me he'd studied extensively. One is very famous; the war that brought the beginnings of what would become WestHem eventually."

"The American Revolution," Lisa replied. "The birth of capitalism and so-called democracy."

"Right," he said. "But the other two wars were very obscure conflicts. Most school kids today have probably never even heard of them. The first was called the Vietnam War. The second was called the Afghanistan War. Both took place in the second half of the twentieth century. All three of these wars have a single thing in common. Do you know what that is?"

Lisa's mind, assaulted by cannabis, could not think of a common thread. She shook her head.

"In all three of these wars," he told her, "an enemy that was better equipped, in better numbers, and that was absolutely sure of victory, invaded a smaller country expecting the conflict to be over in a matter of weeks with their unconditional victory. And in all three cases the under-equipped, undertrained, understaffed inhabitants of those lands defeated those enemies. Soundly defeated them."

"I'm not sure I'm following you," she said, although she was starting to get a glimmer.

"In all three of these cases the enemy—the Russians in Afghanistan, the French and the Americans in Vietnam, and the British in the revolutionary war—were invading unfamiliar terrain at the end of long supply lines. They were fighting an enemy on their home ground, an enemy that was committed to *not* being pacified, an enemy that was fighting for independence from a superior power, an enemy that had something to fight for. In each case, the invaders did not really care for the task that they were embarked upon. They had no passion for the battle. They only wanted to get the job done and get out of what they considered to be a shithole. What do all of the Earthlings call this place?"

"A shithole," Lisa replied. "Or worse."

"Do you think any of the WestHem marines are going to want to die for this place? To give their life to return Mars to the WestHem corporations? Because no matter what kind of bullshit the WestHem ruling council slings via the media, anyone with any intelligence on that planet is going to *know* what the real reason for the war is. That includes the marines. When they start seeing their friends die, when they realize that this war is not a cakewalk, their morale is going to go down the shitter. Troops with poor morale are the perfect setting for defeat."

"Then you think we can defeat them?" she asked. "Drive them off this planet with poor morale? Even though they'll have five times the equipment that we do?"

Brian pulled a pack of cigarettes from his pocket and lit one with a laser lighter. He drew deeply, exhaling a plume of smoke into the air. "I've been thinking about this a lot lately," he told his partner, his friend. "It goes back to those three wars. Now General Jackson hasn't confided his plans in me or anything, but I can make a few guesses as to what he's going to do. Do you know what the major factor in the victory of those three wars was?"

"Home ground?" she ventured.

He nodded. "Exactly. The victors were on their home ground. They knew every nook and cranny of the battlefields. And they all made extensive use of guerrilla warfare. They were all under-equipped forces, with inferior weaponry. They rarely, if ever, hit the enemy head on. What they did was pick at them, piece by piece in their own rear areas. A few squads of harassment troops here and there, squads whose job was to pick off soldiers one by one, when they were least expecting it. The concept is simple. *Never* give your enemy a place where he can feel safe. Even in their own heavily guarded encampments, they were hit by snipers, or mortar fire, or rockets. They made the enemy feel that as long as they were *anywhere* in those godforsaken places that they were in peril, that they could be killed without warning at any time.

"I believe General Jackson is going to employ a lot of special forces teams whose job it will be to do just that. To go out into the wastelands, to their very landing sites, and pick at them. To position themselves along the march and hit their tanks and APCs with lasers. To knock them off one by one and to degrade their morale."

"And that can win the war?" she asked.

"Yes," he said. "Although in all of the above cases it was a long, protracted process that cost a lot of the defenders their lives. They all took horrible casualties doing this. It took years in every case. With the Vietnamese it took nearly a generation. But they all achieved their goals in the end."

"You're saying we're going to have to fight them for years?" she asked, depressed at the thought.

"Well," he said, "there's a basic difference between them and us."

"What's that?"

"The Americans, the Vietnamese, and the Afghans were all under-equipped and poorly trained forces. We, on the other hand, though numerically inferior, have the same equipment that the WestHems have. In fact, we have equipment specifically designed for use on Mars, something WestHem lacks. We also have training that's better than the WestHems."

"So how does that fit the equation?"

He smiled. "I think that WestHem is in for a big surprise when they come over here. A shocking surprise. In any case, to answer your question, this war is far from hopeless. I think we're gonna kick some Earthling ass."

*****

All over the planet, people did as Laura Whiting had instructed. They talked to each other. They discussed the question. In some cases, there were arguments. In some cases, the arguments were violent. In a few they were deadly.

In Libby, a man shot his wife to death when she refused to change her mind on how she was going to vote.

In Procter, two street gang members shot another when he told them that he was going to vote no and they disagreed with his choice.

On Triad, there was another violent voting argument between gang members. Shots were fired in the heat of the disagreement and two were killed.

There were other episodes of violence during the period between Laura Whiting's speech and the vote itself. In the industrial city of Dow, for instance, the regional manager of MarsTrans corporation headed for his office as he usually did the morning after Laura Whiting's speech. His wife, a high society Earthling who hated her husband's assignment on Mars, protested, warning him that it wasn't safe, but he scoffed at her and headed out of the two hundred and eighth floor apartment, intending to take a first class tram downtown and begin calling each of his managerial staff and ordering them to come in. Where did that Martian bitch Whiting get off declaring a work holiday anyway? He was going to show those greenies a thing or two about playing hardball. He made it less than a block from the front of his apartment before an angry group of middle-class Martians, many of them employees of MarsTrans, attacked him and beat him to death.

But for the most part, the presence of the MPG on the streets kept the planet in order. In every city, roving patrols on foot and in clanking APCs took up positions on major street intersections and augmented the police force. The actual incidents of street crime, already at an all-time low, took an additional dive.

The cities of Mars were confined to the Western Hemisphere of the planet and stretched across only nine of the twenty-four Martian time zones. The prime meridian for the planet ran through New Pittsburgh, the first of the Martian cities. The furthest city to the east was Dow, a mining city in the northern latitudes with a population of five million. Dow was three hours ahead of the prime meridian. It was here that the polls first opened on the morning of the vote; at 0800 Dow time, 0500 New Pittsburgh time.

Voting was accomplished by calling up the ballot program on an Internet screen. The main computer that controlled it was in the capital building in New Pittsburgh. The computer had been instructed to allow only those people who were Martian citizens to vote. It obtained a list of these people from the census computer and downloaded their names, social security numbers, and fingerprint information. The voters would identify themselves by placing their right index finger on the pad of the screen they were using.

Once the terminal sent the identification information to the main voting computer and the main voting computer was satisfied that that person was a Martian citizen of voting age that had not already voted once, the ballot was sent. In this case, the ballot had a single issue on it that required either a yes or a no vote. When the voter made his or her decision, it was sent back to the main computer and logged.

The program that controlled voting, aside from being completely tamper-proof (attempts to change the programming would erase the program completely), would not allow the release of any results until all polls had closed planetwide. This was because in the past it had been found that the release of such information as it was collected tended to discourage many people from voting at all. After all, what was the point of casting your ballot if the issue already seemed decided? This was a particular problem among the western time zone cities both on Mars and Earth. Since 2070, the new system of non-release had been in place and all but the media, who used to delight in making daylong newscasts out of Election Day, seemed to like it.

The westernmost city on Mars was Procter, an agricultural city of six million. It was six hours behind New Pittsburgh and Eden, nine hours behind Dow. At 2000 Procter time, the polls were shut down. In Eden it was 0200 the next day. In Dow it was 0500. Despite the late hour, not many Martians were asleep.

The department of voting office was on the seventy-third floor of the capital building. The head of the department, Jackie Yee, heard her computer terminal send a simple message to her. "Voting is complete. All polls are closed. Would you like to release the results?"

She sighed deeply, her body tingling with anticipation. "Not just yet," she told the computer. "Get me the governor."

It took less than fifteen seconds for Laura Whiting's face to appear on her screen.

"Are all votes in?" she asked Jackie. If the governor was nervous, she certainly didn't show it.

"Yes, Governor," Jackie replied. "Would you like me to release the results now?"

"Yes, I would," Whiting answered. "It's time we found out what we'll be doing tomorrow."

"I'll order them released immediately," Jackie said. "And Governor?"

"Yes?"

"I voted yes," she said. "And I hope everyone else did too. Free Mars."

"Thank you, Jackie," Whiting replied, smiling. "Now go ahead and release the results so we can all stop wondering."

"They'll be out in less than a minute."

Jackie instructed the computer to make public the results of the vote. The actual results would now be stored forever in its memory bank and would be accessible to anyone, anywhere with an Internet terminal, which meant pretty much everybody in the solar system. As a perk of the job, Jackie was the first person to actually see the tally. Her screen filled with figures listing the number of voters on the planet that fit the requirements, the number of those voters who had actually voted, and finally, a breakdown of yes and no votes.

"Wow," she said simply, staring at it.

A second later, a counter near the bottom of her screen began to whir rapidly upward. It was an indicator of the number of requests for information from the voting computer. In less than fifteen seconds it had spun well past sixty thousand.

*****

In her office, Laura Whiting sat with Kevin Jackson. Outside the window the stars were visible, shining as brilliantly as the lights from the surrounding high rises.

"Well," said Jackson. "Shall we see?"

She nodded. "Let's find out if we're going to be in jail tomorrow or not." She took a deep, nervous breath. "Computer, access Martian voting computer and display results for last ballot issue."

"Accessing," replied the computer, which had no idea of the magnitude of what it was doing.

It took less than four seconds and the screen lit up with the requested information. Jackson and Whiting stared at it, eyes wide, mouths agape.

"Well, would you look at that," Laura said softly, unable to develop a reaction just yet.

"I can't believe it," Jackson mumbled beside her.

MARTIAN SPECIAL ELECTION 06102186

WILL THE PLANET OF MARS DECLARE INDEPENDENCE FROM THE FEDERAL ALLIANCE OF WESTERN HEMISPHERE AND ENFORCE THIS DECLARATION BY ANY MEANS AVAILABLE? YES OR NO?

PARAMETERS FOR PASSAGE:
1. MUST HAVE GREATER THAN 90% VOTER PARTICIPATION
2. MUST PASS WITH 66.667% YES VOTE OR GREATER TO BE CONSIDERED BINDING

RESULTS
NUMBER OF PLANETARY INHABITANTS OF VOTING AGE WITH MARTIAN CITIZENSHIP:
49,346,412
NUMBER OF ABOVE THAT PARTICIPATED IN THIS ELECTION:
49,005,922

PERCENTAGE OF VOTER PARTICIPATION:
99.310%

WITHIN PARAMETERS?
YES

YES VOTES:
45,820,537   93.504%

NO VOTES:
3,185,385   6.496%

YES VOTES ARE MAJORITY

GREATER THAN 66.667%?
YES

RESOLUTION IS PASSED

*****

Capital Building, New Pittsburgh
June 11, 2146

Like her speech before, this one was going out live all over the planet. The media had been informed of its imminence and had been reporting it since the votes had been counted the previous night. The planet was abuzz with the news of the successful vote and very few people had slept. And like the previous speech, it was being transmitted to both WestHem and EastHem on Earth.

Laura was dressed again in a simple cotton shirt, produced from the vast cotton fields of Mars. She wore no make-up and her eyes were bleary, with obvious bags under them. But her face was radiant and happy.

"Citizens of Planet Mars," she began her address. "Today that phrase has entirely new meaning. By an overwhelming majority, you have sent a strong message to me and to WestHem. We are no longer citizens of the WestHem colony of Mars, we are truly, for the first time, citizens of the independent Planet of Mars. We have voted for freedom. Let yesterday, June 11, 2186, be forever known as Martian Independence Day. Though we have yet to put a constitution in place, I do not think it will be too forward of me to declare this day as our first planetary holiday.

"As I've promised time and time again, a free Mars is meant to be a Mars of the people." She stared into the camera. "Of the *people*, not of the corporations, not of the rich. Our goal should be the betterment and prosperity of Mars and everyone on it, everyone, not just those with money and power. Not just those with political clout, and most certainly not those from Earth who own everything."

She smiled wickedly, knowingly. "Did I say own? I must have misspoken myself. As of yesterday, at the close of polls, this is an independent planet. All industries, including of course, the vast agricultural and steel industries that forged this planet, that made it what it is today, belong to the people of Mars. The goal of these industries will not be profits for powerful corporate conglomerates on Earth, but the betterment of the Martian people. Each and every Martian person will benefit from them. All of you. I give my sacred vow that this will be so.

"When things settle down a bit on this planet, when we get the necessary steps that need to be taken in these first days taken, we will convene a committee to begin work on a new constitution for our planet; a constitution that will guarantee for perpetuity that Mars will forever remain a planet of the people and that the horrible abuses of the old system will never be repeated.

"But in the meantime, we have much to do and little time in which to do it. Our most daunting task of course, is to keep the forces of WestHem from taking this planet back from us. We must *not* allow this to happen. If it does, never again will we be given opportunity to free ourselves. We've made our move, now it is time to enforce it. For that, we need to beef up our military forces. To do that, we need volunteers.

"As I explained in my first speech, this will be a voluntary war. We may be defeated and the fate of the military personnel if that should happen is unknown. You may be killed in battle whether we win or lose. But if we're to win, we're going to need as many new soldiers as we can get our hands upon. This includes men and women, employed and unemployed. You are all Martian citizens and you all should have the opportunity to fight for Mars if you choose. So please, sign up for service.

"We have approximately ten weeks before WestHem marines land on this planet with the intent to return us to WestHem rule. We'll take military volunteers at any time, but we really need people to sign up as soon as possible so we'll have time to train you prior to deployment. The more training we can instill in you, the better chance you'll have of surviving this conflict and the better chance we'll have of remaining free.

"In addition to military personnel, we'll need other things for the coming conflict. Weapons, tanks, artillery pieces, ammunition. All of these things are produced here on Mars in the manufacturing cities near the steel belts. For those workers that are vital to those operations, I ask that you remain in your jobs. You will be much more valuable to us there. We need to gear up production in our war industries and that also means we need to gear up production in the steel fields and the mining industry. I ask that all of these industries, and in fact, all places of employment on Mars, please return to work tomorrow.

"I realize that your WestHem managers will not be there. But you never needed them in the first place now, did you? For the most part, their job was to count and distribute the money and to hire and fire people. All of you that performed the actual work are still Martians though, and I'm confident that you'll be able to run the various facilities in their absence. First and foremost, we must continue productivity on this planet during these trying days. Food must continue to be harvested and packaged, products and services must still be available to all. I wish for all manufacturing and agricultural facilities to please give as much productivity as possible. In the case of agriculture, we will need that food as a trading chip with EastHem if they agree to supply us with fuel for the coming conflict.

"So please, return to work and be productive. Let us have no fighting over who is going to do what in the management levels now that the Earthlings are gone. There is no time for that. Work something out and get back to work.

"As for the unemployed among us, we are going to need your help also. We need volunteers for the military and we need workers for the factories and industries. I realize that there is a certain amount of strife between the employed and unemployed. There are different values, different points of view, and the two groups have not gotten along well in the past.

"Please use your common sense and believe me when I say that this antagonism is of WestHem making. The unemployed have been kept segregated from the rest of society, made to feel inferior while the employed have been encouraged to feel superior. This must stop. We are all in this together.

"Some of our unemployed have not been able to work in generations. Well, this is your opportunity. We are all descendants of a people who left Earth looking for employment, who were so desperate for it that they were willing to leave their planet behind and travel to an artificial environment just to get a job. I know that some of that courage rests in the majority of the unemployed and I hope to see it now. We need you; we need *everyone* to help here. And if we are successful in this coming conflict, you need never be unemployed again. You will also have access to higher education if you so desire. It is you unemployed who stand to gain the most from this new freedom, but we may not be able to win it without your support.

"And for those at the factories and industries that will be hiring these people, I ask that you put aside your hostility towards ghetto inhabitants. Put them to work, train them, and try not to hold any preconceived notions about them. I'm confident you will be pleasantly surprised at the productivity.

"For the time being, we will consider ourselves under planetary government rule with myself as titular head and the remaining members of the planetary legislature as my balance system. All of the current laws and regulations will remain in effect. Public assistance monies will continue to flow to the unemployed as they always have. Workers will continue to be paid at their current rate. Stores will remain open. As you will quickly see, we are perfectly capable of surviving without WestHem's assistance.

"The Martian Planetary Guard will be pulled out of the streets of the cities to commence training for the upcoming conflict. General Jackson will be in charge of future deployments and training sites.

"This is the time for all Martians to pull together towards a single goal. This is not the time for petty, insignificant differences to be aired. We must unite, we *must*! If we do not, WestHem will prevail.

"A declaration of independence will be sent to WestHem and EastHem later today. A copy of this will be available on the Internet for examination.

"Thank you for your time, and please, please, remember my words. Mars is now free. Let's keep it that way."

Continued in Greenies—Book 2

Printed in Great Britain
by Amazon